Lycan's Blood Queen

(Book One of the Randolph Duology)

By Catherine Edward

Supervising Editor(s): L. Austen Johnson, Camryn Nethken

Editor(s): Rachel Powers, Chrysa Keenon

Proofreader: Caira Coleman

GenZPublishing.org

Aberdeen, NJ

ISBN: 978-1-7339420-2-7

Lycan's Blood Queen

Randolph Duology Book One

CATHERINE EDWARD

GenZ
The Future of Publishing

Dedication

In the loving memory of my father Mr. Edward.

To my mom, who always supports me in everything I do. To the paranormal romance author Cynthia Eden.

Special thanks to author Melissa S. Vice, Rucha Kulkarni, Apurva Biswas and Alankrita Verma.

CHAPTER 1

Blood was the essence to his madness.

The hunt was on. The adrenaline in his veins kept the creature thrilled. He found no delight in mundane things. What mattered was the chase.

And the kill.

While his initial thought suggested snagging a human for a quick snack, something changed. Though rain hindered his sense of smell by converging everything together, a persistent scent that stood out caught his attention. One that made him falter before taking the life of an earlier prey. The lucky bastard would live tonight thanks to the enriching and enticing aroma that pulled him its way.

Hunting in the enemy's territory was such a turn on, particularly this wannabe victim who smelled like honeysuckle. Boot-clad feet planted in heavy mud as the hungry predator tilted his head back. His nostrils flared as his senses tingled with the need to devour whoever carried the tantalizing sweetness in their blood. A flavor that begged for death. One plea he would gladly fulfill.

Eyes that saw through the night, aligned in the direction his nose led him, bringing him to a dilapidated building made up of brick and mortar. His tongue flicked out and slid over gleaming teeth, careful of the fangs that sharpened with the thought and anticipation of draining the prey.

But as he stepped forth, his head twisted toward an invading pungent smell.

Dogs. And not one that could be shaken off easily.

Chapped lips peeled back, and a defensive hiss slipped out with a flash of his fangs. At war with his desire to feed and the need to flee, he looked toward the building, then retreated to the woods and escaped into the darkness.

***

Mia sighed, looking at the papers piled on her table. She had been working on her thesis for the past couple of hours, and she needed a break before she started seeing letters everywhere. Having chronic fatigue syndrome amid finals was not something she wanted.

Her hands reached up and rubbed at strained eyes. They were probably bloodshot given how much they stung. She blinked the clock into focus. Half-past seven and she was nowhere near finished with her assignments.

Great.

On that note, she went back to focusing on the task at hand. Being an honors student meant having a boatload of work.

Her stomach all but roared a few minutes later, reminding her she hadn't eaten in the past six hours. Her kitchen stared back, appearing just as soulless as she felt. She'd forgotten to restock it. Not that she cooked much to begin with, but throwing ramen noodles into a pot sounded a lot better than putting in the extra energy to get dressed and stroll through the streets to hunt down a place of choice.

Her stomach rumbled again, giving a final warning before it cannibalized on itself. "Okay, I'm leaving," she told herself as she headed to get changed.

Mia locked the door behind her as she stepped out, rolling her blonde hair into a sloppy bun. Distant thunder and the moist air promised rain showers. Even more reason for her to remain in. She wasn't looking forward to being wet and cold. Probably explained why her building that housed nearly fifty residents was so quiet. It appeared as if they received the survival notice while it missed her.

Despite how she felt about freezing in near rainfall, she reveled in the smell of crisp clarity after being holed up most of the day. The best part about the rain was the enriching scent it carried—of water and earth—the flourishing scent of life. Who would have thought mud would smell so aromatic?

Pushing her fists deep into the coat pockets before they froze off, she headed toward a local diner nearby. Dim streetlights illuminated the outline of buildings lined on the side of the empty street. Rock music drifted from one of the worn-out apartment complexes. One of the lights in front of the nearby apartment flickered. The eerie glow of lights combined with the rolling thunder gave a haunted touch to her surroundings. There weren't many shops in this part of town. Students and bachelors preferred this area for its cheaper rents.

Idly, Mia thought about her father. Where was he? What was he doing? A normal person might just pull out their phone and call him. But that wasn't their relationship. She was used to him not speaking with her often. Occasionally, little signs of his love for her would appear. A note. A sweater. And, books among the others.

Sounded more like a butler than a father. Still, that was all it took to warm her heart.

3

The only time they ever shared a conversation that lasted longer than a minute was when she graduated from high school. It annoyed her when he gave her a credit card, along with a list of rules to abide by. Guess it was easier to keep an eye on her while she was still under the same roof as him. College was a different story. If it wasn't for her career of choice, her father would have been the hammer *and* the anvil to leading a robotic lifestyle.

There had been a list of curfews that alternated around daylight savings and seasonal changes. People not to associate herself with— which comprised of the entire student body and then some—and things not to do in her free time. Clubbing, hang-outs, even driving around with anyone that wasn't on public transportation, were serious offenses to her father. The only thing he didn't monitor was her diet.

Overprotective much? To most, perhaps. Paranoid was her answer—

She bumped into something bringing her back into the present.

"Watch it," the person snapped. A big guy from what she saw. Tall with dark hair and definitely the sensitive type based on the way he glared at her.

Seriously? A wrinkle on his shirt bothered him that much?

"Sorry," she said with little meaning. He could've watched himself too. His pal standing behind him seemed the livelier of the duo. Handsome too with his blond hair and spring green eyes. Yeah, she supposed even Mr. Grumpy fit in that category, with his darker features.

And whew, were they tall as heck, towering over her like skyscrapers. She wasn't short to begin with, but their height and aura seemed. . .otherworldly.

Dangerous.

They sidestepped around her, moving on ahead. She continued on, involuntarily following their lead. Her mundane thought process halting as her instinct suddenly woke up. It was a shrieking alarm that forced her to keep her eyes on them. The same sensation you get when walking into the woods and coming across a mountain lion or a wolf. You stand your ground and hold your guard.

Goldilocks turned his head over a shoulder, a glint in his eyes that didn't seem so nice anymore. Her internal alarm dinged off electric signals all over her, and she almost expected them to do something. But they got in their muscle car parked along the sidewalk, the windows tinted so darkly it obscured her view. The warnings still didn't go away, and she doubted if they were watching her. Only when the angry red Mustang came to life and backed out onto the black asphalt did her senses relax.

Something was off. *They* were wrong. They were all wrong. And she hadn't the faintest idea why or how.

She somehow perceived that.

Her stomach rumbled in the silence of the aftermath. Mia shook her head to clear her concern and schooled her expressions before entering the diner.

CHAPTER 2

Juan suppressed a growl as he walked through the woods with his brother. They rushed here after receiving a message from the border patrol. There had been a breach. Somehow, the intruder slipped through their tight security.

They circled the perimeter, concluding their uninvited guest had escaped into the no man's land once again. The brothers backtracked to where they started—the outskirts of the town. Scrunched leaves and the broken twigs guided them through its path.

"The trail ends here," Juan said. His head tilted, thumb and index finger caressing his square chin. A habit he obtained in his childhood. He squatted to study the wet footprints on the ground.

His gaze lifted, peering into the darkness. Everything was calm, nothing out of the ordinary. The lingering dampness the atmosphere hinted at another downpour. His nose flared, drawing in the different scents from his surroundings—wet sand, trees, rotting leaves, small furry animals that ventured out of their holes in search of food—drifted through his nostrils.

Then there was this stench that assaulted his senses. Corrupt. Damaging. The distinguished smell was laced with thrill—excitement of a predator. *Who is the prey?* Being a lycanthrope, he could smell the emotions of a person. His senses never betrayed him. He has spent years, honing his tracking skills.

The furrow between his brows deepened. "He was alone," Juan murmured, inspecting the tree line again. "And looking for prey."

"They've never hunted this far into our territory before," his younger brother, Matthew, said. "This is the third sighting this week. Two humans are missing."

Juan's jaw clenched. These weren't just attacks, but an open challenge to their pack. One they'd gladly respond to.

The messy footprints belonged to one person. The creature met no one that night. Their intruder was observing. He seemed to have remained at one particular spot a little longer. The spot allowed him vantage point to one particular building. He gazed at the old structure, concluding that the prey resided in one of the apartments.

"Something's amiss." The leeches didn't stalk or target a prey. They attacked out of the blue.

"Brother, did you smell that?"

He inhaled deeply, tuning in his senses before finally catching it. A mixture of citrus and flowery fragrances with an underlying stench that shouldn't belong—

An image popped in his memory. It was coming from one of the open windows. It was *her*.

The girl they ran into earlier. There was a hint of a vampire-esque scent on the female when they met. It set their impulses on fire. But she possessed no characteristic features that can be defined as a vampire.

Was she his accomplice?

He was quick to curb that notion. It didn't make sense. He rubbed his chin out of habit. Perhaps it was a coincidence, and he was actually here for someone else. But they needed to investigate this further. How she went unnoticed for so long was something he couldn't come to terms with.

The omegas that comprised the majority of the pack worked around the city. They should have been able to sense her presence. Last night's encounter could be intentional. She showed no fear or shock. Her heartbeat was normal.

"There's more to this." Every single thought ended with a question in his mind. How did she mask her scent? Witchcraft? What if there were more like her? The thought was unsettling to his beast.

"We should tell him," Matthew suggested after a moment of silence.

Yes, they had to inform the alpha and the king of the lycans—their elder brother, Aaron George Randolph.

"I'll call him now."

The conversation was short and to the point. Not even hitting the minute mark when he hung up.

"He wants us to tail her."

"I'm fucking tired of chasing tail," Matthew said with rolling aggression. "We're better off tossing her ass in a chamber." Get rid of one pest for the day. "A fucking student at our university."

"It's a place with a tremendous blood supply, and no one would suspect a thing," Juan agreed. Smart girl, though. Unfortunately, not smart enough.

"If things were easy, I'd have killed her already."

Nostrils flaring, his brother glared around. Given the tension in his body, he fought the temptation of pacing the forest floor to the dust and back, another of his habits. A natural born predator with an even deadlier side to him begged to be released from its host.

"Easy, Matt." Phone still out, he shot a text to some of the pack members. This girl intrigued him. She didn't have the qualities of a vampire, yet she smelled like one. There was this strange aura around her; he couldn't put his finger on.

What are your intentions?

He'd soon discover.

"We need her alive." For various reasons. But if what she confessed wasn't satisfactory to their ears, she would not walk away fully intact.

She was still the enemy.

***

He stood with his back to her. A large figure in front of the massive fire roaring, more like screaming, into the night.

She took a few steps toward him, her laced boots padding against the ground. As she got closer, the fire became brighter. Engulfing her in the warmth, but also blinding her.

Then she saw the body in the pyre. Charred and blackened. Its head turned to her, a hand reaching for her from the blazing heat, holding tightly onto her boot, screeching her eardrums to deafness. The smell of decaying and burning flesh assaulting her.

A hard grip on her shoulder forced her to face the hooded man.

"Dad?"

"Don't look back."

It was a classic scene in most books and movies she'd seen. The protagonist waking up in the puddle of their own sweat due to nightmarish premonitions, right before something bad was about to go down. And it was happening to her.

Sitting up in her bed, she glanced at the clock which showcased a rather disgusting number. Daybreak wasn't in close proximity. She uncapped and gulped down the entire bottle of water kept under her bed. She set it on the table, lingering on the plastic container a moment longer than necessary.

That hadn't been a nightmare. It had been more like a memory. The fear and pain were too real.

The sense of foreboding didn't end with the dream, though.

Later that day, there was urgency to her step when she left class. There was no logical explanation to it, but something was wrong. And she couldn't help but see her father as the driving force behind it since the resurfaced nightmare.

"Mia!"

Mia stopped just as she reached the double doors that led her outside the building. Stella, the petite young woman, who approached her, was energetic as always. Her sable hair had been recently cut just below her ears, adding a sleek sophistication to her bubbly personality.

Stella usually made her want to drink twenty espressos just to keep up with her, except today wasn't that day.

"Hey." She kept things short and sweet. "Do you want something?"

"Want something?" Confusion crossed her friend's face. "I thought we were going to take our mock exams together."

Crap. She'd forgotten. It wasn't like the weight of desperate worry looming over her had anything to do with her lack of memory.

"Ladies! What's up!"

And here was Peter. The wrangler in decision making. He was a pretty absolute guy, though he lacked self-preservation. The all-American nice guy participated in every college event that was comprised of sports or social involvement. And he had an enormous crush on Mia.

"You guys are taking the mock exams?" Peter asked only Mia, though Stella answered in her place.

"Yeah. We are. We had no idea you were too." She was surprised, not that Mia blamed her. He was nice, but he didn't particularly excel in the science division, let alone participate in the practice exams.

"I signed up the other day."

"Oh, gosh. That late fee is no joke. You should have paid for it when we did last semester. It was like a hundred dollars cheaper."

"Really? I didn't know that," he said, scratching the back of his head and looking away. The blush on his face was a dead giveaway as to why he was doing this.

Thank you, Stella, for the rescue.

Maybe now she could sneak off—"Why don't you come with us?" Stella offered sweetly, like bad karma. "We were just getting ready to leave."

So, she wasn't the saving grace Mia had thought her to be.

Damn it.

"Cool. Mind if I grab something to eat first? There's this vendor that sells badass steak rolls. I'll treat us—"

"I have to make a phone call." She suddenly interrupted him. She didn't wait for them to respond as she stepped to the side, took out her phone and dialed her father. When it ended with a long beep, she texted him and tried not to let her worry develop into a panic.

Everything was all right. Maybe he was just busy or just didn't want to talk right now. Maybe she was worried for nothing, and he was actually throwing away the money he earned to pay for her college tuition, which also included the fees for these tests.

She forced herself to release the hard grip she had on her phone before returning to her entourage, finally taking off some edge by constantly chanting, "Everything is all right." She was just overreacting over a little dream.

As they stepped outside, the feeling of being watched hit her like it did this morning when she was leaving her place. Though she kept it to herself as they crossed the street, she fought the urge to scratch the back of her neck, feeling like a flea was there.

Except it wasn't a flea. Her problems were much bigger than she assumed.

***

The men sitting in the '67 Fastback watched as she entered the brick establishment. Who would have guessed these leeches infested their territory? So far, they've learned she was the only one. They had their people run a mass background check on every faculty member and student.

Matthew tapped his fingers impatiently on the steering wheel, while Juan continued to go through the papers in his hands.

"Nothing useful," he declared, shoving everything back inside the folder.

"Drive," he ordered, and Matthew eased their way into traffic. He observed her from the mirrors when they passed. "Why don't we take her into custody?"

"And warn the others if there are more?" Juan shook his head. "Don't get carried away. Our target is the one behind her."

Matthew ground his molars but said nothing to that. "So, what's the plan?"

"We have her father's name. Ted Lawrence. We start there."

CHAPTER 3

Cold crisp air filled his lungs. But it did nothing to ease the tension. Aaron George Randolph marched to the balcony. His fists clenched.

They were in his territory again—hunting. His beast was on edge. It has just been little more than a week since his last run. Strong muscles in his arms flexed as he tightened his grip on the railing.

They wanted a challenge, and he'd give it to them. He'd hunt them all and burn their asses, erasing their species for once and for all.

The double doors to his makeshift office swung open.

His father strode in, moving further to sit on the leather seat. Aaron inherited all his physical features from his father. Both having golden blond hair and warm brown eyes with high cheekbones and strong jaw lines, but he stood a couple inches taller than his father at six-foot-three.

"Something's bothering you." His father, Jerome, observed.

Instead of answering, the towering male made his way back inside the room and over to the cart filled with an unimaginable variety of tea. He filled the white china with the patience of a sprouting seed, waiting for the water to come to a boil before dousing it over the organic leaves sitting in the teacup. Saucer in hand, he balanced it perfectly with every step and placed it gently in front of his father.

"I suppose you're telling me to mind my own business." The former king closed his eyes, relaxing against the leather couch.

He smirked. "It's nothing you should worry about."

"I could argue that point, but I lack your mother's perverseness. She could carry on an argument for weeks without an end in sight." He chuckled. "But I know my boys. You'll do whatever you want no matter the consequence."

Smiling, Aaron pinched the bridge of his nose before sitting across his father and pulling up the slacks to be comfortable. "Are you trying to score yourself a humble brag, Dad?"

He scoffed. "Definitely not. Your mother won in most departments. I just gladly resorted myself to taking an L whenever I possibly could."

The strapping male seated opposite to the former king visibly cringed at his modern use of words.

"God, don't say that again."

He laughed. "I've got to find ways of keeping myself entertained. Bringing good stories to tell your mother when I meet her again. Otherwise, she'll have my ass for being such a gloom bucket." His oldest son looked across the table at his father, noticing the deep, dark bags under his eyes that once shone with authority and love. Jerome was slowly but surely becoming a skeleton of the male he once used to be. But this was the curse of their race—one mate for a lifetime. Since the loss of his mate, the words have slowly proven themselves true as sorrow etched all his features. Anything and everything reminded the male of his dead mate, their mother.

To live out such a life even after finding your soul mate. . .

Aaron looked away, swallowing hard before standing. He'd been trying to rub the edge off, but this made matters worse.

He thought back to the time when his parents used to live happily, eyes twinkling with joy and love for each other. Often enjoying brunch and evening tea together. Esmeralda Maria Randolph, his mother, was always the voice of reason. He gained that quality from his mother.

"It isn't healthy to hold your beast a hostage for so long, son." A quiet sip escaped his father. "A good run ought to set you both on track."

"No time," he said.

Aaron knew his father was right. He'd have to let it out soon or risk hurting someone. Having a mate would square all that out, but now it was not what his mind was occupied with. The war was looming on their heads. He had no time for anything else. "Juan and Matthew are following a lead, and I'm conflicted about the winter ball." The pack would expect him to choose a mate.

"You don't have to hurry, son. Wait for the right female. You have better control of your beast than I did." Jerome's hand combed through Aaron's hair. A deep sigh escaped his lips as he tilted his head, leaning toward his father.

"Is there any progress with the clans?"

"No." The leaders of the three fellow clans were siblings, and Henry, his grandfather, was the firstborn. They lived together until the war among the supernaturals for the greed of power ripped them apart. The losses were too great, and the brothers didn't agree with Henry's views regarding the war. The estranged brothers now lived with their families and their own packs in different cities. Packs run by betas. Didn't they realize the beasts needed their alpha?

16

"What about the others?"

Aaron sighed. "I suspect Helius is in bed with the vampires." The hot-headed demon king was a constant pain in their asses. His spies spotted said demon with the leeches, not on one but two such occasions. It was bad enough that the demon was already on the fence. Despite his promise to stay away from the war, his sword was now tilting toward the wrong side of the playing field. Aaron knew he couldn't trust that bastard. Demons were tricky. It was for the best to not assume anything with their kind, even if things looked rather bleak.

"And what about the fae?"

"Their three subjects were abducted last week. King Luvon wants help." He stood and walked to his massive desk, sipping his tea thoughtfully. His gaze drifted through the stack of papers waiting for him. He'd send out a team of his best trackers. He wondered how much more successful his team would be this time. The trail always ended cold. It was as if they disappear into thin air. Perhaps that was what they did.

He could see the need to have someone else in the field. Someone, who could trace magic back to its origin.

"Now tell me about the girl your brothers found," his father asked sitting upright, cold fury replacing the warmth of his brown eyes.

Aaron sensed the pain behind that fury. "She's under surveillance."

Anger flared within him. The recent discovery had been a crest to his ever-growing problems. He wanted nothing more than to drag her sorry ass to the torture chambers.

He had never hurt a female before. *But I want to hurt this one.*

Her kind had been their mortal enemies ever since they came into existence.

"Let me know when you have something; and son, be careful with this one." Jerome stood.

His nod was grim. "Sure."

He dialed the familiar number for the third time today. Maximus, his third-in-command hadn't checked in this afternoon.

"John!" He reached out through their telepathic link. A convenient ability the lycanthropes and the werewolves possessed. It helped them to communicate with one another telepathically. It sure came handy often, but they had to be in close proximity for it to work. The link weakened with the distance.

"Yes, Alpha."

"Max is in trouble. Get Frankie to track his phone."

"I'm on it."

"See what the leeches outside the city know of this girl."

"Certainly, Alpha."

He knew a few vampires were forced into this life. Hundreds of them lived on the outskirts of his territory with his approval. However, none had warned him about the intruder.

How dare she barge into my territory without my permission? He refused to believe the things he heard about her. Her innocent appearance helped her blend with the humans. Looks could be deceiving. She has an agenda. That much was clear. Why else she would be in his territory under the disguise of a student?

A trespasser.

What were they planning this time? They were on the move. His hatred was directed to their king who set this in motion. No one knew where he hid his sanctuary, guarding it with the magic of witches. And Lilith, the witch, was the key. Escorting her to Brookedge was the task given to Maximus.

He strolled to the balcony. His clothes ripped as his beast pushed forward. Bones snapped and realigned. Razor sharp claws burst out of his fingertips. Midnight black fur replaced his human skin. The beast of the night rolled its shoulders. He jumped over the railing, landing gracefully on the ground before taking off toward the east.

***

Mia woke up soaked in her sweat. The nightmares were becoming her constant companion, and it troubled her. She checked her phone, frowning when there was no reply from her father. He never went this long without responding. *Is he in trouble?* No. He could protect his own hide.

Hopping out of the bed, she strolled toward her tiny en-suite bathroom for her morning ritual. Mia longed for a run. Sometimes physical exertion helped clear the mind. An annoyed groan hissed out from her mouth entering the small space of the bathroom. At least they had running water though she'd have preferred it to be hotter. The worn-out cabinets that held the toiletries made her wonder if they'd survive this year. She could hardly see herself in the old mirror with rusty edges. The sense of foreboding subsided as she started the shower.

A soft masculine hum reached her ears and her lips stretched to form a smile. These mundane things reminded her how ignorant the humans were. *Would they be still singing if they knew they lived in a world filled with mythical creatures?* Creatures that shouldn't exist. She lived with that blissful ignorance until the incident a couple of years ago.

The thin walls of her cozy apartment offered little privacy. She could often tell when her neighbor was awake or when he was moving around his house. Mia was thankful that he was a friendly guy who never had guests or female friends over. That'd have been awkward.

An audible breath whooshed out of her at the thought. . .

Dressing in a pair of tight jeans and turtleneck long-sleeved T-shirt, she pulled on her sweater. It did little to keep her warm in the ever-growing cold weather. Thanks to the centralized heating system that kept her room relatively warm.

There was nothing much to do with exams around the corner. She was tempted to skip school, but then remembered she had a meeting with the college's Career Services Counselor. The lack of caffeine was catching up with her. She ran out of coffee among other things and made a note to restock her pantry.

While she blamed it on her reluctance to spend what's more than necessary, she didn't want to live under her father's roof. However, with all the academic work, it was hard to find a part-time job without risking her grades. The time had finally come for her to pursue her dreams.

"Good morning, Mia." Logan chirped with his signature smile when she bumped into him in the corridor. She threw him a smile over her shoulder while locking the door.

"Morning. How's work?" she asked as they took the stairs down.

"Busy. How is college?"

"Good."

"Aren't you graduating this year?"

"I am."

Logan worked somewhere in the city. Their conversations were limited. She preferred it that way. *Less is better.* She bid him goodbye once they reached the diner and took the bus to her college.

She couldn't wait to get back to her apartment once the day was over. However, sleep was a luxury she couldn't afford with finals drawing closer. She only had a week to prepare.

"Mia!"

Mia whirled around to see Stella, who ran toward her with a set of books hugged to her chest, hair whipping around her face as she ran.

"Hey, I thought you left early," Mia said as a greeting.

"No. I was in the office, clearing up my dues. Are you done with your thesis yet?"

"Yep," she replied enthusiastically. A sense of accomplishment filled her. She was now one step closer to her freedom.

"So how did your meeting go?"

Mia adjusted her shoulder bag. "Good. There are a few internship opportunities I'm looking forward to."

"That's great. Randolph's on-campus recruiting is the best."

It was at that moment that the hair on her neck stood, and her skin prickled with awareness. Her heart thundered against her ribs, and her senses seemed to have heightened without her realizing it. She turned around to see no one. Hesitant feet moved when Stella dragged her along. She let out a shaky breath as a spot on her back tingled.

"Did you see what Peter did the other day?"

No, and I don't care. Her mind was on the invisible stalker, who set her instincts on fire. Stella distracted her momentarily when a shadow moved past the tree line in her peripheral vision at the far end of the football field. A sudden flash of fear washed over her as her mind replayed the memory she tried hard to forget.

I wish it's just my mind playing tricks.

CHAPTER 4

Ted Lawrence has been pacing the small hotel room for the last hour. The vampires' lair was restless. Supernatural abductions had become a daily occurrence and staying away from his daughter was the only way to keep the attention off of her.

It had been over a year. The longest she has stayed in one place since Phoenix. He wondered if her scent has changed. The curfew forced him to stay away from her, and it unsettled his nerves. Speaking of which, he wondered why his associate hadn't contacted him yet.

Figuring out his next step was crucial now that her finals were so close. They should move away for good. Go far from the impending war. Only if such a place existed. No place is safe till Felipe sits on the throne. His drudges were on the move. They were aiming at something big. That much was evident. Why else would they feel the need to wipe out the harmless supernatural races? The latest news claimed the goblins and gnomes were already on the run.

How long before they discovered the secret he has been protecting? Protecting her became his priority ever since fate crossed their paths in a small town market eighteen years ago. Mia Lawrence— the shy child with wide blue eyes and a bright smile—his daughter.

"Mr. Lawrence!" Logan, his human associate, came barging into the room.

Ted whirled around, and his train of thought derailed as his eyes focused on the young man standing in front of him. "What is it?" he asked, taking in Logan's disheveled form.

"It's about Mia, sir. The lycans are tailing her," Logan said, anxious hands raking through his messy, dark hair.

"What?" Ted cried in shock. He knew it would happen, but he didn't expect it this soon. Lycans were bad news. "Is there more?" he asked, noticing his associate shifting from one foot to another.

"It's. . .them. The royal betas. They are the ones after her. I heard more vampires are lurking around the borders," he said, wiping the sweat from his face.

Logan became Mia's neighbor under his orders to watch over her in his absence.

He should have expected this. The warlock cursed. How did he even think she would be safe in the lycan territory? "You should have informed me sooner!"

"Your phone is dead."

Crap. He hadn't even realized. His medieval brain never comprehended the latest technology and often forgot that he even owned a phone. His carelessness has now paved a way for their downfall.

There was no escape once she came under their radar.

Do they know what she is? How am I going to save her this time?

What would they do when they discovered the truth? He rubbed the back of his neck. Jerome, the former king, wouldn't lose a chance to avenge his wife against the vampires. To wait for them to act would be foolish. He had to act immediately.

"We need to get her out of there. You–"

The door burst open, sending wooden splinters everywhere. Ted's head whipped around, eyes widening. Everything happened in a fraction of a second. Bright amber eyes stared into his soul as darkness consumed him.

***

While she'd have preferred to spend her weekend curled up under her blankets, she had other important things to do, like finding out what happened to her father. She'd gone to a few of his dwelling places outside of town, only to find him gone. No traces left.

Where did he go?

It was unlike him to disappear like that. She was sure something had happened to him, only there was no way to know. Mia's headache returned as frustration mounted. Nothing kept her mind occupied longer than a few minutes. Her father was always at the back of her mind. Her heart constricted as a labored breath hissed out. Fists clenched, desiring to punch through something.

What do I do?

Mythical creatures had been a concept that always intrigued her. Only three years ago, she had merely wondered what it would be like if they walked on Earth. Her encounter was nothing like the ones she read in books—not even close. She could still taste her fear, believing she'd have died that night. Over the years, she tried to think of her attacker as an insane man, practicing cannibalism, but she knew what she saw. Life would've been much better if there was an option to erase unwanted memories.

Lycan's Blood Queen

She knew nothing about the supernatural, except that they were real. Where did they live? What did they look like? That was beyond her knowledge.

Her eyes stung with irritation due to the lack of sleep.

There was always this awareness in the back of her mind. A sensation of being watched. She grew tired of waiting for something to happen and knew she had to move. The few places she checked didn't meet her expectations.

The gnawing in her gut grew as hours turned into days and then into weeks. Her exams were over, and she was done with university. The lack of her father's presence when she needed him the most weighed down on her. He was always there, guiding her, even in his physical absence, like a ghost.

Moving on without him was the harsh reality she must face. While his controlling behavior irked her most times, it also made her feel secure. For the first time in years, she felt alone. Mia choked on a sob. He was in trouble, and there was nothing she could do.

Where are you, Dad?

When she looked out of the window that morning, she gasped. Her eyes grew wide, a smile graced her lips to see the trees adorning crowns of snow upon their usual green glory. The magnificent view took her breath away.

It was one of those days when, again, she wanted to stay in bed and do nothing. It was not every day she got a break—she worked hard to keep her scholarship. She moved around a lot more than she would have liked, and for once, she wanted to stay and savor it.

It was around noon, when she got a call from the career services office informing her she landed an internship and asking her to visit to discuss further details. She called Stella, reluctantly asking her to go to the campus with her.

Regret filled her the moment she stepped out of the warm embrace of her building. Warm breath puffed out, and her fingertips grew numb under the biting cold. The air was as fresh as it could be, but the chill it carried pricked her lungs. Though she previously lived in many cities, she had never stayed in one with icy-cold weather. It never snowed in Phoenix where she spent most of her childhood.

She needed to hurry. Stella would be waiting for her at the bus stop. By the time she reached Abby's diner, Mia shivered with cold. The chill seeped through her clothes numbing her skin. She entered the cozy diner, relishing the sudden warmth and ordered carry out before heading to the bus stop.

While crossing the road to the station, she saw them again. The same men she bumped into a few weeks ago were sitting in a car parked next to the bus stop. The brunette glared at her while the blond was on his phone talking to someone.

"Mia! Hurry! The bus is here," Stella hollered, distracting her from the men. Mia hurried and got on the bus, her brows furrowed.

"What's wrong?" Stella asked.

"Nothing, just wondering about the guys in that car over there," Mia replied pointing to the red Mustang parked on the opposite side. Stella always had information about the town's folks.

"Oh, them. Sexy, aren't they?" Stella winked, causing Mia to roll her eyes. "Are they bothering you?" Her friend's expression grew serious.

Very much.

This shouldn't annoy her. They were strangers. Their presence here didn't matter. But she couldn't ignore the warning bells that went off in her mind for the second time. She masked her annoyance with a smile. "No. Not really. They are just intimidating." Her words were framed carefully.

"I get it." Stella relaxed in her seat. "You have nothing to worry about. They work for the royals." She leaned toward Mia and lowering her voice, "Some girls in our campus claim they are the princes, you know the brothers of the ruling king."

Ah, yes, the royals. The Randolphs weren't popular like the royal family of England. But that intrigued her the most since they owned many businesses and educational institutions in Brookedge.

"That's because they keep their business strictly private," her friend said. "They live in a private estate far from the city."

Had she voiced her thoughts out loud? "What are they doing here?" She noticed the lack of security around them. It surprised her that the royal princes would roam the streets like ordinary people.

Her friend shrugged. "Running errands, I guess."

Mia controlled the urge to shake her head in denial. She doubted the royals ran errands like normal people. They were here for something else.

"You may even notice people bowing down to them as they walked on the streets. For an outsider, Brookedge is like any other state in the US. But, we know it's different."

"So Brookedge is ruled by the king," she assumed, wanting to keep the conversation going.

"You can say that." Stella lowered her voice, "They fund pretty much everything. The governor often reports to the king."

"How do you even know all this?"

"Because my mom works there." She rolled her eyes as if saying she should know this already.

A sudden thought crossed Mia's mind. "How old is their king?" she asked. The Mustang guys looked young, maybe in their mid-twenties.

"He was nineteen when he ascended the throne, and that was seven years ago."

"Oh, that's pretty young!" Mia frowned. How much did she know? She couldn't risk asking more without explaining her sudden interest in them. Her slender fingers absentmindedly massaged her temples. *Perhaps I'm being paranoid.* This was the second time she saw them since that night. Blame it on her intuition, but she felt as if something unpleasant was about to happen.

"Yeah, I know."

The silence stretched for a moment as her mind reeled.

These were not coincidences.

"Here, take it." Stella passed her a fluffy overcoat and gloves, bringing Mia out of her thoughts when they exited the bus. "It's mine. You can use them for the cold."

Mia shrugged it on, savoring the warmth it provided. "Thanks."

"It's nothing. You go ahead. I'll be at the library," Stella replied, and walked away as she went inside.

Just as Mia walked past the principal's office, her spine tingled with fear. Then she noticed the guys in the Mustang entering the same corridor.

They walked as if they owned the place. *They do own this place,* her subconscious supplied. Their eyes locked for a moment when they walked past her, Mia involuntarily shuddered.

She suppressed the sudden urge to hiss. She didn't know why their mere presence set her instincts on fire. Every fiber of her body screamed in alarm when they got close, and suddenly she wanted to get as far from them as possible.

There was no recognition on their faces nor did they throw a second glance at her. *I'm overreacting.* She'd been restless, and it must be the stress. Mia forced her mind to calm down and shrugged off the nagging thoughts as she headed to the career services office.

CHAPTER 5

"Mia, I'm so happy for you. I knew you'd get in," Stella chirped for the sixth time that evening.

"What are your plans?" Mia asked. Her mind churned, not able to focus on the conversation.

"I'm visiting my aunt in Europe. I want to enjoy the break while it lasts."

Her friend's contagious smile did nothing to lift her spirits. The juice corner was not very busy at this time of the day. She nodded as she sipped the remaining smoothie with a small smile. The news should have been exhilarating, but without her father to share it with, her emotions were in disarray. If it wasn't for Stella's compulsion, she wouldn't be here. But it also served as a distraction, even for just a short while.

"When are you leaving?"

"This weekend. I'll be back before our graduation though."

She secured the internship; the counselor had claimed it to be a once in a lifetime opportunity. One of the top companies in the heart of Brookedge selected her to work for them. Though the pay wasn't great, it would get her going until she figured out her next move. The benefits included accommodation and transport, which was a huge relief.

"I'll see you when I get back. Call me if you need anything, okay?"

"Sure." Hugging her friend goodbye, she walked away. As she did, her heart grew heavy again. The storm thundered once, and her mind registered the growing darkness around her. There it was again. The churning in her lower belly that promised nothing good.

Sudden fear crept up her spine, and her legs moved faster. The familiar prickling sensation started from the base of her neck again. The bus stop came in her sight. Mia's heart thudded against her ribcage while she crossed a dark alley. Before she knew what was happening, she was forcefully pinned against a dumpster inside the alley while the stench of rotting corpses filled her nose.

"Finally, I have you all to myself." The man's blood–curdling voice had her hyperventilating.

Her body froze, legs rooted to the ground, too shocked to move. Fear consuming every inch of her body. Her breath heaved with loud sobs erupting from her chest as the macabre creature leaned toward her being. This one was different, taller and deadlier than her previous attacker.

"That's quite a chase you put me through. It took weeks to get you all alone," he drawled sardonically, his nasty breath fanning across her face. Fear halted her breathing, but she could still smell his wretched breath.

Adjusting her sight to the darkness she could clearly see his features. His soulless black eyes stared back at her, there was no mistaking the carnivorous fangs under his pale, parched lips. His skin felt like ice where he was grabbing her, reminding her of the dead.

"Let me go." Her voice came out weak, just a meek whisper. The logical side of her brain urged her to fight, reminding her of the defense lesson she learned as a teenager, but fear rendered her useless once again.

He closed his eyes for a moment, sniffing and running his nose along the crook of her neck, savoring her scent. "You smell so delicious." Fear poured out of her. "Ah, so sweet. . ." A dark tongue darted out licking his lips in anticipation.

Mia jumped back feeling his tongue on her skin. Her eyes widened and something within her snapped. Her skin stung where his fangs pierced the top layer of her skin, and her mind went blank. Suddenly, her heart beat faster. The galloping sound was too loud for her ears. An unfamiliar current traveled up her veins, and she pushed him away with all her might. To her surprise, the ghostly man flew through the air slamming into the wall behind him and collapsing to the ground. Everything happened within a fraction of a second.

She moved away from the wall and ran toward the road, only to crash against a hard chest. A short scream slipped out of her mouth. Warm hands enclosed her small frame as another figure walked toward the creep lying on the ground groaning.

The warmth of the person holding her provided her little comfort until she noticed who the other individual was. The brunette from the Mustang. She turned to see the brunette whose's angry eyes were now focused on the man being cuffed by the blond.

Why is he handcuffing the vampire?

Still, in shock—she couldn't recall how she had pushed him off her. Her legs were on autopilot. When the brunette took her to their car —an Audi instead of the red Mustang they drove earlier—she wanted to protest, but her body wouldn't respond to her brain's command. She

32

didn't even know them, but nonetheless climbed in. Her eyes still open wide, not blinking, and not breathing.

"She isn't breathing." A distant voice reached her ears. Still, she couldn't move.

"It must be the shock. Get her warm," a second muffled voice commented.

"You do it!"

She heard a shuffling sound before the second voice spoke again.

"Hey, breathe!" She felt her feet being elevated and something warm covering her body.

"It's okay. We got you." The owner of the second voice removed her shoes and rubbed her feet, restoring their warmth.

Mia blinked as the blond's blurred face came into focus. He kept speaking in a soothing tone that calmed her nerves while feeling returned to her limbs. Her lungs relaxed, and she gasped for breath, gagging when her brain registered the stench of a rotten corpse.

"We are going to take you home now," the blond mumbled, rubbing her arms and feet. She felt the heat slowly returning to her body. Mia could only blink in response. "You weren't breathing," he informed her while raising a bottle of water to her lips. "Drink."

When she didn't drink right away the blond rolled his eyes. "It's safe. Drink. We'd have let you get killed if we wanted to harm you."

His words made sense, but they could still harm her. Mia accepted the bottle and sniffed the content, smelling nothing. Her mouth opened, taking a small sip. Her mind was still on the creature that attacked her. The brunette started the car, driving forward. She gulped the remaining water down, yielding to the demand of her parched throat. She wanted to thank them, but words failed her.

What are your names? She wanted to ask but deep fear rendered her speechless. The blond handed her another water bottle and the car fell silent. She tried to calm her racing heart as the car drove through the familiar road that'd take her home. *How do they know where I live?* Her tongue stuck to the roof of her mouth preventing her from asking any questions.

The car stopped in front of her building, the blond handed her the bag she was carrying earlier while the brunette opened the door for her to exit. She was glad to leave the car, and thanked her lucky stars that she escaped.

Mia slipped out of the car slightly wobbling on her feet, and her body still trembling in terror. When she encountered the attack three years ago, she wasn't this afraid. Tonight was different. It was more than a one-time incident. Hell, she'd be damned if she thought it was a coincidence. *No. It's more than that.*

She nodded at them in thanks before walking slowly toward her building.

They found me.

The realization brought her nightmare to reality. Her legs gave out when she reached her room, and Mia plopped down on the floor. There was no way she could stay here anymore. They must have gotten to her father, too. Her body racked with the violent sobs that erupted from her chest.

Is he alive? No. He can't die.

She didn't know how long she cried or when her eyes dropped. Her vision suddenly blurred, mind slipping into an abyss that tested her sanity.

Cerulean eyes peered around, not recognizing the surroundings. The deep forest carried the heavy scent of nature. Silence thickened and nothing moved. The crisp, cool air held a warning she couldn't fathom.

The sound of a twig snapped on her right. Her heart beating feverishly against her ribcage as she backed up against a tree, slowly looking around her to find the source of the noise.

"Found you," a slow bone-chilling voice drawled, making her jump. It was the same as the voice of the man who tried to attack her in the alley. The nerves in her stomach knotted, and a shiver ran down her spine.

"We will be rewarded." Another voice piped in from her left. She pushed them and ran as fast as her legs could carry her before she was tackled down. The stench of decaying corpses hit her nose full force, suffocating her. More ghostly creatures poured out of the shadows, baring their sharp fangs at her.

"We won't make it easy this time," the one who tackled her said.

Fear coursed through her veins, rendering her helpless as she thrashed against their hold.

"Please help," she shouted. "Someone please!" The weak echo of her voice went unheard. No one was coming to save her.

Her logical brain had no explanation as to how she ended up here. Eyes closed as a prayer whispered out of her lips. Please wake up. It's a nightmare.

Pain shot through her body, and a scream tore through her lips. A creature had its fangs buried deep in her hand. Her legs kicked. They fangs didn't move an inch. She could almost taste their thrill for the hunt. Growls erupted as more bites followed. Flesh tore, sending waves of pain that rendered her breathless. They were feasting.

"Leave me, please," she whimpered helplessly. "Please, let me go." She continued to cry. Her voice and body continued to weaken.

"We need to kill you before it's too late," a creature growled from her right, his teeth snapped menacingly at her before biting down on her shoulders.

Her vision blurred and she gasped for breath. Each rise of her chest left a burning sensation and had her eyes rolling into her skull. Her body felt like it was on fire, pain licked each and every part of her skin.

Soon the screams stopped, and her body grew numb. Dimly, she heard a howl from the distance, and she felt her attacker's fangs leave her body. Their horrified screams echoed through the night and blood splashed upon her.

Her eyes blinked, trying to focus on her rescuer. Something furry and warm lifted her. Cerulean met amber before everything went dark.

She woke with a start, eyes frantically searching. Her skin still burned, involuntary shudders running through her body. She was still in her room, but the taste of fear had been nothing like she'd ever felt. *It felt real.* She felt like she had almost died, and her death would have been certain if it wasn't for the unknown beast.

What's happening? A frown marred her elegant features. She couldn't shake away the shimmering embers from her mind. Suddenly, warmth washed over her, relaxing her rattling nerves when the embers surfaced in her memory. It didn't last though, a sudden pain started at her temples, spreading to the back of her head.

Stumbling up from the floor, she dragged her numb legs to the bathroom. Slowly stripping out of her clothes as eyes focused on nothing. She got into the shower and allowed the hot water to cascade down her slim frame, washing away the remnants of that day.

The hot water slightly burned her, leaving her skin red. She didn't mind the burning sensation—it felt good. She was just getting out and drying herself when her stomach growled—she had missed dinner.

Checking the time, she realized it was too late to go out for food now. She saw the coffee powder she grabbed earlier that week was left on the kitchen counter.

A strong dose of coffee might be all she needed to clear her thoughts. Mia took her time boiling the water and preparing her coffee. The process distracted her a little. Sipping at sugarless coffee, she grimaced at the bitter taste but continued to drink. She'd be a sitting duck here.

Her mind once again replayed the attack. The Mustang guys saved her, but they weren't shocked to see the vampire. Their faces were scrunched with disgust while anger rolled off them in waves. She didn't imagine the blond handcuffing the vampire. His eyes blazed green when he did so. *Who are they? What is their motive? How did they know where I live?*

Mia paced the floor, her mind in turmoil. *What do they know?*

CHAPTER 6

Ted eyed the male before him. The alpha, no doubt. The strong aura and commanding presence radiating off him was a dead giveaway. He tested the restraints on his hands with little hope to find a loose knot only to realize they were handcuffed. Clever. The surge of power flowing through his veins since his birth fell silent.

"Ted Lawrence. Or shall I call you Galahad?" The alpha's impassive brown eyes with flecks of amber pinned him onto his seat. *How did he find out?* He shouldn't have underestimated their intelligence. Lycans were too good with their sniffing. "I'm sorry you almost died. It was a mistake on our part."

The beast before him didn't sound sorry at all. Not in the least. He remembered waking a few times in a hospital bed, feeling groggy. He didn't bat a lash. This was Aaron George Randolph. The freaking lycan king. Gray eyes focused on him. If the stories he heard about him were true, the beast and the man didn't hesitate to kill.

"I wasn't trespassing, Alpha," he claimed in a tone so sincere. He wasn't caught in the lycan territory. Lycans didn't hunt outside their borders. The warlock still couldn't comprehend how they had tracked him. He always cleaned his trail.

"You weren't," Aaron agreed. "But. . .you planted not one, but two of your people within my territory. Why?"

Ted involuntarily shrank away from him. Sweat coated his forehead and upper lips. The alpha's eyes blazed with the intensity of a volcano, ready to burst even at a minute change in pressure. The prisoner knew better than to irk the beast. They were walking lie detectors and one simple lie could cost him his daughter's life.

"Mia is my daughter, and Logan works for me. They aren't intruders," he said, choosing his words carefully.

"Let me refine my question then," the alpha drawled in a thick voice belonging to his beast. Shining amber eyes were proof enough that the beast lay just beneath his skin. "Why did you plant your vampire daughter in my territory?"

Ted swallowed the lump in his throat, averting his eyes toward the nude concrete walls of the surprisingly clean room, forcing his racing heart and breathing to slow down. It was a skill he had mastered over the years. But for the first time, being in the presence of the lycan tested his acquired talent. The corner of the alpha's lips lifted into a smirk as if he knew what was going on in the warlock's mind. Damn their heightened senses. The lycan's enhanced senses missing nothing.

"My daughter is innocent."

"Your daughter is a leech," Aaron corrected and continued. "Where is your mate?"

"She's never hurt anyone." His voice rang louder than he intended to. The alpha's brows rose, and Ted lowered his gaze, turning his neck to the side. "I don't have a mate," he said swallowing the nervousness. His gaze lifted. "I adopted Mia when she was four," he answered reading the question in the eyes of the king. Perhaps, if he could earn the king's trust, he might spare their lives. His eyes darted from one side to the other. The wheels in his head turned, weighing his options.

The king's sharp gaze regarded him for a long minute before a man strode in, handing him a phone. Aaron pressed the phone to his ears. He watched the alpha's forehead crease and his lips bend into a frown. Ted jumped when he heard the thick rumble roll out of the alpha's chest. Aaron closed his eyes, taking a deep breath expanding his chest that strained against the thin material of his shirt.

Unlike the shifters, he didn't have super hearing. The witches and warlocks didn't have enhanced senses.

"Please. She's harmless," he pleaded as the Alpha disconnected the call, but a hard glare rendered him speechless.

"The only *good* vampire is a dead vampire." The lycan's voice was guttural. His features had hardened, and his eyes showed no trace of a man. It now belonged to the beast so close to the surface.

Ted cringed, noticing the sharp claws, exhaustion washed over him, and he suddenly felt tired. "Please, Alpha. She isn't like the others. Don't hurt my baby girl. She's all I have." His voice grew weak and his vision blurred.

"Tell me something I don't know." The alpha growled punching the steel table leaving a dent in its wake and causing Ted to jump in shock. One wrong word may sign his death warrant along with his daughter's.

"The vampires are attacking her, why?"

"I. . .I. . ."

"Perhaps, you need more persuasion." The alpha flexed his hands just as another lycanthrope poked his head in. A silent message passing between the two. "I'll be back soon, Galahad. Next time, I want the truth." Aaron stood, walking out.

"No. Please. . ." His cry went unheard as the door closed with a bang. He was nothing without his magic. They had injected him with something that rendered his powers useless. It was over for them. He hadn't anticipated this. A blind hope had led them here. Now he would be fortunate if they get a quick painless death.

What do I do?

***

"When?"

John Perron, the Lycan General, matched his long strides as they marched forward.

"An hour ago."

A growl erupted from his throat, the leeches never attacked in broad daylight. This time, they killed three unsuspecting teenagers just a few miles outside his territory. The news had interrupted his interrogation with the warlock. The old goat was holding back a lot of information.

He won't for long.

"The royal betas are on their way to investigate," John continued.

"Get the trackers on route. Show no mercy."

"On it, Alpha."

He did not slow down while the general stepped aside to make the call. Levi, the butler, stood with his leather jacket in hand, and Aaron accepted it with a curt nod. The older man, in his early sixties, opened the door on his right that led to the family garage.

He chose one of the faster moving rides, climbed in, and fastened the seat belt. The passenger door opened, and John climbed in.

41

"Maximus contacted the security team. They were ambushed and the witch, Lilith is injured," John said when their vehicle emerged out of the private road after five minutes.

"Where are they now?" he asked as they eased into the city traffic. His knuckles turned white where he tightened his hold around the wheel. Lilith wasn't just a witch. She was like family, his mother's best friend. And their only hope to track the magic trail to put a stop to Felipe's madness.

"His cell phone was last active near Vertrock. Beta Blake is leading a team to rescue them as we speak."

"Good." Relief flooded him at his cousin's mention. Blake, his cousin never hesitated to vocalize his support whenever someone argued against uniting the estranged packs. However, it took time to thaw the ice in the elder's minds.

"Did the warlock reveal anything, Alpha?"

"No." All he did was beg and claim his daughter was innocent. Rolling the windows down, he allowed fresh air in. His beast was getting antsy.

Finding information on the ancient warlock was easy. While he thought he had cleaned his trail well, Frankie, the tech geek of their pack was able to sniff his ass right to the outskirts of town where he laid low. However, their mission went wrong when one of the assigned lycanthropes accidentally injected him with more of the special concoction than needed. Ted had been in and out of consciousness over the past two weeks as he recovered.

The traffic thinned out as they drove past the dwellings that marked the city border. Turning right, he entered the recently cleared path, which led to the woods. The car slowed to a stop beside a familiar Mustang.

"The crime scene is a fifteen-minute trek from here."

Aaron slipped out of his car, eyes scanning the surrounding area. He filtered through the different smells, focusing only on the ones that stood out. They reached the scene in less than five minutes, barely breaking a sweat.

The victim's mangled bodies soon coming into view. The snow under the bodies was soaked with blood from deep gashes. His chest clenched at the grotesque memory of a similar incident seven years ago. His jaw clenched, closing his eyes to try to school his emotions. The beast within clawed to break free and follow the still fresh trail. It was risky. They had to continue the hunt in human form. The atmosphere around was tense as the cops and forensics team shuffled around with their equipment. His brothers rushed toward him.

"Three males of age nineteen, all dead. Their girlfriends are still missing," Juan said, pushing his clawed hands deep into his pockets. His green eyes glowed.

"*Easy, Juan.*" Aaron sent through the link. "Any leads?" Aaron eyed the positions of the bodies. The parasites never planned their attacks. Their scent was masked, but the fang marks didn't belong to a wild animal as the police believed. It was evident they took their time with these boys. The skin was bitten off in several places.

"The suspects headed south with the hostages. Our trackers are onto them," Matthew said, eyeing the scene.

"We need to rescue the girls at any cost." He could imagine the reporters blowing this up if they caught wind of it. Three girls were missing. Probably dead by now. If they were alive, their time was running out.

"Alpha, the reporters are heading this way. We must leave," John whispered in his ear.

Aaron nodded. Three murders right outside his territory and three more lives in danger. These deaths were on him, as their safety was his responsibility. The alpha in him surged to action. Human or wolf, his beast saw them as part of his pack. His protection extended to everyone lived within his borders. And he wasn't going to sit by and watch as the vampires wrecked havoc in his territory. It was an open challenge, containing a clear message.

Brookedge was in danger.

His feet changed course as soon as they stepped out of view. John followed, no questions asked. It had always been this way between them. Aaron hurried through the forest, legs picking up speed as the distance grew. He threw his head back, nostrils flaring. His beast surfaced, staying just beneath his skin.

Standing in ankle deep snow he felt the surrounding air change, growing colder with every minute. The storm was close. He could sense it. The race was on.

Now it was against nature and time.

**

It was four in the evening when Mia reached the hotel she checked into earlier. That morning, at the first sign of light, she had packed her bags and left her small apartment. Though this didn't offer a permanent solution, she needed a place to crash while planned her next move.

Her teeth chattered. She was used to warm climates and adjusting to this new environment was a challenge. The sidewalks and parked cars sported a thick, white sheet of snow. Dark clouds loomed overhead.

Exhaustion weighed her down, wanting nothing more than to sleep in for the rest of the day. It would be a wonder if she could sleep at all after everything that happened. She had wandered aimlessly through the streets wanting some distraction. Shopping had failed to keep her mind from straying.

Her breath puffed out in smoke as she dragged her tired, numb limbs into the building. Reaching her floor, hair on her arms and neck bristled in alarm. Her senses suddenly alert.

Her gaze scanned her surroundings. Anxiety made breathing hard. An involuntary hiss escaped her lips before she took a step.

Shit! No, no, no. Not again. Frantic eyes searched for the source. The corridors were deserted, except for the security cameras. She could call the cops. But, what would she tell them? *"I suspect there is a vampire in my room."* Hell no. That would gain her free ticket to a mental asylum.

The silence stretched, thicker than the uneasy tension in the atmosphere. She looked around, unable to decide the next course of action. Everything seemed undisturbed, and the door was locked, but the stench definitely was coming from inside. *How could they get past the security? What if they were still inside my room?* Going in was the only way to find out.

Now, she remembered the horror movies. Mia could relate to their need to investigate though they knew it was dangerous. She closed the distance to the door with unsure feet as the odor grew more intense, she gripped her phone tighter. *Should I call the police?* She shrugged off the thought immediately.

Her own heartbeat became intense and her palms grew sweaty as she tiptoed with minimal noise. Sliding the keycard in, she unlocked the door and peaked in. The room was wrecked. Her belongings now littered the floor. Crap. The bastards found her again. Shaky fingers dialed 9-1-1 as she ran out.

Her room had been vandalized, but they couldn't find a single clue, not even a fingerprint. The hotel administration was puzzled, since their security cameras got nothing. The police concluded that the culprits got in through the balcony since the glass was broken. Several questions were asked and promises were made to find the culprits. She just nodded when the hotel offered an upgrade. The administration worried about their reputation while she worried about her life. She'd left the old room for a reason. *And that reason has found me.*

The stench had grown weaker now, but it was there even though the cops seemed oblivious to it. She wondered if they were even able to smell what she could.

I can't stay here tonight, or any night for that matter, she decided as the face of her attacker flashed in her mind. She had nowhere to go. It was now apparent they were stalking her. Going over to Stella's home wasn't an option either.

Helplessness weighed her down as she sagged on her ruined bed.

Where is Dad when I need him?

CHAPTER 7

The storm raged without mercy. Frantic legs pushed through the falling snow. Dark eyes looked over its shoulder every now and then. The predator once chased its prey just for the thrill, but now it ran from an even deadlier predator than him.

Aaron's beast followed, purposefully giving his prey a head-start. His prey's senses were a mess because it sure didn't know where it was headed, and the leech clearly didn't know the even terrain would drop. The slippery slopes led to a fifty foot drop.

The body rolled down the snow-covered slopes of the forest, crashing into the trees on its way down. Its scream ripping through the air. It was funny how they still felt pain considering they were technically dead. He descended toward him with practiced ease. The vampire tried to scramble away and hissed at the sight of Aaron's massive beast. He growled. Vampires deserved no mercy. Aaron crushed his enemy's skull with a powerful paw, and crimson stained the snow beneath his feet. The beast relished his kill. Hunting was in his nature. Howls of victory drifted through the winds.

His muscular chest expanded to its capacity as he let out another howl. He had responded to their challenge, and now no one remained to carry the message of their defeat to their king.

They had very cleverly masked their own scent but weren't smart enough to mask the scent of their hostages. It brought him and the trackers right to their temporary den.

The girls are secure, Alpha. John's voice sounded into his mind.

The omegas descended with cautious steps, body bags secured in their grip. Their human bodies shivering in the cold. He eyed his kill. The snowstorm will hide the blood and wash away any trace of their scent, but the bodies needed to be removed and disposed of—burned to ash. He stood watching on the side as they began working with gloved hands. The pungent odor burned their nostrils.

"We are done here, Alpha." One of the omegas bowed. The parasite's corpse was concealed.

He gave a curt nod and gestured for them to move ahead. His cautious eyes trained on them, body poised to act if anyone slipped in the snow. The omegas could shift only during the full moons and aged like humans, unlike the lycans. Though they had some advantages with their heightened senses and healing abilities, a fall from this high could easily injure or kill them.

His mind drifted back toward the female vampire in town. It was time to bring her in.

I'm done waiting.

***

Mia stared at her cell phone screen for a long minute. No place was safe in this city. She contemplated leaving the country. She still had her father's card to cover her expenses. But would that help? They had tracked her all the way across the continent, from Phoenix to Brookedge. How long could she keep running?

Sleep was far from reach. She pocketed her phone when she heard footsteps approach her door. Her instincts kicking in, she sniffed the air for threat. Whoever was outside her door smelled like a wet dog, trees, cologne, and something masculine. That cologne brought up the faces of two familiar men from her memory. A knock following shortly.

She peeked through the peephole.

"Open the door!" a voice growled.

Opening the door was the foolish idea she would soon regret. The two of men she easily recognized barged in. Eyes scanning the room, noses sniffing the air. Their demeanors changed when their eyes finally landed on her.

"Why are the vampires after you?" The brunette asked tilting his head to one side. Nut-brown eyes boring into hers.

How did they know? "I. . .I don't know what you're talking about."

"If you're doing this to get our attention, then you have it." The blond circled her, eyes on her packed bags. "You're coming with us." His voice held more authority than the brunette's. Mia just opened and closed her mouth, gaping at them like a fish as her brain processed what they said.

"What? Why would I come with you?" she said backing away from them.

"King's orders. You have five minutes. Either you walk with us or we will drag your sorry ass out of here," the brunette said in a calm, confident tone.

King? She knew he wouldn't hesitate to follow through. "You can't. I-I will call the cops!" her threat sounding more like a question. Her frown deepened. Were they really royals? What good it would be if she did call the police? She backed up against the wall as fear consumed her. She knew something was wrong the moment they met. *My phone. It was—*

"If you're looking for this, don't waste your time," the blond said, smirking.

An audible gasp left her when she noticed her phone in his hand. Patting her coat pockets as her eyes locked with his sparkling green ones. "G-give me that."

The blond just cocked his eyebrows and gripped her by her shoulders when she pivoted and tried to run. She squeaked trying to break free from his steel grip. "Never run from a lycan."

Her blood ran cold.

Lycan as in lycanthrope?

The brunette rolled his eyes. "Toss her over your shoulder, and let's leave this place."

The blond ignored him, holding her with one hand while pulling out his phone with the other. "I'm sure we can persuade her."

Her eyes went wide with shock when he dangled his phone in front of her. They had her father. "What did you do to my father?" She launched herself at them, kicking and screaming.

But before she could cause any more damage, a hand went to her neck, and darkness consumed her vision.

CHAPTER 8

The woods were serene and calm, comforting Aaron's raging mind. A deep inhale filled his lungs with crisp cold air. Snow crunched under his strong paws, soaking his fur. The beast welcomed the chill, licking his snout to taste the pure essence of nature. Running was liberating. It was his responsibility to ensure this peace lasted. War ruined everything in the past. He won't let it ruin everything in the future. The nagging in his gut was back. His clawed fists clenched with determination. This time Felipe would be facing him. Amber eyes narrowed as his huge form evaded the oncoming blur of trees with ease. He knew these woods like the back of his hand. The beast relaxed finding nothing odd as he completed the patrol.

His beast was calm when he returned to the castle. Pulling on a pair of shorts they always kept in the backyard, he quickly climbed the private stairs and proceeded toward the royal wing. Though he'd washed himself clean of his enemy's blood by the nearby stream, his mind longed for a hot shower. He was about to take a turn toward his room when someone stopped him.

Oh no, not her.

"There you are! I've been looking for you everywhere. Heard you killed six bloodsuckers today. That must've been—"

Her continuous high-pitched squeaks hurt his eardrums. "I'm busy Emilia," he said through the clenched teeth and turned to open the door. Emilia—a sexy, calculative, determined and delusional lycan—had her sights on him.

"Aaron, wait! It's about the winter ball. Everyone's expecting you to announce our mating."

"What gave you the notion that I'd choose you as my mate?"

Her pale green orbs rolled, and he let her action slide. "It's no big deal. I'm the only beta female in this pack. So, that makes me the perfect candidate for the post."

"It's not a job." He gritted out, and his jaw locked. It took a few deep breaths to calm his agitated beast. "Look, Emilia, I told you several times before. I don't want you as my mate." The winter ball was arranged in hopes to find a mate. While everyone expected him to choose a mate, his only motive was to bring the clans together.

"Why? You don't like me anymore?" She asked, her lips drawing down in a pout. It never suited her.

He never liked her. "Leave."

Her face changed as she let out a disrespectful snort. Gone was her polite attitude, replaced was the bitchy one he despised. "You know that a king without his mate is unstable. You. . .are unstable. Trust me, once we mate and forge a bond you will have no option but to love me."

His fists clenched. "How can you force someone to love you, Emilia? Love should come from within. You cannot force it." His beast clawed his chest to break free. There was no point in having this talk with her. He tried it before. It never worked. She'd always be back to square one. Females were attracted to males of high rank. It was the power and strength that attracted them. "You don't love me, Emilia."

He wanted a female who would look past his position and strength, who would love him for who he was on the inside. Is it wrong for him to want his heart to skip a beat every time he looked at his mate?

"You can't say that. I have loved you for so long. You know this."

"Enough, Emilia! Leave me this instant."

"And who would even look at you when they very well know they would have to get past me first?"

"Do not test my patience," his growl and the shifting eyes were the only indications of his waning patience.

She's not worth it. He reasoned with his beast that was on the verge of shifting. Oh, how bad he wanted to wring her pretty neck using his bare hands. The kingdom faced enough death in the past, and starting it again by killing Emilia was the last thing on his mind. He turned and closed the door abruptly, saving himself from doing something he'd regret later.

An hour of running and it all was in vain. The encounter with Emilia irked his beast, and now he wanted to punch the daylights out of someone. He turned the shower on, keeping the water cold. She was pushing him to prove her point. It won't work that way. Despite what others believed he was in perfect control of his beast and was determined on their destiny.

Confusion clouded him as he dressed in a v-neck and jeans. It wasn't the time to lose his cool around the vampire. The reason behind their presence in his territory should be his focus. He was taking deep breaths when Juan called him through their telepathic link, *"Brother, we are in."*

"Dad, she's in."

"Bring her to the office."

"Why don't we take her to our interrogation rooms? We can make her talk in no time."

Jerome chuckled. *"Not everything has to be dealt with in violence, Son. You should know this."*

"Dad, I wasn't suggesting the torture chamber. It's your sudden interest in this girl that I don't fathom."

"I have a theory I'd like to confirm myself."

"Sounds good," his eyes shifted briefly to that of his beast. Not knowing what's on his father's mind unsettled his nerves.

Time to meet you, Vamp.

Impatience was what had him go downstairs to the family's personal garage. He ordered his brother to bring the girl there as none of the pack members would be around. Panic and unwanted rumors would ruin the little peace they had.

The beast itched to break free. The thought of having a vampire who went unnoticed in their territory did not sit well with it. *Is she the only one?* She could have harmed anyone. *Don't let your anger cloud your judgment.* He remembered the words of his father who had more experience and knowledge than him.

Feet tapped restlessly on the concrete when their sleek black Audi slipped in. "Where is she?" his voice growled out in agitation. His beast surfaced just beneath his skin.

Juan signaled to the back seat, and Aaron opened the door. His beast itched to rip into the vampire—then froze. Her scent hit him with a force that made his knees go weak. It was like a punch to his gut. Blood rushed to his head and lungs protested, refusing to release the breath.

There she was, curled on the back seat, either asleep or unconscious. Since his brothers were involved, he assumed it was the latter. Her face was peaceful and still. Pale blonde hair fanned out and hid most of her delicate features. A sense of calm and peace washed over him, capturing his heart in a tight hold. Thick eyelashes framed her almond-shaped eyes and pinkish full lips with a tint of red formed a small pout. *Are they soft as they appear?*

The thought shocked him. How long he stood watching her, he didn't know. He came back to reality when his brother shook him slightly. No one had affected him the way this female had, and surely, he had never looked at any woman twice. It must be the scent. His lungs were forced to exhale. Then again. He couldn't get enough of the fresh citrus and the floral aroma that captivated his entire being.

He blinked his eyes and tried to shake her image from his vision, but his gaze went right back to her, admiring the soft pout. *How could she be an intruder?* His throat cleared, wondering on how to wake her. Should he just shake her awake? What's her name? His mind was blank.

Dumbfounded—the word wouldn't explain half of what he felt. His legs refused to move. His hand on the door clenched around the handle as the free hand fisted by his side.

She's a leech. A good one and she smelled delicious.

Mouth watered as images of sinking his cannines into her delectable skin played in his mind. *Shut it! It must be the vampire magic.* That sounded reasonable. After all, they were the most attractive predators in the world. There was this strange aura around them that lured their prey in. *Yes, that must be it.*

"Son?"

Eyes blinked again, lips parted. No words came out.

"Son, meet us in the office with the girl." A warm hand squeezed his shoulder. Footsteps walked away, leaving him to his devices. *Don't go.* The shout never left his lips.

He swallowed the invisible lump. With great difficulty, he forced his body to move. Anger flared at his beast, who he could imagine with his jaw on the ground, drooling. Weren't they supposed to be in this together?

She's our enemy! A very beautiful enemy indeed, his beast side responded contradicting his own thoughts. *Looks can be deceiving.* I beg to differ.

A soft moan caught his ears, and his posture stiffened. The angel stirred in her sleep. His throat cleared, "Hello," he sounded almost awkward. Her eyes snapped open. They were wide and blue—the color of the clear sky. His beast was mesmerized.

"Uh. . .hello," greeted an angelic voice, making his beast purr in content. Realization of what that meant dawned on him and that felt like a bucket of ice being poured on him. *She can't be my mate.* That's the most ridiculous thought ever. She was a vampire—his sworn enemy. *What kind of sick joke is this?*

With her hair out of the way, he could now see her face—high cheekbones and a short chin. An angel indeed. "I'm Aaron. Welcome to the Randolph Castle," he managed. She wasn't welcome here. She was a prisoner. Nothing more. The emotionless mask he perfected over the years was on. His mind conflicted, waging war with his beast who wouldn't relent.

"I'm Mia," she replied, climbing out of the car. Her eyes swept to the sides, scanning her surroundings.

*Mia. . .*He tasted her name, savoring the way it felt on his tongue. "It's a pleasure to meet you, Mia." He stretched out his hand, wondering if her skin would be as warm as her aura. Big mistake. When her hand took his outstretched hand, he was once again taken aback by the warmth she radiated. The beast admired how small her hands were when compared to his. Her skin felt like silk. Vampires' skin was cold as ice, they never radiated warmth. He masked his frown and retracted his hand.

"Follow me," he said and started walking. Once they lost contact, he felt the warmth leave him. Another mistake. Never turn your back on your enemy. He couldn't believe himself. He never behaved like this before. *Is she a witch?* He sniffed the air and confirmed to himself she wasn't.

He couldn't explain the overwhelming sensation that drowned him when her scent first hit him. There was no explanation for the way her presence calmed his beast. *She's a stranger.* She was also the most beautiful female after his mother, and the first one to attract him. Faint footsteps and the tiny stutter of her heartbeat followed. A vampire's heart didn't beat.

What does Dad know?

CHAPTER 9

The silence was unnerving. Though she woke a few minutes ago, she continued to pretend she was unconscious. When the car stopped moving, her body stirred fearing the worst. Senses stretched out feeling her new surroundings. She felt them exiting the vehicle, but no one dragged her out as she expected.

Mia forced her body to stay calm when the door opened, and a strong scent of a male hit her with full force. Masculine because it was a mixture of something earthy and sandalwood, probably his body wash.

She was startled when she heard a throat being cleared and a strange voice call out, "Hello."

Her eyes snapped open and locked with a pair of amber orbs shining bright—they felt familiar. *The eyes of the beast in her dreams*! She gasped and moved back involuntarily.

Mia couldn't look away from the pools of amber that captivated her. Handsome was an understatement to define the man in front of her. He was sexy and masculine with his towering six-foot-three broad frame and well-defined musculature.

A deep blush crept onto her cheeks when she realized she was staring at the stranger. "Uh. . .hello," she greeted in a small voice and noticed his shoulders tense for a moment.

"I'm Aaron. Welcome to the Randolph Castle," he greeted.

His attractive voice caressed her insides like a soft feather. It was thick and authoritative. An aura so strong radiated off him. It was commanding and comforting at the same time.

"I'm Mia." Her eyes did a quick sweep around, finding they were alone. *Who is this man?* He must be working for the king. But he also carried himself like one. She was quick to curb that thought. *Why would he come to receive me in person?*

"It's a pleasure to meet you, Mia." The stranger, Aaron, stretched out his hand. She took it and was immediately surrounded by a sense of warmth that comforted her. His features hardened and his hand withdrew.

"Follow me," he said and turned. Her nervous smile fell, her body mourning the loss of warmth and that was like ice cold water being splashed on her. She wasn't welcome here. They had her father and they kidnapped her.

"Where is my dad?" She tried to reign in her sudden panic.

His feet halted and his shoulders tensed. "He is fine."

He is fine? That didn't answer her question. "What happened to him?"

"He was poisoned."

"Poisoned!"

"It was an accident. You need to hurry instead of asking questions."

The nerve of him, dismissing her like that. She ground her teeth but kept her mouth shut. Her dad was a priority. First, she will find him, and then, they'll plan their escape.

Marble stairs came into view as they walked further inside. Modern railings made her wonder if this was a recent installation. When they entered the luxurious corridor, she found the decorations were ancient, yet beautiful. Despite the situation she was in, her mind admired the long corridors and the rich designs on the doors as they walked past them. They must have been walking for at least five minutes, taking numerous turns. *Where is he taking me? What if he doesn't take me to Dad?* He stopped all of a sudden, and she bumped into his back after not noticing.

"Ouch!" It was like hitting a concrete wall. Once again, his warmth surrounded her.

When he turned around to see her rubbing her nose, concern etched his handsome features. "Are you okay?" he asked, trying to take a closer look at her nose. His voice sent delicious shivers throughout her body, making her knees weak.

"Ah. . .Yes. I'm fine," she said, backing away.

He nodded and opened the door to a room that appeared to be an office. "Here we are. Come in."

The room was surprisingly warm and had a homey feeling. Books and files occupied the shelves, and the walls were lined with beautiful portraits. Suddenly, it felt like she was entering the lion's den. A man who looked like the older version of Aaron sat behind the desk. The blonde and brunette occupied the seats opposite to him. If she had her way she'd be pounding her fists into their pretty faces repeatedly.

"Mia, this is my father and former king, Jerome." Aaron introduced.

Former king. Crap. *That meant Aaron is indeed the king. Should I bow?* But his father extended his large hand for her to shake, and she took it as the nervousness once again took hold of her. She squirmed under his scrutinizing gaze.

"You've already met my brothers, Juan and Matthew."

Oh, so the brutes had names. She made no move to greet them. Her eyes narrowed and a corner of her lips curled upward. Their eyes shifted, meeting her head on. Mild rumbles vibrated from their chests. Her senses were suddenly in tune with them. Eyes followed every shift of their muscle as her hands clenched.

"Sit, Mia." Jerome pointed to the chair opposite him.

She blinked and shook her head. An uncomfortable silence settled in the room. She felt their gazes on her as she took the seat. "I need to see my dad."

Instead of answering her, he gave a curt nod to the brutes and they stood, leaving the room.

"You must be very hungry. Eat up, dear," Jerome spoke, breaking the silence and pushing the steaming tray in front of her. "Your dad will be here shortly."

The mini sandwiches, cookies, tea, and coffee provided a warm welcome. But she knew it was all fake. The smile didn't reach his eyes. She lost control for a moment when she saw them. A mistake she won't repeat again.

Always know your enemy. She chewed the sandwich as her heart raced, anticipating her father's arrival. There were a lot of things she didn't know about the people around her. She welcomed the distraction when she accepted the tray. Anything to keep her mind occupied and calm her rattling nerves. Her mind needed to be clear for what was to come.

***

Ted's heart beat louder when the door opened. Whatever they injected him with, the effects were wearing off, and he felt a small flicker of magic in his blood.

"Your daughter wants to meet you," the lycan he recognized as the royal beta said, unsheathing a syringe with a strange liquid.

His body shrunk as far as the confinements of the chair allowed. "What's that?" Ted pulled at his restraints as panic set in.

"It's a perfect combination of witches' gloves and a few other things you don't want to mess with," his smile was wicked. His green eyes shone with malice.

Ted tried to back away, but the chair didn't budge. "Don't. . ." He breathed erratically.

The royal beta chuckled on seeing his reaction, amused. "This won't kill you. It's a small dose to keep your magic dormant while you're here."

A grimace stretched his facial muscles when the needle breached the surface of his skin. An unfamiliar burn spread through his veins and he let out a hiss. The liquid extinguished the small flicker of magic along with his hope.

"We have your precious daughter in custody. Don't try anything funny, Galahad. My brother isn't a patient man."

***

Aaron reclined in his seat, wondering what theory his father wanted to test. He took the passenger seat when his father volunteered to interrogate the girl. Her posture grew stiff when she entered the room. Anxiety rolled off her in waves.

Her demeanor changed as soon as her eyes landed on his brothers. She narrowed her eyes, and a corner of her lips curled upward. The fur of the beasts bristled and their eyes shifted, meeting her head on. Mild rumbles vibrated from their chests and answering growls rolled out of her own. He wondered if she even realized that. It was as if her senses were suddenly in tune with them.

She hissed at his brothers like a snake, her eyes followed every shift of their muscle as her hands clenched. Then, something happened. Her heart stopped beating, and her scent was withdrawn. He sucked in a sharp breath. If she wasn't in broad daylight, they would have no chance of sensing her presence. Her head had tilted as if listening to the beat of their hearts.

Dangerous.

Aaron's eyes flicked to his father as his brothers' eyes widened. He now saw her for what she was—a perfect predator. *What else is she capable of?*

"Sit, Mia." His father intervened, distracting her, and just like that, her heart started beating and her scent hit them with full force. She blinked and shook her head before taking a seat.

"I need to see my dad." Her impassive voice demanded. She met no one's gaze.

Jerome nodded at Juan and Matthew who left with a grim nod.

"You must be very hungry. Eat up, dear," his dad's voice was gentle as he pushed the steaming tray in front of her. "Your dad will be here shortly."

His old man usually created a friendly environment for the culprit in question with tea and snacks, blanketing them with comfort and security that appeared genuine. They often trusted him and blurted out anything he wanted to know.

He didn't think Mia bought his dad's act. His gaze narrowed as Mia treated herself to a sandwich, her eyes closed for a moment as she took a bite. Vampires couldn't stomach human food, they couldn't digest it. The creatures solely depended on blood. They were a form of zombies in this modern world with working brains, minus the deranged skin. He could almost see the wheels in her head turning.

Aaron's mind reeled. Slowly, like a puzzle piece falling in its place, his mind pieced the signs together. That's it. It was the only possible answer with a valid explanation. Rare, yet *possible*.

"Dad is she what I think she is?"

"Yes."

"What does this mean?" His instincts were on full alert.

"I think fate has some other plans this time."

He hated when he talked like an oracle. *"Dad. . ."* his irritation flared.

"Patience, son. This is something you need to handle with utmost care."

The warlock must have known this. But it didn't make sense why he'd want to hide her in his territory. Aaron wasn't known for his patience. But he decided to wait for some more time. Just as his father opened his mouth to speak, a knock came at the door.

Ted was pushed into the room while Juan and Matthew followed. Mia's head whipped around, and in the blink of an eye, she reached him.

"Dad!"

Her eyes scanned him. "I heard you were poisoned."

Aaron's right brow quirked when Ted's eyes flicked to him. "I'm fine now." His smile was tight.

Her body visually relaxed and her voice lowered as she eyed them suspiciously. "What's going on? I don't understand why they want to see us."

"Um. . .Mia, about that. . ."

"Why don't you both take a seat?" Aaron's father leaned back and Ted's shoulders tensed again. "We'll talk. Isn't that why we are here?"

Ted nodded at Mia, and they both took a seat. Shoulders tense, lips tight and eyes suspicious.

"Galahad, isn't it? The son of one of the great warlocks the kings feared."

"Yes." Ted's gaze swept across the room. Juan casually leaned over the door while Matthew perched on the windowsill, ready to act if they made a wrong move.

"My father often spoke highly of your parents. I'm sorry for your loss."

Aaron quietly observed the interesting turn of events. His fingers tapped silently at the leather as Mia looked between her father and the former king.

The warlock cleared his throat, his expression surprised, and his features softened a bit. "It was a long time ago."

"It was a foolish move on your side, trying to hide her in our territory," Aaron intervened. Now that he knew what she was, he didn't think they were here with any intention to spy on the lycans. Again, the attacks could've been staged to make them believe. But the parasite his brothers brought in the other day claimed he was there to hunt the girl whose scent made his mouth water. And, he spoke the truth.

"It was," Ted averted his gaze. "I was just trying to protect my daughter."

"By hiding her in the lion's den?" he asked. "She could've been killed." Had she stumbled on one of his warriors instead of his brothers, she'd have died already.

When Ted's gaze locked with him for a brief moment, they held regret. "I had no choice, Alpha. They were closing in on us—on me. I thought they wouldn't go into your territory in search of her."

"And yet, they came." In fact, the vampire sightings were becoming a headache in the recent months to the point that he had to double patrol. Mia appeared lost, a deep frown on her face as she listened to their conversation. "Why are they hunting her?"

"I'm not sure." Ted frowned. "It must be her scent or they have found out the truth about her. He killed the two before her."

Ah, yes, he remembered now. The two purebloods before her were killed in cold blood. He didn't think Felipe knew the truth. She was the first female to ever be born. He can never get his hands on her. Never.

"Felipe can never get his hands on her." his father's words mirrored his thoughts.

"We can't hide her here."

"Letting her leave is not an option, son."

"Is she a pureblood?" Juan joined their conversation.

"Yes."

"Wow!" Matthew's eyes widened.

"What are you both talking about? Who were killed before me?" she asked, interrupting their discussion. He heard her heart racing.

"It's something I should have told you sooner," her father spoke. "We'll talk later."

When Ted's attention turned to the former king, Aaron knew what was coming.

"Thank you for your hospitality, Your Highness. We apologize for the trouble we caused. We don't want to be a burden anymore."

They weren't a burden. They were a liability. His liability.

"I'm afraid that's not your decision to make, Galahad." Aaron stood to his full height, squaring his shoulders. "The war is coming and *they* are coming for us. You have to stay until we decide otherwise."

Ted stared with his mouth agape.

"My son is right, Galahad. We'd like to extend our invitation for you both to stay here at Randolph Castle."

"That's. . .Your Highness—"

The warlock risked a nervous look toward his daughter. "She—

A knock sounded at the door, interrupting them.

CHAPTER 10

She stared at every person in the room without a clue as to what was going on. There were so many questions she wanted answers for. Everyone seemed to know what she was except her. She couldn't wait to get her dad alone. A knock interrupted their conversation, and she turned out of habit to see who it was.

"I'll get it." Juan moved to the door, his face grim as if he already knew who was on the other side.

"There has been a—" a male voice began. "What do you have in there?"

Before Juan could respond, someone barged inside.

"I knew it! I could smell her all the way here." A tall man in his early forties bellowed. Rage contorted his features as he pointed angrily at Mia. "You not only let a leech inside, but also let her sit in front of you!"

"Excuse me!" Mia exclaimed.

"Richard, stand down," Jerome's features hardened. "She isn't the one you need to worry about."

"She's a vampire, and that makes her our enemy."

"What? I am not a vampire." Her breathing quickened. Her eyes weren't dark nor did she smell like a rotten corpse.

The furious lycan let out a loud growl as he lunged at her with his claws extended, his face turning red with anger. In the blink of an eye, Aaron was in front of Mia, pushing her behind him. He caught Richard's hand in a death grip as he pinned him against the table. Her eyes widened further noticing his long, sharp claws. *What the hell.*

"Stand down, Richard!" he bellowed, his eyes shifting between amber and brown as his beast surfaced.

"Ridiculous. You're protecting a leech. I will never allow this! She must be killed, not protected!" Rage distorted his features. Fur sprouted in his arms and face, he growled with his spit flying everywhere. He reminded her of an angry animal.

She staggered behind, creating more distance. He thrashed in Aaron's hold. A blur of movement caught her eye as she tripped and fell on her ass. Before Richard could get anywhere near her, he was pinned against the wall by his neck. Her protector was too fast—one second, she saw Richard coming at her, and the next he was dangling in Aaron's steel-like grip struggling to breathe.

Their growls reverberated around her.

"Stand down," The guttural voice belonged to the man, who even in a situation like this had her heart racing.

Her father's protective arms wrapped around her, and they looked at Richard, whose eyes were shining brighter. She had seen nothing like this. The former king hadn't moved from his place behind the table.

"S-she's a vampire, Alpha."

Why would he claim that I'm a vampire? Her dad's arms tightened their hold on her, and she closed her mouth from voicing out her thoughts.

Catherine Edward

"Do you think I don't know that?"

What's wrong with these people?

The other man bared his neck in submission. "Forgive me, Alpha."

Aaron did not respond, instead he threw Richard on the floor.

The other lycan quickly scrambled away from him.

"There won't be a warning next time, Beta. Run the patrol for the rest of the week." His masculine rumble was full of authority and her knees buckled hearing the command in his voice. Her shoulders hunched, and she felt a compulsion to bare her neck. It weighed down on her until she relented.

"Leave and do not speak of this."

"Y-yes, Alpha," Richard stuttered.

Her mind vaguely registered him hurriedly leaving the room.

"Are you okay?" Aaron's voice was now gentle.

She was shaking but nodded yes. "Why did he call me a vampire?" It had been gnawing her gut ever since the word slipped from the lycan's mouth. He could've called her anything, but not that. She despised them. They were dark, sinister, and smelly creatures. Her nose scrunched at the memory.

Ted shifted from one foot to the other. "You're a born vampire, Mia. A pureblood."

"A born what!" Mia stood. "I-I can't be a vampire. I'm not bad. I don't drink blood, and I have surely not killed anyone before." Blood rushed to her head, and her vision blurred. The sound of her own heartbeat became too much to bear.

"It's not like that."

She shook her head, "Call me anything but that. I can't be that." Her body trembled as sobs choked out.

70

"I think you have had enough for today. Why don't we save this discussion for another day when you're well rested and more relaxed," Aaron suggested. "My brothers will show you to your room." He gestured toward them.

"Come on, Mia. We'll talk later." Her father ran his hand through her hair.

"I'm not—"

His hands silenced her. "You're not one of them."

With another sob, she sank into his embrace as he led her out.

***

She wasn't faking it. Her emotions were true. The mixture of shock and fear on her face made him want to pull her into his embrace and assure that everything will be all right. Her eyes had changed to pitch black and Aaron didn't miss the panic she was going into.

"Take her to the far end room of the omega's quarters. I'll have John secure the perimeter until we figure out our next step," he shot the orders via their telepathic link.

A born vampire was the most powerful being, and he didn't want to test her limits when they didn't know what she was capable of.

Aaron barked orders to John, then turned to face his father. "This is serious. And, I didn't know you knew Galahad's father."

"I dug into our archives when you were away," he shrugged his shoulders.

"We can't keep her here."

"Yet you can't let her leave either."

"Dad–"

"Either she'll die or will become something worse if he got his hands on her," the warning in his father's tone shot an alarm through his system. His father stood, walking around the desk. "So far, the vampires can only increase their numbers by biting and turning the humans. But imagine if Felipe can reproduce, bring more pureblooded leeches into this world."

His blood ran cold at the mention of their archnemesis. He hadn't thought about it that way. "It'll be a disaster."

"Disaster would be an understatement."

"She seems innocent."

"Don't forget the monster that resides underneath that innocence. We got a glimpse of her abilities today."

Yes, they all got a glimpse. He wondered how she was able to withdrew her scent and stop her heart from beating. He never heard of a supernatural that possessed such lethal ability that put his senses to shame.

"And, she's only beginning to come into her powers. She's still a baby in our terms. He can never ever get his hands on her."

"Then, we should just kill her—" The beast within snarled a warning to Aaron before he could even finish the sentence. It caused an unbearable pain where his heart lay, and his hands clutched his chest.

His father put a hand on his shoulder. "I feel it's too late for that son."

***

When you live in a castle full of supernatural beings with enhanced senses, it is impossible to go unnoticed. That's what happened when the royal betas guided them to their new room. Without the aid of his magic, Ted felt vulnerable but still maintained a protective stance beside his daughter.

The shoulders of the betas were stiff, their bodies poised to attack. The omegas scrambled away from them with their eyes going wide in fear while the deltas, the ranked pack warriors, bristled their fur and snarled, only to be silenced by the alpha-born males.

Mia's small frame shuddered in his arms. and he once again felt like he was holding the four-year-old she once was. His paternal instincts surged forward as he pulled her further into his body and hid her face from their vision. Her occasional whimpers tugged at his heartstrings. The royals radiated too much authority that even made *his* knees buckle.

Despite his initial fear of immediate death, the lycans had let them live. Ted refused to fall for this false sense of security. They weren't off the hook yet. Not in the least. They've just extended the term of their lives until the lycans decided what to do with them. Now, they had a place to lay low. He had to figure something out soon. Logan's face popped into his mind and he assured himself that the human was safe. The beasts didn't attack humans. They protected them.

The warlock had no hopes until the attack. But then, a plan began to take root when he noticed the way the alpha's beast behaved around Mia. His stance was protective, promising sure death for anyone who came at her. The beast had surged forward when a lycan tried to attack his daughter earlier in the office, and he knew enough about their race to read the signs.

A few more lycans joined them when they turned into a corridor, forming a protective circle around them. A tight smile found its way to his lips. Ted's plan was risky, but if he succeeded it was a win-win for both. Mia would not only live and flourish but will also forever be away from the clutches of the power-hungry predator who threatened to ruin their very existence.

"Lock the door from the inside. Do not open unless it's one of us," Juan, the first beta, warned before closing the door.

"Dad," Mia let out a strangled sob. "It can't be true. I'm not a monster. Please. . .tell me I'm not."

"You're my daughter. That's what you are and will always be." His hands clutched her shoulders and forced her to look into his eyes. "You can't change who you are. But, who you want to be is in your hands."

"That's not convincing. I. . ."

"Denying what you are isn't going to help the situation, Mia." He silenced her before she talked. "Not now, sweetheart. We are not safe. We have to be more careful than ever."

Her sob was the only response he got as her tears soaked his skin.

"It's not the time to break down. Rest now and trust me on this, okay?"

She gave him a half-hearted nod and allowed him to lead her to the bed. He watched as she curled herself into a ball. It hurt him to see her like this. His baby girl who gave him hope to carry on with this life.

As long as I breathe, I will not let harm befall you.

CHAPTER 11

Aaron knew what to expect when he called for a pack meeting. Their pack bond had been restless since the news broke out, and they felt betrayed. While he'd have preferred to handle this with little drama, his choices were limited. His beast didn't appreciate the idea of locking her away like a prisoner.

Silence fell over the crowd when he made his way to the throne that stood tall and regal. He could feel eyes crawling up his back with different emotions—betrayed, frightened, outraged. His shoulders were stiff and his stance was wide when he turned to face them.

The omegas appeared small with hunched shoulders, while the warriors bristled. His father and brothers stood by his side as they always did. Emilia's seething face couldn't be missed, not that he cared. Aaron met the gaze of each pack member, holding it until they averted theirs.

"Good evening, pack. I sense the sudden unrest and panic in your mind, and I'm here to address your concerns." He took a deep breath to compose himself and reign in his beast. "We have a vampire and a warlock in our custody. There are certain things I do not wish to discuss now, but I'll ask you all to trust me on this."

Disclosing the truth about her would warrant unnecessary panic. A few members murmured their disagreement as the whispers rose considerably.

"Quiet! Your safety is my responsibility," his bellow was laced with the growl of his beast. "Any decision I make will hold the best interest of our pack." His tone took a hard note as he spoke the next words, "John and his team are carrying out my orders. I've heard about the few incidents earlier. I do not want a repeat." His ambers were shining brightly when he regarded each pack member. "Our guests are under my protection. Do you understand?"

The pack bowed, unable to withstand the weight of his authority and bared their necks in submission before replying in unison, "Yes, Alpha.".

"You may all leave now," he dismissed the crowd before turning and nodding at his brothers to follow.

The crowd dispersed with loud murmurs as they made their way to the office.

"Stay alert and prepare one of the rooms in our wing. She's not safe where she currently is," Aaron mused.

"What about the warlock?" Juan asked.

"Stop the dosage. He's useless without his magic, and for the time being, we need him by her side."

"What if he tries to escape?" Matthew's question was something he contemplated, but decided they wouldn't escape since the dangers of the outside world were worse than their confinement here.

"They have no other place to go," his answer was confident. "Their lives aren't safe outside that room. He wouldn't risk her like that."

"And, what about the human we have in custody?"

"Keep him close until we decide our next course of action."

***

It was nearing midnight when he heard the commotion. Aaron had just returned from another run when the muffled screams reached his ears. When Aaron opened his mind, lifting the temporary barrier that blocked the others from contacting him, the pack bond was raging.

"Brother! We need you right now."

"Situation is getting out of hand."

His pointed ears twitched after realizing the screams were coming from the omega's quarters; he took off in that direction. *Mia is in danger.* It did not sit right with his beast. Going through the multiple corridors would take time. His strong hind limbs pushed harder and he dived into the air, catching the railing and jumping over.

The small room stood still when his beast burst through the glass door that separated the room from the balcony. The strong metallic tang of blood hit his nostrils, and his golden eyes did a quick sweep across the room, finding Mia cowering in one of the corners and hugging her injured father. Blood from his body pooled around them as she frantically pressed a cloth over his gaping wounds.

Talk about a surprise. The vampire didn't as much as flinch at the smell of blood. The control she had over her blood thirst amazed him.

Juan's beige-furred beast stood protectively over them, while Matthew, still in his human form, held a fully shifted lycan in a chokehold. Four unconscious bodies lay in a heap. When the fight resumed, his roar shook the walls. Ted's faint heartbeat fluttered, struggling to hold on.

"Enough!" Their knees buckled. *"Keep coming if you want to die tonight."* His warning held no remorse, and he was poised to see his threat through. They went against his orders. Did they think they could get away with it? Brainless oafs.

The warriors growled in response, their massive jaws snapping at him. A blur of brown raced past him when the first beast made its move. Matthew's powerful paws collided with its jaw, breaking it. A howl ripped into the night as its jaw hung on its hinges. Yet, it kept coming closer until Matthew snapped his neck, rendering him useless.

That move won't kill a lycanthrope. To kill, they must remove the heart or decapitate their head. Grunts and growls could be heard from the corridor.

Fearful blues gazed up to his form. *Is that relief on her face?* Sobs choked out as she looked helplessly at her father. Her tearstained face stirred his protective instincts. The eight-foot beast bent scooping the injured warlock before handing him over to his brother. *"Take him to Paul. Now!"*

Juan's beast nodded once before running toward the balcony, jumping over and landing gracefully on its hind limbs. A surprised yelp warmed his insides when Aaron hoisted Mia onto his back, allowing her to hook her legs around his waist. She clung to his fur as he took off in the same direction. Her soft body pressed against his hard muscles as her grip tightened, making his heart race.

The beast warned anyone who dared to look their way as he moved toward the hospital. He wanted to check if she was injured, but now that she was close, he could smell her blood.

The infirmary occupied most of the first-level of their underground building structure. It could be shut down from the inside and acted as a safety bunker at times of the war.

Lycan's Blood Queen

Dr. Paul Barnes rushed toward them with his staff. The experienced doctor asked no questions as he turned his attention toward the injured warlock, barking orders at his team. Another doctor, Jacob Anderson, rushed toward his beast. When he let her down, the human doctor immediately got to work on her. It helped that Jacob's family worked for the Randolphs for over five generations and knew of their existence.

Her arm was injured although the claw marks were already healing. When he was finished dressing her wounds, more lycans were brought in by the others. Jacob urged them further down the aisle toward the section dedicated for their prisoners. Aaron appreciated his thoughtfulness. It was time to demonstrate what would happen if they went against his orders.

"Call for a pack meeting. I want them all out in the training area in one hour." The injured lycans would be ready by then.

When he looked at Mia's face, he knew he couldn't let this happen again. Aaron's beast extended his furry paw, offering it to her before he could stop himself. The overgrown furball was now in control, and when he tried to push to the front, he was just swatted back into his mind.

To his surprise, she wasn't afraid of him. That wasn't the reaction he got from many, even within his pack, almost everyone feared his beast. To them, he was reckless. The relief in her eyes when he first made his entry couldn't be missed. His clawed thumb caressed the back of her palm before enclosing her hand in his much larger ones. *Soft, small, and warm.* His massive head gestured toward the entrance and she followed.

The look on the faces of his pack members promised an upcoming headache. The beast treated no one with so much care. He took her straight to the royal wing and opened the room adjacent to his chamber that was once the nursery.

His current bedchamber used to belong to his parents before his mother's demise. It had a door connecting to the nursery so he could check on her or reach her room immediately in case of emergency. His mother arranged it that way so she could care for her little ones' needs. None of the Randolph children ever had a wet nurse.

Mia took in the pale blue walls and matching silk curtains. A queen-sized bed occupied the middle of the room, spotless silk sheets covering them. Talking while in beast form wasn't something he preferred. His tongue slurred and words dragged if he tried. He inclined his head to her and went to his room through the connecting door.

***

Mia watched his beast disappear behind the wooden door and turned her attention toward the room. Her body still trembled with the memory of the attack that felt so sudden. She'd been sound asleep and woke to the sounds of snarling to see her father attempting to fight a creature she'd never seen before. When her eyes adjusted to the darkness of the room, she saw what was unfolding.

Her eyes barely kept up with the blur of motions and fear shot through her when she heard her father's screams. Fear had become her greatest enemy since it once again rendered her useless. It felt like déjà vu as her nightmare became real. Only this time it was with different creatures.

One of them had cornered her. It swiped at her with his sharp claws. Pain shot down her arms from where it connected while she tried to protect her face. When a beige colored beast jumped to her rescue, she'd hurried to her father. Her legs felt like jelly. Blood pooled around his body. *He's hurt because of me.* That's when her sobs broke out. She hated tears. Hated that it made her feel weak.

"Dad!"

Another beast pounced at her. The startled scream had barely left her lips when the beige beast pummeled into its massive body. Growls, snarls, roars, grunts, and pain-filled howls shook her. The noises drowned her strangled cry. If this happened three years ago, she would have questioned her sanity.

"Dad, please wake up."

Blood whooshed out of his gaping wounds. She tried to remember the first aid lessons she learned in school. Removing her sweater, she pressed it over his injuries, trying to stop the blood flow. He needed medical help. Her phone sat on the head table where she left it earlier. She would have to cross the room to get it. "Please hold on. Help is coming." She tried to stay confident.

Her chest heaved and hands shook. A beast took position in front of them, protecting them from the onslaught of attacks while Matthew, still in his human form, fought a fully shifted lycan. "Help, please. He's dying." The beige-furred beast's ears twitched, but he didn't turn. His body was poised toward the entrance, ready to attack.

Suddenly, the glass door that separated the room from the balcony broke, sending pieces of glass everywhere. A towering beast with fur black as night and eyes blazing bright golden entered. Strong hind limbs stepped over the debris as his eyes swept around the room.

When their eyes connected, she just knew everything would be okay. She should be scared. His massive form should have sent her running to the hills. He was a predator, who didn't hesitate to kill. Oddly enough though, she didn't fear the beast. He'd acted faster, saving her and her father.

"Apologies for earlier, Mia. It won't happen again."

She turned startled by Aaron's voice. He wore a simple white shirt and jeans. The concern in his eyes warmed her insides. "How is my dad?"

"He is fine. He'll be out of the infirmary in a day or two."

"Thanks for saving us in time."

"It's nothing," his shoulder lifted in a shrug. "That door connects to my room. This used to be our nursery," he said, changing the topic. "No one dares come to the royal wing, so you'll be safe here."

"Thank you."

His pack scared her. If they had left earlier, none of this would have happened. "This won't happen again, Mia. I didn't think they would go against my orders. It was a mistake on my side."

He was a good leader. She liked the way he took responsibility for his pack's actions. "It's okay," she replied, suddenly feeling self-conscious about her appearance. His hands were in his pockets. The front of his shirt stretched, emphasizing his muscles. She had to force her eyes away from him.

Someone knocked on the door, making her jump. It opened and a tan-skinned hand slipped in, placing her bag on the floor.

"That's one of the guards on duty," Aaron told her. "I'll leave you to rest then. If you need anything, just use the intercom. 125 is my extension." He stopped and turned with a hand on the doorknob, "Mia, close the main door and don't open it. Also, leave this open." He pointed to the connecting door. "I won't enter unless it's an emergency."

"Your Highness. . ." She hoped it was the right way to address him. It wasn't like she spoke to a royal every day. Her father called him an alpha.

He turned to look at her.

"It's about earlier. Do you think I'm a v-vampire?" she couldn't shove that thought away. Her father refused to talk about it and forced her to rest when she tried.

His brown eyes with flecks of gold bore through hers. "We'll talk later."

"No!" Mia wrapped her arms around her middle and her teeth caught her lower lip as she averted her gaze. "Please. . .please tell me I'm not." Her father said she was in denial, and she believed him. But she needed to know—a blind hope that someone would say it differently.

She stood unmoving as he came toward her. "Rest. We'll talk later." His hand rose to her face, stopping mid-air before falling to his side.

She nodded, resigned. He won't say it again. *And, he didn't deny it.*

"Good night, Mia. Sleep well," he said and left the room without another word.

"Good night, Your Highness." She murmured into the air. There was no point in thinking about this tonight. She was worn out, and what had happened today was a lot to take in. It drained her mentally and physically.

She locked the main door and collapsed on the mattress with no mood to admire its softness. Her life as she knew it had changed within one night, and her conscience told her there was no return. Her eyes scanned the room, not really focusing on anything. Her mind wandered, and her heart still galloped. Tonight, she had almost died. *Almost.* And, this won't be the last attempt.

Sighing, she got up and busied herself by arranging the small amount of clothing she had here before pulling out a towel and a clean pair of pajamas.

The bathroom was big and luxurious, which was no surprise. It was a relief that she could move around without hitting the walls. White tiles covered the walls alongside cabinets with golden handles and a three-foot mirror that adorned the sink. Every toiletry she could possibly need was in the bathroom.

If it was any other time, she'd have been excited at the sight of the jacuzzi. Her exhausted mind longed for a shower as she prayed for her father's recovery.

She turned on the faucet, setting the temperature just right and let the warm water cascade her tired body. It soothed her aching mind, providing a distraction for a short while before all the events came crashing down. She was alone again and desperate tears exited her eyes, mingling with the water.

Why me? Crying was useless. No matter how hard she tried to shove the thoughts aside, they just kept coming back to her. *How do I accept it? Will I be like the others?*

She stopped crying after a while and forced her wandering mind to concentrate on the sound and feel of the water hitting her body. Her father said he'd do everything in his power to help. Perhaps, she could find a cure. *I'm not craving for blood. It doesn't affect me.* If there wasn't craving, then, it wasn't too late for her. The thought relaxed her.

Her mind drifted to the alpha. *He's so handsome.* Something about him made her grow warm inside. She was quick to curb the thought as soon as it came. *He's a king. Get hold of yourself, Mia. This is neither the time nor place to admire him.* He was off limits. Her mere presence in the castle had led to havoc in less than twenty-four hours. She wasn't welcome here.

CHAPTER 12

The pack had gathered in the snow-covered training yard at the eastern side of the castle. Their gloomy faces stared up at their alpha with mixed emotions. Aaron was conflicted. The issue on hand was delicate. He didn't want them to think that he chose a vampire over them. His father was silent. His brothers stood by his side again.

He shook his head when John handed him the whip. It won't be necessary. Whipping them would have been his usual form of punishment, but tonight he decided against it.

"I am ashamed of your actions tonight," his thundering voice earned a few whimpers from the crowd. "It's a shame you'd felt the need to take matters in your hands when I'm here. You'll be punished for going against my orders."

"Forgive me, Alpha. But they were merely acting on their instincts," Emilia stepped forward. "It's in their nature—"

"I did not ask for an opinion, Emilia. It shows disrespect and their lack of trust. They attacked their brethren and went against their alpha." He squared his shoulders, meeting her gaze that averted to the ground.

"Aaron please—"

"You shall address me as your alpha."

"I'm sorry, Alpha."

"Bring me the collars."

"Yes, Alpha," John gave a curt nod before disappearing inside the castle. Whispers broke out as the deltas visibly shuddered. Their chin touched their chest and shoulders hunched.

When John returned with the silver spiked collars Aaron gestured him toward the misbehaved lycans. The silver ends would release diluted wolfsbane and a few other herbs into their bloodstream if they tried to shift into their beasts. The liquid caused a burning sensation within and drained their energy, exhausting the beasts. It was a punishment usually given to juveniles who had no control over their transformations.

"Lock them around their necks," he ordered to John before speaking loudly to the others. "This is to teach you obedience."

They whined when the collars clicked, announcing the lock was in place.

"I'll tell you once again. Stay away from the girl and the warlock. I'd never do something that would put our safety in jeopardy."

No one spoke as he dismissed them. His eyes burned due to lack of sleep.

"How is she?" the former king asked once they reached his bedchamber.

Aaron sunk into the cushion with a sigh. "Shaken."

"You should have been more discreet."

He knew what his father meant. His beast had walked hand in hand with a vampire, with his chest puffed out in front of the pack. "I wasn't in control."

His father shook his head. "Your actions today have sent mixed messages to the pack. First, you lost control with Richard. Your beast took over and you almost went for his throat. Then, you threatened to kill anyone who went against you during the fight, despite knowing they are your pack."

"I wouldn't have killed them."

"They don't know that." His father's voice lowered. "Pack always comes first, son. For the first time, you put *her* above them."

Aaron realized his mistake. "I'm sorry, Dad. It won't happen again."

He saw his father nod. "I'm glad you chose to collar them instead of whipping. It was a wise decision, son."

"Thanks, Dad." His father always told him when he was wrong and never failed to appreciate him when he did something good. He knew brothers were silently listening to their conversation. "Did Blake call?" he asked Juan.

"Yep, he called while you were away. They successfully retrieved them. Both Max and that witch are gravely injured. It'll be a while before they can travel home."

Aaron's brows creased. His beast grew restless again. His brothers moved closer, sensing it.

"Your beast is edgy," Juan said. "I can feel it." He proceeded to rub his tense shoulders.

"So will the pack," the youngest lycan in the room added, his hands going to massage his eldest brother's scalp.

The prowling beast relaxed, settling on its haunches in his mind. Aaron relaxed further, reclining in the seat.

"Do you mind if I crash with you?" Matthew asked.

"Since when did you start asking for permission?" Juan teased. "FYI, I'm joining you too."

"You boys will never change," their father said, chuckling.

Aaron shook his head and stifled a laugh, feeling light. "See you tomorrow, Dad."

"Well then, goodnight my boys," his warm brown eyes crinkled with laughter as the brothers hugged him mumbling good night.

***

Mia woke up late after a peaceful night's sleep. She'd been so exhausted that she fell asleep immediately. She stretched her body like a lazy cat feeling the softness of her comfy bed as she snuggled deeper into the bed, inhaling the fresh citrus scent of the softest fabric.

A small chuckle brought her out of her morning heaven. She whipped around to see Aaron standing there with a breakfast trolley. He looked more delectable in his figure-hugging workout gear.

"Oh, hi. . ." she blushed, giving him a shy smile. Her heart fluttered as she pulled the sheet high up her chin, trying to hide from his view. Underneath her blanket, she pinched herself to make sure she wasn't dreaming.

"Before you ask, I knocked a few times, and when I didn't get a response, I came in to check," he explained.

"Oh. . .okay," she gave him a sheepish smile, not meeting his gaze. It was embarrassing enough to wake up in front of a man, plus someone as handsome as him.

"I must admit, you looked cute when you stretched like that," he said, making her eyes go as wide as saucers.

Did he see that?

"You look beautiful when you blush."

The deep rumble of his voice caressed her. She felt her cheeks heating up. "I-I need to. . ." she pointed to the bathroom without looking up at him. She scurried out of the bed to get away from him. Mia wanted nothing more than to hide deep inside the closet.

Unfortunately for her, today was definitely not her day. As her legs tangled in the sheets, she fell and landed on her ass.

Ugh! She screamed internally as she wished the floor would open up and swallow her. She yelped in surprise when warm hands enveloped her and lifted her from the floor.

***

Aaron's eyes glistened in amusement as he watched her stumble out of the bed. He had been worried when she wouldn't open the door and when no sound came from inside. He hurried inside, only to see her sound asleep.

It was a sight to behold. She looked so serene in her sleep. Her pajama shirt had ridden up, exposing her midrib. Oh, how badly he wanted to trace that flawless skin of hers.

He swallowed hard as he clenched his jaw to silence the appreciative growl that erupted from his chest. His beast enjoyed the sight. *This is wrong.* When he was about to the leave the room, she stirred and stretched exposing more of that creamy skin.

He didn't understand why he insisted on bringing the breakfast. He could've sent their butler, an elderly harmless human they trusted. However, it was worth it when he saw her stretch out like a cat. He couldn't help but admire how beautiful she looked with her disheveled hair and crumbled pajamas.

When she noticed him and pointed to the bathroom without looking up at him, she stumbled on the sheets and fell down. Aaron shook his head and bit his lip to silence his laughter. He didn't want to make her feel more embarrassed than she already was. He lifted her off the floor and held her close as he carried her to the bathroom. She bit her lower lip and never once looked up at him. He sat her up on the spacious countertop next to the washbasin and lifted her chin, looking deep into her mesmerizing blues.

He could get lost in the depths of her eyes forever. Aaron moved the long strands of her hair away from her face. The beast within was pushing forward. "I like your hair,." he murmured. His long tan fingers played with the blonde strands. She didn't move, and he wanted nothing more than to close the few inches and feel her lips. The sudden urge shocked him. Aaron cleared his throat and shook his head as if to get rid of the dirty images his beast kept supplying. He wanted her. Never in his life had he felt this attracted to a woman before.

"I-I'll let you get ready for the day." His throat cleared. "Come to my room once you're dressed and finished with breakfast," he stuttered out, to which she nodded mutely. Before he knew it, his fingers went to trace the pinks of her soft cheeks. He didn't miss the way her heart skipped a beat when his hands caressed them.

With great difficulty, he detached his hands from her soft body and walked out of the bathroom.

***

What just happened? Mia wondered as her heart fluttered.

Her body heated up when those brown orbs scanned her frame. The golden flecks in his eyes, mesmerizing. His touch left a fiery trail that made her feel things she had never felt before.

I can't let this happen. This place was temporary. She'd soon move out and leave them all. Shaking the thoughts away, she hurried toward the shower to finish her morning routine.

CHAPTER 13

Mia hesitated for a moment before knocking. She didn't know why he asked her to go to his room.

"Come in," a voice said.

Opening the door, she slid in. Her eyes scanned the room, taking in the luxurious interior, the royal blue lush carpet that was soft under her bare feet. Thick and velvety royal blue drapes decorated the huge windows which provided the perfect view of the snow-clad trees. *Was blue his favorite color?* The king-sized bed was also draped in royal blue, confirming her thoughts.

Shaking her head to clear her thoughts, she asked, "How is my dad?"

"He woke this morning and asked for you." He closed the file he was reading and placed it over a neatly arranged stack. Aaron was dressed in a formal shirt that hugged his broad chest. The first two buttons were open, giving her a view of his smooth, tan chest. His long sleeves were folded at his elbow. His wet hair was combed back, and the three-day stubble gave him a rugged yet handsome look.

"I want to see him." Her teeth caught her lower lip as she fiddled her fingers. After last night, she didn't think it was wise to go out. But she had to know how he was.

"You can see him when the doctors discharge him tomorrow." He pulled another file out of the stack, opening it. His warm coffee browns swept over the contents briefly before focusing on her.

"Um. . .Okay." Disappointment flooded her. "I-I'll go then." She moved from one foot to the other and made a move to leave the room. Tomorrow was too far.

"You can stay with me—I mean, you can hang out a little longer if you want to," his voice was hesitant. "I have movies if you'd like to watch one."

Tempting. But no.

"Can you suggest some movies?"

Crap. Too late. *What's wrong with me?*

"Sure." He stood up, going to the entertainment center which sat on the opposite wall of his king-sized bed and pulled out some DVDs. "What do you prefer? Romance, action, or comedy?"

She pushed her hands into the pockets of her jeans to hide their slight tremble. "Action with supernaturals in it, preferably with um. . .vampires."

Aaron rummaged through the DVDs before picking a few. "I have many, but I think both of these series will keep you occupied for a while," he said handing her Underworld and Blade.

Mia took the DVDs he handed to her and contemplated what to watch.

"Here," he handed her the remote before going back to his table.

Taking the remote from him, she sat down on the comfortable couch, mind wandering to the sexy lycan working at the table. Turmoil churned her thoughts. A deep breath of his intoxicating scent relaxed her

92

lungs and calmed her nerves. Her eyes fixated on the screen as she wondered about the changes the coming days may bring.

***

Aaron sneaked secret glances at Mia every now and then, but the paperwork demanded his undivided attention. His family avoided the official engagements and limited their public appearances for generations to maintain their secrecy.

Getting new social security numbers and other ID cards itself was a headache with every system digitalized now. Lycans weren't immortals. They just lived longer and aged at a snail's pace after puberty. Their youthful look warranted unwanted attention.

A feminine sniff drew his attention out from the file he was perusing. Her eyes held a shine as she watched an emotional scene and he watched her, unable to shift his eyes. Bloodsuckers didn't give a damn about emotions. He wondered if they ever felt emotions at all. Because Felipe sure didn't care about the lives he destroyed. *She is different.*

When Mia entered Aaron's room, he almost forgot to breathe. Her scent hit him first. She looked like a fresh morning flower bathed in dew with her still wet hair. The shirt she wore hugged her frame like a second skin accentuating her curves. The black skinny jeans showed off her shapely legs. He noticed Mia inhaling his scent, and her eyes shifted partially, her normal irises mixed with the black that usually belonged to a vampire.

He shook his head, clearing his thoughts. Why he asked her to stay, he still couldn't figure out. The raging beast was still in conflict with his human side. Aaron wondered what that hairy butt saw in her. An enemy to their race. With a long sigh, he shifted to focus on work.

It was lunchtime by the time she finished the first movie. She was silent when he provided lunch, accepting her plate with a small smile.

He watched her take the first bite before starting with his food on instinct. Aaron was confused with his actions. He was an alpha, the provider of the pack. But, he was also the first to take the bite before the others. The only exception was a mate. The lycans always put their mate's need before their own.

They ate in silence, both of their minds occupied. The silence shouldn't have been this comfortable. Her presence shouldn't put his mind at ease. He refused to accept the explanation. His jaw clenched together as frustration mounted.

His father's words infiltrated his thoughts, dousing his brain with ice cold water and forcing him out of whatever trance he was in. The pack came before the family. Their needs mattered the most.

Letting her leave wasn't an option as his father said. Her stay in the castle was unavoidable and with the present war, outside danger increased. The pack could only take so much. Aaron contemplated introducing her to them, and perhaps, once they met her for themselves, their opinion of her might change. At least, there would be transparency. It would be much easier to handle if they weren't constantly at each other's throat.

When he returned to his table after lunch, Mia went back to watch another movie.

The events in his office from earlier replayed in his mind. Mia, whom appeared innocent, was most dangerous of all. If she could mask her presence, then he wondered what else she was capable of. *What if she lost control?* She hadn't. So far.

Like the lycans, the pureblood vampires also had two sides to them. Not many knew what exactly Felipe became upon his transformation. *Because he left no survivors.*

His eyes fell on the remaining files. It was close to five in the evening and he was in no mood to continue to work today. He pushed them away and shutdown his computer before going to her. She had dozed off while he worked.

Mia sported a pout, with cheek in hand, as she lay on her left side. He reached out to trace her soft lips. He wanted nothing more than to feel those lips against his and find out how she tasted. The beast rumbled in his chest, liking the idea as he imagined her lips on his. Aaron cursed, shoving aside the inappropriate thoughts.

"Hey, wake up."

Her eyes cracked open and her sleepy orbs stared back at him; he could hear her heartbeat quickening at their proximity. Her lips slightly parted as her eyes lowered to his lips. *Tempting.* He cleared his throat and gave her a smile. Her breath hitched, and she turned away to hide her blush from him.

"Why don't you freshen up? I'll send over dinner," he said, helping her up from the couch. Blue eyes blinked. His eyes narrowed at her lips before trailing down her bare neck. Cannines lengthened and gums burned. *What would she taste like?* She leaned in to his touch before pulling away.

"Dad, we need to talk."

Aaron watched her leave, then exited his room like a bat out of hell.

***

Jerome could feel his son's turmoil even before he entered the library. He knew the storm was coming. The beast was in war with the human.

"What's happening to me, Dad?"

Pure rage washed over him. It was as if Aaron was once again a juvenile.

"You're in disagreement with your beast."

"I get that. But why? She's an enemy. There are millions of women in this world. Hell, I don't care if it's a human. But her—this can't happen."

"Take it slow, son."

"How?!"

Jerome cringed but held his ground as his son paced the room. Aaron's strong biceps flexed with the clenching and unclenching of his palms.

"She makes me feel weak. I feel powerless when I stare into her eyes. And, I don't like it. This is wrong. It's all wrong. I shouldn't feel this way." His voice was a roar.

Jerome wanted to explain why. That it was just that way between mates. Mates become ones' strength and weakness. Right then wasn't the right time, though. It was important for his son to figure it out on his own. Once the beast found its potential mate, they forged an immediate bond with them. The bond only grew stronger with time.

"What happened today?"

"I. . ." His Adam's apple bobbed up and down. "I asked her to spend time with me."

There was more his son wasn't telling. A ghost of a smile spread on his lips and he was quick to hide it. This could work for his plan. The silence stretched as he waited for his son to continue.

Aaron ran his hand through his hair and rubbed his face. His eyes were distant and restless. "I want to introduce her to the pack. If she's going to stay, then the pack should be able to get along with her."

"Are you sure about this?"

"Yes. I don't want them to feel as if we are hiding something. I mean we are keeping her because we can't risk Felipe capturing her. I'm going to introduce her to the pack members and let them decide the rest. But I won't allow a repeat of last night."

Jerome wondered if his son realized what he was doing. He wanted the pack to accept her. That was a sneaky move though he claimed otherwise. "If that's what you want, go ahead."

Aaron inclined his head before leaving Jerome to his thoughts. The oldest lycan couldn't help the smirk that lifted the corner of his lips. His son was smitten. He looked forward to the introduction.

It was Aaron's turn to prove he was a strong and capable leader. Jerome wanted to see how the young king would react to the pack's animosity this time. Aaron was treading over a thin layer of ice. The conflict was unpredictable, and he was keen to see how his son handled this issue without breaking the pack apart.

His father, Henry, did the same thing when he chose Esmeralda as his mate. An qlpha choosing an omega wasn't allowed in those days because they believed it would taint their bloodline. Jerome refused to even take a breeder when his Esme didn't conceive. However, none of their children turned out to be an omega.

This was Aaron's test. A lycan mating with a vampire had been impossible before Mia. The girl's heartbeat showed that she was different. Maybe, just maybe, this might be their chance to end the centuries-old war.

His long, thick fingers tapped on the mahogany desk as his mind shaped the plan.

Catherine Edward

CHAPTER 14

Mia had been staring at her wardrobe for the past five minutes while her heart thundered against her ribs. She was expecting dinner in her room when Aaron announced she'd be joining him at the dinner table. *That's an idiotic decision.* This couldn't be happening.

Her legs felt like jelly as she pulled on jeans and a turtleneck. What if they attacked her again? She thought she wasn't allowed out of the room. The wound in her arm had healed, leaving no traces of the injury.

Apparently, most of the pack would be there. There was a knock and Aaron entered looking fresh in a white v-neck t-shirt that showed the lines of his taut muscles. She swallowed before averting her gaze down—big mistake. The jeans he wore hugged his body, accentuating his long muscular legs. Is she thought he looked smarter in his office attire, now he looked like sin.

A small smile teased his firm lips. "Come on, let's go." The rumble of his voice vibrated in her core.

Taking a deep breath, she straightened her back. Her stomach twisted into knots at the unknown feeling. Though she appeared calm on the outside, she was screaming on the inside.

Anything could happen when they saw her again. The taste of their hostility was ingrained in her memory.

The brutes, Juan and Matthew joined them in the corridor along with their father. The guards, dressed in jeans and tight t-shirts, formed a circle around them, walking briskly. They reminded her of the bouncers. Their nostrils flared and eyes shifted to that of their beasts when those eyes landed on her. They were quick to mask their emotions, though. Guns peeped from their holsters. The closer she got, the more anxious she became. She wished she was back inside her room, under the comfort of the quilt.

The grand double door drew closer, and her breathing quickened.

"They can sense your fear. It thrills their beasts," Aaron whispered, much to her dismay. She opened and closed her mouth, unable to form any words. That wasn't the assurance she wanted. A slight tremor shot through her body. "Come here," he said, pulling her to the side by the arm. Her fearful eyes swept around them. Others turned a blind-eye to them and kept their gazes straight.

"Mia, look at me," Aaron said, cupping her cheek with his right hand. His left hand held her close. The touch of his hand made the butterflies in her stomach flutter. His thumb caressed her cheek as she locked her gaze with him. "Do you trust me?"

Do I trust him? She swallowed, her eyes searching his gaze. She nodded and his hold on her relaxed.

"Good. You have nothing to worry about."

She doubted that. Her hand unconsciously traced the recently healed skin. The pain of claws slicing her was still fresh in her memory.

His thumb continued to caress her cheek as if sensing her unease. "I won't let anything happen to you." A breath was exhaled from her lungs, and she leaned into his touch. Her eyes closed.

When he stepped away, Mia took a deep breath as she faced the door once again.

This is it.

Her posture stiffened as the butler opened the door announcing their presence to the others. She felt his hand on her lower back. The hall fell silent and everyone stood at once.

Several oak tables occupied the huge hall. It had a magnificent chandelier that hung high in the center of the room. It took her breath away. Portraits lined the red and gold patterned walls. Every inch of the room was such a vision to behold that she could easily spend hours admiring it. Everything was perfect.

One table stood out from the others. Servants lined both sides of the table, assisting everyone to their seats. There were two grand chairs at the head of the table. The royal blue cushions and golden frames with intricate designs indicated to Mia that they belonged to the king.

Mia waited for the chaos to begin. Her pupils constricted. Warning bells were set off in her brain like a fire alarm. She clenched her jaw and held her hands fisted by her sides. A labored breath entered her lungs as Aaron's warning replayed in her mind.

She felt his hand on her back again, rubbing in smooth circles. Suddenly, her mind was at ease. Her shoulders relaxed as she met the gazes of the audience with her head held high. They sniffed the air and sudden tension gripped the atmosphere. The stances of the lycans protecting her widened, their body poised to face any attack.

Low growls emanated from the crowd. Her heart lurched and she stepped back, but Aaron's steel-like hand pinned her to the spot. His palm flattened on her back and warmth seeped through her clothes.

Her nervous gaze did a quick sweep across the dining room. Mia choked on a hiss that urged her to flash her teeth at them. *What the*—She forced her racing heart to slow down and took a deep breath before focusing on the warmth and strength radiating from Aaron. *Don't look at them.* She closed her eyes. *They can't hurt you.*

"Move to stand by your designated seats." His voice thundered.

Her eyes shot open. The subjects moved immediately. Their eyes wary.

"Mia, here, is our guest and is going to be staying here for a few weeks."

She sneaked a glance at him in her peripheral vision. His eyes challenged anyone who dared to look at her. The pack members flinched at the authority and displayed their necks in submission. His deep masculine voice made her knees tremble, and it wasn't because of fear.

"If anyone has trouble with her staying here in the castle, address your concerns now," he said, bringing Mia out of her trance.

A pale blonde woman with snake-like eyes flashed her teeth. But her jaws clamped shut when Aaron looked her way. Mia pressed herself into his side, and the woman's looks turned murderous. She moved away from him and noticed the woman smirk. Everything about her screamed trouble.

"I have no qualms against her presence, Alpha. Just wondering what a vampire is doing at this table." The same woman said in a mocking voice as those venomous eyes narrowed at her. Mia could feel the animosity in her bones.

"You'll find out soon enough. If no one has anything to say, then dinner shall be served."

Mia faced him when his hand withdrew, taking the warmth and comfort away form her body. He gestured to the seat at his right-hand side and she sat, bringing her knees together. Juan sat to her right and

Aaron sat at her left, which was also the head side of the table. Matthew occupied the seat opposite to her.

She lowered her gaze down to her hands, averting her gaze from everyone else, wishing this would end soon. The curious glances thrown in her direction felt like worms crawling over her skin. She pulled the long sleeves, covering her palms. The food was a good distraction.

"It's butternut squash and tomato soup with spinach and ricotta tortellini. Try it," Aaron's encouraging voice urged.

She tuned out the others in the room as she ate. Her mind churned. Mia couldn't handle much food despite its deliciousness. When she pushed her plate aside for the dessert, her eyes briefly locked with the blonde woman who glared at her. If looks could kill, then she'd be dead.

The woman was the epitome of beauty, with perfectly groomed hair and features. She wore a purple sleeveless dress with a deep neckline that showed more cleavage than necessary, but the color contrasted well with her skin tone. Her eyes were a mixture of amber and green that made them appear similar to that of a snake.

Mia's jaw locked involuntarily as she met her gaze. While she wanted to avert her eyes, she couldn't. Her own eyes narrowed at the challenge. Suddenly, the girl blinked, averting her gaze, and Mia felt Aaron's hand gripping hers under the table. Her body relaxed as if a switch was turned on.

When their eyes met briefly, he gestured to the strawberry cheesecake. Mia quickly grabbed it, finding something else to focus on. If there was one thing she was sure of, it was that this silence wouldn't last. These people were quiet because of his presence. She hoped to leave once her father was released. *Yeah, that's it. There is no other way around this.*

103

***

Emilia didn't like Mia. One look at her, and she hated her. No, she *despised* her. For one, she was sitting next to Aaron, who was supposed to be hers. Two, she was a fucking bloodsucker.

Why would Aaron allow a vampire to sit next to him? The place was reserved for the queen. *Me.*

The girl was a tramp. Emilia didn't miss Aaron's attentiveness toward that leech.

Trash.

She wondered what her presence here meant. *Why would Aaron house a vampire?* There was more to this, and Aaron introducing her to the pack only cemented her suspicion. The bloodsucker rubbed her the wrong way. But, the girl's heartbeat would allow her to pass as a human if it wasn't for her strong scent. Emilia's eyes followed the girl's every move as if she was watching her prey. *Prey. She'd soon be.*

Long and slender fingers drummed on the table in a casual manner as she forced her hostility down. The leech had the protection of the alphas. She should be careful with her move.

"So, Mia what do you do?" Emilia fished, hoping to find more.

"I've just completed my four year degree."

"Hmm. . .What about your family?"

Emilia had to tread carefully. She didn't want Aaron to know her dislike for this vampire, which was hard to mask from his scrutinizing gaze. If she wanted information, then she had to behave and get closer to the vampire.

"It's just me and my dad," Mia immediately replied.

"Oh, I hope you like it here." Emilia tried to sound friendly though her expression seemed otherwise.

"Thank you."

"I must admit that I like you, Mia," Emilia lied. "Excuse me for being rude earlier, our history with vampires so far has not been pleasant." Her eyes registered the leech going stiff at the mention of the title. *So, she didn't like being called a vampire.*

"It's okay." Mia's smile fell.

Emilia gave her one last smile before returning her gaze to her dessert. Asking too many questions would warrant unwanted attention. Already the members were leaning toward them to hear the conversation better.

She didn't like her, but she needed to know more. *There is a reason the leech is here and I'm going to get to the bottom of it.*

Soon Aaron stood, announcing he was retiring for the day. He bid them to continue dinner before leaving.

As they exited the dining hall, Emilia noticed Aaron's hand going to Mia's lower back, guiding her out. Emilia seethed. He had never once touched her that way. He had never treated a female like he was treating Mia. Aaron never *touched* another female. Period. His beast disliked skin contact.

Her heart raced as this new understanding dawned. The alpha wasn't just trying to protect the leech. Emilia quickly excused herself from the table to follow them. She followed their scent, putting enough distance so they wouldn't see or feel her presence. She was only allowed near the royal wing during the day because she was a beta female. She knew Aaron had banned her entry only recently after she asked him to choose her as his mate.

Pathetic. There won't be another future queen as long as I live.

Her legs halted when the scent led her to the royal wing. Jealousy burned her insides. While she was aware of the attack last night, she hadn't expected him to take the girl to the royal wing. The usually deserted corridors were now guarded by the elite warriors, the top twenty, that protected the king. *Shit.*

"Going somewhere?"

Emilia jumped. She slowly turned to face John Perron, the bulky lycan who creeped her out, even after all these years. The dark-skinned general had slipped out from the shadows.

Fuck!

"Oh, hey, John. . ." She hadn't noticed him there. Big mistake. "I wanted to talk to Aaron about something."

"He is no longer your playmate, young lady. It's Alpha Aaron for you." His predatory eyes narrowed at her. "You can talk tomorrow, and if I'm not mistaken, the alpha has banned you from this wing."

"I'm sorry." She forced a smile and averted her gaze. The delta-born general was more cunning than a fox. His strength even challenged that of her father's. Emilia turned away.

When she reached her room her mind was churning.

"Miss, is there anything you want before I go?" Chelsey, her personal maid asked.

"No. You may leave." Only a few trusted servants stayed in the castle at night. The rest left after dinner and resumed working early in the morning.

Emilia headed to the bathroom, following the sweet scent of lavenders and steam. The bath was ready—mildly hot and perfect. She loved her baths. It helped her think clearly. A sigh of content left her lips as she lowered herself in the water.

The royals had guests before like witches, warlocks, and even demons. However, no guest ever entered the royals' private chambers. Their guest rooms were in the southern wing. *Why isn't the leech staying in one of the guest rooms?* The elite warriors were handpicked by the king, and their loyalty was only to their alphas. They would blindly protect her if he commanded. *Why is she so special?*

The water was soothing, the scented candles flickered catching her attention. Her lips stretched to form a sly smile. Oh, how much she wanted *him* in the tub with her. She'd been dreaming about him ever since they turned sixteen. Wetness warmed her thighs at the mere thought of the sexy lycan.

One of her hands slipped under the water, parting her wet folds. The ache seemed to grow as she thought about him. She imagined his fingers inside her and moaned out loud as her slender fingers entered her wet channel. It wasn't enough. She wanted him to quench the fire that burned within her.

The mild soap burned her sensitive flesh, but that didn't stop her. She added two more fingers, pumping in and out. "Oh, Aaron. . ." her lips whispered out, imagining his thick cock sliding in. Fangs slid out, catching her lower lip and drawing blood. Her eyes transformed green showing the presence of her beast.

"Ah, yes. . .Fuck me, please. . ."

Her thumb circled her swollen clit, and her free hand cupped her own breast, squeezing the hardened nipple as she imagined his lips on them. The tension rose as her body tuned to the pleasure rippling from her lower half.

With a scream of his name, she let go, panting harder as her head rested at the edge of the oval-shaped bathtub. The orgasm was a relief, but it wasn't enough. Her itch only grew. Fuck. She needed more now.

"Zach, baby, I want you now." She made sure her voice projected her need.

Emilia knew very well knew how to flaunt her beauty to get what she wanted. Only it never worked with Aaron. *I will never stop until I have you for myself.* No lycanthrope held a match to Aaron. Over the years, several deltas warmed her bed. But none satisfied her. Zach should do for now.

The bathroom door burst open as the six-foot warrior entered. He was sexy in his own way. Not beautiful, but rugged and handsome with a killer jawline. She shook her head and blinked. His nostrils flared, drinking in the essence of her lust that hung thick in the air. A growl rumbled out of his chest, and she cupped her breast, teasing him.

Her eyes clouded with lust. He was nothing like the alpha, who stirred her desire and made her insides bubble like hot lava. But he was better than the others. The fool loved her and thought he was courting her. She giggled when Zach hovered over her, pulling her flush against him while kissing her thoroughly.

Hmm. . .I definitely need this tonight.

CHAPTER 15

Aaron let out a relieved breath when they exited the dining hall. He could feel the gaze of the pack on them and the urge to hide Mia from them washed over him. His jaws ground together as he fought to control the need to pull her flush against his body. He let his hand rest on her lower back and relaxed when she unconsciously leaned toward him.

The entire event had gone better than he expected. He thought he'd have to cancel the dinner when she had almost gone into panic mode earlier. When they approached the dining hall, her fear had kicked in. The white of her eyes had blackened, and her heartbeat had slowed. Aaron made the mistake of touching her, which was the only thing he could think of to calm the frightened woman beside him. Her skin was smooth, and he almost got lost in her intoxicating scent. The touch was necessary. That was the only thing he could come up with to distract her. He felt her relax in his arms.

Mixed emotions assaulted the pack bond when they had first stepped into the dining hall. It felt as if he had lead a rabbit straight to a wolf. He had silenced their hostile glances with a growl. Nothing more had to be said. More was dangerous. No one had spoken except Emilia. He felt their curiosity replacing their anger a few moments later.

Dangling her before them was a sudden decision but worth the shot. They needed to work together if Mia was going to stay here. He peeled his eyes off her and focused on his plate. This situation was crappy.

Perhaps, they had thought he would serve her blood. They had been in for a surprise. He eyed Emilia who hadn't taken her eyes off Mia. Low murmurs rose from the far end of the room, spreading to the other end.

The servants brought in the variety of dishes, serving their alphas first. A nervous silence settled down. Aaron took the first bite, suppressing the urge to feed her first. He searched through the bond, looking for any hostility.

"It's butternut squash and tomato soup with spinach and ricotta tortellini. Try it," he whispered, sensing her hesitance.

Several gasps could be heard when she swallowed the first spoon. Now the real challenge had begun. They'd wanted to know why she was so different. And, once they knew, he wondered how they'd react. *One step at a time,* he reminded himself.

Aaron watched his little vampire with an amused expression. His ears had twitched, and hearing her little moans of appreciation sent a jolt of awareness to his lower half.

His vampire. . .

That sounded damn good. A possessive growl formed within his chest.

He felt someone tap on his shoulder and blinked before realizing they reached his chamber. Mia shifted from one foot to the other as his brothers entered his room. He could almost see the wheels turning in her head. "What is it?" he asked.

"Can I ask you something?" Her soft voice drawled. He chuckled when she added, "Your Highness."

"Sure, let's talk inside," Aaron entered her room and leaned comfortably on the wall beside the door.

"Um. . .it's about earlier, can we sit?"

Aaron nodded and moved from the wall to sit on the couch. He expected she'd want to talk sooner. Mia sat on the opposite side and the increase in her heartbeat told him how nervous she was.

"I don't feel like a vampire," her voice cracked. "I thought I'd worry about it later, but after seeing everyone at the dining hall–" she paused taking a shaky breath.

Aaron kept quiet, waiting for her to regain her composure. The past forty hours had been a rollercoaster ride for everyone. Things hadn't been the same ever since she stepped in.

"I always fantasized about mythical creatures," her wry chuckle held no humor. "I've known that I'm one of them for the past three years, but never exactly knew what. Dad never revealed that." Her breathing quickened as tears rolled down her cheeks. "Of all things, why do I have to be a vampire?"

Aaron didn't know how to respond. Her tears tugged at his heartstrings. He moved to crouch in front of her, something he never did before. *What are you doing to me?* The compelling urge to comfort her rendered him speechless. When he took her hands in his, she didn't object.

"Am I going to change like them?" She sniffled. Her growing fear now infiltrated his senses. "I don't want to be like them."

"You won't change," he assured, though he knew it wasn't true. She wouldn't be staying that way for long.

"How can you say that?" Her teary eyes locked with his. "I've seen them twice. They are cold without a touch of humanity. They stink. Why would you think I'm a vampire?"

"Because you smell like one," Aaron answered truthfully.

"But, I don't smell anything wrong," Mia argued and sniffed herself. "What do I smell like?"

Flowers. Aaron took a deep breath. "You smell like roses." *Like freshly bloomed roses.* He cleared his throat. "The blood drinkers usually have this lasting scent of blood on them. It's different from the other living beings, and it's stronger." The metallic stench wasn't unbearable on her. Instead, it was alluring. It was mouthwatering.

"Oh." Blood rushed to her cheeks, and she averted her gaze to the fluffy rug. Her nose flared, a soft movement that caught his eyes. "You smell good, too." The deep crimson on her cheeks suited her better.

"You're stronger than you know." He couldn't help but wonder if she realized her strength.

"I don't feel strong." Her lips trembled. "I didn't feel strong when they attacked us last night."

"I'm sorry about that," he said, his voice was sincere. He almost failed to protect her.

"How can you tell a human and a supernatural apart only by their scent?" Mia asked.

"What do I smell like?"

Mia pushed the loose strands of her hair behind her ears, eyes still downcast. "You smell nice."

"And?" Aaron probed.

"Masculine."

"And?"

"Something more," she said.

Aaron's lips stretched to smile. "Lycanthropes smell like wet dogs and a bit like nature. You know, like wood or mud," he explained. "Likewise, every supernatural being has a distinctive smell that sets them apart from the others." Demons smelled like brimstone—fire and death. And, the good witches—or guardians—reek of incense, oils, and herbs; whereas, the dark ones, lost to the darkness in their mind, smelled differently.

"You called me a pureblood. What's that?"

"The purebloods are born to human parents but become a vampire due to some genetic mutation. A born vampire can survive on human food and blood, but their strength comes only from consuming blood."

Mia visibly relaxed. "So, I don't *have* to drink blood." A small smile found its way to her lips. "I don't want to harm anyone."

You can't stay like that forever. He wanted to tell her but couldn't. The peaceful look on her face was too good to be ruined. He'd let her believe she was harmless if that helped her sleep better.

"It's late. Go to bed. I'll be in my room if you need me."

"Okay. Goodnight."

"Goodnight."

The attraction was undeniable. She was dangerous. He probably was committing the biggest mistake, but his beast stood its ground, claiming it was the right thing to do. With a shake of his head to clear the conflicting thoughts, he left her room. *She's off limits.*

***

Emilia seethed as she paced the confines of her room, her beast restless. Zach had left her room early in the morning after a night filled with pure pleasure. Mia was something else; she smelled like a vampire but ate human food.

The night's incident kept flashing in her mind: Aaron's hand on the leech's lower back, the way she kept looking at him, the scowl on

113

Aaron's face when Emilia talked to her. Her mind flagged every move. The alpha hesitated before taking the first bite. Her eyes didn't miss even that minuscule action.

No. *I'll never let her become his mate.* It was unheard of, but she'd be a fool to believe it was impossible. She'd have to eliminate the threat before it grew into something else. *If someone is worthy of becoming a queen, it's me.*

The dead queen had been weak and useless and had never been fit to be chosen. *What did the king see in her anyway?* He'd crowned her against all odds. Emilia's heels clicked against the marble as she paced.

Aaron, his name had become an addiction over the years. He was the complete package with a crown. Growing up, they spent a lot of time together as children. He was her playmate. Then he avoided her. He'd push her away when she tried to touch him. *That fool hasn't even kissed anyone yet.*

She tried to convince him the right way. *"I like you so much, Aaron. I want you to be my first,"* she'd told him at the tender age of sixteen when her hormones raged.

"Go to your room, Emilia. I have other things to do," he'd replied, shutting her out. She even tried her best to seduce him by inducing her heat cycle, but he wouldn't relent. The beast in him had scrunched its nose in disgust and pushed her away. Unmated lycanthropes went crazy by the pull of the mating scent, but not him.

No one rejects me and gets away like that, Emilia fumed. *What's wrong with me? I've been by his side for years, and he never once looked at me how he look at that vamp tonight.*

The alpha's beast was something to die for. She always watched him whenever he went for a run or trained in his beast form. The ten-foot tall beast was any girl's wet dream with his midnight black fur, which blended so easily in the dark. His fur and skin had a velvety texture which glistened in the moonlight while his eyes shone bright amber. Oh. . .how much she wanted to run her hands over his sculpted chest. She drooled at the mere thought. Lust knew no boundaries, and she was keen to achieve her target.

The wolves were bristling. Omegas bitched when they thought no one was listening. A wicked smile tugged at her lips as a plan formed. She would use this to her advantage. It wouldn't take long to turn the pack against the leech. Then, Aaron or his dad would have no option but to lock her in the dungeons, or the best part, kill her. Emilia's claws elongated as the itch to rip Mia apart grew.

Emilia's hips swayed from side-to-side as she walked to the kitchen. When she went in, Victoria, the castle chef, was testing the consistency of a delicious-smelling batter. It was another new day, and the kitchen staff was busy preparing the meals.

"Hey, Vic. What's for breakfast?"

The omega rolled her eyes, and the groan wasn't missed by Emilia's heightened sense of hearing. "We have bacon, boiled eggs, toasts, muffins, pancakes, and some leftovers from last night." Emilia knew the low breed added the leftovers to the menu, knowing she didn't like it.

Emilia picked an apple from the fruit basket, masking her disgust. "Did you see that leech? Such an actress." She wouldn't normally chat with these low lives, but when she wanted to spread gossip, they were her best bet.

"She seems different," another omega named Saloni piped in.

"Different my ass," Emilia huffed. "She's here with a plan."

Victoria was silent as she checked the batter that one of the omegas was whipping. "Blend all the ingredients together, and whip it until it lathers," she instructed before moving to another omega chopping the vegetables for soup. "Cut it nice and square."

"The alpha wouldn't let her stay without good reason," Saloni replied.

Emilia rolled her eyes. The conversation wasn't going in the direction she wanted. "I'd like to believe that's a lie they've been telling everyone. Aaron punished our own for that bloodsucker."

"That's because they went against our alpha's words," Victoria responded.

"Then how do you explain her staying in the royal wing?"

Her eyes followed the omega, who went on with the tasks at hand, not really paying attention. Victoria was a tough cookie with an unshakeable loyalty toward the alphas.

"You already have the answer for this. Alpha assigned a room in the omega's quarters for her to stay, but the peanut brains attacked her and almost killed her father."

"That's bullshit and you know it," Emilia commented. "Did you not see the way Aaron looked at her the entire time? She's using him." The omegas looked at each other, confusion dancing in their faces. Emilia grinned inside. Her plan was working. "He doesn't like to be touched, but he was touching her the entire time."

Victoria shrugged. "That's not our business." She raised her hand and stopped Emilia from saying anything. "Emilia, you might be the alpha's childhood friend, but stop addressing him with his first name when you're amongst us. We respect our alpha, and most of all, we trust him. He'd never do something that'd risk our lives or peace."

Fury shot through Emilia's veins, and she suppressed the threatening growl. "Keep saying that. One of these days, you'll regret your words."

"Back to work, girls. And, don't pay attention to this nonsense," Victoria chirped going back to what she was doing, leaving Emilia seething.

This wasn't going to work. She'll have to try something else.

CHAPTER 16

Ted eased onto the comfortable mattress. Mia placed the empty bowl back on the cart and handed him a paper towel.

A groan left his lips when he readjusted his position. Pain tugged at him from his injury. He popped the painkillers his daughter gave him and relaxed. Warlocks and witches didn't heal fast like the other supernaturals. It'd take at least a week or two before he could move around comfortably.

"Thank you."

"It's nothing, Dad."

He couldn't believe his daughter survived in the wolf's den. The night of the attack was still fresh in his memory. Guilt and helplessness were the only emotions he felt before darkness had consumed him.

"I'm glad you're okay, Mia."

She gave him a tight-lipped smile. Something bothered her. "I'll plan our itinerary while you rest."

His eyes narrowed at her. He could sense her turmoil. "We can't leave." The lycans would never let her go.

"We can't stay either." She looked away. "We don't belong here," her voice cracked. "*I* don't belong here."

"Mia—"

"These people hate me. I can feel it in my bones. Last night the king introduced me to his pack. They were silent only because of his presence. Else—"

"Wait. The alpha introduced you to the pack?"

"Yeah. It was a foolish thing to do, considering they want to kill me. I felt like a piece of meat dangled before them."

Ted couldn't believe what he was hearing. This was huge. "Did he touch you?"

"Um. . .Yeah." Confusion washed over her. "But not in the way you think. He gave me a little pep talk before dinner, and we talked in the room before he left."

He couldn't talk for a moment, and his heart raced. Mind reeled with the new development and a huge grin broke onto his face. There was only one explanation to it. "Where did he touch you?"

"Dad!"

"Answer me, Mia. You don't understand how important this is."

She swallowed as if contemplating what to tell him. "He just touched my hand." Her gaze averted to the floor and pink tainted her cheeks.

"Just your hand?"

"I panicked and he tried to assure me that no one would hurt me. It doesn't matter. We need to leave."

"I told you. We can't. You're not safe out there."

"I'm not safe here either!" She wiped her frustrated tears and walked to the huge window that overlooked the forest. "When you told me I'm one of you, I never imagined you meant a vampire," her whisper was weak.

Ted sat, bringing himself to the edge of the bed, which wasn't as painful since the painkillers kicked in.

"The way they look at me—it feels as if I'm a pest." Mia shook her head and turned to face him. Her eyes were red-rimmed, something he failed to notice until now. "I want to go somewhere no one knows who I am. Perhaps, you can help me find a cure."

Ted shook his head. "There is no cure for this, Mia."

"Why not? I'm different from them. I don't crave blood. I'm perfectly fine. I can still—"

His features hardened. Did she still think she could reverse this? Once a vampire, always a vampire. The majority would have redeemed themselves if there was another way.

"You're a vampire. A freaking pureblood and nothing can change that. You'll change when the time comes." He stopped her when she opened her mouth. "I'm not finished yet. I know this is hard for you to come to terms with, but you have to understand. Our lives are in danger."

"Kill me, please. I don't want to change. I can't live like this." Sobs wracked her body. Her sadness weighed on him. But she needed to get it in her head. There was no going back.

"I didn't protect you for eighteen years for nothing."

"I'm a monster. How could you protect me? You should have killed me the moment you found out what I am," she cried.

"I said enough!" A burst of energy broke out of his fingertips, pinning her to the wall and stopping her from harming herself. His chest heaved. "Get it together, Mia!" His physical condition wasn't helping him. The magic drained his energy considerably and his hands trembled. His control over her wavered.

"Dad!"

Mia was there to catch him when he collapsed. His exhausted eyes looked at her, and a hand cupped her cheek. "When I found you, Mia, I saw hope. You gave me a purpose to live."

"How can you say that? If this change occurs, I'll be like them. I'll kill others. That can't happen."

Ted wiped her tears. "You don't have to kill in order to live, Mia. But keep denying the truth, and you'll become what everyone fears the most." The warning in his tone must have gotten through to her because she stopped crying.

"What do I do?"

"Accept the truth and move on. I'm here to help you do just that."

"I'm scared." She sounded like the little girl she once was.

"It's okay to feel scared. Fear is good. Now, help me up, will you?" Mia helped her father up, and he leaned on her for support. "Now, listen carefully." He limped toward the bed.

Her blue eyes locked with his grey ones as he sat.

"You're not the only pureblood vampire in this world." A deep frown pulled the corners of her lips down. "Felipe Lancelot is the first of all. He's in a war with the other supernaturals. We've been running from him. He can never find you, Mia."

"I don't understand." Mia shook her head.

"I'll explain. Come here."

***

"Dad, do you even realize what you just said?" Aaron's voice boomed across his father's room. Impossible. He could never mate with a vampire, could he?

"I meant what I said, Son. Felipe can never get his hands on her, and this is the only way."

"Why can't we just kill her or lock her up? You can't force him, Dad." A hard glare from their father shut the youngest son up, who spoke out of turn.

"She's also a weapon," Jerome stressed.

Aaron shook his head. "I can't do this. This isn't the right thing to do."

"This is war, Aaron." Jerome's growl reverberated around the room. His father only used his name when he needed to get a point across. "There is no place for right or wrong when millions of innocent lives are at stake."

Aaron swallowed. He couldn't use her like that. Mia deserved more.

Jerome paced toward him, brown eyes pinned Aaron in place. "Two things can happen if Felipe finds her. One: he'll kill her and that's one less headache. Two: the worst case scenario, he'll mate with her."

An involuntary growl tumbled out of Aaron's chest in warning. Eyes blazing amber as his lips curled up.

"The option I give you now will not only let her live, but also will keep her far away from him. Can you even bring yourself to kill her?"

No. He could never do that. Mia was innocent. She had no choice.

"Your beast thinks of her as a potential mate. Although it's too soon, you've already forged a bond with her. It'll only grow with time." His father's voice took a soft edge. "You're giving her a life by doing this, Aaron. And, with her by your side, you'll be stronger. It's a win-win situation."

"The pack won't accept this."

"They'll understand."

He couldn't and wouldn't take away her choice. Aaron understood his father's point of view and knew he was right. But, the mating meant they were bound for eternity. Relationships shouldn't be built on a lie.

Aaron looked at his brothers. They lifted one of their shoulders into a shrug, and he could sense their turmoil.

"She's born to become the queen of vampires. Mia will be a force to reckon with once she reaches her full potential. Just think, our races could peacefully coexist," his father continued to pacify.

His words made sense. But was it the right thing to do? No. And, this time his beast agreed.

***

Mia sat immobile; her eyes stared aimlessly at the wall. Her body shivered just thinking about *him.*

"Hiding you here was my last option. I thought they wouldn't find you here."

"If you say this guy, Felipe didn't know about my existence, then how come we are on the run?" It didn't make sense.

"Something about you lures the leeches in." Mia cringed. "No offense, sweetheart. It must be your aura. With the ongoing pattern, they'd have found you in no time like they found the others."

"But Dad, we can't stay here forever. They've already attacked me twice, and they'll come again. It won't be long before he discovers my existence."

"You're right. And, it is exactly why you'll do exactly as you're told."

Mia was quick to refuse when he suggested that she was to seduce Aaron.

Preposterous!

"This is the only way, and this is your destiny." Her father's determined voice held no room for argument.

Her emotions were conflicted, but this wasn't something she wanted to discuss with him. She shook her head. Mia couldn't help the flutter of her heart when he suggested the mating. He'd explained it was similar to that of a human marriage, only more of a lifelong commitment without an option of divorce. She was attracted to Aaron. That was natural, considering how handsome he was.

"It won't work." She wanted to laugh at her father's face. How could he even suggest something like this? It's too soon.

"Are you kidding me?" Her father gave her an incredulous look. "That beast is smitten with you."

Mia turned her face away to hide the smile. Her heart skipped a beat. "It's barely been two days."

"One look is enough for a beast to choose its potential mate. And, trust me when I say all the signs are there—thick and bold with blinking, neon lights."

Laughter tumbled out of her chest. It felt good to laugh. Suddenly, the foreboding seemed to leave her. "That's overkill."

"Maybe," Ted shrugged, making her shake her head.

"I think the painkillers are messing with your brain," she stood, smoothing the creases on her pants. "Now, go to sleep. We'll think of something productive once you're well rested."

"It's the best plan, trust me."

"See you later, Dad."

While it was good to hear, it still wouldn't work. Aaron was way out of her league. There was no way it'd work between them. Her father must be really desperate to even suggest something like this. Mia closed the door behind her and walked to her room.

With a sigh, she pulled her phone out. Juan had returned it to her that morning. She had two weeks to plan. This time, no one would be able to find them.

CHAPTER 17

A week had come and gone, but Mia was nowhere near completing her plan. It sounded simple—find a place and leave without a trace. Executing it, however, wasn't easy. Her father had enemies everywhere. She always found herself back at square one.

Her dad was recovering faster than she expected. They would soon be able to leave, if they could find a secret hideout. She had dinner with the pack a few times, but there was no change in their hostility. The murderous glances thrown her way tired her out.

The letter that confirmed her internship stared at her from the table. Mia toyed with the beige envelope as her mind reeled. All those years of hard work were in vain. Education won't save her life from a mad king. Her anger flared at the thought. Her father should have focused on training her to fight instead of letting her pursue a degree that meant nothing now.

A deep breath expanded her lungs. She'd overheard Aaron talking about a few more vampire sightings and knew her time here was limited. Sooner or later, the vampires would find her. Her mind went to Aaron, the sexy lycan whom she had grown closer to over the week. They only talked a little, but his actions and the way he noticed even the small things about her spoke louder.

Mia couldn't believe how soon they'd gotten to a first name basis. She remembered him chastising the blonde girl for addressing him by his first name. She couldn't help the way he made her feel—*special*. His eyes lit up every time they met hers, and he never forgot to appreciate her whenever he had the chance. Moreover, the sexual tension in the air whenever they were together was so palpable it almost hurt.

She pushed the thoughts of Aaron to the back of her mind. Mia knew their attraction would go nowhere. He was a lycanthrope and she was a vampire—a fact she still had trouble digesting. Her father still thought it was a wonderful idea. She always turned him down when he started "the talk" with her.

Aaron didn't hide the fact that he was attracted to her. He often asked her to join him for lunch in his room or sometimes just to hang out. She didn't think he could be anymore obvious. Getting attached to him while planning to leave was probably the most foolish idea.

Mia shook her head. She didn't know how to protect her young heart from wanting him. The initial attraction was slowly turning into a need she didn't fathom. The slow burn of desire flared whenever he was near. She couldn't just stamp it as lust. It was more.

She headed to the bathroom and quickly stripped before turning the shower on. A deep sigh left her lips as she lathered her body with soap. The fragrance of scented roses filled her lungs and relaxed her mind. She was changing into the clothes she chose for the day when someone knocked on the main door. If it was her father or Aaron, they'd call out for her. This had to be someone else. She chewed her lips as she contemplated who it was.

Once dressed, Mia went to the connecting door and knocked before entering, her eyes immediately went toward his makeshift office. She frowned when she didn't find Aaron there.

Where did he go? Who would have knocked?

Mia was lost in her thoughts when the bathroom door opened, and Aaron entered the room in only a towel. His hair was wet and droplets of water cascaded down his torso, sending a jolt of awareness throughout her body. The reason she came in search of him long forgotten.

When their eyes met, she broke out of her trance with a squeak and turned around. "I-I'm sorry. Ah. . .I—"

"Why are you sorry?" His breath fanned the exposed area of her neck, and she whipped around to see he was very close. *How did he get here so fast?*

"I-I—" she stuttered as her eyes zeroed in on his lips. S*o firm.*

Aaron leaned closer, and her lips parted in anticipation. "You haven't answered my question yet," he said huskily as he reached out, cupping her cheek with his large hand. Bright amber eyes bore through her soul.

He tipped her head back as her eyes partially closed, her small hands reaching out to him on their own accord. A droplet of water from his wet hair fell on her shoulder. His eyes followed the trail it left on her soft delicious skin.

Mia gasped when his lips touched the bare skin at the crook of her neck. Her entire body came alive as a need she never felt before burned in her lower belly. His tongue darted out tasting her skin, earning another moan from her. Her head felt dizzy, and with a sudden movement, he had her pinned against the door.

His knee parted her thighs as he pulled her small frame flush against his body, his hands gripping her firm ass and urging her to hook her legs around his hips. His lips trailed wet kisses along her jawline, and his beast surfaced to his skin.

Mia protested when his lips left her neck. She looked up to see Aaron looking at her intently, almost as if asking for permission. He looked wild with his disheveled hair and sharp fangs that glinted under his partially opened lips. His amber eyes seemed to burn as they locked with hers.

It turned her on. She could feel his need pressing against her waist as he held her close. She wanted him to close the distance. Just as he was a breath away from her lips, a knock came at the door. Dazedly, Mia remembered why she came to Aaron in the first place, jarring her out of her lust-filled haze.

***

Aaron's shoulders stiffened, and he released her quickly. He opened the connecting door. "Mia, go shower again and change your clothes," he urged. "They can smell me all over you," he explained when she looked at him in confusion. She nodded before dashing toward her bathroom.

He opened the balcony doors wide, letting in the fresh air. Going to the bathroom, he washed her scent of his body half-heartedly, scolding his beast for slipping beyond his control like that. Aaron didn't know what came over him when he noticed Mia in his room, looking lost. The shock on her face when she noticed him was priceless.

He could smell Emilia outside their room and hoped she didn't smell Mia's arousal. He didn't want her getting any ideas. Emilia was worse than the entire pack put together.

Once he had washed off the scent, he dried himself with a spare towel and hurried to the closet. Pulling out a random pair of jeans and a shirt, he threw them on hurriedly as he rushed to the door. Before opening it, he took a deep breath and forced his heart to slow. He sniffed the air and relaxed when Mia's scent wasn't that prominent now.

Fortunately, his chamber was soundproof, else she would have heard what had gone on inside. The only part of the room which allowed sounds to come in or out was the connecting door.

"Emilia." He frowned when he noticed what she was wearing. It was a pink sundress which barely reached her thighs paired with a colored beaded necklace and completed her look with brown ankle boots. Her blonde hair was pulled tightly into a ponytail.

Who wears a sundress during winter? Again, he already knew the answer to his question. *Emilia.*

"Hi, Aaron! I was here to see Mia. She wouldn't open the door, so I thought I would check with you," she chirped enthusiastically, increasing his confusion.

Why would Emilia look for Mia?

"What do you want with her?" he asked opening the door wide. Her eyes immediately scanned the room behind him and her posture relaxed when she didn't find Mia inside.

"Oh, you know. It's time for breakfast. I thought she might want company," she said and shrugged nonchalantly.

What's with this sudden interest? he wanted to ask. Although Aaron knew she did not mean a word of what she said, he couldn't shut her out. Doing so would raise unnecessary questions, and in turn, create a rift within the pack. He didn't want that now.

"She might be still asleep," he answered going to his phone. He dialed the extension to her room. Her voice came only a second later.

"Emilia is here to accompany you to breakfast," he kept his tone neutral, not wanting to give any hint to the eavesdropper.

"Oh, okay," Mia replied before disconnecting the call.

He heard her footsteps approaching his door. "Come in."

She entered, looking around to meet Emilia and gave her a warm smile which she returned, though it didn't reach her eyes.

"Hey, hope you slept well last night," Emilia said.

"I did. Thank you," Mia responded and returned the smile as she looked at Aaron for his permission.

He nodded with a grim expression, not liking where this was heading. Once she left, he sent the instructions to his general. *"John, Mia is heading to the dining hall with Emilia. I need two warriors watching her at all times. Make sure no one tries anything foolish."*

"Sure, Alpha. His Highness Jerome and the princes have already arrived. I will make sure she's safe and watched," his reply came immediately.

"Okay. Sounds good." Combing his wet hair, he hurried toward the dining room. His beast felt uncomfortable with Mia around Emilia.

When he reached the dining table, Mia was seated between Matthew and Emilia. It was clear his brothers and father didn't like the idea either.

Though Mia looked uneasy, she seemed to adjust well.

"Aaron, do you mind if I show Mia around? She's been holed up in that room all week."

Aaron almost choked at the question as he turned his gaze toward Emilia who had an innocent expression on her face. The pack was slowly getting used to her presence. Though the hostility was still there. "Emilia, I don't think that's a good idea."

"Oh, come on, Aaron. She's a guest here, and you can't keep her locked up all day. She will get bored, and besides, the pack will want to get to know her."

Aaron noticed the pack listening to their conversation.

"I will just take her to the backyard, so we can hang out for a while. I promise I will bring her right back to you after an hour," Emilia pleaded, giving him her hideous puppy face.

He looked at his dad and brothers who gave him a half-hearted nod. "Alright, Emilia. One hour, and I don't want any fuss," he said with a stern look.

"I will take care of her. Don't worry about it," Emilia's voice dripped with extra sweetness. Unfortunately, Aaron could see a few pack members agreeing with Emilia. He looked at John, who nodded cautiously.

What's your game, Emilia?

CHAPTER 18

Mia followed Emilia around the castle. Her hands were pushed deep into her coat pockets to hide their tremble. Suspicious and hostile glares drilled into her back. They weren't going for her throat, but the threat was definitely there. She focused on regulating her breathing and calming her racing heart.

Emilia didn't seem to worry about anything as she gossiped about things that were not familiar to Mia. She squirmed under the glances the pack kept sending her way, internally wishing she could run back to the safety of her room. Sadly, it also reminded her of why she could not be with Aaron. He made her feel wanted, and it felt right in every sense. She wanted nothing more than to surrender in his arms while he claimed her.

The never-ending corridors easily tired her mind as she followed Emilia like a lost puppy. Soon, they made it outside. Mia glanced around.

"This is the backyard of the castle, which leads to the forest," Emilia's face lit up.

Children of different ages were playing in the snow. The sounds of their laughter filled the air. Everything smelled fresh, and cold wind brushed Mia's face. The scenery before her was a distraction from hwe nagging thoughts and put her mind at ease.

"Pretty, isn't it?" Emilia asked again. Mia nodded in response, taken aback by the beauty of the forest. The wind, though chilly, was bearable. She eyed the children throwing snowballs at each other. In her peripheral vision, she noticed the lycans forming a protective circle around the children.

Suddenly, a snowball hit her square in the face, causing her to lose balance and fall on her butt. *Crap. That hurt.*

Mia wiped off the remaining snow from her face and narrowed her eyes at Emilia who was laughing hard and clutching her stomach. Her eyes narrowed, she wanted to throw it right back at Emilia's face, but she held off knowing she was at a disadvantage.

The surrounding members were wary, and if she read their expressions right, they were waiting for her to make one wrong move. It was written all over their faces and stiffened postures. They reminded her of a predator waiting to pounce on its prey. *They are predators.*

Emilia's eyes narrowed at her mockingly. Mia didn't miss her smirk either, which promised trouble. The snake was planning something. That was for sure. With a smile, she stood. Hiding her nervousness, she brushed off her backside.

A boy aged around six or seven advanced forward with a snowball. It sailed in the air before hitting Emilia square in the neck. Some of the snow slipped inside her sundress, soaking her.

"Oh, no you didn't." Emilia's attention switched to the boy.

Mia took a few steps back, stepping beside John and two others from his team. She watched from the sidelines as the snowball war continued between the children and Emilia. Although, she welcomed the change of scenery, Mia couldn't wait to return to the safety of her room.

***

Aaron, who watched the scene from his chamber's balcony, scanned the area for any threat. His sharp eyes were alert.

The phone on his table blared, demanding his attention. He was finishing up a call when a scream reached his ears. He ran to the balcony to see the final moments of Emilia, stumbling down the snow with a boy.

The fresh scent of blood hit his nose a fraction of a second too late because when the realization dawned, Mia was already beside them. She appeared next to the child in a blink of an eye, who was cradling his injured leg.

Fuck.

He jumped over the railing and rolled on the snow before running toward the commotion. A warning hiss sent shivers down his spine. The six-year-old screamed from Mia's arms. Her pitch-black eyes stared back at the guards running at her with their claws extended.

A snarl tore through her lips, and no one saw it coming because the guards flew across the field, crashing to the ground. Three well-trained deltas lay among the snow-debris, and Mia crouched low with the child still in her arms. Her two-inch razor-sharp claws were coated with blood.

Aaron's heart sped up as the scene unfolded before his eyes.

"Alpha, it's my son!" Victoria, the child's mother, wailed. Shaking hands cupped her pregnant belly, shifting from one foot to the other.

"Back off!" he ordered to the pack. They whimpered, but obeyed.

"Mia," he called softly, his steps cautious. It was the blood. No vampire could fight the thirst. She was in control when Ted got injured. Now, her fangs were out and tongue darted out to lick her lips.

"Stay away," he warned the pack.

Mia didn't look at him. Instead, she held the omega-born Louie closer while she rocked him from one side to the other—slow and careful. Her lips murmured something incoherent before burying her nose in the crook of his neck.

Aaron almost screamed as Victoria let out an agonized howl. Louie stopped crying immediately. The control he had over his raging emotions was put to the test as he approached her with his heart in his throat.

When he was close enough, he called her again in a gentle voice, "Mia."

A small mishap could kill the boy. *Oh god, how could I be so careless?* If her fangs were buried deep in the boy's jugular, tearing him away would leave him severely wounded. The task would be to make her retract them willingly. The scent of blood was thick in the air. However, he smelled no fear. Louie's breathing grew even, and his heartbeat slowed down as if he was asleep.

"Mia!" His voice came out harsher than expected. He shook her slightly, ready to act if she attacked. He only relaxed when her eyes shot open, blue orbs blinked at him. Relief washed over him when he noticed her fanged mouth free of blood. *She didn't bite the boy.*

Aaron released the breath he hadn't realized he was holding. He gave her a reassuring smile before pulling the kid slowly from her. She released him with a confused look as her eyes swept around them. He quickly checked the boy for any injury. No bite marks marred his neck, and the wound in his leg was healed with only an angry red scar now visible on his pale skin.

Though the omegas healed faster than humans, it should have taken at least two or three days for the boy to heal from that injury.

136

Aaron looked at Mia with his own confusion. She healed him. Her control over the bloodlust was surprising. *How did she do that? Is this some kind of trick a born vampire could do? Could Felipe heal someone like this?* He handed the boy to Victoria, who immediately grabbed him, crying in relief.

"Protect," Mia murmured without taking her eyes off the boy, her posture stiff.

Aaron understood now. She attacked his guards to protect the boy. "That's his mother. He's safe," he assured her.

"Mia, are you okay? You scared me for a moment there." Emilia asked, concerned.

She just nodded and turned her blue orbs at Aaron, her face paler than ever. "I'm tired," she whispered as her eyes rolled into her head. He caught her before her body hit the ground, hoisting her lithe frame in his arms.

***

Aaron paced in his chamber while his brothers watched him, waiting for him to stop and talk.

"She didn't go for the boy's throat. I mean she should have, right? He was bleeding for God's sake!" he exclaimed for the hundredth time.

"Maybe it's a trait of a born vampire," Mathew's shoulders lifted in a casual shrug.

"I thought—I thought she bit him. I couldn't—"

"You really like her that much, don't you? I can see it in your eyes," Matthew commented, a smile stretched on his lips.

"You want the pack to accept her. Not fear her as they do now," Juan added.

Aaron sighed in defeat. "She's different. I can't fathom the control she has over my beast. The more time I spend with her, the more he wants her."

"That's what a mate does to our kind, right?" Juan asked.

"Yes. But in my case, my potential mate is a vampire—our mortal enemy."

"Not just any other vampire. She's their queen," his brother pointed out. "Dad has a point."

"What if it doesn't work out?" Aaron plopped on the couch, crossing his legs.

"I think it'll work," Matthew's voice was confident. "I don't think she's driven by bloodlust like the other vampires. Even if she was, she can feed on you. Lycans heal faster than humans, and our blood replenishes in less time compared to them."

"You just labeled me as a holy grail of blood."

"Well, if you want to put it that way," Matthew joked.

"Their bites are painful." Juan rubbed his biceps with a grimace. "I don't think that'll work. How do we know if you guys are physically compatible?"

"Only one way to find out," Matthew smirked.

Aaron rolled his eyes. "It's not an easy decision to make. It will have a huge impact on our pack. They would need to accept her as their own. The other packs would too. Do you think they would take kindly to my mating with a vampire?" he asked.

His brothers nodded.

"It's a war. Dad is still serious about your mating with her. And I feel like you should listen to him."

Aaron shook his head. "I can't do that to her, Matt. I won't use or play with her emotions like that."

"No one's telling you to play with her emotions. You already feel something for her. We are just encouraging you to pursue it. See if she likes you back," Juan said.

"What if she doesn't like me?"

"Then seduce her," Matthew shrugged, only for Juan to hit his head.

"She likes you. Talk to her and get to know her better," Juan said.

"It's frustrating. My mate is the one person I shouldn't have any problem choosing. And here I am, attracted to the second most dangerous vampire in the world." Aaron let out a wry laugh, shaking his head.

"Everything happens for a reason. What if you're meant to be? I like to believe there are no coincidences." Juan stretched before picking up the remote and powering up the TV.

"Yep, also today's incident will allow them to look at her with different eyes. Just give it some time," Matthew said.

Aaron's brows creased, and he reclined into the couch. "Only time will tell which path she will choose to walk. What if she changes into someone like Felipe?"

Someone knocked on the door before it opened. Emilia sauntered in as if she owned the place. "How is Mia?"

"I thought you banned her from the royal wing," Juan shot through their link.

"Sleeping," Aaron replied in a clipped tone.

"Oh, I was worried and thought I would check."

"Sounds like you really like her, Emilia," Juan intervened, browsing through the channels.

"Of course, I like her."

"You guys didn't come for lunch," Emilia said.

"We ate here," Matthew replied. Aaron averted his gaze, trying to control the laughter that bubbled within. All her questions were directed toward him, but his brothers answered instead. He could sense her growing irritation. She tried to mask it but failed.

"Can I see her?"

"No." Their answers came in unison.

"What's got your panties in a twist?" Emilia huffed.

"Men don't wear panties, FYI," Matthew snickered.

"We wear something called briefs or boxers," Juan added.

Emilia's jaw locked. "Well then, I'll come back later."

"Sure. You know the way out," Juan pointed toward the exit.

Emilia opened her mouth to retort but decided against it and left the room with an annoyed huff.

"I heard she hit it off with that Zach last week. You know how he brags once the high set in," Matthew said. "He's smitten with her."

Alcohol didn't affect lycans. They had a higher metabolic rate than humans. It broke down the effects of alcohol before it affected their system. However, a few centuries ago, someone found a drug that could create a high for lycans for a few hours.

Aaron knew Emilia had flings. His heightened senses always picked up the distinct scent of other males often saturated in her skin no matter the number of baths she took or how many times she sprayed perfumes. He could always tell which male she spent her night with.

"I thought she was with Kamden," Juan said.

"That was a few months back," Matthew replied.

Aaron tuned his brothers' conversation out. His thoughts wandered back to Mia again. He thought about how badly he wanted to look into her baby blue eyes again. With a sigh, he closed his eyes. His mind reeling with the day's incidents.

CHAPTER 19

The night was eerily calm. The blowing wind carried an unnatural chill. No animals dared to make a sound, and the usual night creatures were absent in the forest.

A castle sat shrouded in darkness at the valley of Verboten Hills. No living being that entered the valley ever came back alive, which was why it was called the Slaughter Hills by the villagers. A vampire made its nightly rounds. His ghostly pale skin glistened in the darkness.

An unfortunate bird made the mistake to pass him. It didn't have enough time to regret its mistake before it was caught and drained off blood. A dark chuckle slipped past the lips of the macabre creature as he continued with the patrol.

Sounds of a whip tearing through flesh resonated throughout the walls of the ancient castle. The moan of pain in response to the lashes was drowned out by the repeated sound of the whip connecting to flesh again and again.

Felipe Lancelot, the mighty king of the vampires, sat upon his throne. His shoulder-length dark mane was combed to the back of his head. His calculating eyes watched as the witches tortured and conducted experiments on the other supernaturals they had captured.

The captives' pain-filled screams were music to his ears. His smooth lips curled up into a smile, revealing his sharp fangs.

"Have you come up with anything, Tanya?" he asked.

Tanya bowed with a seductive smile. "Their blood is not of use, Master. We will have to continue our research with the others," she said, pointing to the helpless gnomes behind her.

Gnomes were ugly, hot-tempered immortals, who lived underground. They were harmless when compared to other supernaturals. Too bad. The witches thought their blood would hold some power.

"Discard of them!" Felipe ordered.

He dismissed Tanya and reclined in his throne. The green-eyed witch was another plaything, nothing special. None of the women were. Tanya breathed because she was loyal and useful.

Getting beautiful women in his bed was never an issue; they swooned at his feet and begged for him to notice them. Unknown to them, he was the seductive predator who wouldn't hesitate to strike.

Felipe reveled in the next scream as he sipped fresh lycan blood from his chalice. His eyes rolled back to his skull as the warm liquid traveled down his throat. The power surge that came with it was more addictive than any drug used by the humans. He wanted the effects to last.

He knew of a witch whose knowledge far excelled that of the witches who worked for him. Lilith. She was the most knowledgeable witch of different herbs and potions. The only other one he knew that could match her was in his dungeons, lost in her own darkness.

"Master," one of his drudges bowed.

"Mhm," Felipe hummed when the sweet stench of fear and piss reached him. *Humans.* The corner of his lips twitched.

"How do you prefer them, Master?"

He no longer liked humans. Their blood made him gag. "Drag them to the drudgelings."

"Yes, Master."

Felipe followed, his dark silk robe swished behind him. The lowlifes cried, begging for a drop of kindness. They wouldn't get any. He hadn't felt that emotion in a thousand years. Snarls and hisses greeted them.

The drudge dropped the helpless hostages down and went to open the metal latch that held the iron door secure. It led to an underground chamber—a tunnel that homed thousands of his drudgelings. They were mindless killing machines he'd been tending to for over a decade.

An overwhelming stench of death and decay overpowered his senses, and Felipe had to stop breathing. Not that he needed to breathe. The habit got stuck with him when he shed his humanity long ago.

His eyes narrowed at the humanoid creatures that no longer held an ounce of humanity. A new development caught his eyes. Their eyes were completely black and bulged out like that of a reptile. Their incisors had become sharper and the front of their mouths had protruded forward. They were evolving.

"Drop them."

The drudge swallowed but obeyed. The hostages screamed and it was muffled soon by the sounds of tearing flesh and gurgling. A shiver racked the body of his drudge, causing Felipe to quirk one of his brows.

"Are you afraid now, Lucas?"

The drudge swallowed and hung his head.

"It's okay to fear them." Felipe's smile was sinister.

"How do we use them if they don't follow commands, Master? In a battlefield, they won't know the difference between us and the enemy. They are a threat even to the rest of us."

"Isn't that why I created them?" Felipe turned away as Lucas moved to closer the door and slid the lock in place. "Get me more lycans. I want their warriors this time." He looked over his shoulder when Lucas didn't respond. "What?"

"They killed every vampire that entered into their territory." The drudge froze under his hard stare. "C-can we take a witch with us, Master?"

Felipe waved his hand, dismissing Lucas from his presence. He didn't care who went as long as they completed the job. His mind went to the fae female who waited for him in his quarters. Pale fingers traced his cheek where she hit him earlier. He liked her feistiness, and it had been years since he'd been with someone who had anger issues. Excitement lit his face as he climbed the stairs.

***

Aaron knocked on Victoria's door an hour after lunch.

"Mom! It's the alpha." Louie, who opened the door, disappeared into a studio apartment of the omega quarters.

"Alpha," Victoria bowed. "Please, come in." She pulled a chair for him to sit. A warm, orange interior greeted him.

"How's Louie?" He eyed the six-year-old who peeked from behind his mother's skirt.

"He's fine, Alpha." The mother beamed. "He doesn't remember anything."

They were silent for a moment. He had come to check on the little boy but was left speechless. He had almost failed in his responsibility. If it was some other vampire in Mia's place, Louie wouldn't be standing here.

"I thought I lost him," Victoria admitted, breaking the awkward silence.

"I'm glad that your boy is fine. I wouldn't let any harm befall him or anyone else."

"We know."

His shoulders relaxed. "Thomas complained that you're not taking as much rest as you're supposed to. I'll arrange someone else to help you in the kitchen," he said, looking at her protruding baby bump.

"Oh, not at all, Alpha. My baby and I are perfectly fine."

He stood and ruffled Louie's hair, making him giggle. "Ask Thomas to meet me later."

"Sure, Alpha."

Worry nagged at his mind when he approached Mia's room. Work had kept him busy, and he couldn't visit her in person even though she stayed in the next room. Ted stood from the chair beside her bed and greeted him with a curt bow when he entered the room with a knock. The warlock still looked pale, but he was healing better. He hadn't left her side since the incident.

"How is she?"

Ted looked at his daughter lying on the bed. "I'm afraid she's changing."

"Isn't that a good thing?"

Ted rubbed his tired eyes. "Only time can tell. Her bloodlust will be at its prime when it happens."

Aaron nodded in understanding. They had theoretical knowledge only of what happened to a human when bitten by a vampire.

The bloodlust during their initial days was uncontrollable if not guided properly. "You can help her through this transition, can't you?"

The warlock shook his head. "I have no idea. Felipe is the only pureblood we know of. We don't have any information about his transition."

Aaron rubbed his forehead. Just what he needed right now. The pack's emotions were conflicted. They were wary of her. It didn't help that her kind were the reason for their painful past. She was their only trump card. Whether or not she'd aid them in defeating Felipe, only time and circumstances will decide. They needed her to figure out the weakness of a born vampire.

Liar. The beast within snarled. Okay, he needed her.

Aaron excused himself and moved to his room. The beast kept prowling at the back of his mind as he carried on with his duties. When dawn broke over the horizon, he couldn't wait to see her.

***

The warlock was asleep on the couch when he checked on her the next morning. He shook her awake. "Mia, how are you feeling?"

Her eyes fluttered open, focusing on him. A small smile stretched her lips. "Tired."

"You've been asleep since yesterday."

"I don't feel like I slept that long," her exhausted voice groaned out.

"You can go back to sleep after you get some food in you."

Worry etched his features upon noticing that her skin was paler than before. He helped her out of the bed and watched as she dragged her tired limbs to the bathroom. His chest tightened, wondering what kind of changes and trouble this change would bring.

The pack wasn't ready. *He* wasn't ready. Would he still feel the same once her transition was complete?

While she was in the bathroom, he woke Ted and sent the warlock to his room, demanding him to refresh and rest. Then he called the butler and ordered breakfast.

He was setting up the breakfast table when she walked back in the fresh scent of roses wafted through his nostrils, making his beast purr. It clawed at his chest and his eyes shifted to the ambers of his beast.

Draped in a towel that did no justice to her soft curves, she walked to her closet with no realization of his presence still in the room. Her hair was damp from the shower, and Aaron watched as droplets of water rolled down the bare skin of her shoulders. He felt his cock straining against his pants.

Inhale.

Exhale.

Inhale.

Exhale.

His canines embedded themselves in his lips, drawing blood. Oh, how bad he wanted to run his hands all over her naked skin. He choked on a growl, turning away from her and walked to the only window in the room. His hands clenched into fists.

Inhale.

Exhale.

Air filled his lungs, expanding them. Her scent teased him. Ripe and ready to harvest.

Fuck.

Can vampires go into heat? This wasn't heat though. Still, her scent had gotten several times sweeter. His eyes closed, drawing her scent in. He buried his claws into his palms, and his blood dripped to the floor.

Need he never knew before gripped his heart, sending jolts of awareness to every fiber of his body. His legs felt heavy when he took another step back. Fortunately, he was closer to the window. He needed the fresh air.

Aaron wrenched the window open, exhaling louder. A gust of fresh and crisp air rushed in, clearing the fog from his mind. Once in control, he was quick to clean the blood droplets from the floor and used the fresh snow to wash away the traces of blood from his hand.

The Lycan King schooled his emotions when she came out of the closet dressed in a pair of pale green pajamas. She still hadn't looked at him. Her attention was on the breakfast he brought in. Her eyes darkened at the sight of food, and he watched as she mauled the dishes as if there was no tomorrow.

Mia gulped down the food without chewing it. A loud growl emanated from her chest as she continued to devour the food on the tray before her. When done, she moved to her bed without cleaning up, and fell asleep when her head hit the pillow.

Aaron couldn't fathom the reason for her behavior. She acted as if she was possessed. He approached her sleeping form with a napkin he dipped into the glass of water and cleaned her mouth and hands before removing the tray. He pulled the blanket over her and left the room with more questions than answers.

CHAPTER 20

"Dad, you called."

"Yes." Aaron's father looked up from the book he was reading. His brows creased. "Is she awake?"

"No. Ted said she's changing."

"Be prepared to face the worst. You know the drill."

"This is an unwanted tension, Dad." If this information leaked to the pack, they'd demand her death. He already knew a few who awaited the chance.

"I know. But, would you prefer the other choice we have?"

Aaron shook his head reluctantly.

"That's what I thought. We'll have to handle this confidentially."

"We'll stick to our plan. We will wait and watch and keep everyone at a safe distance from her."

"So, it's our plan now?" his dad chuckled.

Aaron let the comment slip. "Mia has surprised us so far."

"Can't disagree with that. No vampire had shown so much tolerance for blood. She healed the boy. It's something we need to investigate. What else can she do?"

"Ted has no clue." No one had a clue. Aaron reclined in his chair and stared at the ceiling. A deep sigh relaxed his lungs. He would

149

have to be more careful with her situation and make sure that she wasn't blinded by her instincts. It would be a hard ride for them. He vowed to be with her and guide her toward the right path.

A knock on the door distracted him from his thoughts. His brothers entered.

"Brother, the number of vampires lurking around has increased over the past couple of days. The patrol killed two this morning. Do you think they are here for her?" Juan asked.

"No, they're here for us. Mark and Raymond's clan reported minor vampire attacks in their territory. I feel like Felipe is testing the waters." He rubbed his biceps while his brows creased. "Either that or he needs more wolves to run his experiments."

"What do you propose, brother?" Matthew asked, his body tight with tension.

His chest expanded. "Ready the fighters. We won't spare anyone this time."

***

Emilia paced within the walls of her room. Her jaws ground with an itch to tear through the female vampire. Her frustration mounted. After her failed attempt in the snow, she couldn't find another way to get Mia alone. How long would they keep her locked in?

How could a vampire resist blood? The thought had been eating away at her since the incident.

All she had to do was trigger the leech and trick her into attacking the kid. Then she'd loop in and kill her in defense. Emilia had been ready with her outstretched claws when Mia attacked the deltas.

Then, Aaron stepped in, ruining the game for her. The plan would have gone without a hitch if it wasn't for him.

The pack's reaction wasn't something she expected. She could sense their dilemma, but no one was voicing it yet. Emilia expected someone to protest and demand their alpha for more answers. But the useless mutts tucked their tails between their legs and carried on with their chores as if there wasn't a vampire among them.

"Em, the alpha has called for a meeting in fifteen minutes. Come to the training yard." Her father's voice slipped in her mind.

What now? She immediately left the room.

She stood behind everyone, listening to the alpha. Aaron was discussing the safety measures for the women and children while giving out orders to the deltas. *So, the bloodsuckers are coming for us.* When the meeting ended, a wicked smile lit her expression as an idea clicked.

Let's see how you will escape this bullet.

A few females strutted through the arena, supplying water as they went by.

"Hey, Em!" Keith, one of the warriors, greeted. "Wanna join?" He flexed his muscles suggestively, but she was in no mood for combat. Her freshly done nails wouldn't withstand a shift.

"What's the point of all this?" she glanced around as the lycans gathered for an intense training session.

"Didn't you hear?" he asked. "The alpha thinks we are being targeted by the bloodsuckers. The patrol killed two this morning."

Oh. Emilia huffed, letting him see her anger. "You're all fools," she hissed. "Our problems won't end by fighting these faceless puppets."

"I'm not understanding," Keith murmured. The others had paused what they were doing, and their ears twitched.

"Don't you get it? It's happening because of the leech. We haven't had them infiltrate our pack grounds for at least seven years."

"Why would they come for her?" asked Simon, another delta.

"Yeah, didn't you hear they killed three humans earlier this month? It was before her arrival."

Emilia ignored their questions. "I can't believe this. How could you live with the knowledge of a bloodsucker being so close? She should be locked in the dungeons and tortured for information. Instead, she's given a room in the royal wing next to the alpha so they can fuck."

Keith boomed with laughter. "You've got a good imagination, Em. Don't let the alpha hear this."

"Oh, really. If you can't see what's happening in front of you then you're blind," she pushed at him, making him growl. "Why isn't she staying in the guest wing, where she could be better monitored by the guards?"

"You mean *them*," he pointed at the collared ones who were clearing the snow from the ground. "You know what happened the last time she was left with the guards."

This wasn't working. The peabrains believed whatever their alpha said.

"I'm tired of this. Why can't you see it? She's seducing him! That fucking leech has him under her control, and I swear she's planning something."

There was confusion on their faces now. Emilia smirked as they contemplated her words.

"The alpha says—"

"Use your brains. How could she go unnoticed in our territory for six months?" Her smirk widened when she noticed their fists clenching. "She's hiding something. She's a spy. She's working for the vampire king and these repeated vampire sightings are just the start."

"Victoria said the vampire cured Louie," Mason, who had just walked up, protested.

"Why hasn't she showed her face after the incident? She spared the kid so you'd believe her," Emilia countered. "That's her plan to earn our trust." A smile of satisfaction spread on her lips as the venom in her words spread across their minds. "Do whatever you guys want to. I won't fall for her plan. I'm gonna catch her red-handed and prove it to everyone."

When she left the field, she knew her words had done the job.

***

Mia glanced around nervously as they walked through the backyard. When she had woken up, it had been close to four in the evening, and her father said she'd been sleeping all day. She could tell he hadn't slept judging by the black circles under his eyes. It took her a while to convince him she was fine and to get him to rest. She was taking a stroll through the corridors of the royal wing when the snake-eyed beta female came up to her and demanded they go for a walk.

Though Mia told her she didn't want to go out, Emilia was persistent. She claimed the boy was fine and the mother was thankful she healed his wound.

Mia didn't remember the healing part. She remembered nothing. The members of the pack spoke in hushed tones as she walked past them. Her shoulders hunched, and she looked down to avoid the weird looks she always received. The backyard was empty except for a few omegas carrying out with their daily chores.

Emilia chatted animatedly as Mia toyed with the hem of her coat. Nothing had changed since she'd last been out. The glances thrown her way were still as hostile as ever. She was lost in her thoughts when the omegas stopped what they were doing and turned abruptly, whipping their heads toward the forest, their eyes growing wide.

Emilia growled. Her eyes narrowed toward their right where the tree line started. Fur sprouted on her arms, causing Mia to take a few steps back. Then, she smelled it. The nauseating stench of a decaying corpse hit her with such a force that made her knees shake.

She whirled around, facing the forest. Her eyes scanned the snow-covered vegetation as her heart beat rapidly. She could literally feel all her blood rushing toward her head, making her more alert. Men and women ran. They scurried away like little mice. There were more people outside than she noticed.

No, no, no. Please god, no. Not now.

Her breathing became erratic as the familiar sense of fear turned her legs into jelly.

"A-Aaron," she whispered, looking around. She needed him now. Only he could keep her safe. A group of warriors poured in from behind her, ready to fight as the stench grew stronger. She gagged, fighting to keep the bile down. Suddenly, a group of vampires broke out of the tree line.

The warriors moved fast, shifting into their beasts in mid-air, launching themselves at the vile creatures. Even Emilia ran into the fray. Gunshots went off and a few leeches dropped to the ground only to stand again after a few seconds of being down. Her eyes teared up.

I should run. Hide somewhere.

Growls and the tearing of flesh filled her ears as Mia felt a splitting headache overtake her senses. She fell on her knees, clutching

154

her head as her vision blurred. More creatures charged at them, overwhelming the lycans. Her mind vaguely registered that they were severely outnumbered.

Her body felt light and swayed to the side as she fought with the fear that had overpowered her senses. Suddenly, someone grabbed her around the waist and ran. She was too dazed to realize who it was. The foul smell and cold embrace told her it was the creature she despised.

Mia screamed only to find her voice stuck in her throat as she struggled against the hold, trying to break free. She witnessed many following, each with an omega in their hands.

Panic set in as she thrashed with all her might and head-butted the one carrying her.

He stopped abruptly and adjusted her in his arms before motioning his accomplices toward some direction. Her jaw dropped at the scene before her. A huge black hole that hung in mid-air greeted her eyes. The vampires carrying the omegas jumped in and disappeared one after the other. The hole sucked them in, and the screams of the omegas disappeared within.

Her shock-filled gaze noticed a short woman standing beside the hole with a wicked glint in her eyes. When it was Mia's turn, she felt something snap within her.

CHAPTER 21

"Hurry up!" The witch screeched. "We don't want these fucking mutts. Where are the lycans?"

"They are too strong for us, witch," someone wheezed.

"The master asked specifically for the deltas. Throw her into the portal and bring *them* in."

More creatures poured in, all holding a hostage. Terrified cries and furious growls reverberated around Mia. The headache was becoming too much. When it became too hard to bear, she let go and felt as if her head was splitting in half. When the headache subsided, strength she hadn't felt before pulsed in her veins. Everything around her became more focused when she opened her eyes. She could hear their heartbeats and heavy breath.

"She's not one of them." A long finger was pointed at her. The dirt embedded in her nails appeared too close and the stench of death around her was too much.

"She smelled nice. Thought master could use a quick snack."

The witch shook her head. "Drop her and find some warriors if you want to keep your head."

There was no fear within her, and it felt as if she was in yet another dream. Only in this one, she felt like she could fight them all.

The nature of who she was clawed within her chest. She didn't like the way they talked about her. Violence bristled within her marrow. The need to defend and the need for blood clouded her.

Something shifted in the air as the creature released his hold on her. Mia didn't fall down. Instead, she floated in the air, in the same position, with her head down and her hair covering her face.

"What's happening?" the witch yelled with her palm raised in the air.

A loud snarl stopped everyone in their tracks. The vampires all blinked but didn't move an inch from their spots. Their hold on the hostages tightened.

Blood.

Mia's nostrils flared and head whipped to the source. The warm crimson liquid trickled down the tan skin of the omega she didn't recognize at first. The hostage trembled, and she smelled her piss. Eyes bulged out in fear, almost begging as their eyes locked.

Protect.

This female had served her food once. The warm smile she gave her was assuring in her mind's eye.

"Let her go." Mia's lips flashed her fangs, sharp and lethal. She landed on her feet ever so slowly.

The witch's eyes widened with an inaudible gasp that left her mouth. The surprise was soon masked, and Mia felt her skin tingle. The woman's hands were glowing. The brightness almost blinded her. She could almost taste the witch's maliciousness.

To everyone's surprise, Mia stood, unmoving. Her body absorbed the magic like dry land that hadn't seen rain in years. The surge of power in her veins was addicting. She felt this new version of herself taking the wheel while pushing her consciousness to the passenger seat.

More. She wanted more.

Mia snarled again at the witch and felt a gust of energy leave her, throwing the witch off balance.

"W-who are you?" the witch stuttered.

The energy pulsed.

Whispering.

Murmuring.

The strange syllables that echoed in her brain were incoherent yet compelling.

Then she felt herself move. Her body hoisted the witch up in the air. Mia's cackle echoed through the forest followed by the witch's scream. Blood—strong and powerful flowed into her mouth, nourishing her taste buds.

Mia watched in satisfaction as the witch's lifeless eyes stared back at her. Her face twisted in her final moments of agony. The black hole vanished, and the witch's lifeless body thumped to the ground.

As the thirst for violence subsided temporarily, her consciousness pushed forth. Mia's heart thundered within her ribcage as she tried to take control. No. This wasn't how she wanted it to end. But the invisible force held her immobile in the back of her mind before everything went blank.

***

Aaron's beast halted in its tracks as he noticed the omegas thrashing in the hold of the vampires. The vampires' claws digging deep into the omegas' skin. His eyes found the dead body of a woman who did not belong there. The dark robe and the accessories around her neck stamped her as a witch. The flesh on her neck was torn away, her blood sucked dry.

Who killed her?

"Do not come forward," one of the vampires threatened, distracting him from the corpse. "We will kill them all," he said, placing a hand on his hostage's neck. The hostage's pale hands shook.

The area reeked of wolf piss and defecation. The wolves whimpered just as another cackle sounded above them, and they looked up to see the lifeless body of a vampire being dropped.

His heart stopped when he saw Mia floating above them. Her pitch-black eyes held neither emotion nor recognition. Fresh blood dripped from her chin. Her eyes flashed to Aaron when she heard the other lycans growl.

She paid them no attention, and all they could see was a blur of movement. Soon all but one omega was free. The bodies of the parasites that held them hostage dropped to the ground—lifeless.

Aaron watched with his heart in his throat when she cornered the last one. Clawed hands tightened over the she-wolf's throat.

"I-I'll kill her," the enemy's voice trembled out. His paranoid eyes swept around. He kicked his accomplices, checking to see if they were alive as he backed up.

The lycan king feared for the omega's safety as the rescued ones scrambled away, running to hide behind the warriors. Their hearts beating louder as they waited. One wrong move would end the she-wolf.

Mia tilted her head, eyes following the leech with a smirk. Tension gripped the air with its tightened fist. He almost roared when In a blink, Mia grabbed the omega by her neck, freeing her from the vampire's grip. Tears trickled down Saloni's cheeks, her gaze hopeful yet filled with fear. Mia's eyes shifted to the creature that tried to slip away.

With a hiss, she pushed Saloni behind her before pouncing at the heartless monster that stood no chance against her. A loud screech left its lips as her fangs tore through its throat. She gulped down its blood with greed that Aaron wished he'd never witnessed.

"Take the omegas back to the castle and leave us alone," Aaron ordered, without taking his eyes off her. Everyone left except for his brothers. Their eyes were fixated on the female who once claimed she wasn't a monster.

Gone was the sweet, innocent Mia. The one in front of Aaron was a pureblood vampire, who had tasted blood for the first time. Her body was drenched in it. Aaron let out a breath, concentrating on his human form. Within seconds he had shed his fur and was back in his skin. Pulling on a pair of shorts stashed in a nearby tree, he contemplated his next move.

Now, he needed to calm the unpredictably strong vampire, who was being purely guided by her instincts.

"Stay away from her line of sight and interject only if the situation gets out of hand," he told his brothers, who nodded and stepped back immediately.

"Mia."

She didn't look up. Instead, she dropped the body she was feeding on and moved to another. Aaron winced, hearing her fangs tear through the vampire's jugular, realizing she had just broken their necks earlier. She slurped the blood as if it was the best thing she had ever tasted.

They were beasts, and hunting was in their nature. However, the scene in front of him was savage. He had seen the worst, but an uneasy feeling settled in his stomach.

"Mia, you have to stop." His steps were cautious. She paid no heed to him as she moved to the other parasite. "Mia. . ." He dared to shake her slightly. A hiss was the only warning he got before she pounced on him.

Aaron, surprised by her sudden attack, lost his balance. He fell backward on the forest floor, taking her with him. Uncertain hands held her secure while she straddled him.

The pulse in his neck heated under her narrowed gaze. Her blood-coated tongue darted out as a claw traced his thrumming pulse with an appreciative growl. He saw her nostrils flare, taking in his scent. The parting of her thighs rested on his hips. Warmth radiating from the contact.

Mia was too strong. The position put him at a disadvantage. She could kill him in the blink of an eye. To his horror, the furry mutt inside purred in delight. Lust shot through his veins and fur sprouted from his arms.

She looked startled when his beast purred. She tilted her head, her fangs flashed at him. The sight alone was enough to stir his desire. The shirt she wore had slipped off her shoulders. When her head tilted to the other side, it felt as if she was taunting him with a "come and get me" tag. His eyes shifted to those of his beast and narrowed at the spot that connected her neck and shoulders. The predatory fangs elongated with a burn to sink into her flawless skin, marking her as his forever.

She had pinned him to the ground with both her hands on either side of his naked chest. Her pitch-black eyes stared him down and blood dripped onto his chest from her chin. Her breasts heaved.

The beast tuned out the sounds and smells of the surroundings, focusing only on her. A growl tumbled out of his chest. Her eyes blinked before pressing her palm over his heart, an answering growl reverberated within her ribs.

Claim.

Take.

Possess.

The overwhelming thoughts of his beast floated in his mind. Aaron panted with a need he never felt before. Mia leaned down running her nose along his jaw as another rumble erupted from her chest.

"Mia. . ." Aaron's voice rang thick with lust. Her response was another rumble, and Aaron tensed when he felt her tongue tasting his skin. Her eyes closed when his thumb traced a small part of her bare skin underneath her blood-soaked shirt.

Flipping her over in the blink of an eye, he pinned her wrists to the forest floor. The thick scent of her desire clouded his senses. It teased and tested the restraints of his control.

Aaron swallowed hard. He could almost taste her essence. Her wetness soaked the front of his pants.

"Get a hold of your emotions, brother!" Juan's voice pulled him out of his lust-filled trance.

"Yep, PG-13 please." Aaron could imagine Matthew rolling his eyes while saying this.

It was hard to look at her and not want. Even as she was bathed in blood and reeked of the leeches, the sight appealed to his beast more than ever. His chest puffed in pride for this female and itched to make her his. Then, his brother's voice had reactivated the logical part of his brain. It was neither the time nor place for such emotions. She was not herself and was acting on pure instincts. He held her down when she tried to move.

"Mia."

There was no recognition in her eyes as they continued to roam across his naked torso. Aaron almost lost it when she raised her hips a little trying to get closer to him.

"Mia!" This time he yelled, startling her.

She blinked rapidly and frowned when she noticed her current position. Aaron released her hands when he noticed her eyes were back to their normal blues.

"You okay?"

Red-tainted hands reached to clutch her head and frantic eyes roamed around the surrounding area. A silent scream escaped her mouth when her eyes landed on the pile of bodies she left in her wake. The beat of her heart grew erratic, and she pulled at her clothes frantically when she realized they were soaked in blood.

Deep cerulean eyes bored into him with panic before she scrambled away from him. "Calm down, Mia. You're safe." Her eyes only went wide before she froze.

Fuck.

CHAPTER 22

Mia's memory was vague—she remembered being afraid, being forced away from the castle, and the black hole. She recalled the witch dying in her hands. Her blood tasted divine. After that, it was just fragmented pieces, and they were gruesome.

Everything stopped around her. Silence. Vision and thoughts went blank. Though she blinked, she saw nothing, felt nothing. Strong arms wrapped around her waist to pull her into a hard embrace.

"Mia!"

The voice was distant, she blinked to clear her vision, and someone's face came into focus.

"Mia, it's okay. I'm here now."

Blink. His striking features felt familiar.

"It's okay, my love. Look at me please."

Blink. Her lungs gasped for air to fill them. The thick scent of a male overpowered other senses.

"Focus on my voice. Listen to my heart."

Warmth shot through her palms, and she felt his heart pulsing.

"Breathe, Mia." The gentleness of his voice tugged at her heartstrings. "It's okay. Everything is fine now."

Her mouth tasted different than usual, reminding her of the horror that brought it. Mia spat repeatedly, wiping her mouth. *Oh, God. No!* Violent sobs racked her body. *I killed them all.* She drank their blood. And, she enjoyed doing it. *I'm a killer.* Her head shook from side to side.

Emotions coiled around her throat—disbelief, denial, and guilt. Her breath heaved. With a strangled cry, she broke out of his embrace, pushing him away.

Mia hissed in warning when Aaron tried to move closer. Her gums burned again, and her senses honed to listen to the beat of his heart. The blood pumping through his veins. The smell of his blood was strong—so seductively overwhelming.

"I will never hurt you," he advanced with slow steps.

No. Her mind visualized his hot blood flowing in her mouth. Her mouth watered as she wondered how it would taste. *But, I will.* Sharp fangs sliced her skin when she wiped her mouth. Frantic fingers pushed at the fangs. Mia didn't know how to get those fangs inside. They hurt. She hissed at him again.

"It's okay. Let me come to you," Aaron had both of his hands up in surrender. He inched closer with careful steps. "Breathe, Mia. Take deep breaths." His aura radiated calm, forcing her to relax.

She did as she was told. He smelled like fresh rain and forest. It was oddly comforting. Her eyes closed, inhaling deeply as she felt his arms drape around her again. Her body leaned toward him, taking in his scent and basking in the warmth that surrounded her.

Mia buried her face in the crook of his neck and inhaled. His body shivered to make her stop.

"Take it easy," he said, rubbing her back.

She felt her fangs retract. Her gums still burned, but the sudden urge to taste his blood had subsided.

"I don't want to hurt you." Her voice shook. Tears soaked her cheeks. She had attacked them, killed them, and drank their blood. She scrambled away from his embrace once again and brought her knees close to her chest after dropping to the forest floor. "I'm a monster." Her body trembled and she rocked back and forth, eyes frantic.

"You're not a monster," his reassurance didn't help. He sat down and pulled her into his lap. "Look at me, Mia. You are not a monster." She could sense the doubt in his words. The initial hesitation and the minuscule tremble in his voice were not missed.

"I killed them all. How could you say that I'm not a monster? Did you not just see what I did to them!" Her eyes locked with his and held.

Aaron's eyes closed. It suddenly felt as if he couldn't deny her words and was trying to convince himself. When they reopened, the coffee brown orbs were sincere. "I saw what you did. You saved the life of eight omegas."

"I couldn't stop it," she cried, pushing her face against his chest. "What if I had hurt your people? What if I fail to control this again? I don't know why I did what I did."

The silence stretched for a long minute. "Your dad and I will help you to control this better."

A week ago, she claimed she wasn't a killer. She argued she was innocent. A second was all it took to change her life.

"I'm not a killer. I don't want to kill anyone, not even by accident," she continued. "You should kill me. If this is what happens when I change, I don't want to live."

"Mia. . ." His lips parted and his eyes went wide.

"Trust me, you'd be doing me a favor. I don't want to be like them."

"You won't be like them."

"How can you be so sure? No one has seen this Felipe guy, yet he's a fucking monster. If what you said is true, then I'm going to be just like him. A killer!" Mia controlled the urge to snarl. Her chest heaved and her nostrils flared. She searched his eyes and found nothing. "You have no clue what's going to happen, do you?" her voice whispered out, cracking at the end.

"Let's get you cleaned up."

Mia knew he was changing the topic. She allowed him to help her and followed him mutely as her mind kept reeling. *I'm a monster.*

***

Aaron took her to the flowing stream nearby. Snow crunched under their feet. Mia retracted her feet at the first touch of water, but then slipped into the knee-deep water with a hiss. They carefully stepped around the rocky bed and stopped when they reached a bunch of rocks.

A warm puff of air came from Aaron as he pointed her to sit on a rock. Water sloshed around them. She sat, so that the water now came around her hip. Mia cupped the water and splashed it on her face and body. Her body shivered with cold.

Aaron stopped her and squatted in front of her. Her vampiric scent had intensified stronger than the day before. He helped her remove her shirt and washed it clean of blood. Once satisfied, he used the wet material to gently scrub her skin.

He scrubbed the sticky blood with utmost care while she sat still on a rock. Tears continued to stream down her cheeks. He couldn't take

167

her to the castle the way he found her. It'd strike fear in his pack's minds.

Aaron was conflicted. She had saved the omegas by fighting off the vampires. Her instincts must have taken over. With little knowledge about how it worked, he considered making their juveniles an example. It took a while for them to accept and work along with their beasts. They often lost control and attacked the others.

Mia was a ticking time-bomb, and he didn't know how to help her. He stood and moved to her back. Even as his hands scrubbed her neck, he thought about his father's words. Killing her would be easy. One slice and she'd be dead. His hands shook at the mere thought.

She turned around, fixing him with her blues. "Why haven't you killed me yet?" her question caught him off guard. "They killed your mother. How could you spare me?"

His eyes went wide, he didn't recall telling her about his mother ever.

Who told her?"I heard the guards talking about how you were housing one of the leeches responsible for your mother's murder," she murmured. "I guessed that they were talking about me and my father because there weren't any other guests at the dining table with us that night."

His features hardened. "You had nothing to do with that."

The silence stretched between them. Her gaze averted to the water. Aaron's jaw locked. He had become attracted to her the moment they met. His beast was smitten and he couldn't bring himself to hurt her. How could he tell her this? Their future was uncertain.

"I was so scared when they attacked. They took several people with them. I thought they were going to take me away too."

Damn it. Everything happened so fast he failed to check on the pack members who were retrieved.

"Juan, check how many were abducted. I want the report ASAP."

"Already on it, brother."

"We'll talk later," he absent-mindedly mumbled to her as his mind reeled. He had suspected a witch was in play, and he was right. The vampires kidnapped his wolves. He continued to wash her hair in the stream, scrubbing out the dried blood until she was clean. His beast raged. He had failed to protect them. He couldn't imagine what Felipe would do to them in the name of experiments. The sooner Lilith came, the better. Only she could help him rescue them.

Both were lost in their own thoughts; he stood once she was somewhat clean. It would take a long hot bath to get rid of the coppery scent that had saturated her skin.

Once out of the stream, Aaron eyed the soft towel his brothers left for them. Mia accepted the towel from him wordlessly and wrapped it around her, shivering as she did. He threw away her shirt he was still holding. Stains of blood still clung to the material.

"Brother, they took five omegas. Two deltas are injured. They, along with the rescued ones, are being treated for their injuries," Juan informed him.

"Okay, Juan. Secure the path. I'm bringing her in."

CHAPTER 23

The door to his room burst open, and Aaron instantly knew it was his father. He wiped his body dry before pulling his clothes on.

Are you all right? The question wasn't asked. His father's worried gaze swept over his frame and the tension creases in his face smoothed.

"We had to sedate her," Aaron said. Exhaustion crept into his bones. The past few hours had been hectic. With a sigh, he lowered himself to the nearby couch, placing his legs on the table while his father occupied the other. "She killed a witch."

"I heard." His father's forehead creased. "Saloni said she drank her dry."

"Yep, the witch wasn't the only unfortunate one in the bunch. You should have been there. She was a force to be reckoned with."

"It doesn't make sense," Jerome shook his head. "A vampire isn't compatible with witch blood, son."

Now, that had his attention. "I don't follow."

"Witch blood burns them inside out. Mia should have been dead, but she's not."

Aaron frowned. No. She wasn't dead. She turned out to be stronger than ever. "There is more to this. Talk to Ted, see why she hadn't reacted to witch blood."

His father nodded. "The wolves are shaken. Your pack needs you now, son."

Aaron could feel the unrest within the pack. He was in no mood to deal with them, but it was his responsibility. When he tapped into the link that connected the entire pack, he could hear their thoughts as clear as a bright sunny day. Someone had spread a rumor that the increased vampire activities were because of Mia.

"Juan, I'd like to address the pack. Get them to the throne room. Keep the pups away."

There were things that needed their attention. Dealing with pack politics was something he wasn't ready for. Juan and Matthew had gathered all the available pack members in the throne room by the time he reached it.

A hushed silence fell over the crowd when he stood facing them. "What's going on?"

"She shouldn't be here, Alpha. She's the reason behind the attacks. They want her," said a male omega.

"Sanders is right, Alpha. She's a danger to us all," another omega called.

Ridiculous. His eyes narrowed at the beta female who stood passively among the crowd. "Who told you this?"

The crowd quieted at his question as they looked at each other for answers.

"Answer me!"

"It was me, Alpha."

Zach, the head of dungeon security stepped out of the crowd and stood in front of him with his head bowed. Aaron knew it wasn't him. In his peripheral vision, he noticed Emilia shaking under his alpha command.

"Why would you lie to save your girlfriend, Zach?" he asked, making the crowd go silent again.

"Alpha—"

"Dare lie to me again and I will rip your tongue out," Aaron growled. When Zach had no response Aaron continued, his eyes focused on Emilia. "Step forward, Emilia."

Confusion was clear in the faces of the pack members. Emilia's trembling form stepped forth and stood beside Zach.

"I have clearly told you all that Mia is not your concern. What made you go against my words?" Though his question sounded general it was directed at Emilia.

"She's a threat," her voice though wavered, she held her head high.

"Is she?" Aaron let his beast surface just beneath his skin as he tilted his head.

Emilia shook under his scrutinization. "I don't trust her, Aaron."

"It's alpha to you," Aaron growled. "The next time you forget your place, you'll be whipped."

Shock coated Emilia's features as she gazed at Aaron, averting her gaze when she couldn't withstand the authority radiating from him.

His attention turned to the crowd. "Did you forget that my mother was killed by vampires? Whom do you blame for the vampire sightings before Mia's arrival?"

The beast raged inside, snapping its jaws. "A war is coming. Supernaturals are being abducted. He's wiping out the races. They killed humans and left them right outside our border as a challenge." He paced, eyes fixed on the members who were shaking under the burning intensity of his ambers.

"Mia is their spy. She is—"

"Enough!" Emilia dropped to the ground under his command, whining as he pinned her with his gaze. The beast wanted to sink its fangs on her neck to put her in her place. "I don't have time to deal with this bullshit. Do you hear me?" The vein along his jaw ticked as his claws burst free.

"Have I ever let you down?" The question was directed at the crowd. Whimpers and whines slipped out of their mouths. Heads shook and knees trembled.

"I asked a question. Have I ever let you down?" His face reddened as his chest vibrated with a growl. Perhaps, it was time to remind them all of their places. He was King. Their alpha. Their protection was his responsibility. His grandfather died for it. His mother died for it.

"No, Alpha," a few whined. They were all on their knees now, including his brothers.

"Do you think I would be so careless? Do you think I'd put your lives at risk?" Aaron snarled. The silence stretched except for the occasional whimpers.

"Mia, the only female pureblood is our trump card in this war." Audible gasps echoed from the crowd as he continued. "I'm sure you have seen how she fought today. She killed eight leeches and a witch. Or did you forget that?" The beast was in control. A decision was made. Mia was the rightful female to stand by his side. A queen strong enough to protect and kill.

"Today's incident made me realize one thing," he smiled to himself. "I choose Mia as my potential mate." His beast growled in agreement.

The pack stood gaping at his words. Their jaws went slack and eyes went wide like saucers.

"I'll be at the training yard tomorrow morning at six. Those who do not agree with my decision may challenge me in a fight." His gaze narrowed at them. "You may choose to fight alone or as a group."

Numerous eyes blinked as realization dawned on them. The beast cracked its knuckles. "You may disperse."

***

Felipe jerked from his throne with a hiss on his lips. He felt as if each of his drudges lost their lives. The thin thread holding them to him was cut off. He would have sensed their pain if it wasn't for the distance.

The lycans won again. He had no doubt. Well, he suspected something like this. A deep inhale filled his lungs with air that carried the metallic tang of blood.

Something pulled at his chest. He clutched it just above his heart. The sudden pain was gone as soon as it came. But it spoke a hell lot of volumes.

"Dreven!" His voice had lost all traces of humanity as it growled out.

His eyes darkened as the realization of what that meant dawned. The last two times it happened, there was a discovery of two other purebloods that he later found and killed. Whoever it was, was just coming into their powers. He had to act fast. The drawback—he had to track them the old-fashioned way.

"Master," his most trusting servant and one of the first humans he turned bowed.

"Send a word out to our allies," he rubbed his chest. "We have a born vampire to track."

"Yes, Master."

Dreven left with a bow. No questions asked. That was what he liked about his general.

Felipe's thoughts drifted to the past. He still remembered waking up one morning beside his dead girlfriend with her blood still fresh in his mouth. It was a time when society didn't allow unmarried men or women meet in private. She had been his betrothed.

When he'd learned no one would be in her home that night, he snuck in. Everything went as planned until something snapped from within, and he lost consciousness. Human food didn't satisfy him anymore from that day on. He occasionally hunted unsuspecting humans from the nearby villages.

Over the years, his thirst had left a mountain of corpses in his wake. It was a few centuries later he came across a human who didn't die after his feasting. Dreven was hanging on by a thread, fighting to live. Fascinated by this, Felipe had fed his blood to the victim, wanting to see what it would do.

His blood worked like magic. Felipe watched as the huge gash on Dreven's neck healed. The transformation took an entire day and was painful, but he became a vampire. Felipe then turned many more after that day. Although not as strong and powerful as he, they served their purpose.

Felipe saw humans for what they were—weak and useless. He watched as the governments rose and fell over the centuries. He cackled when the countries fought each other. *Fools.* He'd teach them all a lesson. He'd prove they weren't the superior race. And then, he'd rule over the world with them as his slaves.

To do so, he needed to wipe out the other supernaturals who stood in his way to victory. Whenever he did something, they were always there, protecting the stupid humans.

His senses perked up as his drudges returned with only five lycans in tow.

Omegas. . .

Fury pumped through his veins as he gritted his teeth and narrowed his eyes at the vampires that cowered before him. "Did you forget my orders, Urien?" his thick, velvety voice drawled.

"Master, the warriors were too strong for us. They killed our men, and we had to leave with the omegas we captured. Amanda has not yet come back," one of the drudges answered with his shoulders hunched.

It was highly unlikely that Amanda would get killed. She was one of his elite witches. Lycans wouldn't stand a chance against her dark magic.

The vampire king knew his drudges were dead, but he couldn't have cared less. He could always make more of them. Witches, however, were too precious to lose. They were born with their powers, unlike the vampires.

"Tanya, take the prisoners to our dungeons. Find out why Amanda has not come back yet," he ordered.

CHAPTER 24

It was six in the morning when Aaron stood before his pack in the training yard. His eyes scanned the assembled, finding the deltas waiting to fight him. A huge circle had been drawn for the challenge.

"Those who are fighting me today may step forward," his loud voice rang across the arena. "If you aren't happy with my choice of a mate, this is your only chance."

Around twenty lycans stepped forward while the omegas watched with concern. He didn't bother to analyze his odds against the deltas. Aaron cracked his knuckles and rolled his shoulders as his betas stepped beside him.

"You know the rules to this challenge," John, his general, announced. "You may attack the alpha in groups or alone. Remember, the last one to stand is the winner and will choose the fate of the rest."

"Step forth my warriors," Aaron's lips lifted in a snarl. "Fight me with all you got."

The deltas came at him with claws extended and fangs bared.

"Don't hold back!"

Aaron ducked the oncoming claws, hitting one attacker square in his chest and elbowing another. He turned, kicking the third in his gut and punching the fourth in his jaw, dislocating it.

"Is that all you got?"

His words taunted the beasts, who shifted in mid-air and charged with ferocious growls. Aaron wasn't fazed by this. A corner of his lips lifted and he crouched lower. When they got closer, he swiped his claws across their chests and caught one by the throat.

Aaron sent a roundhouse kick at another, knocking him down. The lycan thrashed in his hold, trying to claw at his hands. Blood seeped through the gashes, but it only fueled Aaron's resolve.

His beast surfaced and he threw the furry mutt to the ground before kicking at his ribs. Bones cracked at the impact and a howl echoed through the trees. Aaron knew the fight wouldn't last for long at this rate. His warriors didn't stand a chance. His fury was directed at them now, realizing how much they lacked in training.

"Come at me," the alpha roared. "Is that all you got?" He paced the ground and puffed his chest. "You're all pathetic. Is this how you fight in a battle?"

They all came at once. Claws swiped at him, drawing blood. Fangs embedded themselves in his body. His knees buckled at the impact. The beasts pounded their fists into his body, and he welcomed the pain. It wasn't enough.

Aaron let them hit him, wanting to see how long they could hold him down. He could feel the fear of the pack, vibrating through the pack bond. With a snarl, he pushed them away from him. He blocked their punches and kicks all the while staying in his human form. The beast clawed from within his chest. He knew no one would leave the circle alive if he unleashed it.

A roar tore through his lips and he punched the opponent closest to him, quickly snapping his neck. It would take a while for him to wake and that was more than enough time for him to be done with them all.

He watched as they came at him again like weasels. Aaron smiled. Blood dripped from his body. He licked his lips and tasted blood. The pain didn't matter. The beast growled, welcoming the challenge.

Aaron lunged at them, snapping their necks one by one. He was too fast for them. Only two warriors slipped from his clutches and attacked him with a calculated precision. *Good moves.* But, he was too good for them.

He crouched, swiping their legs off the ground. When they fell back, he was on top, staring at their eyes with his canines on display. They thrashed in his steel grip, trying to throw him off. Aaron punched their faces and throat. Noses broke and fangs cracked.

With a combined effort, they sliced at his chest and kicked him off of them. Aaron had no time to appreciate their move because they were on him again. It wasn't one of his best positions. Lying on his back, he laughed to himself before stabbing his claws in their bodies. Not going deep enough to make the kill, but enough to slow them down.

Once distracted, He retracted his hand and snapped their necks. "Anyone else?" he asked throwing their limp bodies to the ground.

No one made a move. One lycan, who'd regained consciousness, crawled toward him. The delta wheezed and coughed blood. He could see the pain in his eyes, but the delta still wanted to fight.

"The fight is over, Marmon."

"No. It's not. You'll have to kill me," the delta's snarl broke through the telepathic link. His jaw hung on its hinges and a sigh left Aaron's lips.

Marmon was one of his best warriors. "This challenge isn't to kill anyone, Marmon. I will not kill nor punish anyone."

Aaron reached for him and patted his back before gesturing to the omegas to transport them to the infirmary.

"Alpha, you're making a mistake."

"This is a war, Marmon. I've got to do what it takes to protect my pack. You'll understand this when the time comes."

"They've taken my mate," the delta whimpered, and the pain gripped Aaron's heart. *"She's with child, Alpha."*

"And, I promise to do everything in my capability to rescue her and the others."

His Adam's apple bobbed. *Trust me.* He wanted to tell them. But, he knew better. Felipe left no one alive. He couldn't bring himself to think of what was happening to them. He could only wish they were being held captive and little damage was done before he could find them.

"The challenge is over and the alpha stands," John announced, distracting him from his thoughts. "The alpha has chosen to spare the lives of the challengers."

Aaron didn't spare a glance to the pack as he turned and left the arena. His ancestors always killed their opponents who challenged the alpha. But he couldn't bring himself to kill them, though his beast was more than willing to do it for him.

It wasn't how he wanted to rule. He vowed that no blood of his pack member would be spilled by his hands when he ascended the throne.

***

180

Mia woke to the sound of someone knocking on the door, but she couldn't move a muscle. Yesterday's events flooded her memory as she tried to rub the sleep from her eyes.

Matthew waited in the forest with a blanket when Aaron brought her out. He carried her to her room. To her dismay, she puked all over Aaron the moment he set her on the bathroom floor.

He stayed calm and held her throughout the ordeal as she vomited all the blood she had consumed. The once immaculate bathroom floor was a mess, now looking like a murder scene. Mia didn't care when he stripped her to her underwear and sat her under the hot shower, she had been drained of energy and could barely keep her eyes open.

He'd bathed her, dried her, and wrapped her shivering body in a spare towel before carrying her back to bed. She felt his hands gently removing the towel from her body underneath the thick blanket.

His delicate care had broken the barrier she'd been building around her heart to protect it from falling for him. How could she let go of the male who cared for her and respected her emotions? Her eyes drooped when she felt the bed dip again and someone pulled her body into their chest.

Another knock brought her out of her mind, and she realized that she was still naked under the blanket. The door that connected her room to Aaron's opened and he entered, tension etched in his features. He only relaxed after seeing her. Mia couldn't move. Her whole body ached, and her head felt heavy. She felt as if her body was on fire, and a single tear rolled down her cheek as she looked at him helplessly.

"Mia. . ." Aaron came closer, touching her forehead. His touch soothed her, and she let out a sigh of relief as she felt the burning sensation reduce a bit. "You're burning up." She didn't move as he removed his T-shirt, revealing his taut muscles. He carefully pulled the

T-shirt over her head before he finished dressing her. His fingers were careful not to touch her skin too often as his hands worked under the sheets. "I'll get the doctor," he said before exiting the room.

The pack doctor came within a few minutes. Aaron followed the doctor along with her father into the room. Mia flinched when Dr. Barnes touched her, but she couldn't move away.

"Interesting—the recent events must have boosted her change. Her vitals are similar to that of a lycan just before his shift," Paul mused. "What do you think about this, Mr. Lawrence?"

Mia's father scratched his four-day stubble. "Her body is acting on instinct to stay strong, and she's suffering as she's fighting the urge to feed. It doesn't help that she's around her mortal enemies," he said after a moment.

Their voices grew distant as her mind once again slipped into the dark abyss.

***

Aaron's mind reeled as their words set in. His eyes widened with realization. The signs were all there, and it never crossed his mind. Before the shift, a lycan's body would go through a phase, where a juvenile would consume more food and sleep for days.

"You said she vomited the blood she consumed, didn't she?" Paul asked, and Aaron nodded. "We don't know how it works for a vampire. Since she's experiencing symptoms similar to that of a lycan, I'm assuming that her body and mind would have to be in sync while she consumes the blood."

Aaron understood. "If we force her to drink the blood, her body will continue to reject it until she accepts it." As for the lycanthropes, one should be attuned with his beast and accept him with the entirety of his heart during their first shift. Or else the shift would bring drastic consequences. He assumed Mia was struggling with something similar. Her human side didn't accept her vampire side.

"For the time being, we can do blood transfusions. She's not comfortable with feeding, so the transfusions would be more effective at this stage. It will help her recover," Paul suggested. "Perhaps you can teach her to control her bloodlust if she does decide to feed."

"Do what you have to Paul, but this must stay between us," Aaron said and glanced at Mia, whose face was as pale as a ghost.

"Certainly, Your Highness. I will guard this with my life. I'll start with the procedure."

The lycan king paced the floor, his eyes glancing at the unconscious vampire every now and then. It had taken over three hours, but Paul had performed the blood transfusion and sedated her with a sleeping drought. Mia was fighting the change, which was causing her pain.

Color returned to her cheeks, which was a good thing. He sat beside her on the bed and clutched her small hands in his larger ones. The distance he tried to maintain between them didn't sit well with the beast.

"Lilith is fit to travel," his father announced. Silent footsteps approached them. "Blake is sending two of his trusted guards with Max."

Aaron nodded. His thoughts were on his little vampire. *What if she loses her mind like the others?* If that happened, he'd have no choice. Sadness weighed down his heart. He had just found her. He'd fallen for her despite his struggle to take it slow. A hand patted his shoulder.

"She will be okay, son. She's strong," His father's gentle voice reminded him of his presence. "No vampire could fight the bloodlust as she does. Look at her. Even in her unconscious state, she's fighting the change," he pointed at the IV. The blood, which was supposed to get into her body, was forced back into the blood bag.

Aaron's face was grim when Paul injected another dose of sleeping drought into her system. The blood then entered her body without being rejected.

"Come on, son. You haven't eaten anything since last night," Jerome urged. "She'll need you when she wakes up."

Aaron didn't like the uncertainty of their future. Once inside his bedroom, his father squeezed his shoulder. "I'll send Levi with your lunch." His father excused himself to go to the library, where he spent most of his days after his mate's untimely death.

His brothers came in after a while. "How is she doing?" Juan asked, sitting on the bed to stretch out his legs. Matthew sat on the floor beside him. Both appeared tired and worn out.

"Paul sedated her. What did you find?"

"Nothing. No one has seen or heard about Felipe in a while. He's executing the attacks from a remote location that's unknown to the other supernaturals."

"We know that already." Aaron reclined in his seat. "They had taken the wolves right from under our noses, and we did nothing. Their safety is our responsibility." The atmosphere grew thick with tension. "How do we tell the pack that their members cannot be retrieved? I should have seen this coming."

"A witch helped them."

"That's not a valid excuse, Matthew," Aaron shook his head. "If it wasn't for Mia, they'd have taken more."

"What do you suggest, brother?"

"Make the training intense. At this rate, we won't win the war. We have to be prepared." His gaze narrowed with determination. "Stop practicing with dummies. The fights will be real, and the one to lose won't be served at the table."

"Don't you think that's a bit extreme?"

Mathew averted his gaze to the floor under his harsh glare.

"They failed to protect their brethren, Matthew. The attack was child's play. If they didn't win this, then they'll die when the war actually comes," the beast within growled out. "They need to realize this. Training isn't a routine anymore. It's a necessity."

"I'm sorry, brother."

Aaron nodded. "Juan, take over the training sessions from now on. Make sure every wolf, including the children above six years old, train on a daily basis. The children should be taught to sense the danger and save themselves in a time of need. Exclude pregnant women and new mothers, but they should watch whenever they can."

"Sure, brother." Juan stood and exited the room, followed by Matthew.

Aaron watched them leave, and his thoughts drifted back to Mia once again. Last night, he had felt that he couldn't leave her alone. She was a mess. The stench of her fear suffocated him. He wanted to pull her flush against his chest and provide all the comfort he offered, and he had done just that.

The door opened with a knock, and Levi entered with lunch. Aaron shifted his focus to the food and decided to call back the teams he'd sent to the fae kingdom. He needed them here. With Lilith's arrival, they'd have even more help. Perhaps, he could use her expertise to track the magic trail.

Ted was still out of his element after the attack, and he wondered how much help Lilith could actually offer. Witches and warlocks healed at a slower pace. Time worked against them, but there was nothing else he could do.

His heart went to his pack members who were abducted. Worry and concern for their well-being gnawed at his gut. The vein in his jaw ticked.

The King of Leeches had centuries of experience and knowledge. Felipe Lancelot was a cunning bastard. *Fucking coward.* He had studied his war tactics over the centuries to know how the bloodsucker worked.

Not for long, Felipe. This time I'll be ready for you.

CHAPTER 25

Mia stirred from her deep slumber.

A frown marred her face as she tried to remember how she ended up here. The last thing she remembered was being in the backyard. Her head whipped to the side when she heard a loud buzzing, which was some kind of insect flying past the only window in the room. Suddenly, every detail of her surroundings became noticeable.

Her lungs constricted, refusing to take another breath. *Too much.* The gentle rhythm of her heart was so loud now that her eardrums hurt. It felt like everything was crashing down on her at once. Trembling hands grabbed her head, unable to control the sensations bombarding all at once. Aside from the overwhelming noises and scents, there was this nagging inside her head. It was a voice, barely above a whisper, demanding her to do things. It wanted blood.

Blood.

No. She didn't want blood.

Blood.

Her mouth watered as the delicious scent of blood hit her with full force.

Blood.

No. Help!

*Blood.. .*The dark whisper demanded again and reminded her how it felt so good when the crimson liquid flowed in her mouth. Mia salivated at the dark memory. Her throat burned with a need she never felt before.

Water. She needed water.

Urgent hands reached to the bedside table, grabbing the water jug. Mia emptied the contents in a single breath. Water spilled and soaked her T-shirt. However, it did nothing to quench her thirst. The burning only increased. Her hands wanted to claw her throat out, and her eyes teared up.

What's happening?

Then she heard voices on the other side of the door. Mia crawled out of the bed and stood on wobbling feet. *Aaron.* She needed him. She wanted to scream and pull her hair out. A whimper tumbled out of her lips as her knees buckled.

Her head was growing heavier by the minute as the dark thoughts tried to push through the back of her mind once again. Flashes of her memory returned, reminding her of the goriest things she had done and enjoyed. A need to bang her head on the floor until she passed out rooted itself in her mind. It felt like the only means of escape. *Or I could just jump off the balcony and end it all.*

The voice inside her head chuckled. *That will not kill you. Give me blood and this will stop.*

"Stop!" she screamed. "Leave me alone."

The door swung open and someone ran inside. Aaron knelt beside her, pulling her into his lap.

"Please make it stop," she sobbed. "I can't stand it. My head feels like it's going to explode, please stop it."

"Shh. . .It's okay. Look at me, Mia," Aaron adjusted her in his lap so that she was facing him.

Her eyes focused on his tan skin that seemed to shine. The thing inside her was mesmerized by this male.

"Look at my eyes."

Swirling pools of amber sucked her in. The small flecks of gold in it moved, reminding her of fireflies.

Holding her face with one hand, he took her trembling hand and placed it over his heart. "Listen to the beat of my heart, Mia." The gentleness in his voice calmed her like an evening breeze.

"Focus on me, Mia." She felt his heartbeat vibrating against her hand. He radiated an aura so masculine and raw that it enveloped her. The steady and strong rhythm forced her to relax.

"Now breathe." She followed as she was told.

Suddenly, the grip on her lungs loosened. They expanded, gulping the air. The familiar scent of forest and trees surrounded her. It drowned out all the other smells around her.

Beast. The snarl of her inner voice held disgust, but her body's reaction to him contrasted with the thoughts. Her belly clenched and her eyes traveled down his broad chest, admiring the hard muscles underneath.

Mia leaned toward him, running her nose along his neck to the strong jawline. Fingers ached to trace his stubble. Suddenly she couldn't get enough. She buried her face in the junction where his shoulder and neck met and inhaled.

Blood. The vein in his neck pulsed against her lips—tempting. *Yes. Drink his blood.*

"So powerful and hot," she whispered, licking his neck once. *Just a taste won't hurt,* her mouth watered. Her gums burned as her fangs descended. *I'll just take a sip.*

***

Tingles shot through Aaron's body and his breathing quickened at the touch of her tongue against his skin. The essence of her arousal soaked the front of his pants and the enticing scent filled his nostrils.

His chest vibrated with an appreciative growl. Mia's chest rumbled in response. Her lips sucked at the soft spot on his neck.

Tempting.

Seducing.

Luring.

Her hard nipples brushed against his chest, and he took a labored breath. Aaron buried his face in her neck, inhaling more. He pulled her body flush against him. His cock swelled and fangs descended.

She was still in his T-shirt that rode high enough to expose her inner thighs. Aaron knew she was naked underneath, and his beast reminded him how soft her skin felt when he bathed her. He hissed at his beast. *We can't do this to her.*

Her assault on his neck intensified and the beast purred, his eyes almost rolling back into their sockets. *She belongs to us. She's ours—to claim, to protect, to cherish.* He could taste her arousal on his lips. *She wants us.*

She's a vampire, and she isn't the one in control. That one word was enough to pull his beast out from his lust-filled reverie.

Mia growled, rolling her hips against his obvious arousal. Fuck. He choked on his growl and swallowed the urge to mark her then and there. Aaron turned his head away and forced his fangs to retract. His rational mind told him it was his blood calling to her. Though he enjoyed every moment of it, he knew he had to stop her.

She nipped at his skin, without breaking it. Her fangs dented his skin. Damn.

"Mia, we have to stop."

The pressure on his skin froze and she stiffened. Aaron pulled back and gently held her face in his hands, making sure those fangs stayed away from his neck. Dark eyes bore into him. The goddess before him threatened to break his control. He wanted to ravish her body while tasting every inch of it.

"We can't do this. Not now. Not like this." It was more like he was telling this to himself. Aaron took a deep breath to compose his raging emotions and reasoned with it. "You have to stop. You can't drink from a live source until you learn how to control it. If you don't stop now, I know you will hate yourself for this later, Mia." His hands rubbed her back in a soothing motion.

Her bare neck invited him to sink his fangs in, and he forced himself to look away once more. A tear rolled down her cheek. He saw the fight inside her. A moment later, her eyes shifted back to her normal baby blues and she gave him a weak smile that didn't reach her eyes.

"It stopped," she said, her soft voice was barely audible.

"I know," his thumb caressed her cheek.

"I'm hungry," she told him, and her stomach rumbled to confirm it.

His shoulders relaxed and he felt relieved. "Then let's feed you," he said, leaving her and going toward her closet. "Before that though, you have to put these on." He came out with a pair of sweatpants.

Her eyes widened and she looked down. Blood rushed to her cheeks, and he admired the pink glow on them.

"Um. . .It's better if you shower first," Aaron's eyes momentarily shifted to that of his beast. "Your arousal is too distracting," his voice was laced with a growl, and Mia looked mortified.

A squeak left her mouth as she raced toward the bathroom. The thrilled beast wanted to pursue her, but Aaron had to pull the leash on it once again. *Not so fast, buddy.* The beast whined from within. *All in good time.*

When Mia exited the bathroom, showered and dressed in clean clothes, she didn't meet his gaze. Her heart fluttered. His feet were already walking toward her.

"Come, the food is waiting," he said, tracing her pink tainted cheeks. Her shy smile was back on her lips and he curbed the inner longing to taste them. With great difficulty, he pulled his hand away and guided her toward his room.

***

The delicious aroma of meat and desserts filled her nostrils when she entered Aaron's room. Gratitude filled her upon noticing his family there. "Thank you," she mumbled and occupied an empty chair, sending a tentative smile toward his father and brothers who already had their plates filled to the brim.

"Anything for you," he replied, placing the food-filled plate before her. She took a tentative bite, and before she knew it, she dove in, shoveling the delicious chicken into her mouth.

The thing inside her had quieted down, retreating to the back of her mind. *Perhaps, I might be able to control this if I kept my stomach full.* She would have to check her theory since no one knew. Until then, she needed to learn how to keep her fangs to herself.

The steak, chicken pasta, and grilled vegetables were delicious. She ate more than her usual serving all the while aware of Aaron's hot gaze watching her. The comfort she felt around him and the others was surprising. She pushed the plate away when she could stomach no more.

"Where is my dad?"

"He's resting after his appointment with Paul."

Mia felt embarrassed for her behavior earlier. However, Aaron seemed to handle it just fine. "Thanks for stopping me," she told Aaron once his brothers and father excused themselves from the room.

His hand brushed hers as he grabbed her plate emptying the remaining food on his plate. Her eyes widened and her heart fluttered. Aaron behaved as if this was a normal thing between them and she liked it.

Their knees brushed, and he didn't bother to move like he usually did. Mia liked his closeness. The care melted her heart. Then, the memory of him bathing her yesterday made her blush like a tomato.

You love him, her conscience claimed. She had no words of denial. She knew her actions toward Aaron were not just the lust for blood.

His scent did things to her, she wanted to hold him close and not let go. The warmth that surrounded her when she touched him was nothing like any feeling she had ever known. It was so addicting. *What's happening?* She was a vampire and his mortal enemy. How she could even think of them being together was beyond her. She was just glad they didn't throw her out of their territory, or worse, lock her in the prison.

Her father's words surfaced in her mind, and she wanted to laugh out loud. There was no need for seduction. The attraction was real. She might be inexperienced, but she knew he was into her. *Shut up and stick to the original plan. You're a threat, to them and to everyone.*

The thought of leaving him saddened her; she didn't want to leave. Her headache was returning with all the possible "what ifs" and she looked at Aaron longingly, an unknown feeling pressing her from the inside. Mia shoved the conflicting thoughts aside. When she looked at his face again, she realized one thing.

I love him.

***

"What's going on in that head of yours, Mia?" Aaron asked noticing her frown. The beast caught the longing in her eyes.

Blue eyes blinked. "Huh? It's nothing. It's just. . .um. . .What if I go all vamp on you or others again?" she asked.

The slight flutter of her heart and the erratic breathing was proof enough that she was lying. "I think I can handle you just fine," he said.

She averted her gaze, looking anywhere but at him. Aaron knew she wanted him. But it could be just the primal action of her instincts. He wanted her to want him in both mind and body.

"Lilith is arriving in two days. Until then, we'll give you blood transfusions to keep your feeding needs at bay," he informed her.

Mia nodded without looking at him.

"Don't fight the change, Mia. Accept this side of yours. We had to sedate you, so your body could accept the transfusion."

He watched her throat move up and down. She still didn't meet his gaze.

"Come, you need more rest." He stood, pulling her up. He led her toward her room. Their eyes locked. "And. . ." he drawled.

194

Aaron leaned closer. Her lips parted at his proximity. Her eyes shifted momentarily to pitch-black. His hot breath fanned her ears.

"I know what happened earlier was not just from your bloodlust." His lips traced the sensitive skin behind her ears. "I also know you aren't ready yet." His fingers dug into her hips and stayed there. "Be careful next time. My beast isn't known for its patience."

She almost jumped when his lips touched the skin on her neck. Her breathing grew erratic and his jaw clenched. Fangs descended and nipped at his intended target. "Sleep now, Mia. I'll see you in the morning." He stepped back and closed the door while she stood there stunned, her face flushed.

CHAPTER 26

Emilia was pissed off. The useless mutts had failed at the challenge. That was her last hope to stop the mating from happening. She didn't care what the royals thought. She will accept no one as her queen—much less, a leech.

Aaron had known that she had taken Mia outside that day and had shouted at her for being so careless. "I know why you're doing this, Emilia. Stop it. Remember, you're conspiring against the pack and not just me. I won't warn you the next time." His ambers had burned into hers when he said this.

Rage and humiliation were her companions tonight. She now had no chance of mating with the king. Everyone in the pack now knew she was with Zach. Emilia stayed away from Aaron, but that doesn't mean she could let this go.

Why is this vampire so important? She hadn't seen how Mia fought, and Emilia was sure that wasn't the only reason the royals kept her close.

Mia had a secret. A secret Emilia wanted to unveil. Now, all she wanted was revenge for ruining her plans.

That bald doctor, Paul, had been going in and out of the royal wing the entire day. No one knew what was happening until one reliable source informed her that he was carrying blood bags with him.

Barnes must be feeding the vampire. Only a few had seen Mia after the incident, and she heard the omegas describing that she was soaked in blood. The rescued omegas sang the vampire's praises and reiterated how she fought the other vampires to save them.

The pack's view about the leech was changing, and Emilia had to do something. She needed to find Barnes.

It should be easy to coax the information from him. She despised the omega-born doctor. In her eyes, omegas were nothing but a bunch of weak idiots with a brain. *Weaklings!*

Emilia searched the medical unit for the doctor and found him in his office.

"Hello, Doctor Barnes. How are you today?"

He looked up from a file while adjusting his glasses. "Hi, Emilia. I'm doing fine. What brought you here?"

His no nonsense tone brought a smirk to her lips. "Well, I saw you in the royal wing today. Thought I could ask you if everything's okay?"

"Oh, that's nothing, Emilia. It's just a normal routine," he replied before continuing to read his file.

Emilia ground her jaws, suppressing a growl. She had to tread carefully if she wanted any information from the weakling. "Well, I was worried because you were carrying blood bags," she smiled. "Ah. . .I forgot our guest is a vampire, now it makes sense. It's kind of funny that you're feeding our mortal enemy."

"It's none of your concern, Ms. Philip. You're not my alpha, and I'm not obliged to answer your questions," he responded in a bitter tone, "Now if you don't mind, I have important matters that require my attention." He stood and walked around her.

She was there before he could take another step toward the door. Her five-foot-eleven frame towered over his medium-sized frame. Emilia caught him by his neck and threw him across the room. She watched with a smirk as he hit the far wall and fell with a painful grunt.

Emilia kicked his ribs repeatedly before picking him up by his throat again and pinning him to the wall. The doctor coughed and took a labored breath as his legs dangled above the ground. She squeezed his throat, cutting off his air supply.

"'I may not be your alpha, but I am a beta, and you will *not* disrespect me again," she spat. "No one disrespects me and gets away with that. I will show you pain, omega," she said, tightening her hold on his throat.

Paul's face turned red, and his eyes bulged. Incoherent gurgles slipped out of his lips. His fear was so thick, it clouded her senses and it thrilled her beast. Gums burned and instincts urged to sink her fangs on his neck to remind him of his place.

Suddenly, the ground was ripped out from under her feet, and she was thrown against the wall. It cracked upon the impact. When she scrambled to her feet, Aaron stood with his brothers beside him.

Veins bulged in his neck, eyes bright amber, and his claws extended.

"What the fuck were you thinking?"

The authority that radiated from him was too much. Her knees locked and shoulders hunched. The depth and authority of his voice made her shiver with fright. She crawled to a kneeling position, showing her neck in submission.

A whimper tumbled out. She should have been more careful about her surroundings.

"His ribs are broken," Juan stated.

Emilia's breathing quickened as she noticed the royal betas carrying the injured doctor out of the room.

"You attacked our doctor. What reasons do you have now?"

"I didn't! Al-Alpha, please, listen to me. He tried to molest me," Emilia tried pathetically.

"Shut up!" His beastly claws dug into her skin as he raised her above the ground.

"Paul has a mate, and a mated wolf can never bring himself to touch another female. You know this well, Emilia."

He crushed her windpipe blocking the air supply. Her feet dangled in the air.

"Now you know how it would feel to have your air supply blocked," he spat.

"P-please Alpha. Let me go," she wheezed. "He's just an omega." Emilia tried pathetically.

He added more pressure to his hold. "You have no business in royal matters. You threatened someone who is under my protection." His voice sounded more animalistic; his beast was surfacing.

"I'm stripping you of your position as a beta female. You do not deserve the title that came along with your birth."

Emilia hit the floor with a grunt. *He didn't mean it, did he?*

"W-what? No, please. . ."

"As a beta female, you should be supportive and caring. You should have treated the lower ranking members of the family with respect and protect them. From now on, you'll hold no rank within this pack."

She shook her head. "Please don't do this."

Disbelief wasn't a word that was good enough to describe what she felt.

"You won't eat at the table from now on. You'll take orders from everyone in this pack and do anything they ask of you. You'll eat only the scraps left to you by an omega."

***

Emilia laid next to Zach in his bed, his arms draped around her naked form. Snake green eyes stared at the ceiling.

You'll eat only the scraps left to you by an omega.

The words kept replaying in her mind. All Emilia could hear was a buzz when those cursed words left his curled lips. For the next few hours, she'd been in disbelief, unable to digest the punishment. She hadn't moved until Zach had come to get her.

He'd taken her to his room. Since the others thought they would be mates, no questions were asked. Aaron hadn't spared a glance after issuing her sentence, but she could feel the pack's gazes on her as Zach carried her back. Many eyes held satisfaction and shone with the mockery she once sported.

You'll take orders from everyone in this pack.

She swallowed the hard lump in her throat. Violating Alpha's orders would warrant punishment. Everyone in the pack, including her father, supported his decision as a fitting punishment for attacking the doctor.

Everything happened because of her.

That leech had come out of nowhere and turned her world upside down. Her jaws locked and she choked on a growl. Zach's hold on her tightened and his comfort washed over her. Gone was her dream to become a queen. Dead was her reputation. Now, there was nothing left to do.

That fucking bitch!

Emilia needed a plan. A sudden thought popped in her mind. She eyed the fine specimen of male sleeping beside her. Her nails raked his back, earning a low growl. She knew it aroused his beast.

Zach worked his shift in the dungeons that held supernaturals as prisoners. They were locked there for eternity with no sunlight. If only she could bargain with them for some information.

"Zach honey, are you asleep?" She cooed in his ears. Of course, she knew he was not asleep.

"No, Emi," he said, turning to look her.

She despised that nickname yet still smiled. "Well, um. . ."

"If it's about the bloodsucker, Alpha was clear about his intentions. Why can't you let that go?"

"She's here for a reason. She has seduced Aaron. He's blind and does not know her plans," she complained.

"What are you talking about, Emi? We have talked about this before." He sat up, his brows creasing. "Alpha said his beast chose her. If the alpha says she can be trusted, we should trust her."

"Why don't you believe me? Alpha is being deceived. I know she's wrong." Emilia rolled her eyes internally and sniffled. "I heard her speaking to someone on the phone. She's a spy and is here to find our weakness. They are going to attack at any time."

"You heard what? We should inform the alpha of this," he tried to get up.

Emilia pushed him back to the bed. "I confronted him, but he wouldn't believe me," she said, forcing her eyes to water with fake tears. "Of course, he wouldn't believe me. This is my pack. I-I just can't sit back and watch while the bitch destroys it."

Zach sighed. "You need to have a better control over your emotions, Emi." His hands rubbed her back. This wasn't the reaction she was expecting. He hadn't questioned her about her attack on Paul, but she could sense the questions coming.

"It's not what you think. God! How do I make you all believe?" She cried, tears freely flowing. "I know I've been a bitch before. You know how it is for me," she sniffled. "I have trouble controlling my anger. It's just—"

He embraced her, rubbing her back.

"I've been a bad person for so long, and then you came. Things changed. But, no one will believe me."

"I believe you."

"I know." She continued the act, taking deep breaths. "It is why only you can help me."

"What do you need?"

"I just want to visit the prisoners."

"No one is supposed to go down there without the alpha's knowledge."

"Please, Zach. You have to do this for me. They might know her. I just want to try this once. Please. . ."

"Okay. I'll see what I can do. But just this once," he said bringing her close.

"Just this once," she beamed before reciprocating his kiss.

CHAPTER 27

"How is he?" Aaron asked Jacob, the human doctor.

Paul lay motionless on the bed, his face pale.

"A few broken pieces of his bones had punctured his lungs, but we performed a surgery to remove them. His ribs will take a few more days to heal. He should be on complete bed rest until then."

The alpha ran a hand over his face.

"See to it that Paul rests until he fully recovers. Juan will talk to you regarding an arrangement with our new guest," Aaron said before walking out of the hospital wing and to his room.

Aaron was in his office when Richard entered with a knock.

He looked ashamed and didn't meet his alpha's gaze. He should be ashamed for raising his daughter like that. Aaron felt no remorse.

"I came to apologize on behalf of my daughter, Alpha. Thank you for sparing her life," he said.

"I spared her life only for your sake, Richard. There won't be a next time. Make sure your daughter understands this."

His father's beta nodded in understanding and left him to his devices. It was close to midnight, but sleep was too far off. He thought about hiring a private firm for castle security but decided against it. The human government had offered security several times over the years, but the royals had refused politely. It would affect their privacy.

The beast prowled restlessly in his mind. Aaron stripped out of his clothes and exited through the balcony.

***

Mia felt so much better than the previous day. A new doctor, Jacob, checked on her in the morning. He'd informed her that he would give her a blood transfusion in the afternoon as they had a female in labor today and he needed to be there.

"You look well," her dad entered with a broad smile. She thought his clean shaved look suited him better.

"Hey, Dad. What's with the smile?"

"Nothing." His shrug roused her suspicion.

"Dad. . .You're not good at hiding things."

"I hid you for seventeen years."

Mia huffed. "Don't get me started on that. It's your talent of hiding that got me right into this situation." She grabbed her breakfast plate and ate.

Her father chuckled. "That's fate." He pointed above his head. "And, I brought you straight to your mate."

Mia choked on the juice she was sipping. "Dad, we talked about this."

"I know."

"It's not going to work."

"It already did."

Her cheeks heated up. "I don't know what you're talking about."

"I don't know what you're thinking about."

"Dad. . ."

"All right, all right," he raised his hands in a surrendering motion. "The alpha has announced to his pack that he has chosen you as his potential mate. It's official."

Mia groaned noticing the huge smirk on his face. "We aren't there yet."

"You aren't denying it anymore."

Mia averted her gaze to the floor. She had no response to him.

"I've heard that girl Emilia attacked Paul last night."

"What?" That must've been why a new doctor visited her this morning. Damn. She knew something was off about that girl.

"The alpha had stripped her of her beta rank. It's a severe blow to a lycanthrope's ego. It's the talk of the pack."

"Oh." She refused to think this punishment would stop the female beta. Emilia was cunning and manipulative.

"Enough about her," he stood and thrust his hands in his pant pockets. "I'm heading to the gym."

"Gym?" Her brows rose.

"Yep. Have to hone my skills. Also, heard an unmated witch is en route," he winked, earning a giggle from her.

Mia shook her head as she watched him leave, whistling low as he closed the door behind him. Her father no longer wore that worried crease on his forehead anymore. He laughed and conversed with her as if they've always done that. She liked this side of him and having a father figure in her life felt good.

Her thoughts drifted to Aaron, wondering why he hadn't come to visit her yet.

Was he busy?

She went to knock on the door that connected their rooms, but held back, debating the idea. Why she hesitated she couldn't fathom. Summoning up enough courage, she knocked on his door. No sound came from the other side and no one came to open the door. She tried again.

Where did he go?

She turned the knob with a fluttering heart. *Was he showering?* The memory of him in only a towel surfaced in her mind.

Upon entering, she was greeted by a sleeping Aaron. A smile formed on her lips, and she allowed herself some time to admire him. He looked so peaceful in his sleep. Unruly golden blond hair framed his face. His naked torso was on display with his sheets pooling around his waist. She wanted to touch him and run her hands along his stomach, tracing the taut muscles. Mia knew her staring was inappropriate. She should have turned around the moment she found him sleeping.

"How long are you going to stay right there?" he asked without opening his eyes, his voice hoarse with sleep.

Mia jumped, startled. *How?* His eyes opened, and his deep browns pinned her in place. The golden flecks in his eyes grew intense. The smile on his lips made her heart race. *Oh, my!*

"It's just, I. . .I wanted to see you. I knocked, but no one opened the door, so I thought I would check," she muttered. "You didn't come to see me today," her voice accused as her eyes stared at her shoes.

"Oh, really?" He teased.

"I-I should go," her cheeks heated up, and she turned away from his gaze to hide her face.

Aaron jumped from the bed and caught her before she could take another step. His index finger tipped her chin, forcing her blue eyes to his brown ones.

"You came to see me," his husky voice had her shivering in delight. The gentle touch and the soft caress of his voice were enough to stir the sinful desires she often tried to keep locked away.

Aaron caressed the side of her face, his thumb tracing her lips. Her lips parted in response, body leaning toward his embrace.

"I did come to see you, Mia. You were sleeping like a baby," he said as his thumb pressed against her soft lips. "Did I ever tell you how beautiful you look when you sleep?" he asked, inching closer. She inhaled deeply breathing in his scent. "Is it wrong that I want to kiss you this badly?" he asked, his eyes were no longer brown. They were burning with an intensity that set her blood on fire.

Her eyes closed in anticipation and she sucked in a breath when his lips finally touched hers. Soft and tentative. Her breath hitched as his lips tugged at hers, encouraging to follow his lead. He tasted like mint and coffee. His lips firm yet warm.

She mimicked his moves, kissing him back and opening when she felt his tongue trace her lower lip. Aaron used the chance to deepen the kiss, which almost had her eyes roll back to her head.

A throaty moan left her lips and suddenly every cell in her body came alive. Hard planes of his muscles pressed against her body, making her aware of their closeness. The distant ringing of a phone brought them both out of their bliss. He broke the kiss, breathing heavily.

"Damn," he whispered, resting his forehead against hers. "Stay here, I need to take this call."

Mia could only nod in response. Her legs gave out once he moved, and she sat on his bed. Her lips still tingled from the kiss.

Once he finished talking, he came to sit beside her, pulling her onto his lap.

"I'm sorry about the phone call."

"It's okay." The smile on her lips couldn't be helped. Her heart fluttered again at his closeness.

"That was perfect," he murmured as his lips found her neck.

Her eyes closed and her neck angled to the side to allow him better access. Aaron sucked and nipped at her skin. She thought for sure that he'd leave a mark. His fangs pressed on the skin without breaking it and he stopped.

"Damn! It's getting hard to control myself around you."

That was the sexiest thing he'd told her.

"There is something I need to ask you."

"Hmm. . ."

"Will you be my mate, Mia?"

Her eyes shot open and head whipped around, eyes locking with his. That wasn't what she expected. In the world of humans, this was too fast and too soon to decide. But she wasn't human anymore.

"I know it's too early. I've thought this through. There is no one else that I want as a mate. You're it for me."

Mia gaped. Words failed her. He was proposing to her, and she didn't know how to respond. "Um. . ." she blinked, trying to form a response.

"I'll understand if you want more time," he said quickly, and she jumped at the opportunity.

Her breath quickened. She needed to think. "I need time," she agreed, her voice a squeak. She was already halfway across the room.

When she closed the connecting door to his room, she slid down to the floor. Isn't this what she wanted? Isn't this what her father wanted? Then why couldn't she bring herself to say yes?

She ran a hand through her hair. Why did that question make her nervous? She did love him and that should have made her elated. "Relax, Mia," she spoke to herself. "It's just the nerves."

Damn.

I should have said yes.

What would he think of her for running away like that? She banged her head on her knee. Now, she'd ruined the beautiful moment by doing so. *Okay, relax. Deep breaths.* Crap. It wasn't working. Is this how girls freak out when someone proposes to them?

The mating with Aaron wasn't just an option. It was a necessity for her and for the sake of everyone close to her. She could tell she wouldn't be offered asylum if Aaron hadn't thought of this. Her father had told her why the lycans would want to keep her close.

She was glad things were at least happening at her pace. By accepting his proposal, she'd not only become his queen, but that also meant she'd be shouldering his responsibilities.

There are no coincidences.

When she stood, she knew what she had to do. There was a reason she was born as a vampire. There was a reason why she had stumbled upon her dad at a young age and that later led to the situation in a lycan's territory.

She had a purpose.

CHAPTER 28

"Done," Emilia said to herself, quickly exiting the infirmary. It was easier than she thought it would be. Paul was on bed rest, and Jacob was attending the woman in the labor room, making her task easy. *Anderson, being a human, won't be able to tell the difference.*

"Get ready to explode inside out, leech," Emilia spat.

Zach had been useful today and it took only seven minutes in total for her to finish the job. Her mind went back to the day. A few blood bags given to the vamps and delicious food to the starving prisoners did wonders.

"Tell me your weakness, and you can have this."

Emilia dangled the blood bag before the vampire's starved gaze. She moved back when he lunged at it.

"We cannot withstand the power," he said, licking his parched lips with greed. Dark eyes stared at the blood bag with a longing. His face pushed between the bars, hands stretched, trying to reach the bag. "Vampires don't drink from any other supernatural beings. Not all blood suits us, and the power that comes along with the blood is too much to handle at times."

Emilia threw the blood bag at him. He caught and finished it in a single breath, letting out a satisfied moan. He wanted more, she could tell.

"The blood is the life source for any supernatural, and with it, comes the power," he said eyeing the second blood bag. "A vampire is drawn to blood, no matter to whom it belongs to; the blood calls to us. We came across a witch once, our master had ordered to bring her in alive," he drawled in a thick voice.

"She got hurt and was bleeding."

He licked his lips and inhaled deeper.

"The power and scent were enough for us to pounce. I stood back because I was afraid of what the master would do if he found out." His eyes grew distant.

"The vampires who drank from her started convulsing after a few moments and became violent. Her blood burned them inside out. Their bodies were only a pile of ash."

She tossed the second bag at him. "How much do I need?"

"One drop."

In the next cell, a witch eyed her but made no move to take the food from her hand.

"I need your blood," Emilia said, throwing the food packet inside her cell.

Emilia didn't get much blood from the witches and warlocks imprisoned. They had been starved for so long that she could hardly get a vein. They might be immortals, but they needed food to stay strong.

Casting a spell needed energy, and that energy was mostly fueled by the power of their soul. It partially drained their physical strength, depending on the power scale of the spell they used. Emilia had neither time nor patience to wait.

She'd slipped into the infirmary when no one was looking, heading toward the blood bank. Paul had ordered a new stock of human blood to feed the vampire, She quickly pulled out a bag with Mia's name on it and injected the supernatural blood into it, leaving it in the same place and left quickly.

Zach didn't know what she had done inside the dungeon nor inside the infirmary. But he stood guarding the door like the best guard dog he was. With a smirk, she headed to her room.

I wish I could hear you scream.

***

Felipe threw the lifeless body of the fae female to the floor. *What a waste.* Their blood gave him a power surge similar to that of lycan blood, but only for a short while. Experiments on other supernaturals had not worked out to the way he wanted.

It was easy to lure the fae in. It was a fine skill that he had perfected over the years, the art of mesmerizing his prey. Just one look into their eyes, and they came to him willingly.

He glanced at the female. She was beautiful. However, she was not enough to satisfy his hunger. He would be lying if he said he hadn't enjoyed the pleasure she provided. He had a great time until she started coming out of her stupor.

When she woke, she started to fight him. So, he had snapped her neck like the worthless chicken she was. He licked his lips, tasting the last drop of blood. He didn't believe in wasting blood. But, sometimes, spilling it did please him, especially on a battlefield.

He looked at his kill, satisfied. Not a drop of blood had spilled on his clean white sheets. Pulling his pants up, he quickly dressed.

Might as well go check on the witches' progress. Amanda and the other vampires had not yet returned. He could feel the death of other vampires, but as for Amanda, he had no hope.

He grew bored these days, having nothing to do. He tried several things to irk the lycans but nothing worked. They just avoided him like the plague.

Cowards. But soon, there will be a bloodbath.

His gums burned painfully in anticipation. He had been a silent spectator in the last war and bathed in the victim's blood. He had chosen to stay away because of his lack of army to fight the lycans. Now that he had the witches by his side, he had devised an excellent plan that would bring other supernatural forces to their knees.

"Tanya!"

"Master," she bowed.

"Did you find anything?"

"Amanda is dead, Master. The portal closed upon her death, and no one returned."

"Any updates on Lilith's location?"

"No, Master. She has not used her powers for a while, and the Dark Witch couldn't track her."

"How could she not track her? They share blood. She doesn't need a magic trail to track her!" Felipe bellowed, making the witches cower in fear. "Fools. Torture her and find her sister's location!"

"But she's weak," Tanya murmured.

He was about to respond when he saw one of his drudges running toward him. Felipe quickly sifted through the vampire's memories. He hated long conversations.

"A born!" He appeared in front of his drudge in a swift motion clutching his head between his hands as he searched his memory. This wasn't news, but a mere confirmation of what he already suspected.

Only this time it was a female. The drudge knew her location. Felipe searched further and saw the lycan territory.

The animal scent would have easily masked her scent.

"A female pureblood." He chuckled, his first real smile in centuries. "After all these years." A girl with wide blue eyes and pale blonde hair stared through the window. His nostrils flared wanting to know her scent, and his hands dropped to the sides when he remembered the memories wouldn't share those fine details.

"How old is she?" he asked. Blue eyes flashed and he took a deep breath. He found his heart thundered within his ribs. It hadn't beaten that way in centuries.

"Twenty-two, Master."

Hmm. . .So young. Perfect.

He would finally have a mate, perfect in every way. He would finally be able to have an heir. Over the years, he tried to produce an heir through his many mistresses, but none conceived. His witches were trying to find a solution. Though he didn't need one, having an heir would strengthen his empire.

"Do the lycans know about her?"

"I do not know, Master. Her scent is luring the vampires to their territory. I followed her enough to know she's like you. But the lycans have tightened the security around the borders. Getting in and out is not easy as before. I stayed low and slipped out at the first chance I got."

And without a witch's help it would take weeks for the drudge to reach him. Anything could have happened in this time. The lycans might have found her. But he knew she wasn't dead. He felt her first taste of power. It was a natural connection born vampires had. He used that to his advantage in the past to hunt them down. Because he despised competitions.

Felipe was tempted to go there himself and take her away. Then, he held back. His drudges were enough to do this. "I need her alive, no one is supposed to touch her. She's going to be your queen. Send the message to Dreven to come back." The search was over. They knew her location now.

There had not been a born vampire in the past three hundred years. "Feed the Dark Witch. We need her strong. Once she's ready, we attack again."

"Master, we are ready to go *now*," Tanya intervened.

"And end up dead like Amanda?" His shook his head. "None of you can stand against the lycan force if you face them alone. The Dark Witch in the dungeons holds the power of ten of you put together," Felipe sneered. After the recent attack, they'd be more alert. They have to be prepared for the fight.

He turned toward the others. "I don't want any of those beasts near her." They'd kill her when they realize what she was. "We move when the witch is ready. Prepare a throne, my queen is coming home."

***

For the first time in a long while, Mia felt genuinely happy. Her thoughts were filled with Aaron and the kiss they shared. She had yet to respond to his proposal. There was a permanent smile etched on her lips.

Her room had a comfy couch and a small tea table that faced the television. She now sat on the floor, watching a documentary. Well, she stared at the screen, though her mind was somewhere else.

The door to her room opened, and Matthew entered with her lunch. His smile was warm, and his eyes crinkled. "So, how are you doing today?"

The youngest of the three brothers had warmed up to her considerably in the past few weeks. He was nothing like the guy she stumbled into. Matthew was the sweetest of all—the man acted purely on emotions. Whenever he spoke, she could sense a longing he wasn't good at hiding.

"Much better, thank you."

"Do you mind if I join you?" He placed the tray on the table and sat on the floor next to her.

"Sure. . .I mean, I don't mind if you join me." Her grin widened as Matthew opened the dishes.

They ate in comfortable silence. Matthew kept his eyes on the TV screen, and Mia focused on her food. It had been like this most of the days. They'd often watch a movie or two and sometimes talk about general stuff. He'd tell her about their younger years, and it was obvious that he missed his mother more than anything.

"I heard you like books," Matthew stated.

"I do. I like fiction novels and occasionally enjoy a book on ancient history."

Matthew nodded.

"I can take you to our library later. It has all sorts of books there."

"Thank you! I appreciate it."

"It's nothing," Matthew shrugged. "So, how well do you fight?"

"I can hold my ground. I learned the basics as a teenager."

"Hmm. . .You can train with us in the morning. You'll need it."

Mia hadn't had time to think about training. She appreciated his thoughtfulness. "Thank you."

An hour later, they were still talking and watching TV together. They were laughing at some joke on the TV when someone knocked. Matthew went to open the door to reveal the doctor.

"Hello, Mia. How are you today?" Jacob started pulling out the blood bags.

"I'm good." Mia's face grew pale at the sight of the blood. She knew she needed it, but a part of her despised it. She went to lie down on the bed without replying. She was not in the mood for pleasantries.

She wanted this to be over soon. She flinched when she felt the needle prick her skin and her eyes widened like saucers when the first drop of blood entered her body. Her mouth opened in a silent gasp.

Mia's nostrils flared as her instincts kicked in, her eyes darkened. Her fangs elongated with a burn. The blood was no ordinary blood, it was dark and addicting. The power it brought with it thrummed inside her veins. The dark whispers were back, and before she knew it, the thing inside her took control.

CHAPTER 29

Aaron had just finished the call with Blake when his cell phone rang again. "What is it, Juan?" he asked.

"A bloodsucker was in town. He was following your mate before we tooke her in and was caught on a security footage. I have a team tracking him."

"Okay. Where are you now?"

"Almost there, brother. Five minutes tops."

"Meet me in Mia's room when you get here. Mia is getting a transfusion, I'll be with her."

Turning to the corridor, he saw his youngest brother running toward him with a look of horror on his face.

"Brother! It's Mia—"

Aaron took off toward her room.

"Someone's switched the blood."

Doctor Jacob was shaking with fear outside Mia's room. Aaron rushed past him to move inside the room, his feet coming to a halt when he saw her. His mouth went slack and eyes widened, unable to comprehend the scene in front of his eyes.

Mia floated ten feet above the bed. The blood bag attached to her arm was draining faster.

"Witch blood—but it smells like a mix," Matthew whispered behind him.

"*Dad, we need you here.*" Aaron contacted his father through their telepathic link.

Juan rushed in, "Matthew called—Shit!" He froze when his eyes landed on Mia. He stood there with wide eyes. He sniffed the air, "Supernatural blood."

"Jacob hooked her up with the blood, and by the time I got a whiff of it, she had already begun to rise from the bed. I could get nowhere near her. She just flung me across the room," Matthew said, still shaken. "I immediately got the doctor out of there."

"Who switched the blood?" Juan asked.

"Jacob said he took the bag from our blood bank and the blood bag was already labeled with Mia's name. He thought Barnes had set it up," Matthew said.

"He's human and cannot smell the difference," Aaron mused. "I'll try to get closer." He too was thrown across the room. His body hit the wall and a grunt left his lips.

"Brother!" Juan helped him up.

"She's strong."

Mia's pitch-black eyes stared at the ceiling aimlessly.

"What do we do now?" Matthew asked.

"I have no idea."

All three of the brothers stood waiting for their father, feeling helpless. The former king rushed inside shortly, followed by Lilith and Maximus.

"Oh, my! What do we have here?" Lilith exclaimed.

"Lilith, someone switched the blood." Relief flooded the lycan king at the sight of the witch.

"What blood is it?"

"It's a mix. I smell witch and lycan blood."

"Witch blood burns them from the inside out." Her feet rushed to the bed. Lilith muttered indecipherable words under her breath, and Mia's body began to glow faintly. Her rising pulse slowed down and soon she was fast asleep.

"Oh my, this is amazing."

"What is it, Lilith?" Aaron asked, his desperation obvious.

"Her body is processing the power," Lilith answered, her hands hovering over the pureblood.

"A few days ago, she killed a witch by draining her," Juan informed.

"I've never seen that happen before. Her body is acting normal. We have nothing to worry about," she assured after checking her vitals.

How? If the vampires couldn't tolerate witch blood, how did Mia do it before? She appeared to be asleep now.

"Son," his father gestured toward his bedchamber and he followed, his mind already putting together several questions he wanted to ask.

Aaron watched as the witch process whatever information his father had conveyed to her. Her brows creased as she appeared to be lost in her thoughts for the past couple of minutes.

"A born vampire, huh. . ." the witch mused, breaking out of her trance. "Tell me everything." Lilith was a red-haired beauty. Though she was three hundred years old, she looked like she was in her late twenties. Her kind hazel eyes twinkled.

Aaron glanced at the warlock before retelling everything that had happened since Mia's arrival.

"Where did you find her, Galahad?"

Ted's eyes widened, but he masked the surprise. "In a small town in Colorado."

"There should be a good reason why a warlock like you—who's been on the run from the world's worst man alive, if I may add,—adopted a pureblood."

"She was just a child. I knew she'd be in trouble if someone else found her."

The petite witch stood and paced around. "You don't strike me as a man who falls for innocence. The real reason, Galahad." Her gaze narrowed at him.

Aaron looked between the witch and the warlock. He hadn't known they knew each other.

Ted's fists clenched and he took a deep breath. Sweat coated his face. "I've already told you why."

"That's not entirely true, Galahad. No one can tell apart a human and a pureblood at the tender age of four." The witch walked around the couch, planting her hands firmly on the headrest. "I want you to tell me exactly what happened when you stumbled onto her."

***

Lilith was the last person Ted expected when they said a witch was coming. Didn't Felipe abduct her? But she stood before him in one piece. Her scrutinizing gaze never once left his face and he feared she could read his dark secrets.

The warlock was silent for a moment, mulling over her question. A deep breath expanded his chest. Dark eyes scanned the room as he recalled that day.

He was just passing by and had gone into town to buy some supplies when he met the four-year-old girl. She was in the market with other children. She had caught his eye and smiled.

He tried to turn away from the girl and carry on with his day but couldn't. When his eyes locked with her blue gaze, fog covered his vision. A strange whisper caressed his ears before giving him a glimpse of whom she was and who she would be.

A lethal combination of a predator who wasn't supposed to exist.

Ted knew right then what it was. It was a rare but strong form of magic. He breathed through his mouth as it bonded him to the girl.

"Damn."

It worked like a curse. There was no running now. Wherever he ran, it would bring him right back to her.

He had spent the entire night contemplating. Her innocent blue eyes and the bright smile kept popping into his mind. Only he knew what kind of danger lurked behind that innocence. What was he supposed to do? He tried to shake the foreign emotion in his chest and move on, only to find his way back to the innocent blues.

She's just a child. His subconscious argued. *But, she's a pureblood.* She was the first female to be born with that vampire gene in her body. Was she Felipe's? No. That wasn't possible. So far, the vampires could only increase their numbers by biting and transforming others. But, if mating and reproduction was possible, then it would lead to disaster.

If one born vampire can do so much damage, what will happen when two are together? He knew the answer. All the races would be wiped out from the face of the Earth. Is that why she was protected? How could he forget the last war between the vampires and lycans? It lasted over fifty years before both sides withdrew because of their dwindling numbers. Felipe should never get his hands on Mia, or vice versa. Ted had no doubt what'd happen if they met. Their instincts would force them to pair, and much worse, reproduce.

Who cast the protective spell was beyond his knowledge.

As soon as he adopted her as his own, she was enrolled in a famous boarding school until he could figure out his next move. He had to keep her safe from the other vampires and other supernaturals until she matured. The only way to do that was to hide her among the humans.

***

One corner of Lilith's lips lifted to form a smirk. "The once famous warlock, Galahad, became a nomad during the 1970s. He has been changing names since the late 1800s and swore off any familial connections. I knew all about you, Galahad Mortem. The only necromancer with the power scale so high that it put the others to shame."

Necromancer? Aaron's eyes widened. He thought they were extinct. The ones who call themselves a necromancer these days could hardly wake a corpse much less an army. Now it made sense why Felipe was after the warlock. Ted had changed his name and appearance at least twenty times before he adopted Mia.

Ted nodded with a smile and crossed his legs. He relaxed further and leaned in the couch. "It's an honor to finally meet the High Witch from Cascade Coven. The ones who've seen you perform magic used to bet on their balls that you were a hycinth."

Lilith's smile faltered, and she was quick to mask it. "Hycinth witches are history. No one talks about them now."

223

"Yeah, and it's such a shame."

Aaron had no idea about the covens they spoke of. Lilith's eyes had grown distant when she talked about the hycinth clan. He deduced she knew more than she led others to believe.

"So, what do you think of Mia?" Ted asked. "How she's able to process the magic is beyond my knowledge."

"I don't have an answer to that now," Lilith pushed the loose strands of hair behind her ear. "Vampires cannot tolerate supernatural blood. Felipe is an exception. He's experimented on this with his drudges in order to find a way to become more powerful," Lilith began to pace. "But even he can't stomach witch blood."

"How do you know so much about Felipe?" Ted asked.

"A few decades ago, I was captured along with a few other witches. I escaped and managed to nip him with my knife during our fight. I was able to do a few experiments with his blood in the coming years."

She poured a cup of tea for herself and occupied a seat. "The witch blood does not kill Felipe like it does other vampires, but it doesn't do well for him either. I had to wait a few years for the technology to evolve before continuing my experiments. Recently, I discovered that when supernatural blood was mixed with his blood, the cells evolved more powerfully by consuming the power in the supernatural blood. The effects lasted only for a short while—that is, only for thirty minutes."

"So if he manages to make the effects last longer, then he'd become invincible," Aaron mused.

"That's his plan." Lilith nodded, reclining to get comfortable.

"You know a witch teleported the vampires a few days ago. Can you trace the magic trail?" Matthew asked.

"Of course, I can." She stood. "Do you have her body?"

"Yes, we preserved it as per your instructions," Aaron informed. "You can rest if you aren't feeling up for it."

She shook her head and stood. "I've rested enough." She rubbed her hands together and gestured her head for him to lead the way.

"Come, I'll take you there."

The left the room to go to the morgue.

"You already have a warlock, Aaron. You didn't have to wait for me to do this," Lilith said, eyeing Ted. She was his mother's best friend and was one of the few with the privileges to address him by his first name.

Ted huffed. "I was poisoned and was held as a prisoner here."

"That sounds like Aaron." Lilith chuckled. "How did you like the concoction by the way? Worked like magic didn't it?"

"That was your idea!" Ted pointed his accusing finger at her.

Lilith shrugged. "What can I say. It's one of the best portions I ever concocted."

"If you love it so much, why don't you try it?"

Lilith's teasing smile faltered. She made no more comments after that.

The trip to the infirmary morgue took ten minutes, and Aaron had to stop breathing altogether so he wouldn't gag. The place reeked of mortal remains and chemicals. An omega, who was on duty rushed to the alpha's aid.

"Show her the witch's body." Juan covered his nose using his hand.

The omega attendant pulled over a pair of gloves and his surgical face mask and went to the cold chambers, pulling out her body. Lilith wore the mask and gloves handed to her by the attendant.

Aaron and the others stood far away as the attendant loaded the body onto the examination table. The witch examined the corpse, and Aaron took shallow breaths through his mouth. When he couldn't take it anymore, he exited the morgue, gulping fresh air. He noticed his brothers had exited as well, and their father patiently stood leaning against the wall with a knowing look on his face.

Lilith and Ted were the last to leave after a few more minutes. Aaron straightened and looked at the witch expectantly.

"There is some sort of shield in place that's not allowing me to look past the defenses. I don't know where he's hiding. He must have gotten his hands on a powerful witch or warlock." Lilith's eyes narrowed.

There went the hope for rescuing his abducted pack members. Aaron's shoulders slumped. He had hoped that Lilith could help. "What do you mean by 'shield'?" he asked.

"It's usually a magical barrier witches or warlocks use to secure their hideout. Nothing magical can get past a good protective ward. It's also known to confuse the wanderers and lead them elsewhere," Lilith explained.

"Does that mean the witches won't be able to teleport within our territory if we have something like that in place?" Aaron asked.

"Yes."

"Great. Lilith, then I want you to place a shield around our castle and territory as soon as possible. Could you do that? I don't want any more surprise attacks."

Lilith nodded. "It'll take a few days to complete, and I'll need some things to cast the spell."

"Juan will assist you with anything you need."

"Okay."

"Matthew will show you to your room. Rest for now and we'll talk soon."

"Sure, Aaron."

Aaron gave her a curt nod and excused himself.

"I'm going to check the cameras in the infirmary," Juan said. "I had the guys install cameras overnight after Paul's attack. No one except for the security team knew about the cameras."

"I will go with him." Maximus, his third-in-command stood, smoothing his shirt.

"You should be resting, Max." Aaron put a hand on his shoulder, stopping him. "Your mom and sisters are worried." It hadn't been an hour since his return and the young lycan already jumped to work.

"I'm perfectly fine, Alpha." His third-in-command rubbed above his sternum where Aaron could see a pink scar still healing. His eyes narrowed, and he swallowed a growl. That looked like it was supposed to be a lethal blow. He could've lost him.

"I'm glad to have you back, Max. Rest and heal." His eyes challenged Max to speak when his third-in-command opened his mouth. "No arguments."

"Okay. Can I at least keep an eye on the queen?"

Aaron shook his head. He patted his gamma's cheek with a smile. Maximus was Matthew's age and they grew up together. The younger lycan always looked up to the alpha borns and stuck to their side like a sibling and even addressed their mother as mom.

"Go to your mother, Max. We'll talk tomorrow once you're rested."

Maximus' shoulders slumped. "Okay, if you say so. Can I meet her tomorrow?"

Catherine Edward

"Of course." His third-in-command left with a beaming face.

"He just looks like Larry did in his younger years," Aaron's father recalled.

Larry was murdered along with the former queen, Esmeralda. Max was only fourteen when Larry died. "Yes, he does." His mind drifted to the abducted pack members. With a sigh, he turned to his father, "I need a shower." When he walked away, his heart was heavy.

CHAPTER 30

When Mia woke, she felt power coursing through her veins. The moment Jacob began to pump blood into her body, she felt the power in it. She knew immediately it was not just any human blood. She reveled in that power and felt the blood pounding through her veins, merging with her blood cells and evolving into something more. Her senses were stronger than ever. But, her mind was oddly calm.

A quick shower later, she stood on the balcony admiring the nature. Outside, the sun was setting, casting an orange glow on the snow-covered ground and trees. It was one of those rare days. The sun barely made appearances during the long winter nights in Brookedge. She heard someone speak downstairs.

Different scents from the atmosphere drifted into her nostrils. One, so masculine and fertile stood out over all. Oh, she knew that scent well. *Beast. Her beast.* The powerful blood that pounded through his veins called to her.

Blood.

Her body turned, hypnotized by the scent. Slender legs advanced to the door with slow steps. The strong thrum of his heartbeat grew louder. Hands pushed the door open and eyes black as night regarded its prey. Fangs extended in anticipation.

Blood. . .so strong and warm.

Want it. . .

Need it. . .

Her mouth watered as his alluring scent teased and encased her entire being. Aaron stood in front of the mirror only clad in his towel.

So hot and sexy, *all hers. . .*

The pounding inside her head increased as her eyes zeroed in on him. All the veins in his body were visible to her. Her tongue darted out wetting her plump red lips.

Mia gawked at Aaron's shirtless torso shamelessly, her eyes tracing the contours of his chiseled body. Desire filled her every pore. Every inch of her skin felt hot, and her body ached with need.

Something inside her woke up. It wanted to possess the strong male in front of her. Her insides trembled at the intensity of the force that demanded to claim him as hers. She stalked toward him, her bare feet making little noise. Mia heard his blood pulsing through his veins. She could smell his desire now, and the change in his lower region provided her with a visual confirmation.

Mia felt hot despite the bone-chilling air that seeped in through the open balcony. She was pulled into his tight embrace. The clothes she wore seemed to suffocate her as the heat from his touch swept through her.

"Beast. . ." Her whisper was a seductive rumble. His chest rumbled at her velvety voice and he yearned for more. Her fingers ran over his sculpted chest, tracing each muscle.

"Mine. . ."

***

Aaron stood rooted to the floor as he took in her appearance. Her eyes calculated his movements like that of a predator. His beast was excited to be the prey for once.

Blood, a whisper floated through his mind. Instead of frightening him, her sexy rumble thrilled him. *How did she do that?*

Want it. . .

Need it. . .

A whisper caressed his insides. He stood, unmoving, as he contemplated what to do next.

Aaron's nose flared. The onslaught of her desire caught him off guard, and he wanted to drown in it. His eyes shifted to that of his beast. He stood rooted to the spot, his feet unable to move. Mia was sexy with her wild blonde hair, pitch black eyes, and sharp fangs on display. She inched closer and he stood there, just watching, his calculating gaze undressing her as his beast supplied erotic images to his brain.

How would it feel to have those fangs buried deep in my neck? A jolt of awareness spread through his veins as his member twitched just at the sight of her.

He breathed heavily and pulled her flush against his body, inhaling her desire. His fangs extended painfully, wanting to claim her then and there. The logical part of his brain knew that Mia was driven purely by her instincts. He didn't want her to regret this later, and he had to stop before it escalated further. He wouldn't be able to control himself for much longer if she kept this up. His control over the beast was waning.

"Mia, you have to stop now," he all but growled. "I don't think I can control my beast, and I want you to be sure about this."

His animalistic rumble only seemed to turn her on as she rubbed her nose along his neck and jawline breathing in his scent, grinding her hips against his arousal.

"I want you," she murmured in his ear. "Take me, beast."

Aaron's control slipped and his lips crashed with hers, kissing her with fervent need. She responded immediately, moving her lips in sync with him. Mia let out a moan and bit his lower lip, drawing blood. Aaron groaned as he opened to her.

Her tongue entered his mouth without hesitation, taking, claiming. It was nothing like their first kiss. She was like a wild animal, her kiss dominating. His hands cupped her ass, pulling her tight against him, his erection rubbing against her hips.

Aaron deepened the kiss, earning a throaty moan from her. Her hands roamed over his body as far as she could reach, tracing and feeling every inch of his hard muscles.

Aaron's back hit the bed. Tearing off her shirt, Mia climbed on top of him, once again capturing his lips. Aaron responded to her kiss and traced her smooth skin greedily, his beast out of control. The urge to mark and claim her stronger than ever.

There was no stopping his beast now.

Within a second, he rolled them over, so he was on top of her. He peppered kisses from her jawline down to her neck. He felt her moan and arch up into him, and he let out an appreciative growl. He pulled back enough to tear off her bra, and he just stared, drinking in her beauty.

She's perfect.

He kissed her breasts, licking and sucking at her nipples. Mia moaned, pulling him closer. Her fingers pulled at the curls of his hair painfully. Aaron growled—the beast loved the pain. She tasted so good. He blew air on one of her hard nipples before taking it in his mouth again. Her moans filled the room. He was lost in the feeling of her flesh against his tongue when he felt his back hit the bed again.

232

Mia straddled him, her breaths changing as she pulled him closer. Not a second later he felt her fangs piercing his neck. Hot pain seared through his body, but he didn't move. The pain was shortly replaced with pleasure, making his cock harder than ever. Waves of pleasure wracked his body, and he pulled her mouth closer to his neck involuntarily. He was lost. He had never felt such pleasure in his life. He wanted to be inside her right then, buried deep.

His towel had slipped away. He tore off her remaining clothes and positioned himself between her thighs to thrust into her with such a need he never felt before.

So tight. . .

Pulling out almost completely, he slammed inside her again to continue the rhythm which earned him loud moans from her. Mia growled, releasing his neck and licking the bite clean of blood.

He could feel her womanhood clenching around his member. The lycan king snarled at the excessive pleasure, and his eyes rolled into his head as he thrust harder, increasing the pace. Mia came with a scream, throwing her head back as her hips arched toward him. Aaron ground his hips against her and sank his fangs in the juncture of her neck as he spilled his release inside her wet channel.

Her blood, so sweet and powerful, flowed on his tongue. He could feel the bond forming between them, intertwining their souls for eternity. He could feel her pleasure rolling through her in waves.

Aaron retracted his fangs and looked at her flushed form. His heart felt like it might explode with the love he felt for her. Their eyes locked as he rested his forehead against her. "I love you, Mia," he whispered.

Mia gave him a satisfied smile before passing out from exhaustion.

He had a mate now. *A queen.* His beast felt calm, sated, and satisfied. It prowled in the back of his mind, puffing its chest in pride.

Aaron closed his eyes, pulling her close to his chest. Mia snuggled into him, throwing her arms around him as she buried her face into his chest. That night, he slept peacefully for the first time in a long while.

***

Mia stirred from her sleep when she felt a warm finger trace her cheeks and opened her eyes to see Aaron looking at her with a broad smile. A frown formed on her face as she realized the position they were in.

He is naked.

A shriek escaped her startled lips, and Mia scrambled off the bed.

And she *was naked.* Mia squealed and pulled the bedsheet from the mattress to cover herself. *Real clever, Mia.* By pulling the sheets, she left him naked.

For a moment, she stood gawking at his naked glory. Realizing what she was doing, she closed her eyes and turned away. *How did I end up here in his room? What happened?*

"Mia, are you okay?" he asked, coming behind her, his voice etched with worry.

"How-how did I get here?" her voice trembled.

"You don't remember anything, do you?" He asked in a hurt tone making her regret the question.

What happened?

Frowning again, she clutched her head, her eyes landing on the mark on his neck. A gasp breached her lips when a memory from last night came back at her with full force. She had come to his room. She fed on his blood and took advantage of him.

"Mia, you have to stop now. . .I don't think I can control my beast."

Mia remembered his warning. Disbelief racked her mind. She backed away from Aaron.

I took advantage of him. I took his choice away.

"I-I'm sorry. I didn't mean to," she stuttered as shame filled her. Her knees collapsed, and loud sobs shook her frame. That mark on his neck meant they were now bonded for eternity. The worst part was that she wasn't in control when it happened. She had no explanation.

What have I done?

CHAPTER 31

"Mia, please don't cry. I'm sorry." Aaron's expression was pained.

"No. I'm sorry, Aaron. I took your choice away," she continued to sob. "I-I hurt you," she blurted out as she cried, a fresh set of tears rolling down her cheeks.

"That's not true."

"I forced myself on you. How do you explain that?" she asked, embarrassed. Her small nose red and her face flushed.

"I take it as you seduced me," he said with a shrug. A smile tugged at the corner of his lips.

"I lost control."

"Mia, look at me." He cupped her face with both hands. "You didn't take anything by force. I asked you to be my mate, and you responded by marking me. Besides, you cannot force a lycan to do anything," he said, pulling her close and looking right into her eyes to get his point across. "Unless you're an Alpha."

When she didn't respond, he hooked his finger under her chin, forcing her to meet his gaze. "Last night was the best night of my life." His sincere voice made her heart race again. "I love you, Mia. I found myself falling hard with every passing second that I spent with you.

You're it for me—my one and only. I wouldn't change a thing if I was given the choice." Aaron pressed a soft kiss on her lips.

His voice was a gentle caress, and his words warmed her insides. If those words didn't melt her, nothing would. Mia found herself relaxing as she responded to the soft kiss. *He tasted so good.* Then she remembered something. She had bitten him. *Oh, my God!*

She broke the kiss abruptly and inspected his neck. The wound healed, and in its place were four crescent-shaped marks. It appeared bruised. "Oh, no. It's scarred. I'm so sorry." What if her bite was poisonous? "We should get you checked out."

Aaron chuckled. "It's not what you think."

"No. What if you're infected? What if you change into a vampire?" Her panic rose.

"You can't change a lycan into a vampire, Mia," Aaron smiled. He pointed at his neck, "This is a mate's claim."

Her eyes widened. She now remembered seeing a similar mark on the neck of a few females. She even wondered why they would get similar tattoos. After the initial shock wore off, the realization set it. Lycans mated for life.

Her hand automatically went to her neck, remembering his bite. He marked her too. Urgent legs hurried to the nearby mirror, lips slightly parting when cerulean eyes found the crescent marks on her neck. The bluish-black marks contrasted well against her otherwise pale skin.

"We are mated."

"Yes, my love," he said. "You're mine as much as I'm yours." He kissed her forehead.

With a sigh, she leaned into his chest. A smile bloomed on her lips and lifted her spirits. "That sounded better."

***

Aaron called for a meeting in the office while Mia got ready for the day. They had to announce their mating to the pack. A part of him wondered how they'd take the news. His mate came in wearing a T-shirt and jeans, looking beautiful as ever.

"You look beautiful." He kissed her forehead and inhaled her enticing scent to calm his beast. Warm lips lingered on her skin before he unwrapped his arms from around her body and took her hands in his. "We have to go, my love. They are waiting for us," he guided her out of the room.

She looped her hand in his elbow as they walked together in comfortable silence. The elite guards on duty gave them a curt bow. Their impassive faces revealed nothing. It was how they've been trained since childhood. However, there was no animosity in their gazes.

Mia's hold on him relaxed upon reaching the familiar office. Aaron's family was already waiting for them with an expectant look on their faces. The lycan's nostrils flared, sniffing the air.

A broad smile lifted the corners of his father's lips. "Welcome to the family, Mia." He walked over to them with open arms. Aaron relaxed into the hug as his father patted his back.

Juan and Matthew followed next, engulfing both in a bone-crushing hug. "Can't breathe!" Aaron heard Mia wheeze, which only brought a smile to his lips.

His brothers released her, "What? You're a mighty vampire, but can't manage a love-filled hug from two lycans?" Matthew teased.

"You said it—two lycans."

Aaron watched with a content smile as Mia punched Matthew on his shoulder. His younger brother faked a hurtful expression that earned laughter from her. The melancholic sound made his heart soar.

"Congratulations, Your Highness," Ted grinned from ear to ear. His brows rose, and something passed between their gazes. Mia rolled her eyes before hugging her dad with a smile.

Maximus cleared his throat, "Congratulations, I guess. I'm Maximus, the third-in-command." He came forward introducing himself. "Call me Max."

"Hello," she said, shaking his extended hand. "I've heard about you. Matthew talks a lot about his childhood adventures."

"Max was on a trip when you first arrived here," Aaron said. "This is Lilith," he introduced the witch.

"Hello, my dear." Lilith pulled Mia into a hug.

"Hi, I'm Mia," Mia greeted. A shy smile crept onto her face. "Aaron has said a lot about you." The witch beamed with a nod.

"This calls for a celebration, but we have other pressing matters to handle," the former king's tone took a serious note when he went back to sit behind the desk.

Once the others were seated, Maximus spoke, "Alpha, the number of vampires lurking around our borders has increased considerably. The surveillance team picked up a new face that's not from around here. We caught all of them, except him. There's no trace of him."

"Yeah, Juan told me about that," Aaron said.

"We spoke to the vampires who live outside our borders. They identified the new leech." Aaron winced at the usage of the term, but Mia appeared unaffected. "He was looking for a girl. Many don't know what is going on, but they are feeling some kind of pull from an unknown source. And it's coming from our territory," Matthew said.

"Our source called us to check on the issue and informed that the pull to come inside our territory is growing stronger by the day," Maximus continued. "The vampires who are lost in bloodlust feel it even more."

"That's understandable. A pureblood has a natural tendency to pull other vampires toward them like a magnet. The more powerful they grow, the stronger the pull is," Lilith said.

Mia looked at her in astonishment. "Will I have to move somewhere to avoid all this?"

"Absolutely not!" Lilith waved her hand. "You're their queen by birth, Mia. It's natural for them to want to get close to you. However, this is a game changer. Perhaps, lycans and vampires can coexist."

"But how does that work? It has been this way for years," Juan intervened.

"Well, now that we have the queen of vampires on our side, Felipe will wage war. But we are on even grounds now," Lilith replied with a smirk. "Felipe's drudges will be conflicted; they will have to choose whose side to take. The pull from both sides will be so strong that the vampires will be perplexed as to whose orders they should follow," Lilith said, chuckling. "Two knives cannot be in one sheath for a reason."

"So, only one can survive—either me or Felipe." Mia's face was grim.

No one spoke to confirm her words. They didn't have to. The expression on their faces said it all. Aaron didn't want Mia facing Felipe. With all that was happening, Felipe would know of Mia's existence soon enough, and he would try to take her.

Tension grew thick in the air. Mia exhaled and picked up the mini sandwiches from the nearby tray and munched on them. Aaron noticed his mate ate when she was stressed.

"It's time we started with Mia's training," Ted said. "We have to find out what she's capable of."

"Mia is still going through her transformation. Her powers haven't fully awakened, yet. We can't draw boundaries at this point," Lilith mused. "With age comes power. Felipe is said to have the power to read minds, he can barge into anyone's mind, sifting through their memories without their permission. He can hypnotize and manipulate any vampire or human to do his bidding. I heard that he tried to experiment with this on other supernatural beings, but I don't know of its results."

"You said you were going to try to break into his ward," Ted said. "Did you have any breakthroughs?"

"There seems to be a powerful shield around him, which blocks him from my vision," Lilith sighed.

Her creased brows and grim expression told Aaron she knew or suspected something. The change in her heartbeat and breathing spoke of her fear for this thing. He sensed this earlier when Ted mentioned the witches' coven and when he recalled the story of adopting his mate. *She knew something. But what was it?*

"I expect her transformation will be faster than before now that Mia has consumed supernatural blood. We'll have to wait to see what effect this will have on her," Lilith said. "We can't assume anything based on the facts we already know about Felipe because her body is still processing the magic."

"This isn't the first time this has happened." Ted's information caused everyone's brows to rise and look at each other. "I've been using my magic spells on Mia to hide her scent. A few years ago, when she turned sixteen, my spells stopped working on her. Her body would just absorb the spell, and it had no effect on her whatsoever."

Lilith's face paled and her eyes widened. "What?" Every lycan in the room had noticed the sudden lurch of her heart and the beading sweat on her face. She was quick to mask it. "That's. . .that's—"

"I know," Ted reclined in his seat. "Mia is a miracle."

"What else did you know about her when you adopted her?" Aaron asked.

Ted shook his head. "Nothing except for her given name. The matron said she was left at their doorstep as a month-old baby. There was a note in her blanket with her name on it."

Aaron wiped Mia's silent tears, and she snuggled into his chest. He pressed his lips on top of her head.

"What's her name?" Lilith asked, her eyes curious.

"Mia Walter Edwards."

"Oh." Lilith blinked.

"Is there anything you aren't saying, Lilith?" Aaron asked the question that was bugging him.

"Huh, no," Lilith managed a smile. "Something about her name felt familiar that's all. Nothing that's worth the discussion."

Aaron couldn't think of it as a worthless discussion, but he let it slide for the moment.

"Brother, we have a suspect who has a motive to tamper with Mia's blood bag," Juan announced.

"What did you find?" Aaron asked. He already had a hunch of who it could be but they needed proof.

"The security tapes revealed a hooded figure entering the infirmary blood bank, but we haven't identified him or her yet. Also, someone had gone to dungeons while Zach was on duty. The prisoners didn't reveal the identity of the person, and I can see that they were fed recently."

"So, this someone wanted to hurt or kill Mia, and they gathered the information by visiting the dungeons and bribing the prisoners with food," Aaron growled out. There was only one person inside the pack with such a motive.

"Zach is in custody. Also, Emilia has recently moved in with him. It is her, brother," Matthew's gaze narrowed.

"Yeah, I heard that she's been talking behind the alpha's back," Max informed. "Warriors talk a lot when they are drunk." His shoulders shrugged.

"I will pay him a visit, then," Aaron stood, flexing his hands. He knew how to bring out the truth from someone who was not willing to give it. He could simply command him to speak the truth, but he wouldn't do that. The beast wanted a round with Zach. It wanted to get the point across to anyone who dared cross him. No one should mess with what was his and get away with it.

"My brothers will show you to our personal gym if you wish to train Mia," he said to Ted and Lilith.

"Sure." Ted stood.

Mia's scowl brought a smile to Aaron's lips, and he could tell she wasn't particularly fond of training.

"Can't we start later?" Her pout made him chuckle.

"Felipe isn't going to wait for you to get ready, sweetheart," Ted chastised.

His mate's eyes found his before a sigh left her lips. "Okay. FYI, you waited all these years. You should have trained me sooner."

Ted looked guilty. "I'm sorry and we talked about this. How long are you gonna rub it in my face?"

Mia just shrugged and leaned to Aaron's embrace.

"Max, come with me." He kissed Mia's forehead before leaving. "I'll see you soon."

"Okay."

CHAPTER 32

Mia followed the brothers to the gym with her father and the witch. The gym was big with separate sections for training and exercise. It had all sorts of the latest equipment, with walls that had long mirrors reflecting their images. A mini refrigerator sat at one of the corners.

"Mia, a minute please." Mia turned to see the witch standing in front of her with her palms outstretched. "Do not move," her lips murmured in an odd language, and Mia's vision blurred.

Mia felt a rush of heat spread through her body. Her vision cleared, and she looked down to notice a faint glow on her skin. Lilith's eyes shined bright. As she chanted, Mia felt warmth lick her insides.

The dark whispers inside her head suddenly awoke, and a power pulsed in her veins. The witch's words strangely made sense, and she felt herself repeating the words. Lilith stopped chanting, the shining of her eyes shimmered. The faint glow on Mia's skin shimmered until it faded completely, leaving her skin to its normal hue.

"That's a hell lot of power you hold there," Lilith's voice was a whisper. "I need your blood to run some tests."

"Okay."

A frown marred Mia's features. The vampire didn't understand the sudden flare of fear that was radiated by the witch. Lilith had been behaving strangely ever since they met.

The witch produced a bottle from one of her pockets and asked for Mia's hand. A knife sliced at the tip of her fingers, a bigger incision than necessary. She understood why when the skin healed itself. Lilith had to cut the skin once again to fill the bottle.

You could have just used a syringe. Mia didn't voice out her thought, remembering how old-fashioned they acted at times. Her father often forgot how much technology has advanced. She assumed Lilith must have forgotten too.

"I'll be at the lab," Lilith said.

She was quick to exit, leaving Mia and her father to their devices. Once again, this left Mia puzzled. Her shoulders lifted to a shrug before she turned to face her father.

"Well. . ." his eyes followed Lilith. "That was strange."

"I feel like she knows something we don't."

"I feel the same too," her father's eyes appeared to mirror her thoughts. "The witch is a mystery to many. Someone I plan to figure out soon."

"Good luck with that," Juan snickered from somewhere.

Her father shook his head. "Let's start with your combat training."

"Do I even have a choice?"

"No."

***

The interrogation did not end well for Zach. Aaron confirmed who switched the blood. He knew Zach was just a pawn in Emilia's game. He had only punched Zach to get a bit of anger out.

"Juan, how is she doing?"

"Sprawled out on the gym floor."

"Okay. I want you and Matt to come to the interrogation room. Our suspicions were right."

"We will be there in a minute, brother."

Aaron was pacing the floors of the interrogation room when his brothers entered.

"Whoa! You got him pretty bad," Juan exclaimed.

"Take him to the infirmary and be discreet," Matthew ordered the two guards outside. "If anyone asks, Zach has gone with the team to track the abducted pack members. And, if you want to keep your heads intact, I suggest you keep your mouth shut about my brother's mating," he warned.

The guards rushed in to obey as Juan pulled Aaron aside. "I think we should keep the news about your mating from the pack. Taking Emilia into custody now will only receive unnecessary attention, and knowing her, she would use it as an opportunity to twist the truth."

Aaron shook his head. "This isn't something we can hide. They'll find out if they get a whiff of me." The royals had separate corridors to commute within the walls of the castle, so no one except the elite guards had seen him so far.

"We have something in mind. We just need a few more days to work on it. But first, I suggest you shower and change," Matthew said.

Aaron nodded half-heartedly and left to change.

***

Emilia paced the floor in Zach's room.

He was not yet back from his shift. For someone who comes early, he was very late. She tried to speak with a few guards, but no one spoke a word to her about where Zach was. Did they find out what he did for her? If they did, why had they not come for her yet?

Zach wouldn't reveal her name even if he did get caught. He thought of her as his potential mate. He was so blinded by the love he felt for her that he would jump into the fire if she asked him.

Moving in with Zach was a mistake. But Aaron had left her no choice. He'd revealed her relationship with Zach in front of the pack. Not that it made any difference. Zach had big mouth, which she learned recently. Now the omegas talked without fear and she knew Zach had been talking about their relationship when he was drunk.

When she thought this could be one of the reasons Aaron rejected her advances, her anger was diverted toward Zach. Emilia usually played the men to get her way and always kept her affairs secret. No one knew she was with the other. She made them believe that she might allow them to mate with her sometime.

Zach would pay for running his mouth. *I'll dump his ass when this is all over.* Till then she needed the mutt.

Mia occupied her thoughts again. Emilia had successfully replaced the blood. However, she didn't know if the bloodsucker had consumed it. *Is she dead?* She had heard no commotion coming from the royal wing nor did she see any medical team running for aid.

Slender fingers twisted the hem of the short dress she wore. *So maybe she didn't consume the blood as she should have.* There was no other reason for the plan to fail miserably.

She had no option but to wait.

***

Mia was excited to visit the castle library. Aaron had taken her there after lunch. She waltzed through rows and rows of books, tracing the hardcovers. When she felt his lingering gaze on her, she turned to him with a smile on her face.

"So. . .do you read?"

"I used to. . .before Mom was murdered. I never had time after that with all the work," he said, running a hand through his hair. Though he said it in a casual tone, she could sense his underlying pain.

"So how did the interrogation go?"

His shoulders lifted to form a shrug. "It's her."

"And, you can't act on it," she guessed.

"My brothers suggested waiting until we can catch her red-handed."

Mia sauntered to him. "And, you don't want to wait," she wrapped her arms around his waist, pressing herself to him.

"No, I don't."

She was tempted to run her fingers through his soft and silky hair. He looked sexy in his loose T-shirt. The open buttons gave her a sneak peek of his tan skin.

"So, um. . .what did you do to my dad's lookout?"

Aaron's brows rose, then a smile breached his lips. "We released him from custody when you became more than my prisoner." His hands cupped her ass, giving it a squeeze. "Logan knew too much about us, so we had to keep him close. He now works for the castle."

"Oh." Mia relaxed in his embrace. Her father had requested that she check on Logan after training. Though she knew about Logan's involvement in her security, it had slipped her mind until now.

Aaron pecked her lips, "Once this is all over. I want to court you properly," he murmured in her ear.

"I'd love that," she replied, turning her head to press her lips to his. "So, when are you going to announce our mating to the pack?"

"Juan and Matt want to delay the announcement."

Mia could tell her mate didn't appreciate the delay. "They wouldn't suggest that without a valid reason."

He nodded. "Yeah, they fear Emilia would use this information to stir trouble."

"Was she your girlfriend?" Jealousy coated her tone. She tried to mask it, but failed.

Aaron burst into laughter. He laughed so much that his eyes teared up.

"You didn't have to laugh." Mia sensed the pout forming on her lips. "I just guessed that was the reason. Why else would she so hung up on you? Emilia's hatred is not only based on my origin."

He pulled her to his chest. "You were half right. She's after the throne, but I want nothing to do with her. I never did and never will." His sincere tone warmed her insides as warm fingers pushed the hair from her face. "You're my first," his teeth nipped at her jaw. "And, you'll be my last."

"Aaron—"

He kissed her. Mia couldn't think anymore as his lips claimed hers in a possessive kiss that sent her hormones into overdrive. She felt herself growing hotter by the minute as he pushed her against the bookshelf. A throaty moan left her lips when she felt his hardness press against her hip. Aaron broke the kiss, both of them breathing harder. "I want to show you something."

"Okay." She hid the sudden disappointment that washed over her but then the curiosity poked its head in.

Aaron led her to their room and to their closet. She hadn't had the chance to check his closet out before. He had so many clothes in his collection. She gazed at the variety of shoes, ties, suits, and shirts lining the closet.

"I bought this for you."

She turned her attention to him to see female clothes and accessories neatly arranged on the shelves behind him. Sundresses, formal dresses, casual wear, winter clothes, and a variety of pants, night wear, and matching accessories adorned the shelves. Her lips refused to move. It felt as if she was in a showroom.

"Do you like it?" he asked, hugging her from behind, his warmth blanketing her.

"I love it. Thank you," she whispered, turning to him. This was a surprise. His eyes were now warm shades of honey. While she felt that he went a bit overboard, she also thought it as sweet.

"You can thank me by wearing one of these," he said, pulling out some lingerie. There was hardly anything there. It was completely see-through with a pink thong and a patch that covered her essentials, leaving only a bit for imagination.

"I'm not wearing that," her eyes widened and she stepped back,embarrassed to even look at the piece.

"Or you could choose something else." He sifted through her drawers. "Ah. . .this suits you well," he said, pulling out a red thong and a lace bra with a garter.

She felt her entire blood supply rush to her face and wanted the floor to open and swallow her. She pushed him away and ran out of the closet. If he were not a powerful lycan, he would have been dangling on the wall from the amount of force she exerted unknowingly.

Picking her up by the waist, he threw her on the bed and tickled her sides as she giggled. He stopped after a while, staring intensely at her. She felt a wave of happiness washing over her at the same time her heart leaped with joy.

"I have to tell you something," he sat facing her.

"What is it?" she leaned against the headboard.

"Now that we are mated, we will be able to feel each other's emotions."

"Oh." That made sense. It explained gv the sudden rush of warmth to her heart and the unexplainable anger she felt earlier that day.

"Let me show you." Aaron's gaze shifted toward her lips. His desire washed over her, and her cheeks heated up. Reaching for her lips, he pulled her in for a passionate kiss. Mia moaned, responding to the kiss with the same need that he showed.

CHAPTER 33

She woke to the chilling darkness. Her body floated, surrounded by mist. Mia could hardly see anything with her heightened eyesight. She squinted her eyes and keenly listened for any sound.

What is this place?

How did she get here?

Mia explored blindly, looking for anything as her feet floated above the ground. If she had known a way to wake up in the real world she would. But now, she had no choice other than to follow. She made a note to talk to Lilith about this. The witch would know a way to stop this. She didn't know how long she moved before she saw a light far off.

She moved swiftly, reaching what looked like a castle–dark and sinister. Goosebumps erupted on her flesh, and she felt a strange pull. Her instincts were suddenly on full alert.

She came upon a large bubble that reminded her of a snow globe. Only there was no snow. Upon closer observation, the bubble appeared to be a thin membrane. She reached forward and traced it with her finger, feeling the elastic texture like that of a balloon.

Warmth rushed from the tip of her fingers and spread to other parts of her body. Strange emotions caused her eyes to tear up. Her hands trembled. A strange whisper mesmerized her as she felt a familiar power surge within her veins. A faint glow lit up her body once more.

Another whisper like a snake's hiss caught her attention. It was as if the bubble spoke to her, calling her.

Mia responded to the call by reaching toward the bubble and then pushing her entire being forward into it. It sucked her in and she was surrounded by warmth she had never felt before. She was suddenly blanketed by a feeling of safety and comfort that almost felt like the mother's embrace she never experienced.

Soon enough, she was transported to castle grounds, leaving the bubble behind and intact as she moved forward

Curiosity bubbled from within. The magnetic pull grew stronger with each step she took toward the ancient structure. The castle was not like anything she had ever seen or known before. It was bigger than the Randolph Castle. Darkness seeped from within.

Mia hid behind a tree when she noticed a few creatures coming her way. Just when she thought she was safe to move, she bumped into a vampire.

Crap!

She held her breath as her eyes looked around for a way out. The vampire didn't seem to notice her. He just walked past her. Mia looked at her hands, which appeared dim and foggy.

Mia shook her head and went on to poke another vampire who was talking animatedly to the other. Her hands seemed to go straight through his body. When he didn't react, she floated toward the castle with a relieved smile on her face. That's good.

The darkness was unnerving, but the fact that she was invisible to them encouraged her forward. Mia entered the castle on hesitant legs, exploring its dark corridors. A few torches were lit here and there, casting a dim orange glow.

Who owns this castle? She wondered as she continued to *wander. Soon she reached a basement. She tried to open the locked door or push past it, but she couldn't.*

A distant scream attracted her attention, and Mia rushed toward the source. It was a scream of agony from a man. She was met with a set of grand double doors—the sounds came from behind.

Fear coursed through her body. Taking a deep breath, she tried to push her foggy body through the door once more and she succeeded.

The scene in front of her had her rooted to the spot. Several men were chained to a huge pillar and were surrounded by witches. A woman strode toward one of the men and injected a dark red liquid through his veins, causing him to scream in agony.

Mia averted her gaze; she couldn't withstand the way he twisted and turned within the chains. When she looked again, his body held multiple burn scars that sizzled.

What were they doing to him? On closer observation, she didn't see any hint of fangs. He looked normal except for his pointy ears. He was tall and had long limbs. He was not human.

She was lost in her thoughts when she felt a sudden pull. Something so powerful every fiber of her body came alive as her blood thrummed within her veins. An inaudible gasp left her mouth as a jolt of awareness shot down her belly.

Before she realized it, she was moving toward someone or something. And that someone or something was coming toward her. Just when she was about to push past another door, it opened, revealing a man—dark, handsome and sinful.

Mia froze. A labored breath expanded her lungs and refused to leave. The intoxicating scent of his stayed in. He oozed sex, and the way he held himself regal told her he was none other than the king of the castle.

The stranger's nostrils flared as his frantic eyes looked around. His pitch-black eyes seemed to stare right through her soul as she watched him. Her hands ached to touch him. He was beautiful in every sense. His skin was unbelievably pale, and his hair, dark as night. Predatory fangs peeked from underneath his sinful lips.

There was a strange aura around him, so strong and powerful. Everything about him called out to her. Suddenly, the scene changed, and they were in the throne room.

"Mia," her name on his lips was a whisper that sent shivers down her spine. "You have come to the right place. This throne is waiting for you. I'm waiting for you," he said with his arms spread wide.

"Soon, Mia. . ."

Mia woke with a start and found herself in the same position she fell asleep in. Sweat coated her naked skin. The sheet fell around her waist and cold air brushed her bare skin. She was still in Aaron's castle. She remembered falling asleep in his arms after their lovemaking session. *What was that place?*

"Felipe," she whispered, shocked to the core. It must be him! But how did he know it was her?

Beside her, Aaron stirred.

"Mia," he called softly. "Are you okay?"

She looked at her mate, who looked delectable with his naked torso on display. Her eyes trailed down his body and huffed in disappointment when she couldn't see past his V-line which was hidden underneath the sheets.

Scrambling toward him, she kissed him, and he returned it immediately. Just when he was about to deepen the kiss, Felipe's face flashed in her memory. Mia pulled away with wide eyes as she remembered her dream. The attraction she felt toward the vampire king was unfathomable. She looked into the innocent eyes of her mate. His mark on her skin burned and she hissed in pain.

Aaron's expression faltered as he touched the mark, and Mia sighed in relief when the pain seemed to disappear at his touch.

"What is it?"

"I-I don't know."

"I can feel your emotions, Mia. The mark burns when a mate is attracted to someone other than their mate." His tone held a lot of pain, and it squeezed her heart.

She had hurt him unknowingly. How would she explain? She wasn't expecting to be attracted to Felipe's charms. Mia didn't understand why she even felt that way. It was just a dream, yet her response to him startled her.

"I had another dream. I was in a castle and I think I saw Felipe. He said he's waiting for me. Aaron, I was attracted to him. I don't know how, it just happened. My body and mind were moving on its own and before I realized it, I was in front of him unable to look away," she blurted out. Her mark burned again, and horror filled her when she smelled her own arousal.

Aaron stiffened beside her. Mia's eyes widened when she realized what she just said. She accepted that she admired another man. She didn't have enough time to respond when he pinned her against the bed, his claws digging into her wrist.

His fury washed over her. His eyes changed. A sign that said his beast was in control. His chest vibrated with a threatening rumble. Fur sprouted along his arms and torso. Mia could see him fighting his beast side as his body phased between fur and skin.

I shouldn't have said anything to him.

"You're aroused," the beast snarled. "Mine!"

Catherine Edward

Swallowing the lump that formed in her throat, Mia did the first thing that came into her mind. Shoving aside the fear, she locked her stare with his. *I love him.* She had no explanation as to why she was aroused and why her mark burned. But she knew she would never choose anyone except him. *Only him.* She had to prove that she belonged to him and the beast within.

In a swift motion, she got out of his steely grip, her lips captured his in a hungry kiss. Her legs wrapped around his waist as she fisted his silky hair, opening her mouth wide for him to claim.

Aaron stiffened when her lips pressed against his.

"I am yours, Aaron." Her mesmerizing voice floated in his mind. *"Only yours."*

He responded to her kiss with a feverish need. Felipe was the most powerful vampire. It was a natural reaction for her to be attracted to him, but the fact did not sit well with his beast. Aaron wanted to claim his mate again, to show he was better than the leech. His beast wanted to pleasure her until she couldn't walk without feeling every inch of him within her.

There was no holding back. He wanted to take her hard and fast. The beast surged forward, taking control of his human side. Mia moaned when he switched positions, his lips conquered hers— dominating her. His need to please and pleasure her filled him, stirring her desire. The atmosphere grew thicker with the essence of her arousal in the air.

A loud growl rolled out of his chest, vibrating along her body. His amber eyes shone brightly in the dark. "You're mine!" the beast snarled. His snarl was the only warning Mia had before he tore off the sheet and thrust, plunging deep into her soaking sex. His cock stretched her walls.

Mia threw her head back, baring her neck to the beast and arched her hips forward to meet his hard thrusts. Snarls and growls tumbled out of his chest as he feasted on her tender breasts.

"Oh!" Mia arched her chest toward his tantalizing mouth that assaulted her sensitive peaks without mercy. Pleasure shot from the tip of her nipples to her spine and then to her lower belly.

His large hands caged her slender ones. Soft velvety fur sprouted on his skin as his fangs elongated. Excitement bubbled within the vampire as she noticed the sharp canines that could rip her throat if he wanted.

"Bite me!" she growled, her own fangs extending as the vein in his neck bulged.

Want it.

Need it.

The beast in control of the human side sunk its fangs on her mark. Erotic pleasure pulsed through her veins as he once again marked her as his. His strong jaws clamped around her mark, fangs buried deep in her neck as her body trembled with the pleasure only a mate could provide.

When his hand slipped between them, his claws retracted, not wanting to hurt her in the process. At the first touch of his thumb on her already swollen clit, Mia was sent tumbling into her first orgasm. It shook her to her core and caused tremors to spread along her body.

But the beast was relentless. He kept thrusting as she climbed down from the euphoria and the familiar stress in her lower half began to build again. When she couldn't hold any longer, she buried her fangs in his neck, sending them both into oblivion.

"Mine!" His masculine rumble floated in her mind, his fangs still buried in her veins.

"Yes, yours. . ." she purred, content with the claim.

"Good, because I don't share."

Mia released his neck and licked the wound close as her eyes drooped. Her lips stretched with a satisfied smile as she fell asleep with his fangs and cock buried deep within her.

***

Felipe jolted from his throne. He blinked several times to clear his vision as his brain processed the first dream he had in centuries.

Whoever it was, she smelled divine. His mouth watered at her scent and his fangs extended, wanting to taste her blood. He inhaled again getting a hint of the same addicting scent. It was not a dream. Someone had been here. Why hadn't he seen them?

"Tanya!" He bellowed.

"Master," Tanya appeared and bowed in front of him.

"Someone infiltrated the castle. I want her here. . .now," he ordered as his eyes turned pitch-black with lust.

CHAPTER 34

When Mia woke up the next morning, she was alone in bed. All her sweet spots ached, reminding her of the previous night. Aaron's side of the bed was cold and empty, indicating that he had woken up long ago. *Why didn't he wake me?*

She noticed a small handwritten note on the table which drew a small smile to her lips, quieting her racing heart.

My love,
Something has come up.
I will try to meet you for lunch.
I love you,
-Aaron.

Mia re-read the last two lines, and a smile blossomed on her face. *I love you too, Aaron.* She gave the letter a peck and then hurried to her closet to put it in a safe place.

After a quick morning routine and breakfast, Mia wandered off to the library with Matthew and Max, in tow. Aaron had called Juan sometime during her breakfast, so he had to leave. Max had taken his place.

The brothers informed her that Lilith and her father were in the lab. Going there was not an option considering the pack members would be everywhere.

Mia stopped in front of a few portraits, admiring the details as she went. One portrait at the end of the hallway caught her attention and she ambled toward it, taking in the details.

It was of a beautiful woman. She sat elegantly on a decorated throne. Her beautiful dark brown hair was long. Her bewitching green eyes held joy, and her lips formed a small smile. The burgundy gown had a stylish jeweled neckline. Her arms were covered to just above her elbows. The dress was floor-length and formfitting. It accentuated her curves and complimented her ivory skin well. There was a platinum crown encrusted with diamonds that sat on her head saying that she was a royal.

"That was our mother," Matthew said in a voice so low it was full of pain as he came to stand near her.

Esmeralda was a natural beauty. Her face radiated calm and peace. She could see where Juan inherited most of his features. Mia nodded; she could feel his pain. No words were exchanged as she turned and followed them to the library.

***

Jerome greeted her with a hug as she stepped through the doors. Mia inhaled his calming scent and basked in the fatherly comfort he provided. She let him go when he patted her back twice.

"How are you today, Mia?"

"I'm good, thank you. How is your day?"

"Better than yesterday." His smile didn't reach his eyes.

"Am I disturbing you?" she asked, eyeing the scattered papers and books on his desk.

"Oh, no. Not at all," he assured her with a wave of his hand. "I'm just going through these books to see if I can learn something new about the vampires, specifically Felipe."

Mia nodded. "I had a dream about him," she blurted out. She had to tell someone. "I...um...there was an incident last night." She absent-mindedly traced her mark as she wondered how to break it to him.

Jerome's experienced eyes caught that action and he frowned before understanding dawned his features. "It's understandable." He scratched his chin thoughtfully. "Mia, you're the first female born vampire. It's natural to be attracted to the opposite sex of your own kind, especially someone like Felipe."

"But I'm mated to Aaron. It shouldn't be possible, right?" Mia asked as confusion clouded her features.

"Yes, you shouldn't be attracted to him. However, even though you're mated to Aaron, you're still a vampire. Your body, mind, and soul know that we are your mortal enemies. It is your human side that makes it even possible to be around us," he explained.

Mia followed when he went to sit behind the medium-sized mahogany desk. She occupied an empty chair opposite him as Matthew and Max sat on the couch by the fireplace beside the desk.

"Your survival instincts will always seek the company of fellow vampires. Your powers call upon other vampires for protection. The vampires around our territory are already feeling the pull toward you. There is only so much that we know about the purebloods. I can tell you one thing, though: this attraction is not going to be easy. You will have to be strong, and you will need to fight it," he stressed.

Mia swallowed the lump that had formed in her throat. The mating was for eternity. She would never betray Aaron. Already she felt dirty for even feeling that small amount of attraction toward Felipe. But again, she didn't even realize how or when she got aroused.

She couldn't help it, which scared her the most. It felt as if she was in a trance when it happened. She didn't want to be attracted to Felipe. His face surfaced in her memory again. Felipe was sexier than Aaron on the outside. However, she knew that Felipe was rotten on the inside, unlike Aaron who had a heart of gold.

"I would never betray Aaron. I'd rather die than put him through that pain," she replied, her voice soft yet firm with determination.

Jerome's features softened and he squeezed her hand in reassurance. "I know," he said softly. "You remind me of my Esme." A sigh drifted out of his lips as he reclined in his chair. "You're kind and compassionate like her, I'm sure you would be a great queen and a mother, just like my Esmeralda."

"She's beautiful," Mia whispered. "I saw her portrait outside."

"She was," he corrected. "I had never met a woman with such a kind soul like hers," he gave her a warm smile.

Mia could hear the pain that laced his voice at the mention of his late mate, but she had no words of comfort to offer.

Jerome was quiet for a moment before speaking again. "Seven years back, vampires killed my mate," his voice cracked.

Matthew went to sit on the floor beside his father, taking his hand in his, comforting him.

"She had gone to town to visit a few omegas who recently gave birth. My Esme loved children. She always made sure that each and every pack member had what they required."

Tears were rolling down his cheeks. It broke Mia's heart to see him so vulnerable like this. He looked strong on the outside, but she now saw how broken he was under that façade. "They were ambushed on the way back here. They killed the guards before taking her and my third-in-command. We searched everywhere, her scent had vanished—it was a dead end."

"She was tortured for days before we found a few of her body parts in the middle of the forest." His body heaved as he swallowed a sob that threatened to break free. "A finger here, a hand there. But the bastard never gave us her full body to mourn." At this, his sobs broke free and racked his body.

Matthew hugged his father tightly, letting him cry. Max, whose eyes glistened with tears, walked over to him and put his hand on Jerome's shoulder in comfort. Their pain washed over her. She could hear the mournful howls of their beasts. She could only imagine how hard it would be on the brothers and Aaron, who ascended the throne when he was still a teen.

After a few minutes, the room was silent except for the soft sobs of the former king. Her soul wept.

"We tried to find any clue that would lead us to her killers, but we didn't find any. Felipe has been in hiding, and it's not easy to find a born vampire if they doesn't want you to find them," Matthew continued, pain lacing his voice.

It was sad and painful. They missed her so much and didn't even have her body to mourn. Life was so cruel.

"I'm sorry," Mia said. "I never met my birth parents. I can only imagine how bad it feels."

Jerome calmed down. His eyes red, he suddenly looked old.

"Thank you for sharing this with me. I wish I could take your pain away, but I know I can't. I wish I had met her," she whispered. She had to fight this. Felipe was evil in every way and she should be thinking about ending him instead of her attraction to him.

Mia let out a sigh and straightened her shoulders with determination. She would have to train harder and help them in any way she could. She would have to be ready when Felipe came for them.

***

In the lab, Lilith was busy testing Mia's blood. Ted watched her with a puzzled look. Lilith was performing multiple tests, and he could hear her occasional curses.

She mixed various blood samples with Mia's blood and then added in chemicals. He could tell she wasn't satisfied with the results. Paul, now healed, was at a computer analyzing the set of samples given to him by Lilith.

Logan came in with a knock. He raised an eyebrow at Ted, who just shrugged. The warlock was happy to see his associate alive and well. He was excited to find Logan now working in the castle.

"What did you find?" Logan asked, his eyes scanning the lab. Lilith had been in here since last afternoon.

"I wish I knew," Ted sighed. He'd asked her multiple times and she always responded with "a minute please." When he realized he would get no answers, he stayed silent and just observed.

Lilith pulled up from the sample she was analyzing with a tired look.

"We are trying to find the source of Mia's powers. So far, nothing. All the results I'm getting points toward the witch, which is impossible considering that she's a born vampire," she said picking up another sample.

"What?" Ted wanted to laugh. "That's not possible."

"I know, Galahad. You know, what is confusing is that Mia's blood is different. It is a witch, vampire, and lycan mix. A vampire doesn't become a witch by consuming witch blood. A witch is born with her powers. Her blood processed the power, and instead of burning her, it just boosted some kind of change within her," her voice was tired. "Her cells are replicating the powers, becoming stronger as we speak." Worry etched her features. "My question is how in the hell was it possible for her to digest the witch blood in the first place. There is not even a single sign of discomfort. She just emerged more powerful after the transfer. My spells on her only seem to boost her power, even if it was a simple spell."

Ted stood dumbfounded, processing the information. It was something he'd already thought about but had no answers for. But that was news. What did she mean that Mia was growing stronger by the minute? Did she mean her vampire powers or the witch powers?

"I have so many theories but nothing to prove them," she plopped on the floor. Her red hair was out of place and exhaustion was written on her face.

"Well, I have a theory," Logan piped in. "We don't have any idea about Mia's parents. What if one of them was a witch and she has inherited the powers?"

This had Lilith straighten up.

"Impossible! She's a born vampire!" Ted exclaimed. "I'd have sensed the magic in her blood." Then, he remembered the ancient magic that protected her in the beginning. The one which was strong enough to inflict pain on him. His eyes locked with the witch whose face mirrored his expression. "She was protected with a powerful spell when I found her," his voice whispered out. "That's never happened before."

"What if he's right?" Lilith mused. "This is unheard of, but if what we think is true, she's the first born vampire with witch blood in her. There is no other way to explain the magic in her blood."

How is this even possible?

Ted knew most of the witches and warlocks, and none of their identities matched that of Mia. There were only a few blondes and none of their features matched with that of his adopted daughter's.

Who were her parents?

"Why do I feel like you know something that I don't?" Ted's eyes narrowed at the witch, who averted her gaze.

He could almost see the wheels turning in her head. Her eyes widened for a measure before she stood and returned to her post, pulling out the samples she had ready.

CHAPTER 35

"Master." Tanya bowed before Felipe, who sat at the grand dining table sipping on fresh blood from his golden chalice. Water droplets dripped from his dark hair and her eyes trailed down his smooth chest on display.

"Did you find her?"

"Melisa won't reveal a thing, Master. She acts strange and she became violent when I tried to coerce the information out of her," Tanya said, showing him her bruised and swollen arm.

"Hmm. . .looks like our witch needs a little reminder," Felipe mused, getting up from his decorated chair and slipping his robe on. She moved to help, but he dismissed her with a wave of his hand.

Tanya eyed him with lust but lowered her gaze when he narrowed his with a scowl. Felipe was an attractive man, and she couldn't help the lust that filled her being whenever she looked at him. Knowing what it was like to be with him didn't help matters.

"Control your thoughts, witch," Felipe snapped. He scowled as he exited the dining hall. "Don't forget your place."

"Forgive me, Master." Tanya bowed and scurried after him toward the dungeon.

The dark corridors extended with multiple twists and turns. Tanya had to run to keep up with Felipe's speed. Though he was walking at his normal pace, she couldn't keep up with him.

The Dark Witch had been placed in a secret chamber a few stories beneath the ground. The place was heavily guarded by magic. It took a few weeks and the combined effort of over fifty dark witches to secure the place. Tanya could already feel Melisa's power slowly beginning to break free.

The power of a witch only increased with age, and Melisa, being the oldest, was the most powerful of them all. It was a growing challenge to keep her chained. Twenty years ago, they had to begin putting up a new spell annually before it weakened. But now, they had to perform the ritual almost every three weeks.

Melisa almost escaped once. The vampire king had beaten one of the warlocks to death for letting it happen.

Tanya could feel Melisa's powers even before reaching her chamber. Goosebumps erupted on her flesh as a dark chill climbed up her spine.

Their spells were weakening already, much to their dismay; it was faster than she anticipated they should have. They had just performed the ritual last night. She'll have to perform the ritual again tonight or Melisa would break free of her confines.

"Hello, Melisa. Doing well, I see." Felipe smirked, earning a scowl from the Dark Witch.

She glared at him with her pitch-black eyes. Her arms, legs, and torso were wrapped in chains. Metal hooks on the floor held the chains in place. The length of those chains allowed her to walk in circles.

Tanya stepped back when the witch tilted her head and gave her a threatening grin. She swallowed hard. She didn't know how to convey this to Felipe. He didn't like it when something didn't go as he planned.

Fortunately, her mental shields were up so Felipe could not hear her thoughts. Melisa chuckled. It was as if the witch knew what exactly she was thinking.

"Melisa, I had a dream. Someone visited me. I couldn't see her ,but I could feel and smell her. Who was she?"

"I do not know," the witch growled. Spit flew from her mouth as she pinned her dark stare on the king.

"That is not how you talk to your king, Melisa." Felipe walked around her. "I won't tolerate disrespect, and I won't hesitate to show you your place again." The witch stepped back upon hearing the warning in his tone but she kept her stance stiff. "Now, tell me what that was all about. I know it was not a dream! I could smell her even after she left."

Melisa smirked and tilted her head, her eyes shining like a black crystal. "She. . .is your death," she sneered.

"Enough! The truth now," he bellowed. Tanya could tell that her master hated the nerve of that witch. It had taken ten years to break her resolve and push her to the darkness waiting eagerly to claim her. Even now she looked normal, only her pitch-black eyes indicated that she was still on the dark side.

The witch cackled. The dark eerie sound echoing through the walls of her small confinement smelled like rot, piss, and feces. Felipe backhanded her without another thought.

Melisa's body flew across the room and crashed into the closest stone wall. Instead of a painful grunt or groan, Tanya heard her giggle, surprising her. She stood up, tilted her head again and spat the blood from her mouth.

"That's all you got?" Melisa taunted.

Tanya's eyes grew wider as the Dark Witch advanced with slow steps. Her hands trembled as she got ready to use magic if needed.

"Do you have a death wish, witch?" Felipe's voice boomed.

"Death," she said. "Death is too kind for you, Felipe. But, she's coming for you. You're going to die, I have seen it. I have seen it all!" Her cackle was maniacal as she took in the shocked expression of Felipe.

The vampire king growled, and she could almost see the dark outline of his wings. Tanya retreated to the far end of the room, pressing her back to the metal door. Her master wouldn't forgive what the witch just told him. She swallowed the hard lump in her throat. No one in this world was powerful enough to kill him. However, this witch had the gift of vision which meant it had to be true.

"I'm going to change your vision. Who is she?" He yelled again. Veins bulged in his neck. The bluish-black nerves against his pale skin gave him a ghostly appearance.

"I don't know," the witch sang and laughed again. "Even if I did, I wouldn't tell you."

"It's time to remind you who you're talking to." Felipe nodded to Tanya, who swallowed and brought him the medieval wooden torch. He smirked when Melisa's eyes widened.

Fire and witches didn't get along. They were immune to many things, but fire was not one of them. Witches could conjure fire using their magic, but fire created without magic burned them faster than anything else.

Melisa backed up with wide eyes as Felipe stalked toward her with a devilish grin. "I'm going to punish you for three reasons. One, you disrespected me. Two, you told me that I'm going to die. And three, you had the nerve to deny me the answer to my question."

"No one can kill me, Melisa. If you thought that the female born vampire is going to end me, then you thought wrong. She's just a baby," he laughed. "How good is she going to be against a thousand-year-old vampire?"

Melisa shrieked when the fire licked her pale skin. It sizzled and her flesh burned with a hiss. Her eyes shifted between white and black. Tanya stepped back, her eyes wide. She felt as if she felt a ghost of a burn and unconsciously rubbed her hand.

"That hurt, didn't it? Remember the prophecy? I'm going to make her my queen, and after that, she'll be fighting those pests by my side."

"She won't be yours," Melisa spat. "You're going to die a painful death."

Melisa's screams echoed throughout the dark chambers, followed by Felipe's mad laugh. Tanya slipped out of the room, unable to withstand the torture. She couldn't witness it. She usually enjoyed torturing their hostages. Tanya wiped her sweaty palms on her old gown. She needed to find Marco—they would have to chant the spell and perform the binding rituals once again.

***

Her dad and Lilith joined Mia in the gym after lunch.

Mia was once again sprawled on the floor after accidentally throwing Max across the room, shattering a mirror in the process. What started as fun soon changed into something different as Max kept taunting her. She lost her cool and shrieked in anger. The next thing she knew, Max was flying across the room and into the mirror, collapsing with a painful grunt.

Lilith cast a nervous glance at Mia's father which didn't go unnoticed by her. Max soon recovered from the injury. They had decided to stop the training for the day talk.

Mia listened when Lilith told her about the history of witch covens and the basics of witch powers. Her dad supplied details of their cold war that almost wiped the race from this earth, earning a glare from Lilith.

When Mia hesitantly conveyed the details of her dream to them, Lilith's eyes widened like saucers but she stayed quiet. She paced the gym floor for a while before picking up the knife used for target practice. The sound of the knives hitting their target was the only noise they heard for the next few minutes as they sat in an uncomfortable silence.

Her dad opened and closed his mouth several times as if he wanted to say something but kept quiet. Juan and Matthew's expressions matched Mia's as they sat and waited for Lilith to break the silence which was getting unbearable with every passing second.

"You're a mystery to us, Mia. Your body is still processing powers, and we don't know what is happening. We don't have any idea about the kind of powers you possess. I suggest keeping an open mind. Welcome the change and don't fight it," Lilith said, throwing a knife. It spun and sunk deep into the center of the target mark.

Mia glanced at her brothers-in-law, who just shrugged in response.

"You have had dreams which have come true; I mean at least parts of them. I think you have the power of vision. If you have any visions of the future, listen carefully and look at your surroundings. It will help us to decipher the vision," she said.

"Power of vision?" Her father voiced the question repeated in Mia's mind.

"I told you about Felipe's powers. It's possible," Lilith shrugged.

"Okay." Mia nodded and caressed her hungry stomach. Her hunger had increased considerably. She ate twice as much as the men that morning. She knew this wasn't normal, but Aaron had brushed it off saying it was her body adjusting to the new changes.

"I'm going to eat," Mia announced.

"Alright. Well, there is not much you can do for today, anyway. Let's meet tomorrow at the same time," her father responded with a smile that didn't reach his eyes.

Lilith just nodded, still throwing the knife. Mia thought it odd, but shrugged it off as she exited the gym with Juan, Matthew, and Max.

***

"Her body is preparing for something big," Lilith stated when Mia was out of earshot.

"I can see that. The burst of energy she exerted while throwing Max was not normal. The power exceeded the scale of a normal witch. Hell, it was equal to my powers!" Ted ran a hand through his hair.

"What do we do? How are we supposed to tell Aaron?"

"Maybe we should just speak to the former king and see what he thinks about this situation?" he suggested. "He might provide us with some insight. King Jerome is a knowledgeable man."

"I agree. In this state, Mia is a danger to everyone around her. She should never lose control. It would help to find out her real parentage."

"I tried that a few years ago, and there was nothing I could find."

"What are we supposed to do? My power of vision is very limited. I can only see things that have happened in the past through their memory. I wish I could see like my sister; she could see the past, present, and future."

Her power of vision? His eyes narrowed.

"Where is your sister now?"

"We haven't met in a long time. I don't even know if she's alive."

"What are you not telling me, Lilith?" he asked. "The witches with the power of vision are rare. If I'm right, there was only one alive, and she was rumored to have died in an attack."

Lilith swallowed. "That's not entirely true. The witches in Cascade Coven have the power of vision, too. We just knew to hide it well from the others."

Ted didn't buy her story. The witches in the Cascade Coven were no better than the guardians—the light witches who never used magic to harm others. *Except for her.*

He could tell she wasn't being truthful. Her eyes blinked rapidly, and she wiped her sweaty palms on her dress without meeting his gaze. For a witch who carried fire in her eyes and words, she now appeared small and vulnerable, like a kid with the worst nightmare.

"I don't need supernatural senses to tell you're lying," he said. "I know there is something strange about you. Just remember you're not only risking yourself but also my daughter. I won't be a patient man if anything happened to her."

He meant every word and he said this while staring into her eyes. He didn't care if she was stronger than him. No one risked his daughter's safety. A part of him wanted to shake the truth out of the witch, but he refrained since she was close to the royals. He didn't want this to create any problems for Mia.

Lilith's eyes widened, and she quickly exited the gym. She knew. He could tell. It was written in her eyes. Lilith knew exactly what his daughter was. *I'll find out what you're hiding soon, witch.*

CHAPTER 36

Mia paced her room, feeling restless. Aaron visited her shortly before leaving for an urgent meeting all the way across the country to meet with fellow lycan clans. She should have told him she wasn't well when he asked her. He'd felt her skin and his face frowned with worry when her temperature was hotter than usual.

She reassured him she was fine. She even smiled wider, saying it was nerves because he was leaving her for the first time after their mating.

While she shouldn't have lied to him, he had important matters to attend to. As a king and the alpha, his pack duties came first. She didn't want to set a bad example.

The weather grew worse by the day. The snow covered everything in the vicinity. Losing interest in the serene sight from her balcony, Mia wondered what would happen now that the fellow lycan clans had raised alarms. Word had apparently spread that the Randolph's had provided asylum for an unknown vampire.

Her mate had a heated argument over the phone and went to meet the others in person to settle the misunderstanding. The pack had been under strict orders to keep this confidential; how the other clans got wind of Mia was a mystery.

Aaron traveling in person meant that they would know about his mating sooner than the Randolph pack in Brookedge. They couldn't risk a rift between the clans. Not now when everything worked in their favor.

Max had accompanied Aaron. He was the best negotiator.

She touched her swollen lips with a sigh. The chaste kiss Aaron had given her had turned out to be a mini make-out session. He had to tear himself away from her with great difficulty. Her tongue darted out, wetting her lips where Aaron's taste still lingered. She already missed him and didn't know if she could sleep well without him.

Juan and Matthew were having a movie marathon while she sulked in the background. Her dad and Lilith were once again at the lab, doing God knows what. Other than her mating, she could tell her father wasn't pleased with how things had turned out.

Around lunchtime, Mia felt it again—a gnawing in her gut. It was as if something was clawing at her to come out. She suddenly felt thirsty. Too impatient to drink from the pitcher in her room, she ran to the bathroom and turned on the sink, gulping the cold water furiously. No matter how much water she drank, her thirst only increased. Water sizzled from where it touched her skin.

"Mia, are you alright?"

Mia was drenched in sweat and was lapping at the water greedily when Juan came in. She whipped around to see him. Her eyes, shifting between pure white and pitch black as if they couldn't decide which color they wanted to settle on. Her retina and sclera were merged into one.

Her nostrils flared as a rich scent of blood wafted through her nose. She hadn't fed since morning. After the blood switch incident, she had been drinking only from Aaron. They had stopped the blood transfusions.

Her gums burned as her fangs extended. She could feel a prickly sensation in her hands and toes as her nails turned into claws. Juan backed up a few steps. She watched his every move with a tilted head.

Mia felt an unfamiliar burn course through her veins, and the clothes she wore were suffocating her. She wanted to stop, but she couldn't. It was as if something within her had pushed her consciousness behind, and she was just a silent spectator as she fought the invisible confines.

***

Juan stared at Mia with wide eyes. He sensed something was wrong when she rushed to the bathroom and came in to check on her. Now as she pinned him with her predatory eyes fixed on him, he froze. A vampire with their claws and fangs out was never good. Her crouched position told Juan that she would attack if he moved.

"Uh. . .Matt! I think she's going all vamp again."

Matthew appeared in the doorway not a second later and cursed under his breath.

Something clicked within Mia and she broke out of her trance, shaking her head violently. Her eyes now shifted to their normal blues for a moment before going back to black.

"Leave!" she growled. "Need blood. Don't want to hurt you." Her animalistic voice was so guttural. She plopped down on the wet floor and brought her knees to her chest. She mumbled to herself as she rocked back and forth. The brothers couldn't decipher the incoherent words, except for a few like *blood, can't hurt, don't hurt, control.* Her control was slipping, and her resolve seemed to falter with every passing second.

Juan and Matthew hurried out of the bathroom and locked the door behind them.

"Matt, get the blood bags from the infirmary. I will stay here and watch her," Juan ordered. He quickly called Dr. Anderson, Ted, and Lilith before mind linking with his father. Paul went to their hospital in town to attend an omega, who went into labor that morning. Just when he was done, the bathroom door was kicked open. Splinters of wood flew across the room.

Juan gasped. Mia didn't look like herself. He had never seen a vampire with fangs that large or claws that sharp. Her claws looked like that of a lycan.

Lycan blood, he cursed under his breath as he stood rooted to the floor. He couldn't hurt her, no matter what she did to him.

"Blood. . ." she whispered with a tilted head. "Give me your blood!"

Juan swallowed nervously. Could he let her drink from him? Would it hurt? *She never hurt Aaron but what they had was different.*

Matthew and the others arrived at the scene as Mia stalked Juan to the corner of the room. Juan backed away until he felt the cold wall pressing against his body. He eyed his brother who motioned him to stay still.

"Mia, here is the blood," Matthew shouted and threw a blood bag over to distract her from Juan.

Mia caught the blood bag, drained it under a second, and threw the empty bag on the floor. All the while, she never took her eyes off of Juan. Matthew threw the second bag at her. She caught it and gazed at it with a scowl on her face. "No! *Your* blood," she said, poking Juan's chest with her sharp claw.

Juan cast a nervous glance at his dad, who looked at Ted and Lilith.

"Mia, honey, you can't drink from him," Ted spoke soothingly as he tried to approach her.

Mia whipped around. Her body rose off the floor, floating above the ground. She tilted her head as she regarded them, and her nostrils flared as she inhaled their scent.

"Blood. So rich and tasty. . .I will drink from all of you today." The main door slammed shut and the lock turned in place. The doctor's face paled. She cackled before turning to Juan once again.

"I want you to give me your blood willingly."

Juan's body shook as he fought against her command. He didn't think her command would have such an effect on him.

"Mia, stop it this instant. We're family!" his father bellowed.

Mia's posture faltered for a moment as her eyes shifted to her normal blues. Her body dropped to the floor. "Help!" She wheezed in her soft voice right before they turned pitch black and her body elevated from the ground once again reminding Juan of a possessed woman. She hissed at Jerome, challenging him to make a move. Lilith shook her head at Jerome, who averted his gaze, baring his neck to Mia in submission.

Juan couldn't let her bite his neck—only his mate had that right. He raised his hand and rolled up his sleeve, using his claw he made a small cut and offered his blood to Mia who whipped around at the scent of his alluring blood.

He winced when her fangs pierced through his skin, embedding them into his vein. The initial pain he felt has subsided and a wave of warmth and comfort washed over him. She retracted her fangs when he felt himself getting weaker with the blood loss.

She had almost drained him in under a minute. "Not enough," she growled, but he noticed her eyes shifting to blue for a millisecond. "Can't hurt," she mumbled to herself, pushing him away as she fought for control.

Mia clutched her head as she scrambled away from Juan with a look of horror on her face. They could tell she was fighting her instincts threatening to take over, but she failed once again.

"Blood!" She growled as her eyes regarded the others in the room, choosing her next prey.

Matthew stepped forward and offered his hand to her. Mia looked at him, her eyes momentarily shifting to its normal blue as tears sprung from her eyes. Her fangs pierced his skin not a moment later. It wasn't as painful as he had thought it would be. Juan showed no sign of pain either.

It wasn't how Aaron explained it to them earlier. At the first touch of her bite, Matthew felt a wave of warmth wash over him and almost cried at the comfort it provided. He felt as if he was with his mother once again.

Her fangs retracted, and she pushed him aside when she had taken enough. Mia panted, clutching her chest while her eyes switched colors. "I'm sorry," she sobbed before her control snapped once again.

Her battle with her inner self was evident, but Matthew didn't know what she was fighting against. He thought about the juvenile transformations and guessed Mia was going through something similar. But what she would transform into was something beyond his knowledge.

He moved toward Juan to help him and his body swayed. His father was there to support him. Matthew dropped to the floor beside Juan as Dr. Anderson rushed to them. His fingers trembled as he checked the brothers.

A few feet away Mia clawed at her body, ripping her clothes as she fought the change. Her screams shook the castle walls and mild tremors shook the ground. Blood whooshed from the gashes where she clawed at herself.

Matthew averted his gaze. Pain tugged at his heartstrings. He wished there was a way to help her.

***

Lilith's steps almost faltered as she noticed Mia elevating in the room.

Her powers were blocking anyone from moving toward her. The males had their head bowed and their gaze averted not wanting to see her naked form. Meanwhile, Lilith struggled against the invisible hold, wanting to get to Mia.

Mia let out an inhuman wail and her back arched at an odd angle as her body twirled itself in the air. Lilith noticed ridges forming on Mia's bare back as her skin took on a velvety texture. *She's changing.* Lilith's eyes widened with realization. This was happening faster than she thought.

Her claws extended further and her once pale skin was changing into the darkest shade of blue with every passing second. Her bones extended from her back and Lilith winced at the sound of them cracking and reforming.

Mia screamed as every inch of the bone came out from her back, forming a skeletal frame in the shape of wings. Lilith gasped, looking at the leathery wings

"Look at her," Lilith whispered.

"But she—"

"She's fully covered," Lilith said, cutting off Jerome. In a week moment when Mia's powers faltered allowing Lilith to get close enough, the witch had draped the young queen in a thin white bedsheet.

They all looked up and gasped at seeing the elegant creature that hovered before them.

Mia's skin was now a mixture of black and royal blue with a velvety texture. Her face still held her normal human form, except her eyes which were now pure white. Her hair had royal blue streaks, which contrasted well with her natural pale blonde locks. Behind her, a huge pair of feathery wings flapped, sending a rush of air at the spectators. They had never seen or heard of something like this before.

Lilith gasped. *The rumors were true.* An old text described Felipe as a creature of the night with wings. But, this was the first time she witnessed the true form of a vampire.

"Mia!" Ted cried.

Mia paid no attention to her father as her form continued to float several feet above the ground.

***

"Alpha, many vampires are coming toward the castle. It is as if they were walking in a trance," John's voice infiltrated Jerome's mind with an urgency.

"Let my children come to me." Mia's calm yet dangerous voice floated through all of their minds.

Everyone looked at her, flabbergasted. *How did she do that?* Only a lycan had the ability to communicate through the telepathic link. Mia's mating with Aaron must have given her the ability to get into their minds.

"What are you?" Jerome whispered, unable to swallow the lump that has formed in his throat.

"I am your queen," she answered in a calm tone as the others gawked at her with their jaws open.

John kept sending updates on the happenings outside the castle. The pack members carrying out their daily chores could hear the screams and the tremors. They had been scared of them.

Inside the dungeons, the vampires who had been caught trespassing rattled in their cage, wanting to be free.

While Jerome and the others contemplated a suitable approach to calm her down, something snapped within Mia and she collapsed to the floor. Her body transformed back into its human form. Ted rushed to her side and hoisted her small frame from the floor to place her gently on the bed.

The vampires outside the castle broke out of their trance, confusion marring their faces. "Take them to our holding cells. But don't harm them," Jerome ordered.

Emilia watched carefully at the happenings with her father. Both knew that Mia was the reason for the events, and Emilia smiled internally.

It appeared as if the vampires hadn't come here on their own; something within the castle had attracted them. She didn't know what it was, but the screams and tremors were proof enough to confirm her suspicions.

Finally, she must have consumed the witch blood. That explained why the doctors ran behind Matthew with multiple blood bags in their hands. Aaron was not in the castle and this was her best chance.

She smiled as the opportunity presented itself.

CHAPTER 37

"Is this not proof enough?" Emilia's taunting voice drifted around the pack members.

"Emilia! Don't," Richard warned. He caught her hand, trying to pull her back.

"Don't what, Father? You want me to hide the truth from them?" she asked, her voice dripping with venom.

"What truth?" A delta moved forward.

"The truth the royals don't want us to find," she said. She'd been stripped of her rank. Nothing mattered to her anymore. "That bitch is behind this. We were happy and content with the way our lives were. But she came in and suddenly. . .BAM! The vampires attack and abduct our members. Now she's summoning the vampires into our territory."

"We don't understand," one of the omegas said.

"She's planning this!" Emilia hissed. "She's putting up an innocent act and fooling you all. Why doesn't anyone see this?"

"Alpha won't hesitate to end her life if she so much as harms any one of us," the same omega replied.

Emilia chuckled without humor. "Keep saying that. One day the alpha is going to say she's your queen. It'll be too late then."

"It's time he chooses a queen. I don't see why he can't choose her if she's what his beast wants." A delta shrugged.

Fury licked Emilia's veins. *Fools!* "You're forgetting one thing. *She. Is. A. Vampire!*"

"A vampire who fought Felipe's men when they attacked us." Another delta stepped forward. "We all know who she is. Didn't the alpha met us head-on in the challenge?"

"That was an unfair fight. You all know this. Now we have a serious problem here. It could be her plan to make you all believe differently. They still took five omegas, didn't they?" Emilia watched in satisfaction when the pack fell silent. "She's clever. She staged the attack and fought them to gain your trust. This is all her fault!"

"That's enough, Emilia. You've spoken too much." Richard caught her elbow and dragged her. "Disperse and carry on with your duties," he yelled to the others. "You'll forget this conversation and move on like it never happened."

"Dad!"

"Quiet!"

She struggled in his hold as he took her inside the castle and into his quarters. Her mother came running toward them with a worried look when he pushed her in. "What happened?"

"Your daughter cannot keep her mouth shut. That's what happened." His furious gaze pinned her to the place she stood. She'd never seen him this angry. "I told you several times to stay out of royal matters. I'll warn you again. If you want your head attached to those shoulders you like to flaunt, then stop it right now."

"I stated the truth."

"I don't care what you stated. Don't speak about it again."

"Mom. . ."

"Listen to your dad, honey. We thought we were clear when we said we wanted you to stay away. The alpha isn't known for his patience, yet he let you walk away the last time."

"He stripped me of my rank."

"And you deserved it!" Emilia flinched at her father's growl. It was as if she was a pup again. "I warned you, Emilia. I told you it's none of your business."

"It's in every—"

"Claudia, speak some sense through her thick skull if you want your daughter to outlive us." Richard cut her off and stormed out of the room while she stood gawking at the door he banged shut.

***

When Aaron landed in Vertrock, he got the call from Juan. His shock upon hearing the incident almost made him turn around.

A string of curses left his mouth. He was the one to blame. He should have stayed behind with her when he felt her discomfort. Mia had told him she was fine and forced him to leave. The urgency of the meeting didn't give him an option to postpone it either.

The upcoming alliance was very important. He was negotiating to unite the clans once again. The young generation was more than willing to fight against the vile vampire army to put an end to Felipe once and for all.

"We should get going, Bro," Max chirped beside him.

Aaron clenched and unclenched his fists as he stood outside his private jet. *I can just turn around and fly back.* The meeting had to be postponed.

Max seemed to sense the change in him. "I understand that you want to go back to your mate, but I can't do this alone, Alpha. The royals won't listen to a gamma's reasoning. Stay for one hour. We meet them. Explain what happened and then we leave."

Aaron took a deep breath and looked at their private jet once more. Max was right. The elders—his grandfather's brothers and royal betas—wouldn't listen to him. "Okay, one hour."

The short drive to the grand mansion was tense with Aaron's beast raging inside. He wanted to get back to his mate as soon as possible. Although he understood that the pack came first, he couldn't help it. Vertrock was a beautiful place with mountain valleys and a lake that stretched for miles. However, he couldn't concentrate on the greenery that they passed.

Soon, the mansion came into view. Although not huge like the Randolph castle, it stood in its own glory with white painted walls and high ceilings. An elderly butler greeted them at the entrance and led them to a large meeting room. Aaron was surprised to see the leaders of the other two clans present there.

"Cousin, it's a pleasure," Blake Clayton Randolph, his cousin and the leader of Mark's clan, greeted him with a huge smile. Aaron returned the greeting with a smile of his own. The men shared a simple hug with a pat on their backs as they always did.

"Thanks for coming on such a short notice. I thought it would be helpful if the other clans were here as well," Blake said. He sniffed the air and his eyes narrowed, but Blake made no comment as he led Aaron to the chair.

"Hello, cousin." Aaron's other cousins, Dawson Elliot Randolph and Arthur Edmund Randolph, greeted him next with a hug. They now led the Raymond and Christopher clans, respectively. The clans were named after their grandfathers Mark, Raymond, and Christopher.

"Congratulations on the mating." Arthur winked before going to his seat.

"Nice to meet you all in person," Aaron said. "I wasn't expecting everyone."

"Long story short. Their packs were attacked last night. So, we moved them to Vertrock," Blake said.

Aaron nodded in understanding. Arthur and Dawson's clans were smaller in size and had very few deltas. They wouldn't be able to hold together against the vampires.

"Our fathers will be joining us shortly. You've already met Uncle Cayne and Uncle Holden last year," Blake said. Uncle Cayne was the son of Raymond; whereas, Uncle Holden was the son of Christopher.

The room silenced when Cayne and Holden entered. Aaron could feel the authority radiating from their beasts.

"Aaron, it's nice to see you. How is my brother, Jerome?" Cayne greeted him with a bear hug. His eyes crinkled with laughter.

"Likewise. Father is fine," Aaron replied with a full-blown smile. Cayne, though he looked tough on the outside, was an easy man to speak with. He was also the first person to push his son to negotiate an allegiance.

"Aaron," Holden said in a clipped tone and gave him a curt nod.

He didn't feel offended as he knew that was how Uncle Holden was—always serious. He couldn't blame him. Holden, like Uncle Andrew, had lost his mother in the war. A reason that caused the pack to split into three.

"Where is Uncle Andrew?" Aaron asked, noticing his grumpiest uncle missing from the group.

"Here," answered a stern voice. Uncle Andrew looked so similar to Aaron's father. They had similar dark brown hair with matching eyes, only he didn't smile as often.

"Good to see you, boy! I'm not sure if I want to congratulate you, considering that the mark doesn't belong to one of us," he said, his nose scrunching in disgust.

Aaron nodded. His beast raged within, but he took a deep breath. He could not lose his control now. This meeting was not only important for him, but also for the pack. Their future depended on it.

"That is one of the reasons of why I'm here today," he replied. The expressions on the faces of the elders were not pleasant at the mention of his mating, while the younger ones gave him curious glances. He could tell they were all waiting for their chance to speak.

"I'm intrigued." Blake leaned forward on his elbows. "Cousin, you know well how our beasts are. She's our mortal enemy, yet she managed to tame your beast. She must be special."

His comment earned a displeased growl from Holden and Andrew. Cayne, on the other hand, shook his head with a small smile.

"Yes, she's special." His smile was warm. Mia's name had that effect on him. Her name was enough to pour ice-cold water on his red-hot fury.

"When we got wind of the news about a vampire taking asylum in your territory, we weren't expecting *this*," Blake said with humor.

"How did you know of it to begin with?"

"An anonymous phone call from a male," Arthur replied. "We all received it."

A phone call? It must have happened before he ordered them to keep it confidential. Still, it was treason.

"What's her name?" Dawson asked with an enthusiastic tone while Holden grumbled under his breath. Aaron heard the word leech, but he let it slide.

"Mia," he replied, and Dawson's grin widened. He reminded him of his brother Matthew. They were similar in so many aspects.

"She must be a beauty to have you wrapped around her finger. I can tell by your goofy grin," Arthur's hazel eyes twinkled when he laughed.

Aaron smiled with ease. His cousins were easy to be around. They thought alike and often admitted their admiration for him, expressing their desire to unite their packs like old times.

Unknown their fathers, the cousins had met often since they turned sixteen. They had often sneaked out for camping trips and vacationed on islands disguised as a study trip. Though Jerome found out about the trips, he never once stopped them. The last time Aaron went, his father let him use the private jet and sent his most trusted guards for their protection.

Aaron had no doubt his cousins would respect his choice of mate. They didn't fuss about her being a vampire, unlike their fathers.

"I came here since I believe the matter at hand should be discussed face-to-face rather than over a phone. Mia, as you're already aware, is a vampire," Aaron began. He was secretly relieved that his grandfathers were not there. They weren't known for their patience and he was in no mood to put up with their bitterness.

His cousins nodded and looked at him expectantly while the elders watched with passive expressions. He knew they were just waiting for him to finish. Anger and disagreement clouded their expressions. They would try to make their sons back away from the alliance. This time he wouldn't let that happen.

The pack had been without an alpha for so long. Sure, they were capable of leading it, but it would only grow harder with time. The beasts and wolves wouldn't accept a beta in the place of an alpha. Being an alpha was not just a position. It was a responsibility. Only the alphas could control the wolves.

Just when he was about to speak again, the door burst open and two female lycans sauntered into the room. Their heads held high as they took confident strides toward them.

"We're not sorry to disturb. You should have invited us," one told Blake before turning to examine their guest.

"You must be our elder cousin, Aaron. I'm Leila and this is my younger sister Malaika," she introduced. Her brown gaze radiated mischief. Leila was the queen of pranks.

"Hello." Aaron smiled, shaking their hands. Blake never let them join their trips or attend the winter ball. He had seen them only in photos and spoken with them a few times over the phone.

"Oh, Maricella will be here any—" she was cut off as the door opened. A young female lycan entered with a bright smile. Her silver eyes beamed when they landed on him.

"Aaron!" she squealed, and engulfed him in a bone-crushing hug, causing him to laugh. For a young lycan, she had amazing strength. He'd met her once when she snuck up to one of their camping trips. Dawson had been furious that day because she outsmarted him.

Aaron rolled his eyes when she sniffed him with a frown. "Sorry, but that scent is so familiar. Except, it's kind of mixed with the scent of a vampire," she said, scrunching her nose. Her brows creased, and he smoothed her cute frown with his fingers before pushing her toward an empty chair.

"That's because he's mated with a vampire," Leila rolled her eyes and crossed her legs.

Maricella shook her head and her nostrils flared again. "No. It's different. I—"

"Enough with the pleasantries," Holden said, cutting them off. "I would like to get on with this meeting."

Aaron sighed as his cousins hurriedly took the seat beside their brothers. It wasn't like he wanted to drag this thing on. The sooner he left the better.

"I can't believe he's mated to that thing. He has paved the way for our downfall, and I don't quite understand why we are even here discussing this," Andrew growled, his eyes blazing with anger.

"I have a very good reason behind my mating to her, Uncle Andrew. Mia isn't what you think she is."

"Mia!" Maricella exclaimed. Her enthusiasm was met with many glares she ignored. "You mean Mia as in Mia Lawrence? The girl with curly blonde hair and big blue eyes?"

"That's her," Aaron answered with a puzzled look. *How did she know Mia?*

"Oh, my god! She's a vampire now? Was she bitten?" Her eyes were wide, disbelief crossed her features.

"She was not bitten. How do you know her?" Aaron asked. A deep frown pulled the corners of his lips down.

"We went to the same boarding school. She was my junior—"

"Enough!" Holden silenced her. "What valid reason do you have, Aaron?" he asked and narrowed his eyes that were viewed as a challenge by Aaron's beast.

Max tapped on his hand. "Alpha, may I?" the gamma asked as if reading his mind.

The lycan king nodded without breaking his eye contact with Holden. His uncle's shoulders shook under the intensity of his glare but he held on. Though they had separate packs to lead, it didn't make them an alpha. The beast itched to be let out of its cocoon so that it could teach them a lesson. Aaron pulled on the mental leash and locked his jaw. Holden was family and he needed to tread carefully.

"Mia, our queen, is a pureblood." Max stood. He let the information sink in. "She was adopted by a warlock when she was a child, and when her scent started changing, he had transferred her to our territory to protect her from the vampires. When our royal betas discovered her they took her into custody. During her stay in the castle, she had saved our pack omegas. She killed eight vampires in a fight, hence proving her loyalty to the lycans."

"And it seems the loyalty is rewarded with a crown," Holden snickered. "That still doesn't explain why it was necessary to mate with her. You could've used her as an ally if she's an asset."

Holden had a point.

"If you had thought this through, you would have already known the answer to this, Beta Holden."

Aaron smirked at Max's use of the term beta, reminding Holden of his place. His uncle growled in defiance.

"Queen Mia is the only female born vampire. That makes her a potential mate for our nemesis. Alpha Jerome did not want her to be with Felipe. So, he thought if his son could seduce her and mate with her, she would never fall into the hands of the vampire king. Their mating would seal their fate for eternity."

Andrew and Holden shared a look, their brows knitted.

"This is war," Aaron repeated the words of his father. "I have to do what it takes to secure my pack. There is no place for right or wrong when millions of innocent lives are at stake."

CHAPTER 38

Aaron reclined in his chair and waited for his uncle to respond. While what he said wasn't entirely true, he didn't lie either. That was his father's initial plan. But their mutual attraction had rendered the plan useless, and there hadn't been a need for seduction. Others didn't have to know that.

Andrew took a deep breath and Aaron could see the conflict in his face. "How sure are you about this? What certainty do you have that she won't run to Felipe if given a chance?"

The question stirred Aaron's fury, but he locked his jaw as last night's events popped into his mind. Andrew spoke the truth. Mia was attracted to Felipe and she couldn't help it. Her instincts drove her straight to the vampire king.

"I trust her," was all he could say. "She's kind and compassionate." Her cries when she found she had killed the vampires still echoed in his ears. "She still holds onto her humanity, and I believe that won't change."

Andrew shook his head, his fingers tapping on the desk. "You're risking everything, Aaron. Vampires are dangerous creatures. From what you said, I'm guessing she's still young and hasn't grown stronger yet. What if she lost control or she reaches her prime?" He shook his head again as if he saw no point with this mating. "We don't know how compatible she is with a lycan. You're a king. You need an heir to the throne."

Aaron's jaws clenched. "We have a war to fight before we start talking about an heir," he reminded them. "If it comes to that, Juan will step up as the king."

His cousins nodded. Blake sat upright. "You have a mole inside your pack," he said cutting off Holden who opened his mouth to say something. "We got an anonymous call again yesterday. The caller said Brookedge now had a vampire queen. That was why I insisted on meeting you in person."

Zach was in custody. Who was that caller? No one except those in his close circle knew of their mating. He needed to investigate this further. "Thank you for telling me this. Also, I owe you for your timely help in retrieving Max and Lilith."

"No need for formalities. I did what you'd have done for me if I were in need." Blake shrugged. "Now that that's settled, I would like to pledge our allegiance to you. In fact, it's time we united our packs again."

"That's great news," Aaron said, beaming.

"I didn't agree to this," Andrew growled and Holden agreed.

"It is for the best for our packs, Father. Felipe is targeting us, and we won't be able to keep up for long. Aaron is right—we need to unite and fight against him." Blake reasoned as the younger generation, including the women, nodded in agreement.

"Your grandmother is dead because of the war!" Andrew bellowed.

"Aunt Esmeralda is dead because we didn't end Felipe in that war. If we had fought together all those years ago, we would have gotten rid of him for good." Blake jumped to his feet.

"Uncle Andrew, if Mia is a pureblood, then having her on our side is an advantage," Dawson added. "Besides, we don't have the numbers to fight Felipe. We barely made it out last night. They left the best of our warriors injured."

"I agree with Dawson and Blake," Arthur spoke. "We can't hold them on our own if they attack again. We fight ten bloodsuckers and twenty of them show up the next time."

"Your plans to join the packs will ruin them!" Andrew stood, growling at his son. "This is insane."

Blake's features hardened. "A pack without an alpha is no pack at all. We need Aaron. I need him. The beasts and wolves are growing anxious without a connection to their true alpha." He ran a hand through his hair. "The juveniles are having a hard time during their shift because they need him to help them through the transition, and you're punishing them by denying access to their alpha. This is torture. We belong together."

Andrew's hands fisted at his sides.

"Aren't you feeling it, Dad?" Blake asked. "That gnawing in your gut. They're calm when he's near. Do you feel how calm our beasts are now?" Blake's gaze bore into Andrew's. "It's like we are once again children in our mother's lap." Blake took a deep breath and sat in his chair. "Ignore it all you want, Dad. But I'm uniting the pack."

Andrew grumbled under his breath and abruptly left the room followed by Holden.

It was true. Lycanthropes were social creatures. They needed an alpha. It was their stubbornness that allowed them to stay apart for this long.

"I appreciate the initiative," said Uncle Cayne, who had remained silent all this time. "Do what you must. They'll come around." He winked at the youngsters before following the others out.

Blake turned to face him. "We are family, and it's high time we act like one. It will take some time before we move our entire pack to Faircrest, but we can work it out eventually."

"Sure." Aaron was pleased with how the meeting was turning out. But he had to be somewhere else. "If there's nothing that requires my attention here, I would like to return to my mate." He stood.

"You're leaving already? Can I come with you please? I want to see her," Maricella asked, practically bouncing up and down in her chair.

"Ah, sure. If that's okay with your brother." He looked at his cousins who were in deep conversation among themselves.

"Nah, he wouldn't mind."

"Actually, we all would like to come. Our fathers and grandfathers can manage the packs in our absence," Dawson said. "We can also arrange for the pack migration while we are there."

"You're most welcome to come."

"Excellent!" Max clapped his hands. "I'll go and see that it's all arranged."

Aaron had not expected this. However, it could only work for the best. But it also meant their travel would be slightly delayed.

***

Emilia smirked as she watched the pack members rally toward their king, wanting an explanation for the incidents that had occurred. She hoped her human acquaintance had done the job. Aaron would have no option but to kick the vampire out when the other clans put enough pressure on him.

Soon, I will have you out of this castle, leech. Or better, I will have them lock you up in the dungeons so that I can torture you as much as I want.

"As I said before, your king is away on a business trip. We will discuss this matter again in his presence. Mia is not a threat, and there are certain things only your king can explain. All I ask from you is to believe your alpha. My sons would not hesitate to lay their lives down if it meant the safety of the pack," Jerome announced.

The omegas nodded in agreement as they whispered amongst themselves. The warriors bowed without another word and dispersed while Emilia fumed.

Aaron wasn't in the castle and the small incident with the vampire was her only chance to ruin Mia's rising fame. She made the pack demand the king for answers, but the former king was clever enough to shut the pack's mouth with his words.

She would have to plan something else before Aaron got back. She had to provoke the pack.

Something. . .

Anything. . .

Emilia silently crept away from the meeting and went back to Zach's room. He had not yet returned, and when she confronted John, he told her that he was sent with the search party that was looking for the missing omegas.

That meant Zach wouldn't be here to do her bidding, and the other warriors wouldn't be of any help. She was no longer the beta female she used to be. Emilia fumed when she thought how her life had changed over such a small mistake.

Her anger was directed toward the bloodsucker. That was the reason for everything. She'd lost her respect and the hard-earned place within the pack because of her. Emilia couldn't brush off the smug look on the faces of the omegas when they ordered her to do things. She massaged her temples and choked on a sob that was filled with frustration and anger.

Emilia blamed herself for being in the position she was in now. What was she even thinking, attacking a lower ranked pack member like that? She could tell Aaron used that chance to get rid of her. Her fingers tapped on her arm restlessly as her mind sifted through different ideas.

"Ugh! For fuck's sake. . .Give me something!"

She paced the room. Fury bubbled within her marrow. Her gaze darted everywhere in the room as her mind reeled. Emilia threw a perfume bottle at the mirror with a growl, breaking it.

"I see you could use my help."

Emilia whipped around, pinning her hard stare at the stranger. Her lips curled up to reveal her fangs. "Who are you?"

"A friend." The hooded stranger crossed his arms.

Her nostrils flared. *Friend my ass.* His thick voice was far from friendly. And she didn't know him. The lack of scent unsettled her nerves and she suppressed a growl. He must have have been watching her for a while if he knew what she wanted.

"Reveal yourself."

The stranger removed his hood and she was taken aback by his attractive features. He had cat-like eyes that gave him an exotic look with his dark hair and dark complexion.

"How did you mask your scent?"

"Anything is possible for a warlock." The stranger shrugged. "Enough about me." He widened his stance, tying his hands behind his back. "I know you need help to dispose of the leech."

Her brows shot up in surprise. "How can you help?" Her cunning mind worked ahead of her logical side of the brain.

"I can do so many things to help. For one, you can mix this concoction in the drinks the lycans consume."

"What does it do?"

"They'll lose control and run like the wild beasts they are."

Her eyes narrowed at him. "And, how's that's supposed to help me?"

"It'll provide me with the distraction I need to abduct your queen."

"*My* queen?" Her growl was vicious. "She's no queen." She was on him in an instant, claws digging into his neck. He didn't flinch. A smile stretched his lips as he removed her hand from his neck.

"Looks like you don't know that juicy part." He chuckled. "Your precious alpha is now mated to the leech you despise so much."

"No way. We'd have known if he did."

"Did you ever think about why he hasn't been around lately?" His question churned her belly. "We both have the same goal in mind, Emilia. Why don't you help me, so I can help you in return?"

"What do you get from this?" Emilia grew suspicious of this stranger's intentions. She tilted her head, staring into his eyes, searching.

"I have my reasons. Let's say, I have unfinished business with my old pal Ted Lawrence."

Emilia nodded after a moment of contemplation. "As long as you take her away, I don't care." Disappointment flooded her while she thought about how she wouldn't be able to kill her the way she wanted. But she had to take this chance. If they were mated as this warlock claimed, then she had no time left.

"Give it to me." She extended her hand, and he placed the small bottle in her palm.

"Good luck."

Emilia smirked at him with a nod and eyed the whiskey-colored liquid. The task was simple. Mia won't be here after this night. A wicked smile stretched her lips, and she looked up to see the stranger was gone. With a shake of her head, she exited her room with a determined look on her face.

CHAPTER 39

Shame filled Mia when she thought about her actions earlier. No matter how many times she apologized to Juan and Matthew, she couldn't shake off the guilt that gnawed at her gut. The dark thing that took control and made her do those things had silenced. She cursed herself and blamed it for losing control.

First, out of the blue, she killed the vampires—and she didn't even remember doing it. Just when she thought she was in control, she snapped again and fed on her brothers-in-law.

She could've accidentally hurt them or killed them. That thought was horrifying. Her body shuddered involuntarily. It was possible that they wouldn't have fought her even if they could. She felt all too powerful when it had happened, her body felt light. There were not enough words to describe how she felt. And, that scared her.

She felt superior and mighty, and she had seen them as creatures below her. She had wanted them to bow before her. She couldn't stay here anymore—the longer she stayed, the more dangerous she was to them.

Jerome had tightened the security around the castle and royal wing. It was impossible to escape their watchful eyes. Where would she go? What would happen if Felipe found her? How can she live without Aaron?

She rolled around in the bed for the umpteenth time. The sun had set, enveloping the room in darkness. Her thoughts wandered. Aaron mentioned something about a prison they had in the castle, a few stories beneath the ground where no sun or moon could reach. Maybe she could request them to lock her down there. That should do it. She must be confined before she hurt someone else.

A fresh set of tears leaked from her eyes, wetting her already damp cheeks. She felt like a coward for staying in her room, but she had no other option. How long before she hurt someone again? Who was she to take a life? Would she be able to live with the guilt if she did hurt Aaron's family? They might not agree to it, but it must be done. That was the last thought before her eyes drooped.

A deafening roar woke Mia up from her deep slumber. She didn't know how or when she fell asleep.

Her eyes blinked rapidly to clear the sleep. Her fangs and claws elongated as her instincts were on high alert. The door to her room swung open and her brothers-in-law rushed in. Light flooded the interior, its brightness almost blinding her.

"Mia, are you okay?" Juan asked, giving her a quick once-over.

She only nodded as the remnants of sleep still clung to her brain. But her instincts screamed to jump off the bed and fight.

"Okay. Stay here until I come back. Matt will stay with you," Juan said quickly before nodding curtly toward his brother and exiting the room.

Mia swayed a little, sleep tugging at her. She patted the empty side of the bed and snuggled further into the comfort of the mattress. Matthew sat on the other side and stretched out his legs as she once again drifted off.

***

Juan was sleeping in Mia's old room with his brother, when they heard the commotion outside. The warriors howled for help, before the brothers had hurried to Mia's room to see if she was there. Once he was sure she would stay in the room, Juan ran to the commotion site.

It was when he reached outside the castle walls that he noticed a few warriors running amok, attacking anyone who tried to catch them.

"They are under the influence of something!" his father yelled from across the field.

"Fuck," Juan cursed as he shifted into his beast form and ran toward the lycans. They weren't responding to alpha commands.

Juan's beast ducked at the last moment, avoiding a hard blow and delivering one that knocked out the same lycan who attacked him. He elbowed the other and kicked it in its gut before punching him square in its jaw. Bones cracked under the impact and the delta howled in pain. Juan counted a total of nine and his dad has subdued three on his own. Juan ran farther, knocking out the lycans to subdue them all.

The sane warriors dragged the unconscious lycans to holding cells, and the omegas eyed at their formal alpha for assurance.

"Alpha, I found Knox unconscious in the dungeons. Paul is attending to him. Also, the prisoners were fed once again," John informed.

A warrior approached the former king, but he silenced the warrior before he opened his mouth.

"Go to the holding cell and stay with your brethren," he ordered.

"Alpha, I-I—" the warrior stammered.

"Not now, warrior. I have urgent matters to attend to," Juan' heard his father say in his alpha voice. The depth and authority in his tone made the warrior shudder.

The old king sighed once the warrior bowed and left. "Son, things are getting out of hand. We can't delay the pack meeting any further. Arrange a meeting as soon as your brother gets here."

"Okay, Dad."

"How's Mia?"

"Asleep."

"Good. Go and get some rest, I'll handle the guards in the infirmary."

"Dad, where are Lilith and Ted?"

"Lilith said she was going to meet someone. She was really worried about this new development. Mia is more powerful than we thought," he said, lowering his voice.

"Yes, she is. She only submits to Aaron."

His father nodded. "That's why we need him here as soon as possible. We should make sure that Mia is not exposed to anyone else until then."

"He should be here any minute now, Dad. It's been almost five hours since he last called."

"Okay. Be sure to brief him once he gets here. Did you make arrangements for our guests?"

"Yes, Dad. All done."

"Okay. See you tomorrow morning then."

"Sure you don't want me for anything?"

"No. I'll handle the rest. Stay close to Mia."

Juan nodded with a sigh and watched his father go in. He knew Emilia had struck again. Stripping her of her rank had set her off. The selfish beast was not known to give up that easily. The punishment wasn't enough. It was time they ended this. He could tell Emilia had grown destructive, and that'd put the lives of the pack at risk. Nothing can save her this time from their wrath.

***

Aaron was perplexed at the latest development. When they reached the castle, he excused himself from his cousins and ran to his chamber, wanting to see Mia.

Matthew was watching TV in his room, and he grinned in relief when he saw Aaron, greeting him with a brief hug. "She has been sleeping for most of the day. We will talk tomorrow."

Aaron stopped Matthew and caught his hand. "Thank you for everything, brother."

"You don't have to thank me. She's family." Matthew smiled with ease.

Aaron nodded and went to lay beside Mia once Matthew left the room. Her face looked so pale and despite drinking blood, she seemed so weak. He frowned and pulled her close to his chest. A sigh of content left her lips and she snuggled into his chest.

Her body felt colder, lacking her usual warmth, and her heartbeat was slower. *Is she sick?*

"Mia."

She hummed but didn't open her eyes.

"Did you feed today?"

When she didn't respond, he raised his wrist to her lips and pressed it against her human teeth. "Drink from me, Mia," he urged.

Mia hummed again but made no move to feed on him. He made a small cut in his wrist using his claw. When the droplets of his blood touched her lips, her nostrils flared and her tongue darted out to lick it off. Her fangs embedded into his vein not a second later.

A comforting warmth spread through his body as she fed on him. She retracted her fangs after a few seconds and licked the skin shut before snuggling close to his side. Aaron only relaxed when he felt her temperature and heartbeat return to their normal rate.

Juan informed him about the pack meeting and the small commotion that happened in his absence through their link. Anger flared from within. He'd put a stop to Emilia tomorrow.

The pack's silence over Mia's issue didn't mean they accepted her with all their heart. He could sense their mixed emotions with her.

This new change in Mia didn't help either. He remembered how Juan described the incident to him—he had said it was beautiful and terrifying at the same time. He didn't want the pack to witness Mia's new form, at least for now.

They had a long way to go, and the path they chose wouldn't be easy. Mia had to learn to control her bloodlust and the powers. Only they didn't know how long they had before Felipe would come for them.

Aaron refused to believe Felipe was still unaware of his mate. The bastard had to know, and there was no telling what he had planned. Either he'd try to kill her or take her. Their mating only complicated things for them. A sigh slipped past his lips as he adjusted his mate in his arms. He fell asleep holding her as his mind thought about the next morning.

***

Emilia seethed in anger. She'd been doing that a lot lately.

"Useless cowards!"

A majority of the pack sucked up to the royals.

Emilia kicked at the bed. She had risked everything, and it was all in vain. She had knocked out the unsuspecting guard and bribed one of the witches for more blood. Slipping past the security cameras in the infirmary wasn't easy. She had temporarily shut off the power supply, hoping that'd disable the cameras, and fortunately, they stopped working.

Emilia didn't know how Mia escaped the witch's blood last time. This time, she added it to the batch that was kept on the lower shelf.

Her next stop was the warriors' hangout place at the far end of the eastern wing. No one suspected a thing when she slipped inside. She was a frequent visitor before being stripped of her rank.

When the bartender invited her to serve the drinks, she'd accepted the offer with a victorious grin. Everyone used the opportunity to order her around, and that worked in her favor this time. She mixed the concoction with their drinks, and when chaos erupted, she fed lies to the frightened omegas.

When a warrior went to the former king demanding answers, the old bat seemed to sense this and stopped the warrior from talking. He used his alpha command and the warrior went back to the castle like the good little puppy he was. The warlock bastard who promised to abduct Mia while using the chaos as a distraction, failed.

Emilia knew Mia was unharmed. One of the alpha-born was always close to her, watching her like a hawk. She paced the floor. Her chest heaved and she suppressed the urge to roar.

She had been patient for so long, and tomorrow, she would be caught. She knew it. The guard she took down knew it had been her. The drug she injected him with would keep him unconscious for ten hours, and when he woke up, he would tell the king she was behind everything.

I should have killed him instead of sedating him. But her beast wouldn't have allowed it. Her beast side could understand her hatred toward their mortal enemy, but it wouldn't allow her to hurt one of their brethren.

Emilia went to the infirmary, only to retreat to Zach's room when she saw the former king there. He sat guarding the unconscious lycan. There was nothing she could do before he woke up. Now that Aaron was back, she couldn't breach the security of the royal wing either.

She knew the moment that the two guards took position outside the room she was in, she was done for. Emilia paced like a caged animal. Too late.

"Fuck!" she screamed and kicked the stone wall. *I won't go down without a fight.*

CHAPTER 40

The cold winter air bit at her face, but it had no effect on raging mind. Mia gripped the railing harder as she stood on the balcony with her eyes cemented on the serene snow.

She had woken up during the ungodly hours of the morning to see Aaron had returned. Her entire being seemed to dance from seeing him. She vaguely remembered him feeding her last night.

Mia wondered if he knew what she had done in his absence. She knew the brothers kept no secrets between them. Would Aaron see her as he did when he learned about her real nature?

Why did it have to be me out of everyone in this world?

She had been content with the normalcy and happiness she had in her human life. Mia hated what she had become. No matter what Aaron or his family said, she couldn't digest that she now needed blood to stay strong. Once she got used to having blood, she couldn't go back to her normal self. The blood thirst killed her from the inside out. She didn't like drinking it from the blood bag, either. She wanted lycan blood because its power was addictive.

A single tear escaped the confines of her eyes and froze on her cheek due to the cold.

Mia thought about her friend Stella. She'd have come back. It was almost time for their graduation. The one she wouldn't go to. Mia had switched off her cell phone to stop the calls from Stella and Peter. She had no answers for them.

She didn't understand the changes she was going through. Lilith wasn't being much help. She could sense her father's discomfort. His visits were short, and he often made excuses.

Her instincts were forcing her change to speed up due to her close proximity to her mortal enemies. Her body recognized them as her enemies while her mind didn't agree. The conflict was out in the open now. She realized the arguments she used to have within her mind wasn't just her own, but others' as well.

Mia felt the presence of three different entities within her. One was herself before she was dragged into this mess, the second was her vampire side that lusted after blood, and the third side—she didn't even know. It was often silent. She could feel it bristling within her often, but other times, it was as if it was sleeping. At times, she wondered if she was losing her mind. She didn't know how to explain this to her mate.

It was nothing like how Aaron explained about the connection he shared with his beast. The thing within her had a mind of its own, and when it took control, her human self loses consciousness only waking up to fragments of memories.

When she tried to explain this to her father, he had frowned. After a deep thought, he told her that she should learn to control both sides for them to coexist. Frustration mounted when she thought how no one had an idea about these changes she was going through. She wished someone had the knowledge to help her out. All they did was compare her changes with things they already knew and make assumptions based on that.

Mia wanted to tell this to her mate. Perhaps, talking would help reduce the stress this caused her. Aaron had been urgently called away by his brothers, and he hadn't returned yet. The wind howled in the distance, and her keen senses picked up the slight change in weather indicating an impending storm.

A sob slipped out of her lips and her shoulders shook. The vampire queen gazed off into the distance as helplessness weighed her down.

***

The kitchen staff buzzed around the huge kitchen, which occupied most of the ground floor. Victoria sashayed amongst the crowd with the grace of an experienced omega with her baby bump.

The alpha and her mate, Thomas, had told her several times to rest, but she just couldn't abandon her duties. To be honest, she trusted no one else to handle the kitchen like her. Her family line had been in charge of the kitchen for generations, and she found peace in the work.

The delicious scent of butter sizzling in the pan had her stomach rumbling. She had weird cravings during this pregnancy. She was glad that lycanthropes burned a lot more calories than normal humans, or else she would have looked like a pregnant cow at this stage of pregnancy.

"You know you're not supposed to stand on your feet for too long," her friend Elise urged her to sit.

Victoria gave a fond smile to her childhood friend before accepting the plate of crispy bacon and juicy sausages swimming in spicy onion gravy. She moaned in approval as the taste invaded her senses. She finished the breakfast in record time and set the empty plate on the table. A contented sigh left her lips as she leaned comfortably on the chair and rubbed her protruding belly.

Faint whispers were getting louder as the maids chatted feverishly with the kitchen staff. Victoria's head snapped toward the maids. She listened to their whispers as they talked. Apparently, one of the maids got a whiff of Aaron while he was going toward his office, and she claimed that their king was mated.

Her brows creased in confusion as she wondered why their alpha would keep important information like that a secret. She pushed the chair aside and rushed toward the maid in a few long strides.

"Is it true?" she growled. Victoria hated gossip and never allowed the staff to spread rumors which had no truth behind them.

"Yes, Victoria. I know for sure. He smelled like the leech that is staying in the royal wing."

This further confused Victoria. The alpha stated his beast had chosen Mia, but the mating was a surprise. Usually the royal couple held a mating ceremony, which was similar to the human weddings before they marked each other in private.

"Quiet, everyone," she ordered. Victoria might be an omega, but years of experience and her caring nature had given her maternal control with the females in the pack. "We do not know if that is the truth. However, even if it was, it is a decision for our king to make."

"But, Victoria. . .she's our mortal enemy," one of the kitchen staff argued.

"Just because she's a vampire doesn't mean that she's our enemy. I agree we all have a scarred past. My parents were killed when I was barely thirteen," Victoria admitted. "But Mia healed my child when he got hurt, and she saved our omegas by killing her own kind. Look, I do not know to what extent we can trust her, but I owe her the benefit of the doubt. What if she had never wanted to be a vampire? Alpha said she was born this way. She didn't choose this."

"I get it that she's different. But, how can we trust her? What guarantee do we have that she won't turn on us? Whether she had a choice or not, there's no changing what she is now."

Her gaze jumped to her friend. "We omegas are known for our intelligence. I suggest that we keep our mouths shut in this matter and trust our king. Alpha Henry sacrificed his life in the war, and Alpha Jerome lost his mate to the vampires. Our alpha must have a good reason for doing this. He doesn't have to explain everything to us."

Silence washed over the small crew of maids.

"I don't think our alphas are foolish enough to provide asylum to a vampire if they thought it would harm us."

"Vicky, providing asylum is one thing, but mating? That's beyond the boundary, don't you think?" Elise reasoned.

"If any of you had qualms with his choice of mating, then you should have entered the challenge ring."

"No one from this pack is strong enough to defeat our alpha. You know that. That was an unfair fight." Elise rolled her eyes.

Victoria shrugged. "You know it's not. Our warriors were given an option to fight in groups. Alpha bend the rules of his ancestors because he knew the other didn't stand a chance. The alpha could've killed them if he wanted. He had every right to do so. The alphas before him never spared their opponents' lives in a challenge."

"But he was supposed to mate Emilia." Elise wasn't giving up.

"His beast never chose her," Victoria spat. What the fuck was wrong with these women? "I've been watching them for years. Besides, I'd rather have Mia as my queen. Emilia is a senseless power-hungry bitch. You all know this. If she became queen, then it would have been our doom. She even turned on one of us," She hissed, and several murmurs of the agreement broke out from the crowd.

Just when Elise was about to speak, the old butler Levi arrived.

"What's the news, Levi?"

"This is the only place where a butler is treated like a puppet. I'm supposed to be in charge of you, Victoria."

"That's because I hold the seniority here."

Levi raised both of his hands in surrender as he chuckled. His pale green eyes crinkled as his sixty-year-old self shook with laughter. "I'm not gonna argue with that again."

Victoria winked with a shrug.   "Anyway, I'm here to inform you that the alphas have arranged a pack meeting in an hour, and everyone is expected in the throne room. Also, you're to prepare a feast for dinner." His tone was all business.

"What is it about, and who are our guests?" She'd learned of their arrival in the morning when she was requested to prepare special breakfast for their guests. She asked no questions then.

"They are Alpha's cousins from the three other lycan clans. Guess it has something to do with an alliance."

"That's great. They haven't visited Brookedge in ages." Victoria beamed.

"Yes, it is great," Levi agreed.

"Did you happen to meet our king?"

Levi shifted uncomfortably on his feet. "I did see the mark on our king's neck. It was a mate's mark."

Victoria frowned before composing herself as she glanced at her fellow omegas, who cast her a look saying, "we told you so." "My perception of things still doesn't change. I will gladly accept Mia as my queen any day, especially over Emilia." Her gaze now fixated on the butler. "Why don't you check in with our guests and find out their favorite dishes?" she asked.

"Yeah, sure." Levi left with a relieved look.

Lycans loved their food. And, she'd make sure their stomachs were full and content while they negotiated the terms with the alpha. It was about time they united the packs. She turned her back, going to the kitchen island and preparing the list of dishes for dinner as the others, one by one, returned to their stations.

***

Aaron paced the floor of the office, tension lacing his features. His brothers had no hard feelings against Mia's actions the day before, and he felt grateful. However, the guilty look on Mia's face tugged at his heartstrings, and he had no time to comfort her as his brothers summoned him for an urgent meeting that morning.

This time, Felipe had attacked the fae again and took approximately twenty as hostages. Another attack on Blake's pack, fortunately, had no casualties. The women and children were already on board of an economic airplane en route to Brookedge. The warriors had killed the parasites, leaving no loose ends.

The former leaders of the other clans were shaken when they came in. Blake's suspicion was right. Aaron spent a solid three hours early this morning sorting out the itinerary and protection for the remaining pack members. He had to plan their travel to different destinations before bringing them to Brookedge by road. Bringing in hundreds of people overnight to Faircrest would warrant the unwanted attention of the local authorities.

Matthew was giving Aaron one of his best poker faces and blamed him for being so careless in the morning. Aaron stumbled into a maid when he left his chamber in a hurry, and Matthew was sure by this time the news about his mating would have spread across the pack.

Blake had suggested they meet the pack sooner, so the news didn't stir any hostile emotions. He also said that they should bring Mia only after they were sure about their pack's reaction. Though Aaron had been open with his intention on mating her, they couldn't have cared less. Blake believed that the news itself was something that would take time for them to take in and seeing Mia would only fuel their anger.

Mia's guilty face kept flashing in Aaron's mind. Even now he could feel her conflicted emotions through their mate bond and the beast urged him to go to their mate. "I'll be on time for the meeting." He walked out. His mate needed him.

CHAPTER 41

Aaron found Mia on the balcony. She was gazing at the snow with a serene smile.

Her sleeveless, white chiffon dress sprinkled with blue stars danced in the cold breeze. She looked like an angel with her long blonde hair that ran past her waistline and ocean blue eyes.

He hugged her from behind and kissed her bare shoulders, earning a sigh from her. She leaned further into his chest with another sigh and they stood there, relaxing in each other's embrace.

"Your hair has gotten longer, and I love the new addition," Aaron said, caressing the blue streaks in her hair, which complemented her eyes.

"It happened yesterday after, you know—" Her gaze averted from him.

Aaron tipped her chin up with his finger as he turned her toward him. "I know, my love. There is nothing to be ashamed of, and you know what, I'm amazed at how well you're taking it all."

"I'm not—"

"No, love. It's not easy to accept what you are and adapting to the changes like you have done so far. I understand that you're scared of hurting us, but I trust you, Mia. Our family trusts you, you won't hurt us." He caught a lonely tear that escaped her eyes, "I'll take these as happy tears. I wouldn't have it otherwise," he said, kissing her soft lips. "I know everything has happened so fast, but I'm connected to you in a way I can never explain, Mia. I need you in my life like I need air to breathe. Just seeing your smile makes me happy. I wish to start every day of life with you beside me and go to sleep every night with you in my arms. Does that make sense?"

Mia nodded as more tears followed the first one. A warm feeling of love washed over him. It was like they had known each other for several years.

"I love you, Aaron," she whispered and pulled him down, kissing his lips. His hands traced her luscious curves as he deepened their embrace.

A few seconds later he broke the kiss abruptly, his eyes now glowing. "I won't be able to stop if we keep this up, and considering that we have a pack meeting in less than an hour, I should get going." This would mark his first appearance in front of the pack after their mating.

"Should I come?"

"Not now. I stumbled into a maid this morning and the news has probably spread like wildfire by now. Stay here, until I come to get you."

Mia nodded.

He kissed her again before muttering an "I love you" and exited the room when someone knocked at the door, announcing it was time.

***

When Aaron entered the throne room, the pack stood in silence and bowed. His tall form commanded authority. His father sat in a throne that was placed a step below Aaron's. His mother's throne was empty.

Juan and Matthew stood on each side of Aaron's throne. His cousins stood near the stairs that led to the throne. They all gave him a curt nod.

A few gasps and low growls erupted from the crowd. The loudest of them all belonged to Emilia and Richard. He could hear a few omega females giggle as they whispered to each other while the omega males just disregarded them. His ears twitched. The whispers died as soon as he sat on his throne, and the pack looked at him with expectant faces. Aaron noticed Victoria standing in the front row with her mate and son, sporting a calm smile.

He kept his legs braced apart and his hands remained loose arms of the throne. The beast within pushed a little beneath the surface, gauging the crowd for their reactions. "It's with great happiness that I announce that our packs are now united. My cousins from Mark, Raymond and Christopher's clans have come here to make the necessary arrangements for pack migration."

The crowd applauded and cheered, welcoming the guests as he continued to introduce them. His cousins grinned widely as they accepted the warm welcome.

"Thank you, cousin." Blake nodded to Aaron and stepped in front. "We thank you all for your hospitality. It is a pleasure to be here," he addressed the crowd.

The cheers and applause died down to silence when Aaron stood. He walked to the edge of the stairs, His stance widened as he pushed his hands deep into his pockets. Their expectant gazes were now fixed on him.

"As you all are aware by now, I'm happy to announce that I now have a mate," Aaron said.

Their reactions were as expected—huge grins, jaws hanging open, furious gazes, growls of displeasure. Nothing new there. He noticed Emilia trying to move forward, pure rage contorting her features. Richard caught her hand, shaking his head mouthing, *not now.*

"The crowning ceremony will be organized in the coming days." His eyes scanned the crowd, expecting someone to oppose. Not that it would make any difference. They had their chance and they failed.

"We will never accept a leech as our queen!" Richard stepped forward and got a chorus of murmurs in agreement from the back. "She may be your mate, but she doesn't deserve the throne.

"I didn't see you at the challenge." The alpha cocked his head to the left side. It was a given that she'd become their queen if he mated her. The beta should know better.

Richard lowered his gaze, hands fisting at his sides.

"You betrayed us by mating that *thing*." Emilia jumped forward. Fury radiated from her in waves.

Her very presence was infuriating. It was times like these that he wished he wasn't their alpha. If he wasn't their king, he wouldn't have to think about how her death by his hands would impact the others. Now he had to think. Richard was a loyal bastard, and the beta jumped in front of claws to save his father's life on many occasions. It was that debt tied his hands from taking her life.

"Betrayal is a strong word, Emilia. Especially, coming from you. It makes me wonder about your actions lately. Care to explain why you attacked the guard who was on duty in the dungeons?" he asked. His voice may be calm, but the intensity of his anger could hardly be contained.

"What nonsense are you talking about? I would never do such a thing."

Aaron nodded to one of the guards, and a moment later, they brought in Knox, the dungeon's head security guard. Emilia paled, and the guard growled low, his lips peeled up to display his fangs in warning.

"Knox, why don't you tell the pack who attacked you last night?"

Knox's gaze flicked toward his alpha and he bowed. "Alpha, I was in charge of the security in the dungeon when I caught her scent. She attacked me when I went to investigate. She injected something into my neck, and I passed out before I could send a distress call."

"Liar!" Emilia let out an animalistic roar. "He is lying."

"It is the truth, Alpha." Knox kept his stance straight, unbothered by her threats.

"You unworthy delta. You dare testify against me?" she lunged forward only to be blocked by the elite guards.

Aaron dismissed the guard with a wave of his wrist. His gaze narrowed at the culprit. "Now that that's been clarified, why don't you tell the pack about tampering with the warriors' drinks, causing them to run amok and attack their own pack mates? Maybe you want to reveal the reason for attacking Paul and switching the human blood bag with witch blood to kill Mia."

The audience gasped. Aaron motioned to one of the guards and Zach entered. Emilia's eyes widened when she noticed the cuffs on his neck, arms, and legs. She took a few involuntary steps back.

Zach looked like hell. He looked tired and starved. The pants he wore the last time he left for work had dried blood and hung loosely on his hips. Aaron shoved the pity aside. The guard deserved it for going against his orders. The mutt should be glad his life was spared.

"You seduced Zach and used him to get into the dungeons, so you could bribe some of the vampires and witches for information. You switched the blood, knowing full well that witch blood is lethal to vampires. You led Mia outside the castle twice. Your only motive was to create chaos, and when that failed, you tried alternate means," he said, pointing a finger at her.

"You have no proof." She straightened her back and faced him with a new-found determination. Her features hardened. Gone was the soft fake politeness she often sported. Her face was now home to malice. It was as if she removed the mask she'd always worn.

"I didn't," he agreed. "I let you off the hook because I had no evidence to prove my claim." He motioned to Juan, who clicked the button on the remote in his hand. A giant white screen dropped from the ceiling on the right-hand side of the room where a video was projected.

It was a clip from the backyard of the castle and the scene from when they played in the snow with Mia. When the video ended, Juan replayed a particular scene in slow motion.

Emilia's eyes widened like saucers when she noticed what it was. It showed how she tripped Louie using her leg and pretended to fall on top of him, her claws extending a bit to scratch his leg enough to draw blood.

"See it for yourself, Emilia. How do you explain your action of attacking an innocent child?"

A smirk lifted from the corners of his lips. His brothers had just installed the cameras in the backyard that morning. Fortunately for them, one of the cameras used at the moment had caught the action that was missed until Juan noticed it recently.

Emilia stood baffled as angry murmurs and low growls erupted from the omegas. All blood drained from her face.

CHAPTER 42

Victoria's expression turned from horror to anger in just under a minute.

"YOU!" She pointed her finger at Emilia. "You tried to kill my son," she yelled and tried to pounce. Louie hid behind his mother, and Thomas held his pregnant mate to keep her from attacking.

"Richard, I warned you the first time. You failed to keep your daughter in check," Aaron said, now addressing his father's beta. Richard hung his head, ashamed of his daughter's actions.

"That doesn't explain why you had to mate with a leech. She's a threat to our community, our mortal enemy. I was protecting my pack. I did the right thing by trying to get rid of her fucking ass," Emilia growled. Her eyes shone with malice.

The lycan king almost lunged with a growl, only to be stopped by his brothers. His eyes blazed with fury as he let out a loud threatening roar. The beast forced a partial shift.

She's baiting you, brother. Juan hissed as Aaron fought for control.

"See, that's what I mean. She has done something to you. You're willing to attack me, your own pack mate, for that leech!" Emilia shouted.

A few acknowledging shouts came from the back.

"Enough!" Victoria yelled. "It is in the nature of a lycan to protect his mate. The actions of our alpha hold no other motive, unlike you."

Emilia growled as Victoria continued.

"Emilia, I accept that you consider Mia a threat. We all did at first. But that still doesn't explain why you tried to harm Dr. Barnes, my son, or Knox!" she accused and crossed her arms over her chest.

Aaron calmed down and his eyes returned to their natural brown. He couldn't express his gratitude toward Victoria in that moment —she had defended his mate.

"You're all trying to find my mistake while forgetting the fact that he's mated to that *thing*. She's a freaking vampire, a leech who sucks blood. You betrayed us, Aaron!" Emilia wasn't giving up. A few angry growls were heard from the deltas. But they didn't make a move.

Aaron was growing tired of the "she's a vampire" conversation. They all knew that.

"What are you looking at me for? Ask him. His pack is supposed to come before his own needs. I get it that bitch seduced his virgin ass, but he could've at least waited until he knew how his pack felt about this. He didn't. He doesn't care for us like he says. That leech just walks out of nowhere and becomes our queen? That's unfair." Emilia continued to yell. "As a beta female, I feel responsible for the pack's safety, and I will fight for it to the very end." She turned toward a warrior. "Kamden, the leeches killed your mother during the war. Judah, did your brother's death during the war mean nothing to you? Reid, I pity your family who was drained for nothing. Jeffrey, the vampires tortured and drained your mate dry in front of your very own eyes. How could you forget that?"

A loud growl erupted from the far end of the throne room and four deltas roared into their shift. Others in the room took a defensive stance, and the males moved in front of the females, guarding them as they moved out of the way.

This was the very thing Aaron feared. The sneaky female had a way with words. She never hesitated to do anything to get her point across. The bitch was now opening old wounds. Her words cut to the core and the pain radiated from the members at the reminder.

Aaron, let the power of his beast surface and his nails extended to long, sharp claws. With Mia's blood in his body, he didn't have the need to shift to fight four fully shifted lycans. Perks of their mating. His beast loved to bite and Mia loved to be bitten while they made love every time. Now, her blood increased his strength tenfold. He stopped the elite guards and gestured them to stay in their positions as he readied himself for impact. His beast growled in anticipation. Just when the lycans were a few feet away from him, a wisp of white blurred past him. The shifted beast that charged at him crashed against the wall and Aaron watched him fall with a painful grunt.

Aaron's beast growled his disapproval when he saw that the white blur was none other than Mia. She stood there, barefoot in her knee-length white dress.

"Didn't your papa teach you well?" She cocked her head to the side. The lycan on the floor eyed her with pure hatred and lunged.

***

Mia had been standing on the balcony. The throne room was only on the floor beneath their chamber, so her supernatural senses easily picked up the conversation happening inside. She hadn't been able to stop herself from going down there when the lycans shifted. She wanted Emilia for herself more than anything.

She moved out of the lycan's way when he swiped his claws at her and appeared behind him. "I wouldn't do that if I were you."

The beast roared again and try to punch her by twisting his body. Mia sidestepped and caught his clawed hand with a smile. So much pain radiated underneath the fury. He appeared more like a wounded animal to her. "I understand your pain, Jeffery. You didn't deserve what was done to you."

Her whisper was met with a growl. Mia didn't flinch. Grief rolled off him in waves. "It isn't me you want to hurt. You want him, the mad king. Think about your son. If you want revenge, think wisely. Don't let the anger cloud your judgment."

He retracted his hand and turned away from her, grumbling and growling. His furry paws fisted at his sides. Droplets of blood from his palms leaked to the floor. The other lycans were subdued by men she'd never met before. The room was silent except for a few sobs here and there as the pack grieved for their fellow mate.

"I promise you, Jeffrey. We will get our revenge, and when we find them, we will make it painful."

"P-promise by bl-blood," his beast stammered trying to hold back the fury.

Her eyes gleamed. "I, Mia Walter Edwards swear on my blood that I will help you find the vampires that killed your mate." She sliced a thin line on her palm and pressed her right hand on the bloody paw of the beast. A glow appeared around their attached hands. He regarded her for a moment longer and bowed his head, placing a hand over his heart.

"M-my q-queen." He bowed.

"Get up, Jeffrey. Apologize to your king."

Jeffrey nodded and proceeded to Aaron, doing as he was told.

Mia was about to walk toward him when Emilia gripped her neck from behind, "Not so fast, you bitch. I challenge you, as you're not fit to be a queen. You're a weak and pathetic vampire who is no match for my claws!" she bellowed. Her claws tightened on Mia's neck with every intention of drawing blood, only it wasn't doing any damage. It barely produced a scratch mark.

"Stand down, Emilia. Let. Her. Go." Aaron's face tightened.

"No, I will not! Everyone here has a painful past because of those blood suckers. They killed our queen. I will not stay back and watch while this bitch takes over the throne. We won't kneel before her; I want her head on a platter," she growled. "Fight me, bitch, or are you too much of a coward?"

Mia didn't move, and her eyes didn't leave Aaron's as she fought to control the monsters in her head. They demanded her to eliminate the threat that instant. Her eyes shifted back and forth as her fangs extended.

"Emilia, stay calm. Our alpha won't betray us," one of the male omegas tried to pacify.

She backhanded him, her other hand loosened its hold on Mia's neck. "Shut up, you filthy omega. You're all pathetic and unworthy. You don't deserve to be in this pack."

Omegas around her gasped and looked offended at the insult. Matthew, who was close to Mia, pulled her out of Emilia's reach before she turned and he backed her toward Aaron.

"Enough! You have lost your mind, Emilia. My mother was an omega. Such behavior will not be tolerated," Aaron bellowed standing tall, flexing his muscles.

His anger washed over her, and it only fueled the rage that bubbled inside her.

"Emilia." Richard caught her hand. "Leave this instant."

She shrugged off his hand. "That is why you should have chosen a strong queen. Queen Esmeralda was weak, she couldn't protect herself. This bitch is no different. They are all pathetic and weak." Venom dripped her from voice.

"Esmeralda was anything but weak," the former king roared.

"You have done enough damage. Go back to the house. Now!" Richard growled low under his breath.

"I can't believe you're doing this! You should support me. The king betrayed us by mating a vampire. She's manipulating everyone. Can't you see that?" Emilia turned to Max. "How could you be so blind? Vampires killed your father. How could you stand guard to this vampire bitch?"

"She didn't have anything to do with my father's death. He died a warrior's death protecting our queen. I am proud of him." Max crouched low ready to fight. "It's you, who is blind."

"What has she done to you? You want to fight me—for her?" She pointed her angry finger at him. "Do you not realize you're no match for me, Gamma."

Mia put her hand on Max's shoulder and squeezed gently. The "I am a beta female" card was pissing her off. This female must realize she was stripped of her rank.

"Aaron, you're a coward. You don't think as a king. If, for once, you hadn't thought with your dick, we would never have this vampire here."

"Enough, Emilia," Mia hissed. A sudden rush of rage engulfed her, anger rolled from her in waves, and the air around them crackled with an invisible energy. The thing inside her was awake now, Mia could feel it. For once, her entire being was in agreement. *No one disrespects my mate in front of me.*

"Then come on and fight me, bitch."

Mia's lips twitched. "If that's what you want, then we'll fight."

CHAPTER 43

Mia didn't let her nervousness show as she gazed at the arrangements. They moved outside of the throne room and to the training arena in the backyard now covered in snow.

The human in her didn't want to hurt Emilia, but the other entities within her wanted blood. They wanted to teach everyone a lesson. To show them what she was capable of. Jerome stopped her on the way out. "Trust your instincts, Mia. You're stronger than anyone here," he said, his eyes sincere.

She nodded as Matthew put his hands around her shoulders. "I've been waiting for this moment all my life. Go and break some bones, will you?" His enthusiasm was infectious, drawing out a smile from her lips.

"Do anything you have to. Wipe that smug expression off her face." Juan flanked her other side.

Aaron hugged her. "You've got this, my love." His hands rubbed her back and his lips placed a lingering kiss on their mark. A wave of warmth rushed through her, consuming her racing heart. Mia took a deep breath and nodded.

A hush fell over the crowd when she walked to meet her opponent. Everyone had moved back, forming a circle, allowing space for her and Emilia to fight. She could almost taste their anticipation in the air. The wolves loved fights.

Mia closed her eyes and focused on the powers pulsing in her veins. The vampire within her licked its lips at the challenge. Excitement and thrill bubbled in her chest. Claws burst free from her hands as if they had a mind of their own, and her gums burned with anticipation.

"Come on, bitch." Emilia glowered, her fangs gleaming. "I will make it slow and painful. I will tear each of your limbs off your body before killing you to show them how weak and pathetic you are." She cocked her head to the left. Snake green eyes now glowed with her beast just beneath the surface.

The dark whispers in Mia's head cackled. *She doesn't know what we could do to her.* Mia realized it was coming from the third entity. *Show her. Show them all. . .* The dark and sinister thoughts widened her eyes before she pulled the leash on them.

Taking a deep breath, she shoved the dark thoughts aside. *I am in control.* She flexed her hands, releasing the breath ever so slowly.

"In your dreams, Emilia," Mia replied in a calm and composed tone, never once taking her eyes off the female lycan. She crossed her hands in front of her chest.

Emilia pounced without warning—claws and fangs flashing.

Mia stood rooted to the ground as the furious female came at her. Razor sharp claws aimed for her throat. She was so fast that in the blink of an eye, she was near Mia. But Mia was faster. She moved from her position at the last possible moment and Emilia crashed to the ground, face first with all the grace of a bull in the matador's ring. The crowd sucked in a sharp breath as they watched with bated breath.

Now it was her turn to smile. "Didn't see that coming, did you?" she taunted. Whistles erupted from somewhere in the arena. The dark whispers tugged at her mind strings, demanding control. Her jaws locked, focusing on the opponent, who was staggering to her feet.

Emilia's face contorted with pure rage. She lunged, shifting mid-air. *That's impressive.* She moved out of the way again and the beast ended up on the ground once more.

The lycan recovered faster than the last time and spat the snow out of her snout. This time she stalked Mia like a predator would stalk its prey. Mia stood unmoving, when she was close enough Emilia slashed out with her claws only to slash the air. Mia vanished into thin air like a ghost, appearing behind Emilia.

"I thought I was no match for your claws," she teased in a ghostly whisper.

Emilia turned again to slash, but Mia had moved, reappearing at the far end of the arena with a smug grin on her face. The beast howled with rage. "Stop running and fight me, you bitch." Her voice was guttural with no hint of humanity.

Mia's eyes darkened and her fangs burst out as she pounced. She was too fast for Emilia, and the female lycan was thrown halfway across the field, splattering the snow everywhere.

The beast stood and ran toward the vampire queen at full speed. Mia stood her ground attacking her only when she was close enough. Mia jabbed her in the chest, stopping her forward motion. Emilia coughed blood.

Her opponent panted hard. "You're trained well, bitch. I won't go easy on you next time," Emilia drawled and stalked her again.

She wasn't expecting her to give up right then. She just gave her a wide predatory smile, flashing her own fangs at Emilia. "Oh. . .I'm a bitch alright. But I'm the queen bitch." She emphasized each word and a flick of her finger sent the overgrown beast flying across the field.

Mia blinked, looking down at her hands. *What the hell just happened?* She only thought of throwing her opponent across the field. The dark whisper in her head bristled. *She hadn't seen that coming, did she?* It chuckled. *See, we could do great things together.*

The crowd that surrounded them gasped and scrambled backward. A chuckle from the east side reached her ears. *Matthew.*

No. *I don't want us to work together.* The more she toyed with Emilia, the more thrilled the entities within her became. Losing control was the last thing on her mind. *Not happening.* But this female was a threat to her mate, she was a threat to all and she must be dealt with.

"You changed the blood." She was done toying her. "You fed me the witch blood."

The crowd started conversing in low murmurs once again.

"You used the guards and bent them to your will. Sleeping with them and giving them false hope was so unladylike. Don't you think?"

Loud growls could be heard from the crowd. The glowering lycan had no words of refusal to the accusations.

"You wanted to be the queen, so you tried to seduce *my* Aaron." Mia's voice was guttural, her claws itched. "You attacked Paul. You betrayed your own crown by going against your alpha," she growled. "If you thought I was no match for your claws, then you thought wrong."

Mia closed the distance and hoisted the beast up by her throat. It slashed at her, but it hardly scratched the surface of her skin.

Mia threw Emilia across the field. "I told you I'm so much more." Drinking Aaron's blood had made her immune to the lycan claws, the only effective weapon that killed any vampire. She learned during her trainings that bullets and stakes didn't work on the vampires as the stories claimed. She kicked at the beast's ribs.

There was a loud crack and Emilia screamed. A furry paw clutched her side as she tried to scramble away. The vampire queen caught her by her scruff. The beast howled and shed its fur as the shift was forced. A jolt of magical electricity passed through her system and Emilia—now in her human form—twitched on the ground. Her screams echoed through the field as her claws were broken by Mia—one by one.

Mia laughed as her once strong contender now whimpered in pain. She continued to toss her across the field. Each impact sent the snow flying. Emilia's bones cracked and her limbs twisted in odd angles.

*More. . .*the monster residing in her demanded.

A silent sob infiltrated her senses, and her gaze sought out the crowd for the source. She frowned when she found Richard kneeling in the snow, crying silently for his only daughter. Something shifted within her. *If I kill her, a father would lose his only daughter.* And the pack would look at her as a killer. They watched her move intently and she decided she wouldn't let her anger cloud her judgment.

Her claws retracted as she forced a breath. Protests clouded her senses, and she was quick to shove them aside. *Enough!* She warned the forces waging war from within and let out a relieved breath when they quieted down.

"I will let you live this one time for the sake of your father. His loyalty to the throne will be rewarded with your life," she said, throwing Emilia's battered body in the snow.

Richard ran to his daughter with tears in his eyes. Blood pooled around her body. Her eyes glared at nothing, and her face twisted in pain.

"Take your daughter away; I don't want to see her anywhere near here again." Her gaze flicked to the beta. "I'll let her stay in the infirmary until she's fit to travel. After that, she must leave and never look back."

"Thank you, my queen," Richard rasped with a bow. He lifted him, rushing toward the infirmary. It was ironic how the doctor she once harmed will now save her life.

Zach's struggles caught Mia's attention and she went to him. His eyes lowered to the ground as he swallowed hard. "She doesn't deserve your love." His eyes teared up and his sobs choked out. "But your beast chose her. He'll die without her."

Zach's hazel eyes grew wider. He gave her a frantic nod, his gaze pleading.

"Go to her," she whispered. "Leave him." The guards who held the battered delta shifted their uneasy gazes toward their alpha.

Aaron nodded at them. Zach took off after Richard.

Did I do the right thing? She didn't care.

A startled yelp left her lips when someone of her height tackled her. She staggered a few steps at the impact, claws rose toward the source only to freeze when she realized it was a female. When the girl finished squeezing the daylights out of her, she let go and gave her a happy squeal, pinching Mia's cheeks.

"Oh, Mia. . .I thought I would never see you again," the girl gushed.

The huge grin plastered on her smile was blinding. Her mousy hair and hazel eyes looked so familiar. Mia knew her but from where?

"Ah. . .um. . .I'm sorry, you look familiar, but—"

"It's me, Maricella!" the girl exclaimed.

Mia's eyes widened as the name registered in her brain. *Maricella. . .*she remembered a girl from her boarding school, her first friend, the one who often gave her chocolates and gifts.

"It's you." Mia hugged her.

"Can't breathe." Maricella wheezed. "You're stronger than you look, do you know that?"

Mia grinned. "I never thought I would see you again."

"You totally stole that from me," Maricella complained with a goofy grin. "Wait, let me introduce you to my family."

Shortly, Mia was surrounded by a group of lycans she never met before. Two women and three men. Her mind reeled with all the names, and she shook their hands with a shy grin as her eyes searched for Aaron. As if reading her mind, Aaron was beside her the next moment, pulling her into his embrace.

"You were very brave today, my love," he said, kissing her lips.

Mia snuggled into his chest. They parted when they heard a throat being cleared. Victoria stood with a huge grin on her face, and Louie ran toward Mia, hugging her legs.

Mia bent down to kiss Louie on his chubby cheek and the boy giggled. "Thank you for saving the day once again," Victoria said. "Don't worry about the pack. They will come around when the shock wears off."

"Thank you. I heard what you said earlier. I can't express my gratitude in words." Mia smiled.

The omega's grin widened. "It was nothing. No one expected you to spare her life. What you did was amazing. You will make a good queen just like our Esmeralda."

"Victoria!" a male called.

"That's my mate, Thomas. I should get going." She turned to leave. "Oh, tonight I'm preparing a special feast. I'll send in one of the maids to get a list of your favorite dishes," she called over her shoulder as her mate dragged her away muttering something about how she needed more rest and how she paid no attention to her health.

Mia smiled warmly. The pair radiated love and happiness. She turned toward her mate. Aaron smiled, kissing her forehead as Matthew came barreling toward them.

"Hey, Mia. . .what you did out there was freaking awesome!"

"Thanks," she grinned. "Where did Dad and Lilith go?" She hadn't see them since morning.

"Oh, they went down to the lab this morning and haven't come out," Juan said.

"Okay." The frown was back on Mia's face. What were they doing down at the lab?

"Mia." Aaron nudged her. "The pack omegas are here to thank you."

An elderly female stepped forth, pressing her cheek against hers. "Thank you for sparing that child's life. You proved to be kind and forgiving. It's an honor to serve you, my queen." The omega bowed.

A sudden rush of overwhelming sensation washed over Mia. More females stepped forward. No words were spoken, they all pressed their cheek against hers and bowed before moving away.

"It is how the wolves show their affection." Aaron's hand was on her lower back as she met the pack females one by one.

"Cousin, a moment please," Blake called and Aaron squeezed Mia's shoulder in assurance before leaving her side. Matthew stepped up beside her as she greeted each female.

Aaron returned just as the last female excused herself. "Mia, I believe you will have a lot of catching up to do with Maricella here. Why don't you take them inside? I have to finalize a few things for the new members who are moving in."

"Sure." Mia nodded though that wasn't what she wanted to do now. Then again it had been a while since she had company and she could use some. It was a welcomed distraction.

341

"I'm coming with you," Matthew said.

"Matty, you're not a girl." Juan rolled his eyes.

"Exactly, they could use a guard."

"Not really cousin." Leila waved her hand. "I can take down your ass any time of the day."

"Is that a challenge?"

"Maybe."

"You'll pay for that!"

With a sigh, Mia followed the bantering cousins.

CHAPTER 44

The day had passed quickly. With Emilia out of the way, the pack females had warmed up to Mia considerably. It wouldn't be long before the others accepted her. Aaron excused himself from the grand feast arranged in Mia's honor and retired early to his chambers with his mate.

"You were very brave today, my love." He pressed his lips to her forehead.

"Do you think I did the right thing by sparing Emilia's life?"

"Yes, I do," he responded after a moment. His warm gaze locked with hers. "While it was in your right to kill her, you chose to spare her life." He grabbed her knuckles, kissing them. His lips were feather-soft on her skin, leaving a warm trail. "You're too good for this life. For me." His large hands cupped her cheeks. "You put yourself in Richard's shoes. Emilia is his only daughter. Killing her would destroy him. What she did warrants death, but you spared her life and proved that you're far better than her in every way. I'm so proud of you, my love."

"Do you think they'll see me as one of them now?"

"They've accepted you as their queen now, haven't they?" His thumb caressed her lips.

"Yes. But they had no choice in that matter. They challenged you and failed. It doesn't have to mean they accept me."

"You have a good heart, Mia. They *will* come around. Give them some time."

"Okay."

His lips brushed a kiss, warm and gentle. "You need to sleep. We have a meeting with the high ranking officials tomorrow. Lilith had a breakthrough earlier."

"What did she find?"

"A magic trail ended in a town near Verboten Hills. But what we have isn't enough. We can't just burst into his den." A defeated sigh escaped his lips. Aaron rested his forehead on hers. "I've never felt this helpless before."

Mia tightened her hold on him and snuggled to his chest. "It's okay to feel helpless, Aaron. I'm sure you'll save them this time."

Aaron nodded. "Come on. Let's call it a night. I just want to hold you in my arms and forget all my worries tonight," he whispered into her hair and inhaled her comforting scent.

Mia nodded and climbed into the bed. A deep sigh slipped out. She turned, snuggling into his embrace. "Good night."

"Good night."

She felt his hot breath fan the top of her head before his lips pressed a kiss. The comfort lulled her into a deep slumber.

***

The room was still dark when she woke the next morning. It was seven a.m. and Aaron was still asleep beside her. She carefully removed his hands draped over her body before tiptoeing outside to the balcony.

The cold wind assaulted her when she slipped out of the glass door. The snow had gotten worse and the trees were barely visible. Huge furry beasts broke out of the tree line, making their way toward the castle, which she assumed was border patrol.

Her gaze shifted to the view again. A hot cup of coffee sounded like a divine idea during this weather. She might do just that before heading to this meeting Aaron spoke of last night. She'd need all the boost caffeine could provide.

Closing the balcony door, she hurried to the bathroom for a quick shower. She was lathering her body with soap when the bathroom door opened and Aaron entered. His sleepy gaze scanned the bathroom and his eyes widened as he noticed her naked form, wet under the shower.

Gone was the sleep from his eyes and her cheeks heated when he quickly stripped, getting into the shower with her. He pulled her flush against his body and traced her wet skin with his lips, trailing long hot kisses against her sensitive peaks. Mia gasped and held onto him as the familiar heat pooled in her belly. All her worries vanished into the steam that coated the shower doors.

***

Two hours later, they were just starting the meeting when Maximus' urgent voice boomed through the speakers. Outside the meeting room, the castle's emergency alarm blared—a warning to the pack members to rush to safety.

"Alpha, we need you now. Vampires have infiltrated our territory! Two hundred yards toward the east. Expecting the impact in less than two minutes."

"Fuck!" Aaron jumped to his feet. A growl rumbled out. "Juan, lead the women and children to safety. Take Leila and Malaika with you.

Matthew, ensure the castle's security. John, come with me. Blake, Arthur and Dawson prepare a team of ten each and standby for my orders."

Aaron noticed his mate's confused face. But there was no time for pleasantries. Before Mia could respond, he was running to the huge window in the room. Clothing ripped as his beast broke free. In a blink of an eye, he jumped down the second-story of the castle, landing gracefully and taking off toward the east.

"Mia, stay within the walls of the castle with Matthew. Maricella, stay with Mia." He shouted orders through their telepathic link as he ran. *"Snipers take positions! Shoot anything that doesn't belong."*

"Alpha, they infiltrated our territory despite the protective shield," a warrior shot through their minds.

Their team of five intercepted the vampires when they broke out of the tree line. Aaron caught two, decapitating them. His razor sharp claws sliced through the bodies of the next three that came at him with their claws and fangs bared.

Hot searing pain shot through his arms from where a leech bit him. Before Aaron could engage, the creature retracted its fangs. Its body fell convulsing. Blisters formed on its skin. His eyes widened and he stood unmoving when two other creatures bit into him. When they convulsed and died before his eyes, he displayed his predatory fangs. *Witch blood.*

Mia had consumed witch blood and Lilith had said her body was processing the powers. But why would they react this way to his blood? He had bitten her while they made love in the shower. The blood helped speed up the healing of the wound. His arms flexed. It didn't make sense. Her blood enhanced his strength. Maybe this was one of a

346

perk. Another group of vampires broke through the tree line. With a roar, he barreled into a group of five that charged at him.

"Alpha, incoming from the west," Max's voice informed.

"Blake, lead a team to the west. Dawson and Arthur, prepare back up teams and standby." Aaron twisted his body in time to evade deadly claws. He crushed the creature's head. Thick crimson liquid coated his fur. He wiped it with the back of his paws.

John's pain-filled howl caught his attention. The alpha turned to notice they were being surrounded by more parasites. His beast bristled and hackles rose when his gaze landed on their new threat. Amber eyes narrowed, noticing the creatures that appeared mutated. They attacked his team in groups, cannibalizing whatever they came in contact with.

"What the fuck are these?"

Screams and howls infiltrated the pack link. *"We need backup!"* Blake yelled. *"Looks like the bastard's experiments have paid off."*

They were humanoid creatures with protruding reptilian-like mouths and tails. Their internal organs were visible under their translucent skin. *What the fucking deranged things are these?* There was no time to think.

His movements were a blur as he rushed to his brethren's rescue. Rage ignited from the deep within. His paws crushed their skulls as his claws ripped their translucent-looking skin into shreds. Too soft. Too easy. Their guts spilled.

The beasts around gagged at the overwhelming stench of rot that washed over them. This was nothing like anything they've fought before.

"Beasts! Formation O. Band together. Guard each other's back."

The beasts formed a circle facing the enemy their backs toward each other. Their stance widened as they poised their broad frames for impact. Aaron could hardly keep up with the conversation exchanged via the pack link. They could hardly breathe with the creatures coming in.

His chest heaved after the last wave. Blood dripped from his claws and his fur felt sticky. The beasts flexed their muscles. They were soaked from head to toe with blood that had also turned the snow crimson.

Aaron grabbed a lower branch of a tree, tipping it to his mouth. The fresh snow melted, nourishing his parched throat. The beasts on his team followed suit, taking quick refreshment while they awaited the next attack.

"Updates!"

"Eleven down. The western perimeter and the castle are secure."

"Alpha, there is some activity on the south. Not clear what it is." Max's voice came in.

"Dawson, what's the status?"

"My team is with Blake. Arthur's team can head to the south."

"Good. Arthur, go to the south. We are ten minutes away from the location. Call for back up if you need us."

"Brother, we killed twenty-nine. The castle is secure. I can go to the southern perimeter with Arthur," Juan said.

"Sounds good." Aaron's gaze scanned the area. *"Knox, run the perimeter. Howl if you smell trouble."*

"Yes, Alpha."

"Mia, what's the status?"

"All well. We are transporting the injured men to the infirmary."

"Okay. Keep an eye on the north. I have a very bad feeling about this." His instincts were on high alert. Ears strained to hear anything out of the ordinary. Clouds darkened as thunder clapped somewhere.

"Alpha, I see some unusual activity on all the sides."

"Mia, take my cousins to the north. Stay close to the castle. Max, send in the backups." Aaron reached for his father. *"Dad, where are you?"*

"It looks like someone is teleporting in the north. I'm heading there with Lilith and Ted."

"I thought Lilith's ward ensured protection from this surprise infiltration."

"Things are more serious than it looks, Son. There is only one who has the ability to break through Lilith's magic."

"Fuck! Tell me it isn't the Dark Witch." Aaron's features hardened at the mere thought of the name that wreaked havoc a few centuries ago. The most feared name in the supernatural world had vanished suddenly, and no one had heard about her for ages. Now, her return only meant destruction.

"I'm afraid it is."

CHAPTER 45

The hair on Mia's neck bristled as the dark entity within her awoke with full force. Her gaze narrowed at the sky. A hiss slipped past her lips. She was now at the open balcony in the first-story of the castle with Matthew and his female cousins.

An unnatural twister materialized out of nowhere and moved faster toward their castle. The dark whispers inside her head grew louder as it neared.

"Lilith, someone is teleporting!" her father's shout reached her ears.

"I can see that," Lilith retorted.

The witch spread her arms, murmuring an ancient dialect as an invisible energy swirled in her palms. She pushed the shield forward, guarding the lycans from being sucked up into the twister. Mia saw her dad hurry to Lilith's aid, casting a spell of his own, and together they pushed until it simmered.

Thick black smoke filled the arena, and once it cleared, there stood a witch with hundreds of vampires by her side. The witch took a deep breath as if savoring the fresh air, when she opened the eyes, they were as dark as the tendrils of magic snaking around her.

The new witch was beautiful despite her dust-coated skin and matted hair. The black gown she wore was tattered.

"Long time, no see Lilith," the witch drawled wickedly, toying with the knife she wielded.

"Melisa. . .now it's clear why I couldn't track Felipe. Didn't know you were one of his slaves." Mia could sense the disdain in Lilith's voice.

"I'm no slave!" The Dark Witch growled and her eyes gleamed. Mia felt the atmosphere pulse with energy. She could almost taste it. The power in her veins thrummed, spreading its tentacles as if reaching for the invisible energy.

Mia breathed through her mouth, her eyes shifted between blues and white. Like a magnet, it was luring her in. She could sense the way it brushed against her skin. Tingles erupted from where it touched. Her skin absorbed it, eliciting a pale golden glow.

"Do you know her?" Mia's father asked.

"Every supernatural knows of me, Warlock. They call me the Dark Witch." The witch's cackle was bone-chilling. She said her name with pride, and her lips quirked to a side as she regarded the others.

Mia saw the shock coating her father's features. *Who is she?* She must be someone powerful. So strong. She could tell by the way the air crackled around them with energy. Her blood called to her.

"You have no business here, Melisa!" Lilith said.

"Coming to visit my baby sister today is not my business, I agree." The Dark Witch drawled, placing a hand on her hip. "You're just a bonus. I didn't know you were working for the mutts."

The lycans around growled at the insult which she ignored. "I'm here for the girl. Hand her over to me, and I shall leave you all unharmed."

The lycans growled and shifted, ready to fight. Mia watched the scene unfold. She couldn't believe that the witch who stood with hundreds of vampires beside her was Lilith's sister.

"Lilith can't fight her," Mia said. "The witch is stronger than her."

"What do we do?" Leila asked.

"We are severely outnumbered. There's too many vampires to fight." Malaika moved beside her, adjusting her sword.

"Aaron, what's the status?"

"Nothing here, it looks like a decoy. We are heading north. Can you hold until we reach you?"

"Su—"

Their conversation was disrupted by a warning howl, and Mia heard her mate curse under his breath. *"We are under attack. I repeat we are under attack. Beasts take positions."*

"Fuck! They are attacking us from all sides. We won't have any backup," Mia hissed out.

The witch had a protective shield around her. Her eyes could easily see through it. She wondered if Lilith and her dad could see it as well.

"Bring me the girl and I shall leave this place," Melissa bellowed again. Darkness cascaded around her like a snake with a hiss as its tendrils teased her ghostly pale skin.

"No," Jerome growled.

Within seconds, a pregnant omega was dragged by an unseen force and was forced in the hands of Melisa. Mia stiffened in alarm at the sight of Victoria, her protective instincts kicking in at full force.

"How the hell did she do that?" Leila's eyes widened. "I locked that woman in the safety bunkers."

"Now, you have something to bargain for." The witch laughed, drawing a knife on the omega's cheek without breaking the skin. "There are six more pregnant wolves in your safety bunkers. Nothing is immune from my magic. I thought you knew that, sister."

"Let her go!" Lilith growled. "She has nothing to do with it."

"Oh, she has nothing to do with it, all right. The girl doesn't belong here either."

"You don't have to do this Melisa. You gain nothing out of this."

The Dark Witch tilted her head. "You may be right. But still, bring the girl!"

Victoria trembled in Melisa's hands. Her mate pounded at an invisible wall surrounding the witch and the vampires, hopelessly trying to save Victoria.

"He can't get in," Mia said. "No one can."

"Leave her!" Jerome bellowed as he moved forward, but again, he could not get past the ward, which surrounded them like smoke. It was similar to the bubble Mia had seen in her vision and something shifted within her.

Her father and Lilith chanted. Their spells not breaking the invisible shield. The vampires chuckled darkly at their unsuccessful attempts to pierce the smoky ward.

Mia could feel them; hear their thoughts. The darkness inside her bristled again.

Melisa drew the knife across the omega's skin, this time drawing blood. Victoria screamed and tried to get out of her hold, but Melisa held her in a steely grip.

Jerome and the others pounded at the ward.

"Give me the girl." Melisa stressed each word, her knife now dangerously close to Victoria's belly. "I can feel your eyes on mine, girl," the witch now addressed Mia directly. If the witch hadn't been so focused on Lilith, she'd have seen her earlier.

Tears rolled down the omega's cheeks, her hands hugging her belly. Victoria's light brown eyes met Mia's pitch-black ones.

The Dark Witch raised her knife. The omega's eyes never left Mia's. She had stopped crying. The fear in Victoria's face disappeared, replaced with confidence as Mia's demeanor changed.

"Get ready to feast, leeches!" Melisa shouted.

The vampires crouched low, baring their fangs and claws, ready to attack any minute. Mia could feel how the omega's blood drove them crazy.

"Stand down!"

The vampires tensed, looking around. Their frantic eyes searching for the source.

Mia climbed onto the concrete railing, balancing herself. Her hands flexed as she let her instincts guide her. Her cerulean eyes scanned the crowd, and the creatures cowered at the onslaught of power radiating from her. They knelt, making themselves appear smaller.

"Oh, there she is," she smirked.

"What are you doing?" Maricella whispered. "She's a freaking witch."

"This isn't a training session, Mia," Matthew warned.

"I've got this."

The jump was graceful. The lycans stopped their pounding and turned to look at her. Mia sensed Matthew following her. "Matthew, take your cousins and these warriors to your brother's aid. He needs backup." They stood unmoving, looking between the witch and their queen. "Go now!"

With a bow, they hurried to their alpha while Jerome, Lilith, and her father stayed. They had no choice but to obey the command.

"Hello, my dear. Good to meet you at last," Melisa said, getting everyone's attention. She had yet to notice the way the vampires behind her cowered and lowered themselves to the ground hiding their head with their hands.

"Can't say the same, Melisa." Mia moved forward, vanishing into the thin air before materializing beside Melisa.

The Dark Witch's startled gaze flicked toward her. "How is this possible?" Frightful whimpers caused her to look behind her to see the vampire army cowering on the ground with fear. A frown tugged the corners of her lips down. "You were supposed to be a normal girl," Melisa said, confusion flashed in her features, and her grip on the omega loosened.

"I still am," Mia said without taking her eyes from the witch. She slowly held her hands up for the omega to take, which Victoria did immediately. The scent of the Victoria's blood drifted through Mia's nostrils, making her own boil with fury.

"You made a terrible mistake by hurting her," she told Melisa and pulled Victoria toward her. "You don't get to leave after harming one of my pack members."

"You're just a child, Pureblood. I'd advise you to think twice before you do something rash." Melisa hissed, flashing her teeth.

Mia smirked. *She doesn't have fangs. I do.* "Hmm. . .let's see about that shall we." She grabbed Melisa by the neck before she could move. The knife-wielding hand came toward her, and Mia disarmed her with a blink of an eye. The weapon fell down with a clang as the witch's eyes grew wider. Mia's free hand held the omega in a tight grip as Melisa dangled two feet above the ground, kicking the air.

Mia slowly crushed Melisa's throat. "You like using your knife a lot, don't you?" Her eyes turned from pitch-black to pure white and a large gash formed on Melisa's cheek. The omega healed swiftly; her cheek turned smooth and flawless as if she was never hurt before.

"Go to your mate," Mia said, releasing Victoria and she scurried away.

"How did you do that?" Melisa choked, her eyes shifting from black to brown for a moment. It gave her a more humane appearance.

"I'm not like anything you have ever seen before." She brought Melisa to her eye level. "When I'm done with you, you will regret all that you have done so far," the vampire queen continued. "If you have experienced pain before, what I am going to show you will be far worse and will make you pray for death every second," Mia whispered in her ear before biting down hard in her jugular vein.

The witch screamed and thrashed in Mia's arms. Her struggles stopped after a while. Tears dampened the witch's cheeks as her eyes flickered back and forth between white and brown.

The protective bubble around the vampires came crashing down, and they whimpered from the power radiating off Mia. Everyone around her was forced to their knees.

A dark force of magic hit Mia when she bit into the witch. Dark and dangerous, yet familiar. The magic whispered to her, and the strange hum mesmerized her. When the blood flowed into her mouth, so did the witch's powers. It was not only addictive, it also coated her with the warmth that now brought tears to her eyes for no reason.

The dark whispers inside her head went amok. Mia's eyes closed. She was able to see the attack of the castle from all sides in her mind's eye. The creatures that lusted after blood attacking the members of her pack. She saw the lycans struggle and a growl rumbled out of her chest.

There was this strange pull toward the attacking creatures. Her vampire side rushed forward, taking control. They felt wrong. Not even a drop of humanity was left of their being. They felt nothing but lust for blood. She gritted her teeth. These creatures were born out of pain and their suffering must end now.

You don't belong here. She could see their aura shrouded in darkness. She focused on every creature made of evil. *Die!* Most of the creatures fell. Their bodies convulsed and blood oozed from their nose, ears, and mouths before they went limp. Dark, soulless eyes stared into nothingness. Those with little light left to their aura were spared.

The invisible tendrils of energy retracted to Mia, and the vampire within gave back the control once it was sure there was no threat left.

"Lock her in the dungeons." Mia threw the unconscious witch to Lilith's feet, who stared at her with her mouth agape.

The remaining vampires pressed themselves to the ground, begging for mercy. They were here without choice. She could sense their pain and struggle. She turned toward them. "You still have a chance of redemption, and I will let you live if you obey my rules," she said, receiving frantic nods. "You must control your bloodlust and feed only once a week. You'll be supplied with blood bags. Stand guard and protect the people here. If you ever think of harming someone, I will end your life with just a thought." She learned she could do that. The first time, she did it on instinct. "This chance is given to you only because you were given no choice when you were changed."

Strong paws thundered toward her. The ground vibrated beneath her feet. A smile breached her lips and his intoxicating scent lifted her spirits. Aaron's beast stopped a few feet from her. Her brows creased, and the beast shrugged its massive shoulders. An understanding smile stretched her lips on noticing his blood soaked fur.

"John, lead them away," Jerome told the general and turned to the vampires. "Go and wash yourselves clean."

John's beast nodded. The vampires followed him with a last look toward her, heads bowed.

"I need a shower." Mia turned.

"I'll join you in a bit," her mate's voice floated in her mind.

"Sure, my mate."

CHAPTER 46

Felipe roared as he trashed the throne room. He felt it all; the pain, their screams. Despite the distance it sliced through his heart. Hundreds of drudgelings killed all at once.

"Tanya!"

"Master." The witch rushed in and halted in her tracks, noticing the wreck. The witch took a few steps back.

He continued to punch holes in the walls, sending debris flying. The once regal room now held the remnants of his anger. "They failed!" his voice boomed. "They all failed, including the Dark Witch." He backed her to the wall. "How did this happen?"

"I-I don't know, Master." Tanya trembled, lowering her gaze.

"The plan was simple. All they had to do was to distract the mutts and abduct my mate. Where did it go wrong?" he shook her.

"I felt their bonds severing. Melisa is the most powerful witch in this world, or was I informed wrong?" Felipe threw her to the floor. The drudgelings he trusted so much were all dead. He was foolish to send them in. He crafted them so perfectly, yet none remained.

Tanya whimpered in fear but kept quiet.

Did Melisa plan this? She was growing stronger every day. It would have only been a matter of days before she broke free. The Dark

Witch fed off their spells and sucked their powers when they were in her presence.

"And you haven't thought of telling me this?" Felipe's voice boomed, and it was too late before Tanya realized her mistake. His furious gaze turned toward her. Those were her thoughts he heard.

"Master. . ." Her eyes went wide like saucers and she scrambled away.

He backhanded her and picked her by her scruff, "What else are you hiding, witch?"

"No-nothing, master. . ." Her hands gripped his as the sweet scent of her fear coated his nostrils.

"Hmm. . .I'll see that for myself," he mused, and Tanya screamed when he bit into her neck. The force caused her to double over in pain. His hands held her in a tight grip.

Tanya screamed and kicked, trying to get out of his hold. After a moment, Felipe threw her on the ground as if he got burned by fire. He wiped his mouth furiously as her blood burned his throat. He bent down, clutching his stomach.

"Get out!" he bellowed, and Tanya scurried out of the throne room as fast as she could.

The witch's blood burned him from the inside. He clutched his chest and suppressed a hiss. The eager drudge rushed toward him when beckoned over. Only the drudge hadn't known his fate. He bit into his slave's neck and drained him dry.

"Fools." He threw his almost lifeless body on the floor. They were always eager to please him. Only he didn't give a shit about them. He never cared for anyone.

Fury blinded him and he'd forgotten for a moment that Tanya was a witch. However, the memories he gained from her blood were worth it. The witches in his custody were hiding their thoughts from him.

Huge mistake. They would pay for it.

***

Victoria engulfed Mia in a hug when she entered the castle. "You saved my child," she said as Mia patted her back—an awkward movement. Pulling her aside, she gently caressed the omega's protruded belly. The child kicked, making its presence known.

"Your boy is very healthy, but you have to take care of your own health, Victoria. You're weak," she scolded softly. Thomas came beside her, circling an arm around his mate's shoulders.

"I'll forever be in your debt, Your Majesty." He bowed. "Alpha chose well." His smiled with an ease.

"Thank you, Thomas."

The deltas now looked at her with a newfound respect and bowed when she walked past them. She excused herself from them and headed to the bedchamber wanting solitude. She stripped out of her clothes and stepped into the shower stall, not bothering to close the glass door.

Mia knew the exact moment Aaron stepped into the room because her senses perked up. His feet made no noise as he approached her. The steady beat of his heart and the desire gripping the atmosphere were the only indicators.

His hair was wet from a recent shower and the fruity scent told her, he'd scrubbed clean before coming in. Her upper body twisted to get a better look of his stark-naked torso. Cerulean eyes drank in his well-defined musculature—from his broad shoulders to his strong thighs. The entities within her hummed with appreciation. This fine specimen oozed sex and confidence. And, he was all hers.

Mia almost came when his raw lust and desire washed over her. The beast's heated gaze swept over every inch of her body and she shivered. The heat trail left by his eyes ignited her desire. Toes curled when their gazes locked. Blazing amber eyes of his beast held a promise to devour her. Wetness pooled between her thighs.

One step after the other, her mate approached—fangs and claws exposed—like a predator stalking its prey. Excitement bubbled within. She wanted to be his prey.

A lust-filled gasp slipped out of her lips when he gripped her waist and drew her closer. Skin to skin—she felt the hard planes of his body pressed against her back. Warm water cascaded around them. He closed the glass door, locking them in.

Fuck. Mia didn't know if it could get any hotter. The air grew thicker with the pheromones that released into the atmosphere. Her breasts heaved, and she breathed through her mouth, tasting his desire in her tongue. Her eyes closed, head resting on his chest.

The soft scent of citrus infiltrated her nostrils. Mia suppressed a moan when she felt the feather-light touch of a sponge on her sensitive skin. She relaxed in his arms, sensing the need of the beast to groom its mate.

Aaron lathered her skin and used his hands to massage both of hers, taking time to clean her now soaked nailbeds. His lips brushed her bare shoulders as he worked his way to her breasts. Mia gasped when his fingers rolled her hard peaks between his fingers. Expert hands kneaded the soft flesh, eliciting a moan from her.

Mia rolled her hips as pleasure shot from the tip of her breasts. His lips found the sweet spot on her neck, sucking on the skin before nipping it. Once he was satisfied with her breasts, Aaron moved down, leaving a soap trail along her naval line.

When his hands traced her pelvic bone, her hips arched. Her body grew hotter by the minute as the erotic pressure built in her veins. It begged for release. But he was in no hurry. Aaron soaped her inner thighs and continued to her legs, paying no attention to her aching core. His slow torture tested the restraints of her control tethering on the edge.

A low growl rumbled out of her chest as she pushed her hips toward him. His chest vibrated with a deep chuckle. Instead of moving to her demanding sex, he just rose up and turned her to face him , before he wrapped his arms around her back to run the sponge over the skin there.

She ran her hands over his torso. When her tongue darted out to wet her lips, his eyes followed the movement. She traced his abs, twirling her fingers around his nipples. His jaws clenched. The steady movement of his hand behind her back faltered. Mia smiled internally as she worked to break his control. She wanted him to ravish her; take her hard and fast against the wall.

His nostrils flared as he drank in the essence of their combined desire.

Slender fingers continued their exploration along his torso. When she reached his v-line, a smirk lifted the corner of her lips. Tracing his strong hip bone, she ran a finger over his pelvis, openly admiring his groin. The tip of his bulging cock glistened with his excitement. Her soft pink tongue darted out to wet her lips, and his chest rumbled with a growl. The beast puffed out its chest, attempting to appear bigger. Her blue eyes briefly locked with burning amber eyes before her appreciative glance trailed south again.

Aaron's hand slipped between them, a finger traced her swollen folds. He dipped one into her wet channel and spread her wetness to other areas. The small bud of her center throbbed, but he was such a tease. His fingers continued to circle around it, stimulating her.

Her hand gripped his balls, tracing the engorged vein. Mia knew the moment his control snapped.

Aaron slammed his lips on her, kissing her with a feverish need. Her mouth opened eagerly to taste him. His sinful tongue made love to her mouth. Their wet bodies molded together.

The pressure of his fingers increased in her apex. Blinding pleasure soon consumed her senses, sending her soul flying above the clouds. When she climbed down from the high, Aaron pushed her against the wall, slamming into her not a second later.

A loud moan tore out of her lips. Her legs wrapped around his hips. He grabbed her hands, pinning the above her head. Mia watched the way his body rocked against her. The friction caused the pressure to build on her lower half. Her ragged moans and his grunts drifted around them to mix with the sound of water pelting their naked skin and wet slaps of flesh against flesh.

When she came with his name on her lips, he followed shortly after, shooting hot ropes of his essence inside her. The water washed down the sweat. But her mate wasn't done yet. He rested his forehead across hers only for a moment before releasing her and kneeling down.

Mia panted and her belly clenched with anticipation when he parted her legs, lifting one leg over his shoulder. Amber eyes focused on her sex that was growing wetter by the minute. His long fingers parted the folds of her womanhood, revealing her throbbing clit to him. When his lips wrapped around that little bundle of nerves, her eyes rolled back into her skull.

It didn't take long before she came apart for the third time that day. His ruthless tongue continued its assault, making her double up with pleasure. When she tried to push him away from her sensitive core, he simply pinned her to the wall, limiting her movements. Mia didn't know how much she could handle as the pressure built again pushing her into another orgasm. Her head reeled when he twirled her around in a quick motion. Hands pressed against the wet tiles for balance when his legs parted her thighs.

A strong hand secured hers above her head again and the free hand grabbed her hip. Not a second later, he entered her, stretching her walls. She could only moan as the overwhelming pleasure shot from her core to the other parts of the body.

Her beast was on a mission. And, she loved every bit of it.

CHAPTER 47

Jerome took a deep breath, and for the first time in years, his lungs didn't hurt. His ribs weren't protesting with each breath like they always did. The pain was still there, but the first taste of revenge was so sweet, and it washed over the bitterness occupying his heart.

A tear slipped out and trickled down his stubbled cheek. It was hard to keep living after his mate was forcefully ripped out of his life. She was the axis of his entire life. He rubbed his chest over his heart. It was a challenge to keep breathing and to live each day. And this victory was like a soothing balm to his ache.

For the first time in centuries, there were no casualties on their side. It'd take a few weeks for the injured ones to heal, but they were breathing. That was all that mattered.

He stood in his room, facing the castle grounds with Esmeralda's clothes in his hands. Her scent was fading, but it was still there. It was the only thing that kept his beast sane. Their mortal enemies stood guarding the castle grounds in the distance, now bathed and looking more civil, although jumpy whenever a lycan passed by.

A portrait of his mate hung on the wall. The warm smile gave her a livelier look. The artist had made it with such perfection that her eyes always followed him. It made him feel as if she was present.

"Why did you go, Esme?" Tears soaked his cheeks. She was the calm in the storm. The light to his darkness. That morning he'd begged her not to go, but she had just smiled at him and said he was being paranoid.

He should have trusted his instincts. He should have trusted the foreboding that churned his belly.

It was too late by the time he felt a heart-wrenching pain that felt like his soul was being ripped into two. All he got to see were her bloodied clothes. She was gone. She and his third-in-command, Larry, were missing along with three other elite warriors. The mate bond had been silent since then. A void had filled his heart.

Larry's arm had been found in a stream nearby—chewed to pieces. The dismembered bodies of the two guards had been scattered around their territory, tossed carelessly as if their lives didn't matter.

Howls and cries of the mourning pack members had echoed throughout the forest. It was the first time that Jerome had seen sturdy lycans break down and cry—including himself. The headstrong alpha had found that he could cry. He never had before. Sure, there were a few happy tears when he held his sons for the first time.

It took two days for them to collect all the pieces. The omegas had their noses pressed to the ground, crawling as they searched for the remains. Tears soaked the blood-stained soil. They didn't know what happened to the third guard. He was never found.

The burial had been an emotionally exhausting event. They had to bury the remains together since they didn't know which piece belonged to whom. Felipe proved he was a fucking bastard again.

A week later, they received a box that contained Esme's decayed fingers from her left hand and a toe.

He shoved away the depressing thoughts. That wasn't how he wanted to remember the love of his life. Jerome closed his eyes and forced himself to remember her shy smile.

He was ready to give up on life and follow his mate, but the beast wanted revenge.

The thirst for revenge had fueled his resolve to live. And, his three sons were the pillars of his strength. They had suffered a lot with losing their mother, and he didn't want to add more reasons for their suffering. Aaron hadn't been ready when he ascended the throne, taking on responsibility that demanded so much from him.

After all this time, finally, revenge had come. *Revenge will be so sweet.* Esme may not come back, but he would at least have some peace of mind when he passed from this world. If possible, he'd hope to hold the bastard's head in his hand as he did so. He wanted to die knowing justice was served.

***

Ted approached Lilith who was feverishly running the tests in the lab. He planned to confront her when she slipped away.

"You! What do you know about my daughter?" His face tightened.

Lilith's head snapped toward him, and her gaze locked onto his furious eyes. Her throat worked up and down. His gaze followed the brief action before jumping back to her face. The witch was sweating, her lashes flickered.

"I asked you a question, Witch. What the fuck is your relation with the Dark Witch? Is she your sister?" The vein in his jaw ticked as his hands fisted at his sides.

"Yes."

Ted froze, his nostrils flared with anger. "You're a fucking hycinth. I knew it." Because her magic far exceled the witches at the Cascade Coven. He always doubted there was more. His nails dug into his palms. He wanted to punch through something then. He shook his head and paced. A few moments later, he stopped. "What does Mia have to do with this? No one is magically strong enough to fight Melisa. How did she do it?" He closed the distance between them, gripped her shoulders, and shook her. "Why wasn't the Dark Witch fighting?" his head tilted.

Lilith whimpered under the onslaught of his anger. The witch could've pushed him off her, but she didn't. She was a fucking hycinth. He could sense the guilt radiating off her.

"How did Mia break into that ward when you and I couldn't? Answer me!"

"Because Mia is her daughter!" she pushed at his chest and his feet staggered.

Daughter? That meant—

"Mia is a hycinth."

Lilith's face was crestfallen as her knees collapsed. Ted's throat constricted as the truth weighed him down. *A hycinth!*

His vision blurred, and he took a few staggering steps behind. *His daughter is a hycinth.* His knees gave up as his mind took a trip down his memory lane.

Hycinths were members the most vicious coven of witches that terrorized the supernatural world for centuries. They were the highest in the hierarchy, and, therefore, the most respected. In a world where power was everything, one witch wasn't satisfied with what she had. Her greed for power had led to the downfall of their coven.

The Great Witch Serafine made a deal with the devil himself, who granted her a wish in exchange for her soul. The first-born female of their coven would be the most powerful of them all. The old witch didn't know that the wish came with consequences. They were born not only with power, but they also held the darkness of the devil himself.

Every firstborn witch born in the hycinth clan was lost to their darkness and wreaked havoc on the supernatural world. When the others couldn't take it anymore, they devised a plan to end their reign. Nearly fifty witches banded together and ambushed the firstborn witches to kill them.

The fear for the Hycinth Witches had cost them their lives. None were spared. They hunted every last witch until the Dark Witch rose from the depths of hell itself. No one knew which coven she belonged to. Rumors claimed she was a hyacinth. Then, suddenly, she vanished, leaving the world at peace.

Now, she was not only back but had a daughter. That also explained the powerful protection spell placed on Mia. Damn. The Dark Witch had the gift of vision. She must have known that he'd stumble upon her daughter.

"Hycinths are extinct." At least that was what everyone believed, *until now.*

Lilith continued to sob. "Our grandmother Joanne escaped the attack and went into hiding. That concoction you were injected with, it was grandma's receipe. It allowed us to pass as a normal witch. No one suspected us."

Ted was silent for a moment. "You knew, yet you didn't bother to tell us. Mia's life is in danger because of you." The accusation came with ease. His anger was directed at the witch who hid the truth from him. She caused this.

"I wasn't sure," Lilith whispered. "I hadn't seen Melisa since she lost herself to the darkness. We had no contact, and I thought she was killed. Then, I came across Mia and it was like déjà vu." Her gaze lowered. Tears stained her cheek and guilt washed over him. He didn't want to be the reason behind her tears, but she risked his daughter's life.

"You ran tests using her blood."

"I did."

"You knew she's your niece."

"I knew we were related," she admitted. Her voice still low and ridden with guilt.

"Still, it was a possibility you overlooked. Do you even realize what you have done? Do you have any idea what Melisa's blood would do to Mia?"

Violent sobs racked Lilith's body, and she broke into tears in front of him.

"If you had warned us earlier, I'd have stopped her from consuming witch blood. Her powers began to unlock itself since she accidentally did so. Then, she was injected with a cocktail of supernatural blood. Those witches, whose blood she consumed were nothing before Mia's power scale and she survived. But this. . .this was suicide. She had no time to process the powers."

Ted shook his head and stood, slightly wobbling.

"I'm sorry."

"You should be." His voice hissed out. "I hold you accountable for whatever happens to my daughter. And, I swear I'll end you if her life is in danger because of this."

He then turned and walked to the exit.

"Where are you going?"

"To the alpha," he said. "He must know what his mother's best friend was hiding all along."

Her gut-wrenching sobs were the last thing he heard when he banged the door shut on his way out.

***

Tanya shivered in fear watching their master float above them in his vampiric form. The witches and warlocks cowered in a corner. They hunched their shoulders and knelt, trying to appear smaller. Blood whooshed out from the wounds Felipe inflicted on their bodies.

The room they were in was destroyed as he unleashed his power on them. Despite being witches with magic, they felt helpless. He was not only faster, but also had years of experience and knowledge that compensated for his lack of magic.

Felipe growled and tilted his head. Blood dripped from his claws. He hadn't bothered with the slight sizzle when their life source burned his skin. His thick black wings flapped lazily, and the black, velvet smooth skin peeked from underneath his royal blue robe. Red malicious eyes scanned each one with a wicked glint. She knew he could read their thoughts as clear as a day. There was no hiding now. It was one of his greatest skills that granted him leverage over his enemies. He always knew what they were up to and killed them all if it was the wrong move.

It was not every day they saw their master in his true form, and when they did, it was never good. He had punished them for hiding the truth from him.

"Melisa was outgrowing your powers," he drawled, a dark rumble that sent chilling tingles along her spine. "And you decided to play gods." His features hardened. "Had I known this, none of it would have ever happened." A clawed finger pointed at them, and Tanya lowered her gaze to the floor. "I lost the most powerful witch I had because of you."

"Ma-master, we will bring her in," Tanya stuttered.

"No, you can't," he said, his voice deadly calm.

She swallowed, risking a glance toward him. The rules were laid out clearly. Melisa would extract the girl, kill anyone on site and wreak havoc. A compelling spell bound the Dark Witch. Only the Dark Witch didn't return. No one came back.

It made little sense. Since they used her own blood to activate the spell, there was no way she could've broken the compulsion by herself. The spell worked like a curse. It would cause immense pain if she tried to break it. She'd die if she did not complete it. They didn't know if the witch was even still alive.

"Why is she so important, Master? You have us," one of the warlocks pleaded.

"You don't get it, do you?" Felipe's voice held a dangerous edge.

Tanya pressed her back to the wall when his feet touched the ground again. The warlock cowered as his vampire master stalked toward him. He winced when Felipe's claws dug under his chin, drawing blood.

"Melisa is a first-born hycinth." Felipe smirked upon hearing their collective gasps. "I know, right?" He paced to the center of the room. "You're nothing compared to her powers. It took centuries to get ahold of her; then, decades to break her."

Tanya swallowed. The tales she heard while growing up were true. And, if Melisa didn't want to be found then they never would. It wasn't like they could just march to her door and bring her back.

"Exactly," Felipe said, and Tanya schooled her thoughts. Her head bowed, averting her eyes to the floor. "But first, I must know if she's alive."

"Master." Someone walked in and bowed.

Tanya looked up to see it was Dreven, the second-in-command. Her curiosity rose.

"What's the news, Dreven?"

"She's mated to that mutt."

"What?!" Felipe's wings bristled and pinned Dreven to the wall. The pointy edges of his wings drew blood.

The witches pressed themselves more to the wall.

Dreven's shoulders hunched and his gaze lowered. He did not so much as flinch. "Their alpha knew of her origin. The bastard seduced the pureblood and tricked her into mating him. He had her warlock father locked in his dungeons. I heard his cousins talking. She doesn't know this yet."

Felipe's fists clenched. Blood dripped from where his claws dug into his palm. "Then, he must die."

His cold voice sent unpleasant chills down Tanya's spine.

"Then, he will die, Master." Dreven's eyes shone with malice and his fangs flashed. This was why her master favored him. "She's always guarded. I couldn't get near her. However, I know of their secret passages and exits."

The king turned to the others in the room. "Leave!"

Tanya scurried along with the others out of the room, feeling relieved. She couldn't help but wonder what her master would do now that the female vampire was mated. With a groan, she limped to her shelter.

CHAPTER 48

Melisa could hear an odd beeping around her, as well as the clean smell of disinfectants that infiltrated her senses. While she didn't recognize the scent, she preferred this compared to the toxic stench of her earlier confinement. A strange sense of peace had settled in her mind and she relished in it. It had been years since she last felt such peace. She laid there unmoving and just listened. Even the beep sound was oddly comforting.

What is this place?

Suddenly, the events that led to her situation came flooding back to her. The realization of danger that she was in settled in her mind. Melisa tried to move her limbs. Exhaustion washed over her, and when she couldn't move after several trials, she gave up. With her energy drained, her body was unresponsive. It would take weeks for her to recuperate. There was no way she could warn them of the imminent danger.

The door opened and soft footsteps approached her. A pair of warm, soft hands clutched hers and sobs erupted from the person. It was too hard to miss the familiarity of the touch and the feminine sniffles.

"Come back, sister. I need you," she heard her sister whisper.

"Lilith!" she wanted to call, but her lips wouldn't move. Her tongue never formed the words. It was glued to the roof of her mouth. Melisa tried to move again. She had to tell her. She had to warn them. Mia needed help. The Dark Witch could only hope that Lilith had connected the dots and found Mia's origin.

How do I warn her?

She helplessly listened as her sister's soft footsteps walk out of the room. With everything out of her hands, she was resigned to her fate and waited as the magic in her cells slowly regenerated one at a time.

Her thoughts wandered to the day that sent her somewhat normal life spiraling down. The nightmare that often haunted her replayed behind her closed lids.

***

The sun was about to set for the day, casting a golden glow on her surroundings. The chilly evening breeze played with her long ebony hair as she sat on the porch rocking her two-week-old daughter.

Melisa admired the beauty of her little girl. Mia was the spitting image of her father with a curly blonde mane and mesmerizing oceanic blue eyes. Baby Mia's hair shined in the last rays of the sun, making her look like a little angel. Melisa loved the way her soft pink hands gripped her finger, never letting go even in sleep.

"Honey. . .I'm home!" The lovely voice of her human mate brought her out of her trance.

She greeted her husband with a kiss, which he deepened by tilting her head back. Her veins heated up with a need she felt only for him.

They broke apart when the baby fussed. Mia wiggled her legs free, kicking in displeasure. Carl's blue eyes, the color of the clear sky, crinkled with laughter. She watched in contentment as he grabbed their daughter, cooing sweet things to the little one.

Carl. The love of her life was a true gift from the gods. Despite the bad things she'd done during her life, they blessed her with a mate who loved her to no end. He knew what she was, and yet, he loved her with all his heart.

She was quick to brush off the joyous tear when he threw his arms around her. Her daughter looked at them and gave a heart-stealing toothless grin. *My family.* She now had the only thing she ever wanted.

That night, she lay cocooned in her mate's embrace, her fingers playing with his chest hair. Their daughter, who was now bathed, fed, and changed, was asleep in her crib next to their bed.

Melisa's eyes caught ahold of the simple platinum band that adorned her ring finger. Her heart felt so overwhelmed with love and happiness that she almost forgot her past—that was, until she felt an unpleasant tug at her heart.

"What is wrong, love?" Carl asked. His fingers smoothed her frown.

"Not sure, honey. I feel something," she said, rubbing her chest above her heart. The tugging she felt in her heart was not a good sign— it meant someone or something had tried to get past her protective ward. "We need to leave this place, my love. I have a terrible feeling," she said. The childbirth had taken a toll on her powers. Baby Mia had drained her during pregnancy, and she was now at her weakest. Vulnerable.

Alarm crossed his features and, in an instant, Carl was on his feet, scuttling around their home, grabbing and packing things. He knew who she was and how she was running from Felipe. Yet, he took the risk.

Felipe Lancelot, the first pureblood vampire to walk the earth. The power-hungry, mad king was abducting the supernaturals—to torture and then use in the war. Now he wanted her for her powers.

She was on the run when she met and fell in love with Carl. For a human, he was the most courageous man she'd ever met.

I'd gladly walk through the fire and go through hell if it meant I'd spend another second of my life with you, he'd said. *You're worth it, Melisa. I'd do that and repeat it all again.* And just like that, he'd pulled her out of the darkness that had been eating her alive. Carl was her light.

They had been running for a while before settling down in West Creek, an unincorporated community in New Jersey. When their daughter was born, she thought life couldn't be more perfect. How wrong she was to think that?

Carl had known the risks. He was now packing baby Mia's things, throwing everything they owned into sacks. He raided Melisa's potions cabinet, pulling out a neon green solution and then hurried to the kitchen. Her brows creased, wondering what he was planning to do with it.

She watched as he rubbed a few drops to the side of his neck and joints. That potion helped to mask scents, and he was now diluting it with water. He then poured the solution in a spray bottle and sprayed it all around their house. He paid more attention to where their daughter's crib and things once sat.

He is masking her scent.

It made sense now. Carl was always thoughtful. The people who came after her weren't human. They were creatures of the dark with enhanced senses. This would throw them off the grid. *Oh, God!* If they knew she had a daughter. . .Mia was a first-born hycinth. A female. And she would be stronger than her mother one day.

Melisa tried to summon the familiar power in her blood but couldn't. She felt useless without it. Even simple magical acts drained her of energy. It would take at least a week before she could perform magic without feeling weak.

After several failed attempts, Melisa tapped into her power source. Her vision became blurry and she couldn't make out the features of anyone she saw. They had broken past her protective ward and were now approaching her home.

"Carl. . ." she called from the bed, exhausted after her attempt.

She stared at her husband with glassy eyes as she tried to speak. "Leave with our daughter," she rasped. "I'm of no help." If they started now, they could make it. Carl can take the car and—

"I will never leave you or our daughter," Carl opposed.

No. He didn't understand. They were coming for her. If they got what they wanted, they'd never look for her mate or her daughter. No one knew she had a mate. Not even her sister. Lilith, her baby sister thought she was dead. She fooled everyone but Felipe. That bastard somehow knew she was alive. And he had a way of finding her wherever she went. Melisa knew the obsessed king would stop at no cost.

"Please. . ." she pleaded. "Take her and go away."

"It's too late for that." Carl shook his head and continued with the task at hand. He moved her, lowering her to the floor before moving their bed and the carpet to reveal a wooden trap door. Then he was carrying their daughter to safety—the basement of their home.

Her vision blurred and body became semi-paralyzed. She knew there was nothing she could do to save her mate or daughter. The mop of blond hair appeared again, climbing out from the underground room.

Soon, her husband hoisted her up. She hardly had any energy left to keep her eyes open. Her head lolled to the side, unable to hold steady any longer.

Carl paid no heed to her pleading look as he took her to the basement. He laid her on a makeshift straw mattress beside their daughter before bringing in baby Mia's things.

Now there were noises outside their home. Carl made eye contact with Melisa before placing a lingering kiss on her soft lips. The kiss felt as if he was bidding goodbye. She whimpered, tears now flowing free. She wanted to reach out and catch his hand, stop him from going out there.

"Please. . ." with tears streaming down her face, she begged again.

Her eyes widened when he pricked his finger. He produced a bottle of potion from her collection. *No, not that.* The potion tied one's tongue and rendered them speechless for a limited time. And mixing his blood with it would extend its effects on her. A hycinth witch like her could only be controlled with mate's blood.

He was already pressing the bottle to her mouth, tipping the contents. Her arms flailed, and she tried to spit it out. He closed her nose, suffocating her for a few seconds so that when he released her, she gasped for breath, swallowing the contents. A splutter of a cough racked her body.

"I will keep you both safe," he whispered before going to their daughter and kissing her. More tears leaked from her eyes. Pain and fear clutched her heart in a tight grip.

Please. . .

Carl rubbed a drop of sleep potion on Mia's head. Then he left them, locking the cellar door above them. Melisa did not miss the tears in his eyes, and she could hear shuffling before all hell broke loose.

She lay there, crying silently and praying that her daughter stayed silent throughout the ordeal as she tried to find the strength to move her numb body. She heard shuffling from above. A loud bang sounded, and the intruders burst into their home.

"Hmm. . .Salt and chili? You think this will keep you safe, you worthless human?"

A cold shiver ran down her spine on hearing the shrill voice. An image of the witch she'd known popped in her mind—red hair, long face, short chin, pointed nose, and soulless black eyes. Aris—one of the worst witches from Felipe's coterie.

"Where are they?"

Oh, no. She recognized that voice so well. Uriel, Felipe's third-in-command.

"Do you think Melisa is fool enough to stay put? She left the moment you breached the ward," Carl's voice taunted them.

Carl, please. . .don't do this. Melisa choked on a sob. They'll kill him.

"Fuck! We missed her again," Aris cursed. "Kill this bastard!" the woman yelled. "Make it painful."

No!

It was too late. The snarls and growls had begun by then.

Melisa screamed internally and cried harder when she heard her mate's agonizing scream. No sound could slip past her lips. Not with that potion still in effect. *Carl, oh, Carl. . .What have you done?*

Her heart felt like it was being ripped apart, and she could feel his pain in every fiber of her being. Her vision darkened, and she slipped into a dark abyss, feeling only pain.

The next time she woke it was to the cries of her child. She found her daughter lying beside her as her eyes adjusted to the darkness of the room. Her hands reached out for the crying baby and fed her on autopilot. She tried to remember the recent events as the sounds of her hungry child gulping milk filled the small cellar.

The witch felt something snap inside her and a familiar power surged through her veins. Anger rose as she remembered her mate's fate. Her lips curled up in a snarl as wave after wave of pain, sorrow, anger, and thirst for revenge filled her entire being.

Her senses heightened, and she listened for any sound from the room above. When she heard nothing, she stood and adjusted her hungry daughter. Mia was latched onto her breast as if it was her lifeline.

Extending her free hand, Melisa concentrated on the power that thrummed inside her and released her power onto the door. It burst open, showering wooden splinters all over the cellar. Climbing the wooden stairs, her eyes scanned the destroyed room, taking in the scene. Blood coated the interior of her home.

Her eyes landed on a male corpse covered in blood. The face was turned away from her, and she see crusted blood soaking his blond mane. Melisa averted her gaze immediately—she couldn't stand the sight. She didn't want to remember Carl like that.

She didn't want to see how haunting his dying moments were. Her eyes closed, and she forced herself to remember his smile, those beautiful dimples he had on his cheeks, his joyous blue eyes. The memories that were once warm and sweet now brought nothing but pain.

Her mate was gone. She felt the darkness that lived inside of her spiraling out of control. She didn't have long. Soon, it would consume her like it did before. This time Carl wouldn't be there to bring her back. He wouldn't coo sweet nothings in her ears as she fought off the darkness.

A coldness spread throughout her heart. She now had no mate to thaw it. She was lost. Her daughter fussed in her arms. Mia. . .she wasn't safe. The bastard won't stop. He will never stop until he got her. *Have to save her. My daughter will never fall into your hands.*

With an aching heart, she exited the house and burned it to the ground using her power, destroying all evidence and memories. Melisa left the place she once called home behind, taking only a heavy heart and her daughter cradled safely in her arms.

It was a few days later when Melisa found the monsters that killed her mate. They were tucked away in a cave in the woods. The darkness slithered out, fueled by her rage and sorrow. She relished in their agonizing screams that night.

Aris. . .oh, the sweet red-headed witch now burned faster than coal. The woman who ordered her husband's death screeched. Her loud screams echoed through the cave walls. The other witch rolled on the cave floor, trying to put off the fire. But it didn't work that way. *Because it is my fire.* She controlled it. The bluish-black flames died when Aris was only a pile of ash.

Uriel was missing, but she knew she would find him later. She turned toward the creatures that clawed at the invisible wall and unleashed her fire at them. Their agonizing screams were music to Melisa's ears. She cackled maniacally in rage as she watched her enemies burn until only their ashes remained. She then summoned the wind and scattered their remains all over the forest floor.

Pure satisfaction filled her as dark tendrils of energy swirled around her. She was still weak by her standards, but her strength had been building over the last few days. It wouldn't be long before she reached her prime. Then, she'd have her revenge.

It tasted sweet on her tongue, and the darkness beckoned further.

A sudden cry behind Melisa cut her laugh short, and she turned to see her daughter was awake. Guilt flooded her. How could she forget her precious little girl? She composed herself before picking her daughter up and feeding her, quenching her hunger.

The dark tendrils of energy retreated at the touch of her daughter. A few teardrops slipped out. *Mia isn't safe anymore.* The last time she lost control, she'd attacked her own sister. She'd fled home afterward. Ran as far as her legs would take her and never went back. Then, Carl came along. He healed her darkness with his love.

More tears followed as her legs moved, walking away from the cave. She knew it had to be done. For the sake of her daughter. *I must leave.*

***

She eyed the lonely human orphanage. The matron here was known for her kindness, and she'd witnessed it herself over the past couple of days.

Melisa circled around the tree she'd been hiding behind. The sky was dark with only a few stars. The faint glow of the light from the orphanage illuminated her daughter's face. She lowered her lips to kiss Mia's forehead when a familiar jolt of electric energy tugged at her.

A beautiful woman with curly blonde hair and raging blue eyes floated elegantly in the air. The sky darkened, and thunder clapped above her head.

Fresh blood coated her mouth and her dark brown silk gown danced with the wind as she dropped a limp body of someone familiar on the ground.

"Death is too kind to you, Felipe!" the girl bellowed.

The hint of sharp fangs under her curled lips appeared lethal.

"I'm being kind enough to deliver it to you for the wellness of the others around you. You do not deserve to walk on this earth." Her strong voice rang with an authority that forced the other vampires to their knees.

Her hands lit up with a red glow as she pointed them toward the limp figure. Soon, his agonized screams filled the war ground as she cackled maniacally.

The witch gasped when the vision ended. She looked at her daughter again with disbelief, before her lips twisted up into a full-blown smile. "I have your demise right here in my hands, Felipe," she whispered.

With a steady hand, she held Mia close, their faces an inch apart. Melisa looked deep into her daughter's eyes, and she began a whispered spell.

"I protect thee. . .

From the evils that lurk in the shadows,

That are craving for your blood and flesh.

I hide thy alluring scent and powers,

From the malicious eyes,

Who mean nothing but harm.

I hide thee. . .

Until the time comes,

My blood within you shall protect you."

Melisa chanted repeatedly until a golden glow enveloped her daughter, disappearing into her ivory skin. She smiled in satisfaction and blew softly over her daughter, who giggled and kicked her legs at the touch of tingling magic on her skin.

"Stay safe, baby girl," Melisa said, her voice thick with emotion. Her eyes glistening with unshed tears. The vision had also given her a sneak peek into her daughter's future.

She waved her hand over her daughter, reciting the ancient spell and drawing the intricate pattern in the air. The atmosphere grew thick with magic as the spell came alive. "You won't be alone. A protector will come." The spell she chanted would make sure of that. For it worked like a curse.

"Momma is in danger and cannot take you with her, only harm awaits her path," Melisa said and her voice cracked. "Momma loves you, so did your Papa. When the day comes, we will meet again."

She kissed Mia's temple before leaving her in the crib outside the orphanage. Melisa slipped a piece of paper that stated that her parents were dead, and she'd written her birth name on it. She didn't want her baby growing up with the thought that her parents threw her away. This way, at least she'd know she wasn't abandoned.

Melisa slunk into the shadows and watched as the matron of the orphanage opened the door and picked up her daughter, cooing sweet words to the infant as she cradled her close. A protector would come, someone with ancient magic in his veins. Until then, this was the safest place for her baby.

"We will meet again, my baby girl."

A silent tear escaped her eyes as she watched her daughter's blonde hair disappear behind the door.

CHAPTER 49

Ted was about to knock on the former alpha's door when it opened wider. Jerome stood in his night robe with a bottle of whiskey in his hand.

The warlock had first gone to Aaron's chamber, but when he found it was locked from the inside, he left without a word.

"What keeps you up at this time of the night, Warlock?" the former king asked as he retreated into his room, allowing Ted to enter.

"I have an important matter to discuss," Ted said.

The king just quirked his eyebrows as he settled down on his chair by the window. He waved a hand toward the other chair. His gaze flew out, staring at the night sky.

Ted inhaled. "Melisa is Mia's biological mother."

"*What?!*" The king was up in an instant. Blood drained from his face.

"Their DNA is a perfect match, and it matches with Lilith's as well." Ted swallowed. He had to reveal this matter carefully. "Mia is a hycinth."

"Hycinth," Jerome's whisper was barely audible. The bottle from his hand slipped to the floor, spilling its contents.

He nodded, and his shoulders sagged. "Firstborn."

"Fuck!" The king cursed, running a hand over his face.

"She's not stable. Mia is more dangerous than Felipe. Vampire, lycan, and witch blood course through her veins. Drinking her mother's blood unlocked her powers" Ted said.

"What do you suggest?" Jerome's features hardened.

There was nothing they could do. "Only Melisa can help, but Mia drained her powers, and she won't be waking up anytime soon."

"God. What do I tell Aaron? The pack? Ted, the pack will be frightened. They can't handle that." The former alpha jumped to his feet.

Just as Ted opened his mouth, a loud scream echoed throughout the castle and the entire place shook with violent tremors. Ted's eyes widened as his gaze locked with Jerome's with an alarm. Together they ran toward Aaron's chamber and what they saw froze them to the floor.

***

Aaron hissed, clutching at his bleeding biceps. His amber eyes regarded his mate, who was in her vampire form. She flapped her wings and clawed at her skin frantically as it skin lit up with a fiery red glow.

What the hell is happening?

They had been asleep, and hen he heard her scream, he woke to see her changing form. He tried to get her down. But when he reached for her again, she slashed across his chest, drawing blood and hurled him across the room. He landed with a thud.

"Mia!" he warned. His beast pushed forward. Claws broke out from the tips of his fingers.

She snarled at him again. The wind whipped at his hair, and she hoisted him up in the air and flung him away. The lycan king shifted in mid-air. His beast roared in warning.

The door to his bedchamber broke open, and the elite guards entered. He caught her leg when she tried to fly through the open balcony. *Not that fast.*

"Stop anyone from coming in! Do not intervene." He heard Blake barking orders.

He pulled her down, trying to hold her hands from doing any more harm. Blood trickled from the wide gashes. She fought harder, clawing at his hands. He turned his face away from her claws when she tried to gouge his eyes out.

"Fucking calm down!" he growled into her mind.

The room shook. Things were being thrown across. Her vicious claws slashed at him, and she bit into his hand. Her wings he now noticed were no longer soft. The feathers that appeared silken were actually hard and razor sharp. The pointy edges cut through his thick skin, drawing blood. She twisted her body and kicked at him. He was once again thrown to the side. His body crashed into the wall, creating a dent.

The beast roared. The last straw to his humanity slipped as the beast surged forward to take control.

"GET OUT!" he raged at the others and charged at her. She was floating in the air. The fiery glow brightened with every passing second as she let out an inhuman screech. The portraits that hung on the wall fell down.

Aaron ducked, avoiding her claws and was behind her in an instant. Pulling at her legs, he pinned her to the floor as her wings flapped frantically, trying to fly away. His beast straddled her from behind. He pinned her clawed hands to the floor and used his knees to pin her wings as she kicked at the floor uselessly.

"Enough, Mia!"

Racing heartbeats caught his attention and his blazing amber eyes snapped to the lycans still standing inside the room.

"I said get out!" his voice boomed once again. The others, who had been too shocked to move, scurried out of his chamber. The beast snarled at his mate.

"Calm down!"

She kept thrashing. Hurting her was the last thing on his mind, but she left him no choice. She was lost and she had to snap out of it before she hurt someone or herself.

His head dipped, biting her neck. Sharp fangs pierced her skin as her rich blood filled his mouth. Mia screeched again and tried to throw him off, the more she fought the more he pushed her down. She was stronger, but not strong enough.

The carpet underneath them burned and sizzled as she let out a burst of energy which barely singed his skin. He clamped his jaws tight and pinned her legs using his.

He concentrated on their bond and pushed his compulsion through it. The atmosphere grew dense, and he felt her panic and confusion. *"It's okay, Sweetheart. It's me, your mate."*

He pushed further and moved the hand pinning down her wings to caress her shoulder blades where it emerged from within her body.

"I'm not gonna hurt you."

A shudder ran through her body and her wings flapped—softer and weaker. Her screeches turned to muffled groans and then to pleasure filled moans. He sensed when the wildfire of desire burned through her veins because it washed over their mate bond.

Aaron eased his fangs off her neck only for her to protest and arch her back. The air grew thicker with her arousal. His cock hardened. Her rage was simmering. But she wasn't back, *yet.*

Lycan's Blood Queen

With a growl, he freed her hands, but kept his hold on her wings. Mia was panting hard but did not move. He continued his caress on her shoulder blades, running his knuckles over her wings. It elicited another moan from her.

His beast slid the control to his human side, and the fur receded into his body. His human hands now traced her silken skin that looked exotic in royal blue mixed with black.

"So beautiful," he murmured.

The red glow simmered under his touch as he ran his fingers along her length. She gasped softly. He eased his hold on her wings. They were no longer attacking him.

Aaron couldn't resist the lust building within. She was exquisite. His fingers slid between her thighs. Mia let out a whimper when he teased her wet folds. He was curious. Instead of pressing his thumb to find the opening like he wanted to, he turned her around.

Juan was right when he said she looked both frightening and beautiful. The exotic creature that lay underneath him was his mate— dark and dangerous.

Mia whimpered again as he ran his fingers along the valley of her breasts. Her nipples were hidden beneath the silken fur. His gaze slid to her face. Her lips were parted, wild hair fanned on the floor. He was tempted to kiss those lips—soft, plump, and red.

Aaron bent, pressing a soft kiss there. His tongue darted out to taste. Her mouth opened eagerly beneath him, and she kissed him back with a fervent need. A long throaty moan drifted around him as her tongue massaged his. He growled his appreciation. His hands cupped her breasts and froze when he felt her claws in his back.

She locked her legs around his waist and pushed herself up. Her hips gyrated against his arousal. Aaron broke the kiss and gazed into her eyes. Only he saw no recognition in them. It was the same look she had when they consummated.

"What's my name?" he whispered seductively, and she blinked as if his question caught her off guard.

His hand teased her breasts, never touching the way she wanted him to. She arched her back and growled in frustration. "Not until you come back, Mia. Tell me." She was guided by her primal instincts then.

Her mouth opened and closed, her eyes shifting between pure white and pitch black. Not the blue eyes that belonged to her.

"Who am I to you, Mia?"

She growled again and locked her legs around his waist, her hands chaining along his neck as she tried to bring him closer.

"No!"

She blinked again at his refusal.

"What's my name? I'm not doing this until you tell me my name and who I am to you," he growled.

The air thickened with pheromones that drove his beast crazy. His jaws clenched. He wouldn't touch her until she was back to her normal self. She had to regain control of her instincts.

Rage contorted her features. With a growl, she pulled him down and wiggled her hips against his hardness.

Aaron growled back at her in warning. This wasn't his Mia. He let his anger radiate. Her hands lowered with a whimper. Her now snow-white eyes brimmed with tears.

He almost caved in. No. This wasn't her. It was that thing inside her that was beyond her control. He knew his mate would hate herself for it later. He wouldn't let that happen, he won't let her lose control like this.

"That's it! Mate or not, I'm not touching you until you're in control. I want you to say my name and who I am to you," he said in a stern voice and stood.

Mia snarled and tried to pull him back down.

"I said no! Whatever this thing is took your choice on our first time together, and I'm not letting that happen again. I'm yours, but I won't touch you until you shift back and control this thing."

Mia shrieked, and the fiery red glow was back on her skin again. Her claws slashed at him and he moved out of her way.

"Fuck this! Fight it, Mia. You heard me, snap out of it!"

When she wouldn't listen, he turned his back to her and quickly pulled on a pair of shorts before covering her with a white sheet. His skin tingled as she tried to stun him with her magic.

"Doesn't work, Love. We are mated, remember?" He smirked and knotted the sheet so it wouldn't come off. The vampiress hissed and lunged at him. Her legs kicked at him, but he pinned her against the wall. He quickly dressed her in a pair of pants while she fumbled with the sheet.

"You can come in now, Lilith," he called.

***

When Lilith slipped inside their chamber, guilt washed over her.

Mia hissed at her when she went near. The vampiress lunged for the witch and Aaron jumped in front of her.

She glanced at her niece, who had crossed the invisible border of insanity, with tear-brimmed eyes. There was only one way to help Mia and she would do anything to bring her back. Unlike the normal witches, only a mate's blood could control the Hycinth Witches. It was one of the reasons, she never chose a mate.

"I'm going to need your blood," she said to Aaron. "The only way to bind a hycinth's power is to bind them with their mate's blood." *I won't lose her to the darkness.* Not if she could help it.

A sudden thought crossed her mind. *Does Felipe know Melisa is a hycinth?* He must have known. There was no way he could've imprisoned Melisa without her mate's blood, and the binding spell wouldn't work if the mate was dead. Lilith's eyes widened. That meant—

Mia's father is alive.

CHAPTER 50

Felipe walked through the dark corridors in the restricted part of his castle. His pitch-black eyes glistened as he glided smoothly through the darkness. The fresh blood of the fae he consumed thrummed in his veins.

He stopped when he reached a heavily guarded door. The guards bowed and opened the door for him. The vampire king crossed multiple corridors deep into the earth until he reached an iron door where more drudges stood guarding it.

The door opened with a screech, and he scrunched his nose as a gush of stale air attacked his senses. His gaze sorted out the mop of blond hair in the darkness as the smirk on his face widened. It was time to use his trump card.

"Carl, the time has come for you to obey your king."

"What are your orders, Master?"

***

The foundation of the castle shook as she screeched—a gut-wrenching scream—that promised pain and death. The dungeon walls cracked under its intensity and Lilith sobbed watching her niece writhe in pain. Aaron gazed at Mia with a dumbfounded expression. Her struggles tugged at his heartstrings, but there wasn't anything he could do. He couldn't digest that his mate was a hycinth. She hissed in warning at anyone who dared to get closer.

The lycan king knelt beside his mate, his tears pooling onto the stone floor. Mia looked nothing like the innocent human he met. The one in front of him was a predator primal in its instincts.

There was no recognition in the dark pools that had replaced her baby blue eyes, her fangs were ready to rip anything, and her clawed hands twisted against the magically reinforced chains. The wind whipped around him and tousled his hair as her wings flapped angrily behind her.

"Mia. . ." He called, and his beast howled as their bond twisted with dark thoughts.

She snarled in response but held back when the chains would allow no movement.

"Aaron, I need more blood," Lilith said softly.

Aaron nodded, and he felt no pain when Lilith drew his blood. He'd give until the last drop if it helped her.

Lilith continued to chant in an ancient dialect, a language of the witches, which was long forgotten by many. As the intensity of her chant increased, the air around them crackled with energy.

Aaron's blood twisted in the air, weaving themselves into a rope of sorts. Invisible tendrils of magic fused with them making it strong.

Lycan's Blood Queen

Mia screamed as it bonded her. She hissed a warning and let out a string of curses in an ancient language he didn't understand. The witch continued to wave her hand in the air; the blood mimicked her movements, binding Mia's dark powers. The intensity of Mia's powers lessened, but she continued to thrash in the chains.

Lilith sealed the dungeon with magic. "It's over," she said. "She won't and can't hurt you. But I can't say the same for the others."

Aaron didn't move. Would things be different had he known of her origin before? He didn't think so. When he had seen her the first time, he wanted her right then. He touched her cheek, and she bit into his palm. He didn't as much as flinch as she sucked on his blood.

They were all victims to the cruel game played by fate. Who'd have thought this specific female would change his life forever? His beast chose her despite their differences. He was ready to fight against the odds to have her.

When she'd taken enough blood, he used his free hand to unlock her jaw clamped around his palm. By then, she was snarling, growling and hissing.

Would it change his love for her? No. Helplessness weighed down on him. He hoped she found her way back to him. Because the human side of her would fight this. He knew it was still inside of her. It was only a matter of finding control. At least he thought that was how things worked for the witches.

***

Darkness. . .

Twirling pits of pure darkness swirled around her.

She would hear a wisp of something evil, trying to claw at her skin, whispering dark things in her ears.

Pain. . .

She felt as if her head was being gutted as the excruciating pain shot from one end to the other.

Screams. . .

She could hear the screams, so agonizingly painful, yet oddly soothing. It was like music to her sensitive ears.

The vampiress growled and snarled, but her powers did not affect them anymore. She tilted her head. Her eyes narrowed at the threat—the witch—and she promised a painful death for subjecting her to this. If the witch understood her threat, she didn't show it on her face.

"Aaron. . .Son, get up. We have important matters to discuss," another voice whispered.

Mia's eyes were fixated on the king. Her dark pools were locked with the ambers of the beast. She could hear the howl of his beast in her mind as an unknown sadness settled over their bond.

Aaron nodded. "I'll be back, my love. I won't give up on you. . .or us. I'll bring you out of this," he whispered. His voice thickened with emotion. "I won't stop."

Mia snarled and watched as everyone turned to leave her alone. The chains that bound her arms and legs rattled as she tried to pounce. But an invisible force held her from lashing out. She didn't want the beast to leave her. The dark whispers in her head lessened in his presence, and she wanted him closer to keep them in check. She wanted him closer as the time went by. Her eyes bored into the eyes of a beast.

The young hybrid queen couldn't fathom what was being done to her. She fought against her restraints. She despised the witch who bound her using her mate's blood rendering her helpless. When he turned his back, a small part of her mourned the sudden loss of his presence. No one noticed the lone tear that escaped her eye as she stared at the retreating back of her beast.

Don't go.

The End.

Read on for a sneak peek of the sequel The Hybrid Queen, coming soon from GenZ Publishing.

Catherine Edward

Sneak Peek

The Hybrid Queen

(Book Two of the Randolph Duology)

By Catherine Edward

Prelude

Darkness.

Twirling pits of pure darkness swirled around her. She would hear a wisp of something evil, trying to claw at her skin, whispering dark things in her ears.

Pain. Excruciating pain gutted her from the inside out.

Screams.

The never ending, so agonizing screams felt soothing. It lured her like a soothing music to her sensitive ears. Something was wrong. She shouldn't feel this way. Shouldn't be drawn to pain and misery.

Stop it.

The weak sound was a distant echo in her head as the pressure built. The feeling—both liberating and confining.

When the pain built close to the explosion, a loud scream tore through her lips. The castle shook. The next scream was gut wrenching as something inside her gave one last tug of resistance. As the scream stopped, sudden rush of relief filled her.

She breathed deeper, flexing her arms. Energy crackled in the air. Her magic stirred. *It's over.*

Just as the fiery figure that resembled her physique emerged to the surface of her skin, something else rose above it. Dark, strong and filled with malice. This one—with the wings like that of a demon—strangled the other and pushed it back. Scream after scream tore from her lips as these two forces fought within her for domination.

Behind the closed lids, she watched, becoming a hopeless spectator of her destruction. One made of fire and other creature of darkness.

Gashes and burn marks appeared on her body. When the magical force got to the surface, the binds in her arms and legs forced it down. The other one, the chains did nothing to lessen its hold over the magical entity.

The winged creature caught the fiery presence in a choke hold. The light dimmed and the energy drained as it went limp. She tried to stir, this time though, the demonic creature gave a laugh. With a cackle it pressed her down and soared up.

***

He scrunched his nose as the stale air assaulted his sensitive nostrils.

He wondered how he came here as he progressed through the dark corridors, his body feeling a strange magnetic pull toward something or someone.

He looked around at the vampires and witches held captive. They didn't seem to notice his presence as he glided past them. The pull intensified as he went deep inside the ancient looking dungeon.

His heart thudded against his ribcage as he took a turn around the corner, his eyes soon finding the source.

An angel with wings so dark was chained to the wall of an old cell. Her eyes dark as the night sky stared into nothing as she thrashed in her confines.

She was the most beautiful vampire he had ever seen.

Lycan's Blood Queen

So elegant and exotic...

Her wings flapped dangerously, and she tried to claw at anything and everything. Her entire look was so primal that it aroused him to no extent.

"Come..."

A whisper could be heard, and he was sure her lips didn't move.

The angel smirked as if reading his thoughts.

"Come and get me, my King."

He heard the same whisper again and his dark eyes met hers. She smiled, showing her fangs as her tongue darted out to lick her lips.

The sweet look on her face was soon replaced with something more primal as she snarled at him.

"Release me!" She screamed.

She pounced on him and threw him against the wall. His claws extended as his instincts took over.

"Get me out of here!"

Her shrill scream pierced his ear drums as she hit him square in the chest, sending him stumbling down the darkness.

Felipe twisted in his bed, his claws ripped through the black satin sheets and a terrorized scream brought him back to the reality.

He had pinned the source of scream to the bed as his black eyes stared at her. She looked nothing like the angel in his dreams.

Dreams?

He never had a fucking dream before.

"Tanya!"

He yelled, leaving the terrified witch who served him as the flavor of the night. She scurried out of the room like a rodent and soon the red-haired witch entered the room.

"Master," she bowed.

"I had a dream and I saw a female vampire chained to the wall. She was calling for me. What is the meaning of this?" He bellowed.

"I never heard of this before the master. But it could be a vision of sorts. You are the King of Vampires and she might be using it to send a distress call," Tanya assumed.

"Only vampires created by me can contact me that way, Tanya." Felipe frowned in confusion.

"Master, what if she is the one you are looking for. If she is a born, she might have similar powers like yours or maybe different ones, which allows her to contact you." Tanya looked at him hopefully and Felipe nodded.

Her explanation made sense. Now, he had to discover everything he can about this female vampire.

Felipe closed his eyes, trying to reach the vampires who are alive. He cursed when he felt something blocking his connection with them.

"I can't contact the ones who are living as the prisoners. Bring in Carl, make sure he is cared for. I need him well and alive for this task." Felipe ordered.

Felipe smirked as Tanya hurried out of the room.

I am coming for you, my queen.

A NOTE FROM THE AUTHOR

Thank you so much for reading Lycan's Blood Queen. This is the very first story I wrote back in 2016. It went through a lot of rewrites since then, and I'm very happy with the end results. I really hope you enjoyed this story. If you liked it, do consider leaving reviews on Amazon, Goodreads or Bookbub. Reviews encourage the authors and help readers to discover new books.

If you'd like to stay updated on my new releases, giveaways etc., do subscribe to my newsletter.

I'm also active on Twitter, Facebook and Instagram. Also, you can join my Facebook group "Catherine's Book Café." I love to hear from my readers.

See you soon with the sequel The Hybrid Queen. Have questions? Check out my website to read FAQ's.

Love,

Catherine Edward

Catherine Edward

Acknowledgements:

This is also to all my kind readers who encouraged and supported me every day. I wouldn't be here without you. I'd also like to thank my wonderful friends and authors Brett Hicks–without whom this story wouldn't be possible, Daniel McNeill–who helped me brainstorm ideas for the vampires, Viorra Thompson–who helped me choose this title, Mama Maggie, Rachelle Mills & my pack girls at #InternationalWildflowerPack for motivating and inspiring me in a lot of ways. Also special thanks to authors Alyssa Urbano *(AerithSage)*, Jennise .K, Richa Resa, Sarah Royal, Amy N. Johnson, Kassandra Young (K.A. Young), Ysa Archangel, E.S. Young, Mel Ryle, Sissi .O. Simons, and Jo Lee Hunt for always having my back.

Website: www.catherineedward.com

Email: Catherine@catherineedward.com

71296718R00248

Made in the USA
Columbia, SC
25 August 2019